Kylie Chan started out as an IT consultant and trainer specialising in business intelligence systems. She worked in Australia and then ran her own consulting business for ten years in Hong Kong. When she returned to Australia in 2002, Kylie made the career change to writing fiction, and produced the bestselling nine-book Dark Heavens series, a fantasy based on Chinese mythology, published by Harper*Voyager* worldwide. She is now a fulltime writer based in Queensland's Gold Coast, enjoying the beach and writing a new science fiction series.

Books by Kylie Chan

Dark Heavens
White Tiger (1)
Red Phoenix (2)
Blue Dragon (3)

Journey to Wudang
Earth to Hell (1)
Hell to Heaven (2)
Heaven to Wudang (3)

Celestial Battle
Dark Serpent (1)
Demon Child (2)
Black Jade (3)

Small Shen

Dragon Empire
Scales of Empire (1)
Guardian of Empire (2)

KYLIE CHAN

SCALES OF EMPIRE

DRAGON EMPIRE TRILOGY 1

HARPER
Voyager

Harper*Voyager*
An imprint of HarperCollins*Publishers*

First published in Australia in 2018
This edition published in 2019
by HarperCollins*Publishers* Australia Pty Limited
ABN 36 009 913 517
harpercollins.com.au

Copyright © Kylie Chan 2018

The right of Kylie Chan to be identified as the author of this work has been asserted by her under the *Copyright Amendment (Moral Rights) Act 2000*. This work is copyright.

Apart from any use as permitted under the *Copyright Act 1968*, no part may be reproduced, copied, scanned, stored in a retrieval system, recorded, or transmitted, in any form or by any means, without the prior written permission of the publisher.

HarperCollins*Publishers*
Level 13, 201 Elizabeth Street, Sydney NSW 2000, Australia
Unit D1, 63 Apollo Drive, Rosedale, Auckland 0632, New Zealand
A 53, Sector 57, Noida, UP, India
1 London Bridge Street, London, SE1 9GF, United Kingdom
Bay Adelaide Centre, East Tower, 22 Adelaide Street West, 41st floor,
  Toronto, Ontario M5H 4E3, Canada
195 Broadway, New York NY 10007, USA

A catalogue record for this book is available from
the National Library of Australia

ISBN: 978 1 4607 5326 2 (paperback)
ISBN: 978 1 4607 0790 6 (ebook)

Cover design and illustration by Darren Holt, HarperCollins Design Studio
Cover images by shutterstock.com
Author photograph by Adam Hauldren
Typeset in Sabon LT Std 11/15 by Kirby Jones
Printed and bound in Australia by McPherson's Printing Group
The papers used by HarperCollins in the manufacture of this book are a natural, recyclable product made from wood grown in sustainable plantation forests. The fibre source and manufacturing processes meet recognised international environmental standards, and carry certification.

1

'Corporal Jian Choumali.' The base commander flipped through a paper file on his desk, then glanced up at me. 'Take a seat, Corporal.'

'Sir.' I saluted, then perched uncomfortably on the hard plastic chair across the desk from him. The commander was a throwback to the old school: white, male, straight, educated, and oblivious. He'd never spoken to me before, and I doubted he even knew I existed before now. It must be serious for me to be in his office, although I couldn't recall any major recent infractions. The current cohort of recruits were no worse than usual, and as far as I knew Sar-Major wasn't pissed at me. I raised my chin, ready to take whatever he was about to throw at me.

'Exemplary record,' he said, almost to himself, as he flipped through the file. 'Only twenty-four years old and already assisting Sergeant-Major Shirani to train the new recruits. Half-African, half-Chinese. Perfect.'

I opened my mouth to correct him that I was Welsh, not African or Chinese, but let it go when he leaned his arms on the file and smiled at me, making me even more uneasy.

'What do you know about the *Nippon Maru*, Corporal?'

'Everyone knows about it. They're two years out from Kapteyn-b, and close enough to do a thorough scan. It came back positive. They've confirmed that the planet is habitable. We received the message last week.'

I was surprised at the turn of the conversation, then felt a bolt of excitement at the implications. The whole world had been watching the Japanese generation ship's regular transmissions as it made its dramatic three-hundred-year interstellar journey to the colonisation planet. The oldest occupants of the ship were the tenth generation to be born aboard, and were lauded as heroes on Earth. Their messages were full of determination to make the project succeed.

'Nobody believed they could do it,' the commander said, closing the file. 'But it looks like they made it.'

'So we're sending a ship now?' I said.

The commander eyed me piercingly and I winced. I had to resist the urge to display more intelligence than my carefully crafted 'dumb grunt' persona. The last thing I needed was attention from the higher-ups.

'What have you heard about this, Corporal?' he said sternly.

'Nothing more than what's on the network. But you just said I'm perfect. I'm mixed race, I'm smart and young, and as you said yourself, I have an exemplary record.' I leaned forward to sense his emotions more closely. 'Are you asking me if I want to go on the *Spirit of Britannia*?'

'How on earth do you know that's what it's called, girl?' he said, aghast.

Girl? What public school had produced this dinosaur? I opened my mouth to say something about racism and sexism, and slammed it shut. It was a waste of time explaining any of that to Commander Oblivious if the compulsory awareness training hadn't changed his attitude.

'*Nippon Maru* means *Spirit of Japan*,' I said. '*Spirit of Britannia* is the obvious choice. Ten pounds says the North Americans are working on a ship called the *Uncle Sam* or the *Bald Eagle*.'

'*George Washington*, actually. You owe me ten pounds.'

'I'll present it to you after my next pay,' I said.

'So, Choumali?' The commander pushed a manila envelope across the desk to me. The use of paper was a loud indicator of its high-level security. 'The ship lifts off in two years; we need to move before the Chinese do and claim Wolf 1061, the closer planet, otherwise the journey will take twenty-four light-years, to Gliese 667, instead of fourteen. Getting to Wolf 1061 first will save us a hundred and fifty years. Say yes to this mission and you'll be a heroine, lauded and worshipped until you go.'

'Am I being ordered?'

'No. It's an offer. There are disadvantages – apart from the obvious ones of living the rest of your life on the ship. The *Nippon Maru* lost half its population in transit, so reproduction will be strictly controlled on the *Britannia*. During the voyage you will be inseminated with two children from two different fathers.'

That shook me – I'd never thought of having children. This was a huge opportunity though. What would Mum think? She needed me.

I looked the commander in the eyes as I pushed the envelope back to him. 'My father is dead; there's only me and my mother. I can't leave her.'

'She will be compensated handsomely for your pioneering spirit. She will receive five million new pounds a year for the rest of her life.'

My breath left me for a moment – five million a *year*? – then I pulled myself together. 'Is that how much a human being is worth?'

'If that human being is you, then yes.'

'Then why aren't I being paid more now?' I said, deliberately baiting him to give myself time to think. Would five million a year be compensation enough for losing me? I'd have to ask Mum about it …

'Because right now you're not a representative of His Majesty's Royal Army on a generation ship headed to Wolf 1061. You're just an infantry corporal with a bright career ahead of you.'

I only half-listened to his reply. I was thinking of my mother's reaction. More importantly – did I want to go? The reply came thundering through the core of my being. *Hell yeah!*

'I need to speak to my mother about it,' I said.

The commander waved one hand over the envelope. 'There's a week's leave for you in there.'

'How many other soldiers on the base are you offering this to? If too many of us accept, will you make us compete for places?'

'You're the only one on the base, Choumali. We're being extremely selective in this first round. The second round may be more competitive.'

I felt a quick rush of concern that the army knew my secret, but the commander wasn't projecting the edginess that most people did in the presence of a telepath. He didn't know.

I picked up the manila envelope and stood. 'I'll let you know in a week, sir. Thank you for the offer.'

He rose and held his hand out, and I shook it, dazed at the suddenness of the whole thing.

'I'm honoured to offer this to you, Corporal Choumali. You – and other young people like you – are the hope for Euroterre's future. Do us proud.'

*

The train thundered out of the tunnel and the wind slammed into the side of my carriage. Rain gushed down the windows, and people changed to drier seats as it entered the carriage through the degraded seals. Mist poured out of the ceiling vents as the air-conditioning system fought the increased heat and humidity.

The rails ran on a causeway through what had once been the green centre of England but was now the sea. Mum lived in a small village halfway up the mountains of Old Wales, where people struggled to maintain a subsistence lifestyle. My salary helped her to retain comforts most of her neighbours couldn't afford. I rested my head on the rattling window and thought about what she could do with five million new pounds a year. She could pay for the paperwork to live with our extended family on that. China was rich and green where the land was above water. Mum could follow her heart and help support her sisters and their children, and never have to worry about food again.

And I'd be travelling to the *stars*. I would never see the end of the journey, but my great-great-something-grandchildren would have a whole new pristine *planet* to live on. I fingered my bag containing the envelope. Of course, if Mum didn't want me to go, I wouldn't.

I glanced out the window and saw my mother's eyes in my reflection. My eyes, with their epicanthic fold, were the only Asian part of me; the rest was one hundred per cent my African-heritage dad. He was tall, lean and muscular, with dark skin, a wide nose and full mouth. I had his hair as well, a black frizz cropped close in a military standard cut. When I was a child everybody had said that I was definitely his, as if there was any doubt when they saw my parents together.

The train slowed as it reached the base of the mountains and went from travelling over water to land. It stopped at the first station and a few people left.

The words '*Spirit of Britannia*' were mentioned on the screen at the end of the carriage and I focused on it.

'With the upcoming success of the *Nippon Maru*,' the news presenter said, 'His Majesty's government has announced that the United Kingdom of Great Britain and Western Europe will be building a generation ship as well, to travel to the third planet of the red dwarf star Wolf 1061, fourteen light-years away.'

A graphic of the star appeared on the screen. What would the planet's light be like, I wondered – would everything be tinted red?

The next station was mine, and I lugged my duffel bag over my shoulder and went to the door. The wind and warm rain howled into the carriage as I put my head down to exit. I was the only one leaving the train, and the car I'd ordered was waiting for me. I rushed through the pouring rain to climb in, told it Mum's address, and sat back, fluffing my short black hair to free it of water.

The car rattled and swayed over the potholed road – something felt severely wrong with the suspension. The village probably couldn't afford the required maintenance, and finding printable designs for the parts for such an old model would be a nightmare. I'd have a look at it during the week I was visiting Mum and see if I could do some minor repairs.

I opened the envelope again and flipped through the mission orders. I'd read them so many times I had them memorised. My role on the starship would be security officer, estimating the risks in space, and reporting back to Earth with my findings. My secondary roles were raising two children – two children! – and teaching the next generation how to use military hardware in case they had to defend themselves. I'd never considered having kids, that was my partner Dianne's thing, and now I was being ordered to be inseminated with two of them.

I shifted uncomfortably. Was two years enough time to learn all I needed to about being crew on a starship? I smiled to myself. Starship crew. I liked the sound of that.

The car arrived at Mum's cottage, and I hoisted my bag and ran through the rain to the front door. Mum must have been watching for me, because it opened just as I reached it. I ducked through the doorway into the refreshingly cool entry hall, and trod on something small and hard that resulted in hysterical, high-pitched yelps.

I dropped my bag and picked up the puppy to comfort it, and was rewarded by frantic licks. I checked the dog over; she was fine. I'd just stepped on her wagging tail.

'Sorry I hurt you, puppy.' I leaned down to hug Mum with my other arm. 'Where's old Puppy?'

Mum guided me into her tiny living room, just big enough for a sofa and screen. A folding table stood to one side, and a rough brick bench marked the kitchen. The sweet, rich smell of steaming rice and eggs filled the cottage.

'Some itinerants came through and stole Puppy. I didn't get to him in time – they roasted him over their fire and ate him. Bastards.' She put the kettle on. 'Mr MacDeen gave me the new puppy, but I had to trade for her.'

'That's fine; I don't mind doing some digging. I'm here for a week, and I'm sure the rain will stop.'

Mum poured water into the pot. 'That's good, because the top field needs clearing. And I traded a new terrace field for Puppy.'

'She's worth it.' I turned the dog over in my lap so I could scratch her belly, to her squirming ecstasy. Her oversized paddle-like paws suggested she would grow to be much bigger than old Puppy.

'Hopefully she'll be a better guard dog,' Mum said scornfully. She set the cups on the table and filled them with tea. 'What sort of dumb dog *lets* himself get eaten?'

'You need better names for your animals, Mum,' I said with amusement.

'I have rice from the new bottom terrace you made for me, and eggs, and chicken,' Mum said, ignoring me. 'I had enough surplus coffee from this year's harvest to trade with Mrs Chandra for four chickens!'

'Are they all called Chicken?'

Mum leaned across the table and tapped my arm. 'Don't be rude.' She settled back in her chair and folded her hands over her belly. 'Not any more. One of them stopped laying six weeks ago and now it's called Dinner.'

Every time I saw my mother, the lines on her face were more pronounced; a combination of her steady weight loss and her outdoor life in the harsh climate. She was the thinnest I'd ever seen her; she obviously wasn't eating the extra rations I was sending. She was either hoarding them or giving them away to other villagers in greater need.

'So tell me why you're here when you weren't due for leave,' she said. 'Is everything all right with Dianne?'

'Yeah, she and Victor moved in together. They've gone domestic. They say I'm welcome any time; there's room for me as well.'

'And how do you feel about that? You and Dianne were good for each other. You've had this on-and-off thing with her and Victor for years; I was hoping you'd finally settle down, maybe give me some grandchildren.'

I didn't hesitate. 'I'm glad for her, but I'm happy where I am.'

'You don't seem too worried about her setting up house with Victor.'

I shrugged. 'I'm very fond of both of them, you know that. We're good friends. Close friends. But not ...' Mum always cut to the heart of things and drew the truth out of me. 'I love her dearly, but I don't think I was ever *in* love with her, Mum.'

'That was obvious.'

'And something else happened.' I placed the envelope on the table.

Mum glanced at it, then back at me. 'They found out you're a telepath,' she said, her voice flat with dismay.

'No. They want me to crew the *Spirit of Britannia*.'

She spoke firmly and without hesitation. 'They are not having you. They took your father, they're not taking you! You're all I have.'

'They'll give you five million pounds –'

'That's five thousand new pounds! That's only two years of your salary, and you'll be gone for the rest of your life!'

'That *is* five million new pounds,' I said.

'Oh. Still not worth it. My daughter is not for sale!'

'Five million a year, Mum.'

She froze with her mouth open. 'A year? Five million a *year*?'

'The ship leaves in two years. If I go on it, you'll get five million new pounds every year for the rest of your life.'

'But I'd lose you! Never see you again!' She spoke like a news reporter: 'Mrs Choumali, was it worth the money to have your daughter effectively *die*?'

'I'd still be in regular contact, the same way the Japanese were.'

'It takes five years for messages to go backwards and forwards from the *Nippon Maru*.' She waved her hand at the inactive screen. 'They sent the message that they were nearly there five years ago. They could be dead and we don't know!'

'That's only at the end of the journey – and neither of us will be alive then. At the beginning, the lag will be hours, a day at most. We could talk every week, the same way the crew of the *Nippon Maru* did.'

'That's more often than we talk now,' Mum said. She rose and went into the kitchen. 'Come and put plates out.' She checked the rice cooker, then pulled the central pot out of the magnetic coil. 'I will not take money as compensation for losing my daughter. You are not for sale.'

I shifted the puppy from my lap, put the bowls on the table, and used the argument I'd been saving for this moment. 'I want to go, Mum.'

She turned to see me. 'How much do you want to go?'

'I want this more than I've wanted anything in my life. I'll be crew on a *starship*, Mum. This is the greatest opportunity I've ever had.'

She relaxed and smiled broadly. 'Well, why didn't you say that in the beginning? That makes all the difference in the world. This is wonderful!' She embraced me, her head on my chest, then put the omelette on the table and sat. 'Our family, in the stars. A new planet with *sane* weather.' She reached across the table, took my hand and squeezed it. 'I am so proud of you.'

I released the breath I hadn't been aware I was holding. 'That was easier than I expected.'

'Come, eat rice and chicken,' Mum said, 'and tell me about the mission. My daughter – starship captain! I cannot wait to tell Mrs MacDeen. She thinks she's so superior because her son is in university.'

'I'll be a security officer, not captain,' I said, and put some chicken omelette onto my rice. The fresh natural food smelled wonderful and my stomach clenched with hunger. 'And you can't tell anyone yet.' I scooped the fluffy flavourful rice into my mouth and put the bowl down. 'So tell me about your plans for a new terrace field.'

'No, I want all the details about the *Spirit of Britannia*,' Mum said, and smiled slyly. 'Any room on board for an old rice farmer?'

'It leaves in two years –' I began, and the puppy climbed back into my lap.

*

I took a deep breath and eased my back. The new terrace was nearly finished, and water had already started to fill it. I fitted the rocks into the retaining wall until I ran out, then squelched back to the barrow to collect more.

I stopped, gazing out over the mountains. The peaks surrounded the village, with glimpses of the flat ocean between them a great distance away. Another huge storm was brewing on the horizon, thick with black clouds and scattered lightning. The walking trail down from the village was a grey line through the vegetation, and one of the village children was guiding a flock of sheep along it, up to the safety of their pen.

I pulled at my T-shirt; the heat and humidity had saturated me with sweat. I puffed out a quick breath and took more rocks from the barrow. If I didn't finish the terrace before the storm hit, it could be washed away by the deluge. I carried the rocks back to the wall, pushed them firmly into it, checked they were stable, and stretched my back again.

'Jian!' a woman shouted, and I looked up towards the houses. It was Dianne.

Cursing my mother's big mouth, I slogged through the mud, scrambled up the wall onto the next terrace, then repeated the procedure twice more before I was at Dianne's level.

She was short and black, with a rounded body and a warm generous smile that always melted my heart. She spread her arms for an embrace and I wanted more than anything to lose myself in her soft breasts and unconditional love.

I pulled at my T-shirt instead. 'I'm soaked, love, and probably stink. Let me do you a favour and give you a hug after I've had a shower.'

She took my face in her hands, pulled me down and kissed me soundly anyway, and I cringed at the contact between my soaked clothing and her silk shirt.

'I don't care,' she said. 'Now come up to your mum's house and tell me what the big news is.'

'She didn't tell you all the details?' I said as we walked along the narrow cobbled lane to my mother's cottage.

'Only that I needed to come see you *right now*.'

'Interfering busybody,' I said under my breath, then raised my voice so Dianne could hear. 'I was coming to see you after I visited Mum anyway.'

'Sure you were. Like the last three times you were "coming to see me". Sure.'

I winced. Dianne was right: I always put my career first ...

'... put your career first,' she was saying, 'and me and Victor second. I knew it would be that way right from the start, so don't worry about it. But your mum says you have big news for me.' She tapped me on the arm. 'And I might have big news for you.'

'Victor asked you to marry him?'

'Nope,' she said smugly as we reached Mum's cottage. 'Better than that.'

I turned and studied her carefully, then my heart leaped with delight. 'Holy shit, Dianne, you're pregnant. Look at you – you're fucking *glowing*.' To hell with it. I ignored the sweat and hugged her anyway, then planted a huge kiss on her mouth for good measure. 'Hot damn, girl, my mum's going to be absolutely fucking *thrilled to bits*.'

'What about you?'

'Of course I am too!' I said, opening the door. 'But I have big news as well. Come on in and I'll tell you all about it.'

2

I stepped off the ferry onto the island where the space elevator cable up to the *Spirit of Britannia* was located. It disappeared into the clouds above, and appeared to be tilting as if it might fall on me.

The island was a treeless grassy knoll with rocky cliffs all around, except for where the ferries docked. The stinging ocean wind swept across its surface, making the elevator cable sing with a deep bass thrum. It was strange – and exhilarating – to be standing on such a flat clear area. I was accustomed to everywhere above water being covered in layers of terraces that were dense with crops and tiny dwellings. Perhaps my great-great-something-grandchildren would live on a new planet where the land was this open and free.

'Proceed to the buildings over there,' an officer shouted from further up the hill, and I and the other cadets who'd arrived on the ferry – forty women and two men – followed her directions to the plain concrete structures at the base of the elevator.

After three hours of induction I was in a group of ten dazed recruits following an uninterested lieutenant through the corridors of the island facility. We were all too exhausted from the induction to say much. My arm still stung from the multiple vaccinations; and the burgundy-coloured coverall that had replaced my Euroterre uniform was stiff and scratchy.

I checked the new secure tablet I'd been assigned. It was a heavy-duty model, water- and shockproof, and held more terabytes of information than I could read in a year, along with stern security warnings about sharing any of it, even with fellow recruits.

We arrived at a corridor with five doors on either side, and a set of double doors at the end.

'These are your quarters, with a shared bathroom at the end of the corridor,' the lieutenant said. 'Settle in, then Commander Alto will speak to you.'

Each door had a name on it and a fingerprint lock. I thumbed my door and it opened to reveal standard single accommodation that could have been in any barracks, with a narrow bed and a small desk. My duffel bag was already on the floor next to the bed.

I put my new clothes on the bed, the tablet on the desk, and peered out the window. The ferry terminal was at the bottom of the hill, and half-a-dozen young people were boarding, their body language projecting different levels of shame and defeat. I realised they were failures. Rejects.

I straightened. Not me, I'm doing this.

The tablet pinged: there was a briefing in the lecture theatre in five minutes.

I quickly stowed the clothing in the small closet, and headed out the door to join the other cadets heading towards the theatre. We were all wearing different-coloured coveralls, probably identifying our skill sets. I noticed the same female-to-male ratio as on the ferry: there were twenty people living in this corridor, and only one man.

We turned a corner and I nearly walked into an Asian man in a green coverall. He was as tall as me and slightly overweight, with scruffy hair and a square face.

I stopped and said, 'Sorry,' then realised who he was. 'Edwin?'

'Corporal,' Edwin Benton said, grinning. He flashed me a salute. 'How's the wife?'

I saluted back. 'Not wife. Partner, and expecting.'

'Congratulations!' His face fell. 'And you'll do this anyway?'

'We talked about it and she understands. We have a common partner, so the kid will be very well taken care of. They both support me.'

We turned together and followed the crowd towards the lecture theatre.

'That's good to hear. Your child will be very proud of you,' he said. 'What's your role on the ship?'

'Security. You're med?'

He nodded. 'I received the offer shortly after I finished my residency at QE4 Hospital and graduated.'

'Of course at the top of your class.'

'No.' His smile turned wry. 'Too much partying away from the barracks. I came third.'

'I need to take you through basic again.'

'I'm sure the colonisation officers will do exactly that.'

We picked our way along a row inside the lecture hall, and sat where we had a good view of the stage and the other recruits. The theatre held about two hundred and was filling quickly.

'Your burgundy coverall is security,' Edwin said. 'My green is med. I can see blue, bright turquoise, fluoro yellow and a horrible mustard orange. Any ideas?'

'The blues and turquoises are obviously civilians – long hair – and they're grouping together and talking,' I said. 'They know each other already. Scientists?'

'That's what I think. Similar colours for similar fields?'

'I recognise that blonde woman in blue,' I said. 'Physicist.'

'She's next to a turquoise. Astrophysics?'

'Probably. There aren't many military here; it's mostly civilians. I hope we won't see any conflict between the military and civilian participants.' I shook my head. 'Look at me – career soldier wanting to avoid conflict.'

'That's the best sort of soldier, ma'am.'

'Ma'am?' I said, amused. 'You're a commissioned officer now, *sir*.'

'And starting again from the bottom with this. The gender ratio makes me feel extremely privileged to be selected. But the ship will only take five thousand, and we won't have the genetic diversity to be viable. We'll have to take a hold full of frozen semen and fertilised embryos.' He grunted with amusement. 'Me and the other men are like emergency rations.'

'Oh, don't sell yourself short, Edwin. You're one of the most intelligent recruits I had the privilege of throwing head first into a deep hole full of freezing mud.'

'Surprisingly I never felt honoured by that.' He straightened. 'Here they are.'

A group of men and women walked onto the stage, all of them much older than us. One of the men stepped up to the microphone and the room went quiet.

'I am Commander Richard Alto, head of the project,' he said.

He was mid-forties, tall and slender, with the dark brown skin of South Asia above the collar of his naval uniform. His narrow face was full of intelligence and I immediately liked him – then recognised him. I searched my memory. Mid-forties, Alto ... I remembered who he was at the same time Edwin obviously put it together and made a soft sound of astonishment. Richard *Alto* was the war hero who'd thrown himself onto a bomb twenty years ago to save the five-year-old King. I studied him carefully, looking for signs of the aftermath of the bomb, and couldn't see anything, but I was too far from the stage to make out details.

Commander Alto continued, and I was aware of a slight speech impediment now I knew what I was hearing. 'Before we begin, it's important that you know the current situation. The rest of the world hasn't seen this yet.'

He stepped back and the room lights dimmed. A screen descended from the ceiling and a projector flicked on.

The captain of the *Nippon Maru* appeared: the now extremely famous Haruna Harashi. Her face was pale and drawn, and she was thin to the point of emaciation. The ship's biomass had provided only just enough food for them to avoid starvation.

She spoke in Japanese, and the translation scrolled across the bottom of the screen. 'Dear citizens of our homeworld. My sincerest apologies for the delay on this transmission.' She bowed, the top of her head fuzzy onscreen, then sat back again. 'Here is the surface of Kapteyn-b. We will be landing in twenty-three Earth months.'

The planet looked barren and lifeless; and the audience buzzed with quiet comments.

'They made it,' Edwin said softly. 'Go, Haruna!'

'There is no life on the planet,' Harashi said. 'We can terraform it. There is sufficient water and carbon dioxide to start a life cycle.'

The buzz of conversation became more animated; this was extremely good news.

'We have lost some crew. We have reported the degradation of the ship over time. When we reached Kapteyn's gravity well, it broke up.' She bowed again. 'We lost four hundred crew before we could stabilise the ship. I will provide the list of fallen heroes at the end of the transmission.'

A few people in the audience moaned in sympathy at the idea of making it all the way there only to die just before landing.

'We hope that we have sufficient biomass in the remaining parts of the ship to begin terraforming when we land.' Harashi took a deep breath and wiped her eyes. 'Wish us luck, beloved homeland, because we aren't sure that we have enough seeds and water to feed everybody. We will not give up. We will survive.'

The translation said 'survive' but I definitely heard Captain Harashi say the word 'seppuku'. She was talking about mass suicide, because they had a good chance of failure and a quick death was preferable to slow starvation. Charming.

'Here are the details of the lost crewmen and women,' Harashi said, glancing down at the tablet in front of her.

The projection blinked out and the screen retracted.

Commander Alto stepped back up to the microphone. 'That's the situation on Kapteyn-b as of five years ago. The ship was falling apart around them, and it's possible that they didn't land enough biomass to begin the ecosystem.' He looked down at his tablet, then up at us. 'We may encounter similar difficulties. However, we have their experience to work from. We know, for example, that a ninety-five per cent female crew with a cargo of frozen sex-selected semen and fertilised eggs is much more practical than fifty–fifty – hence your demographics. We can use the *Nippon Maru*'s scans to more accurately ascertain the nature of your destination planet. But ...' He raised one hand. 'There is a good chance that the *Nippon Maru* failed, all the colonists died without establishing anything, and we will be accused of sending you and your children to their deaths. Cryogenics is still too unreliable; a third of the test rats don't survive being frozen more than a year and we're looking at a voyage of hundreds. If you don't want to be associated with a project that may fail monumentally, you can leave now before we share any classified information with you.'

The room was completely silent.

'If you leave now, you will be escorted from the base with our thanks, and no negative implications for your career. You are all valued members of your professions and Earth needs your help to sort out the problems we have here. But if you stay, you are committed to seeing this project through to the end. Once you have been fully briefed, your knowledge will be classified. Even if you're not evaluated as suitable to go on the ship itself, your role will be in support on the ground.'

Two women stood up.

'I thank you for your participation,' Commander Alto said. He nodded, and one of the administrators rose to show the two women out.

I snorted quietly to myself. 'Failures.'

'If they aren't completely committed, we don't want them along,' Edwin said.

'Last chance to decline,' Alto said.

A woman leaped up and nearly ran for the door; a last-minute attack of nerves.

You'll regret this later, I thought at her. She couldn't have heard me – I hadn't said it telepathically – but she turned and stared at us, then shook her head and sat again.

I hunched down in my seat. Maybe some of my opinion had leaked out. I needed to sit quietly and shut it *down*.

'That was strange,' Edwin said. 'It was almost –'

He was silenced by Commander Alto talking again.

'There is a contract on your tablet,' he said. 'Read it carefully and thoroughly. It is a contract with the nation, with Parliament, and with the King himself. You agree to tell us,' he paused for emphasis, 'anything at all that may relate to your ability to fulfil your role on the *Spirit of Britannia* that may not be on file. Previous attempts at pregnancy that ended in miscarriage.

Reproductive issues. Psychological issues. Past history of trauma that may impinge on your handling of the stressful nature of the voyage. You've heard the problems experienced by the passengers on the *Nippon Maru*, including their extreme fear that they'd all be agoraphobic when they reached Kapteyn-b. If any of you suspect that you may have latent telepathic or empathic abilities ...' Commander Alto appeared to look straight at me, and I shrank lower in my seat, suddenly finding my tablet extremely interesting. 'Let us know now so we can bring them on, because they will make you even more useful as crew.

'In the meantime, like most first days on the job, your main task is to read the manuals while we perform a thorough physical and psychological evaluation on you all. Get to know each other, and identify *now* people that rub you up the wrong way, because you will be spending the rest of your life with them. Colour codings are in the manuals; and I will be speaking to each of you individually to confirm your willingness to participate, and to accept your signed contracts after the evaluation. Return to your quarters, read the contracts, sign them, and I'll speak to you on the other side.'

*

It was two weeks before I saw Edwin again; we ran into each other in the cafeteria. He waved me over, and I joined him and his medical colleagues, all in green.

'I'm interested to hear what they're doing with you,' he said after we'd made the introductions.

'Whether it's as intense as what we're doing,' one of the other meds, Lena, added.

'It's more than intense, it's overwhelming,' I said, waving my tablet. 'I'm studying every First Contact situation in Earth's history to see how they usually pan out, and to be prepared if it happens to us.'

'Isn't it true that most of the time it ends badly for the less developed civilisation?'

'Always,' I said. 'At first I thought: how is this related to me defending us in space? And then I realised – I'll be armed, and

I'll have the choice whether to respond with violence to any alien contact. It could end very badly if I make even the smallest mistake. Especially if we're the weaker civilisation.'

'Oh geez, yeah,' Edwin said.

'So it's more than just defence. It's diplomacy and history and socio-political relations. The main goal is for me to know when to shoot and when to ask questions.' I looked around at them. They were all wan and exhausted, same as me. 'You've already had your med training, you're qualified doctors. What more can they teach you? Zero-g surgery?'

'More basic than that,' Lena said. 'Today was surgery without scalpels, anaesthetic, antiseptic, sutures or bandages.'

'Fun and games,' Edwin said.

'Is that even possible?' I said.

'It is if we improvise using a small tool kit that all of us carry,' Edwin said. 'But after we're finished, we have to scrounge for replacements from general supplies aboard the ship. You really don't want to hear the rest.'

Lena pushed her finished tray away, folded her arms on the table and rested her head on them. 'I'm so wrecked. This is worse than residency.'

'You can always quit and go home,' I said.

'Nope,' she said into her arms. 'I had The Talk. I'm staying and finishing this bullshit. I am going into space.'

'The Talk?' I said.

'You haven't been told about it? A few of us have had it,' Edwin said. 'Commander Alto takes you for a private chat in his office to confirm your place on the ship. I think he's starting with medtechs and then working his way through the colours.'

'I'm so busy reading the stupid histories that I barely have time to eat,' I said. 'Let alone talk to my cohort. I think there's two or three other security people I haven't even met yet.'

'Yeah, sometimes we go days without seeing each other,' Edwin said.

'Everybody panics until they've done The Talk,' one of the women said. 'Scared they won't be confirmed. Then when they are confirmed, they panic that they're actually doing this.'

'Super-stressful,' Edwin said.

'We have to be resilient enough to cope with it,' Lena said. 'It will be even more stressful when we're launched into space in a claustrophobic can with a limited social network of people we may intensely dislike for the rest of our lives.'

'Are you sure you don't want to give up and go home?' I said.

'I lie awake every night convinced I can't do this, and decide to quit when morning comes,' she said. 'I never do.'

'A few people are doing that,' Edwin said. 'Up all night freaking out, then back into it the next day, just as committed as ever.'

'I'm not,' I said. 'I'm determined to get there. Any hints on ensuring you're confirmed by Commander Alto?'

'I don't think you'll have any problem,' Lena said. She rose and picked up her tray. 'I'm turning in. I don't care how early it is. I'm completely wrecked and I need to write a letter home.'

She returned her tray to the rack and went out.

The *Nippon Maru* came up on the screen and we all turned to watch. The commentators started to dissect the situation on the Japanese colony ship.

'They have nothing new to add,' Edwin said. 'Everything they could say, they've said.' He put his cutlery onto his empty tray. 'We just need an update from the ship to know what's happening.'

'We may never hear from them again,' I said, still watching the screen.

3

It was six more weeks of psych and physical examinations and training before I was called in for The Talk.

I went up three floors to the admin level, and introduced myself to Alto's assistant. 'Jian Choumali to see Commander Alto.'

The young man didn't look away from his screen, he just pointed at some chairs. 'There, and wait.'

I sat. The room had once been bright and modern, but the white paint had peeled in places, and there was a brown patch on the wall where the commander's assistant had been leaning on it. The door was painted white as well, with Commander Alto's name on it, but it was thin ply and I could hear voices inside without making out what they were saying.

The door opened slightly and I craned my head to hear.

'No, I understand,' the woman holding the door said.

'Your choice,' Commander Alto said. 'Are you sure this is what you want to do?'

She opened the door wider, and I saw she was wearing the rose-pink jumpsuit of Human Resources. 'I'm sure, sir.'

'Very well,' Alto said, and she nodded, came out, and closed the door behind her.

'Are you staying?' I asked her, full of curiosity.

She broke down, sobbing. She made no attempt to wipe her face, just stood with her hands by her sides, weeping uncontrollably.

The young man behind the desk sighed loudly with impatience, and guided her into one of the seats. He took a box of tissues from his desk and dropped it into her lap, and she nodded her thanks, still crying.

He returned to his desk, looked down at his screen, then up at me. 'Corporal Choumali?'

'Sir,' I said, sitting straighter.

He gestured with his head. 'Your turn.'

I looked from the weeping HR woman towards the door, then decided to ignore her, tapped on it, and went in.

Commander Alto's desk held a pile of paper files, but apart from that it was clear. A bookcase contained a number of old paper books, and some happy photos of him with family members: his mother in a sari, his father in a suit, and his wife and child – both dead, killed in the '64 floods – smiling at the camera.

I gathered myself and stood at ease across the desk from him.

'Name?' he said without looking up from the tablet he was reading.

'Corporal Jian Choumali.'

He gestured towards the chair across from him. 'Take a seat, Choumali.'

I sat. 'Sir.'

As he flipped through notes on the tablet, I took the opportunity to study him more closely. The prosthetics were good – they'd been made to mimic his skin colour – but half of his face was glossy and unmoving, and obviously fake. His right hand was larger than natural, and he wore a glove over it. He used his left hand – still natural – to manipulate the screen.

'Corporal in the army, IQ one hundred forty-four, impressive results on the testing.' He looked up, and the pupil of his right eye was silver, not black. 'Do you know why we recruited you, Corporal?'

'You just listed three of the reasons,' I said, doing my best to ignore the prosthetics. 'I'm also mixed race, providing genetic diversity, and I suspect another reason is that I'm bi. You'll have far more women than men on the ship, and there'll be fewer issues if we women can pair up in supportive relationships.'

'Are you still sure you want a place on the ship? The *Nippon Maru* never contacted us again, and it's very likely they failed.'

'We need to do this, sir. Our atmosphere is shrinking. Sea levels are rising. We have to colonise other planets if we're to survive.'

'True,' he said. 'So are you sure? You have good security clearance; you could return to your position in the military if you wanted. You don't have to stay here. You were building a successful career, and your base commander would be happy to have you back.'

'I want to go, sir.'

'Very well. We need to know if there's anything that could jeopardise or enhance your participation in the mission. Anything at all. If there's a skill that we don't know about, tell us now.'

I looked down at the table. They knew who my father was, and they had to suspect I had the same abilities.

'You know everything about me,' I said without looking up. 'You just said that I passed all the tests with flying colours.'

'That's true. But we need to be absolutely sure that you can follow orders and fulfil your obligations, and not hide anything from us. You were ordered to tell us anything that we might need to know, Choumali.'

I hesitated, then said, 'Yes, sir.'

'Well?' He leaned forward and studied me intensely. 'Is there something you want to tell me?'

I looked into his eyes, past the weird silver pupil and the rubbery facial prosthetics. His emotional aura was full of curiosity.

Crunch time. I wouldn't be sent home for being telepathic. But if they found out I'd been lying about it, they'd throw me out immediately. I had to make the commitment, but it would change everything; most of all, the way the other recruits interacted with me. As a psi, I'd become an outsider instead of one of the clan.

'All right,' I said, and sighed with feeling. 'You probably know this already, but I'm a projecting telepath. Mid-level empath.'

'Good.' He scribbled on the tablet with his stylus, his emotions not changing at all. He'd already known I was a telepath. 'That was a deal-breaker, Corporal. If you didn't tell us the truth, you'd be going back to the base.'

'I can't go back to the base anyway. You'll tell the military that I'm psi, a freak. I'll lose every single one of the friends I made there.'

And Dianne, I added silently. The minute Dianne and Victor found out I was psi like my father — which I'd assured them many times I wasn't — it would be over for us and I'd never see our baby.

Commander Alto smiled lopsidedly through the facial prosthetic. 'We don't need to.'

Everything came together in my head. 'They know?'

'Of course they do.'

'Why didn't they put me in the Corps then, like my father?'

'Because it killed him. And we have rules about families. That's why we've allowed you to lead a nondescript life as an infantry corporal, when with your skills, talents and intelligence you should really go to the Academy. You obviously made the choice to be unremarkable, and we respected that.'

'But not now?'

'You agreed to go on the *Britannia*, Corporal. You signed the contract.'

'I suppose I did. Will I have psi training?'

'You'll be evaluated. You'll still be one of the security officers; the telepathy is a bonus. Your main task will remain the same. We have yet to choose your secondary skill set, but you're talented with equipment so perhaps engineering. You can help complete the ship's construction. We need as many skilled hands as we can find.'

'How many security officers will the ship have?'

'We want twenty, but we'll see how we go after the orbital training. The other security people keep quitting, saying it's too hard. Do you have any other questions before we move you up to the ship? You have been fully briefed, haven't you?'

'Yes, sir. I cannot wait to see it.'

'Your new home,' he said. 'Provided you can handle the microgravity until we have the habitat spinning.' He picked up the tablet and swiped it. 'Call home and say goodbye to your family. You're going up in the elevator next Friday.'

'That soon?'

'You were one of the last to receive The Talk. We confirmed people who were more likely to drop out first, so we could be firm about the numbers.'

'You were sure I wouldn't drop out?'

'Your supervisors often used the word "driven" to describe you,' he said.

'I'll take that as a compliment.'

'In this case, absolutely. Dismissed.'

*

'This is Dr Dianne Liebowicz, thank you for calling me,' Dianne said onscreen. 'I'm not here right now, but leave a message and I'll call you back.'

'Hey, it's me,' I said. 'I'm confirmed! I'm leaving next week, and I wanted to see how you're doing. Call me back, okay? I called Victor, but he was probably using the grinder on his latest sculpture and never answered.' I hesitated, searching for the words. 'I love you,' I added lamely, and disconnected.

Dianne was busy with a postdoctoral study of heat-tolerant stonefruit, and was spending most of her time away from her tablet, up to her elbows in dirt. Both she and Vincent were buried in their work, same as me.

I sighed and pinged Mum, and she answered immediately.

'Jian!' She smiled broadly at me. 'Did you know you're famous? They interviewed me!'

'That's great,' I said. I took a deep breath and galloped through the words. 'I was just confirmed. I go up to the ship next week.'

She was silent for a long time, watching me. Emotions swept over her face: pride, loss, grief. 'And no final hug goodbye?'

I shook my head. 'You know about the quarantine thing.'

'Dammit, Jian. It's really happening, isn't it?' She choked on the words.

'Yeah,' I said through my thick throat. 'A few more days and I'll be gone.'

'Listen to me,' she said sternly, seeing my distress. 'You are doing something wonderful. I support you. Even if I can't give you a real hug, I'm sending you a million virtual ones. I love you, Jian, and I am so proud of you. I agreed to this months ago, and I still agree.' She put her hand on the camera lens, blacking out my view of her. 'Go do great things. I am so proud.'

There was a knock on the door. 'Jian?' Edwin said on the other side. 'This is pretty urgent – can we talk?'

'Just a minute,' I said to him.

'It's okay, talk to your friend,' Mum said, the screen still black. 'You're right: we'll be in contact all the time anyway. I'm not losing you.' She sniffed loudly, and spoke through her tears, 'I love you.'

'I love you too,' I said, and she didn't reply. 'Mum?'

She'd disconnected with the screen still black.

I wiped my eyes with a tissue.

Edwin rapped on the door again. 'Let me in? I need to talk.'

I went to the door and opened it.

'Oh shit, sorry,' he said, and sagged. 'I came to say goodbye.'

'What? Nearly three months of misery and you succeeded – and now you're quitting? This isn't like you. We'll need talented people like you on board. You're the best med –'

He cut me off. 'My father has cancer. If I'd been with them instead of here, I probably would have seen it.'

'Oh, that's awful. So you're leaving?'

'I need to take care of him, and my mother. My sister is with them, but I'm a doctor and they trust my judgement. The oncologist has given them a whole suite of treatment options and they can't decide what to do. They need my advice. They need me there.'

'I understand,' I said. 'I'm glad you found out before we hit the point of no return.'

'My father didn't want to tell me,' he said bitterly. 'He wanted me to go without knowing. I'm glad my sister had the sense to ignore him.'

I put my hand out, and he shook it. 'I'll make sure to send you updates on how much we're suffering.'

'Don't worry, the two remaining medtechs in my cohort will be doing that too,' he said.

I lowered my voice. 'And I hope your dad will be okay.'

'He won't. That type of cancer has a very low survival rate, and they've been dithering about treatment for too long. He has about six months.'

'I'm sorry.'

He smiled sadly. 'I'll eat a big fat steak in your honour.'

'I'll take a photo of the stars in yours.'

He nodded to me, wiped his eyes, and went out.

I went to the window to watch the ferry arrive to take the last few dropouts home, then banged the sill with my fist. Nothing would stop me from doing this.

The screen pinged behind me and I turned. It was Dianne. I sat and opened the comms. Her usually immaculately styled hair was a tangle, and she was wearing a scruffy T-shirt. She squinted at the camera.

'Oh, sorry,' I said. 'Are you sick?'

'Not so much now I'm in second trimester. Oh.' She smiled and looked down at something offscreen. 'Nah. Not sick at all.'

She wiggled sideways, and Victor's face popped up next to her, just as scruffy.

He grinned and ran his hand over his blond curls. 'Since she hit second trimester all she wants to do is eat –'

'And fuck!' Dianne said in unison with him. 'Something to do with the hormones. I don't mind.' She nudged him with her shoulder. 'And neither does he.'

Victor grinned his silly I'm-sleeping-with-two-women grin that always warmed my heart.

'Your mum said I had to call you right away,' Dianne said. 'Did something happen?'

'I've just been confirmed. I'm going up to the ship in the next few days.'

Dianne broke down. She cast around, then grabbed the corner of the bedsheet and wiped her eyes. 'I'm so proud of you,' she said through the tears. Victor smiled indulgently. 'So when are you moving up?'

'I can't tell you exactly. I'll let you know when I'm there.'

'Good,' Dianne said. 'I'm glad we won't know when you're going up. They're keeping you safe. You are so important.' She put her hand on her belly and looked down. 'You hear that, kid? Your mum's a hero.'

'I'm a mum,' I said softly.

'Starmother,' Victor said. 'Don't worry about Dianne. I'm looking after her, and I'll look after our kid. You go save humanity.'

'You are such a hero, Jian,' Dianne said. She ran out into the kitchen. 'I'm fine!' she shouted. 'Go! It's just the hormones. I'm really proud!'

'We're both proud,' Victor said. 'And your kid will be as well.'

'Don't you go choosing a name for him or her without my input,' I said sternly. 'Do you know if it's a boy or girl?'

'Not yet, the ultrasound's next week,' Dianne said, coming back into the bedroom with a box of tissues. Her hair was even more bedraggled, and I'd never seen her look more beautiful.

My tablet pinged. I was due for a sociology class.

'I have to go,' I said.

'Go, lovely,' Victor said. 'We're *fine*.'

'We are,' Dianne said. 'Call us every day, okay? And if you give us some warning about when you'll call …' She smiled suggestively. 'You can contribute to the hormone wrangling.'

'Sounds like a plan,' I said. My tablet pinged again. 'I have to go.'

Dianne blew me a kiss as Victor kissed her on the cheek. 'I love you!'

'I love you too,' I said. 'Both of you.'

'All three of us now!' Victor said, just as Dianne switched the screen off.

4

On Friday, I packed my duffel with the basic kit and a few mementos from my life: a letter from Dianne, one of Victor's little sculptures, and a couple of my mother's handwritten recipes from the family in China that I would never have the chance to cook myself. I checked the room carefully, making sure I'd left nothing behind, then exited the building and joined my five fellow burgundy-clad security officers.

Lieutenant Ng, in her black executive coverall, was waiting at the base of the steps that led up to the elevator pad. It was a bleak and miserable day with cold stinging rain, and we huddled to keep warm, stamping our feet.

Ng raised her voice to speak to us. 'In five minutes the rest of our cohort will be sent out of the building and up to the station. You're on crowd control. Line them up at the base of the stairs here, and we'll load them onto the elevator in small groups. Your tablets have the order for loading the space elevator – put them in line according to the list. Any questions?'

She waited while we all considered, and nodded when we said 'No, ma'am' at different times. 'Good,' she said. 'Walker, assign tasks.' She turned and went up the stairs to the platform.

'Breathe deep,' Nelly said. 'It's the last fresh air we'll ever breathe.'

'Oh, thanks a *lot*,' I said. 'I really needed reminding about that.'

'Our last day on Earth,' Leticia said. 'Shame it's such a pisser.'

'Here they come,' I said, seeing the first of the crew leave the building.

Emily Walker, the head of security, opened the list on her tablet. 'They finally made a decision about the groupings. They're mixing them up so they can't form cliques on the elevator. Positions: Jian and me down here. Nelly, Rachel and Leticia, go to the elevator pod and make sure they use the correct berth.'

'Ma'am,' we said, and moved to guide the other crew, cool and professional.

The entire crew of the ship would be rotated through enforcement roles throughout the trip to avoid a situation like the Stanford Prison Experiment, but as security we had to maintain a slight distance from the rest of the group to ensure our roles were respected. We wouldn't be part of the clan, but when everybody found out I was psi, I'd become even more of an outsider. Nobody had told my cohort yet, but it was only a matter of time, and word would spread quickly.

*

'Choumali as the aggressor on Brett. Sherazi, you have to neutralise Choumali,' Commander Alto said.

He was standing at the side of the cylindrical gym that had been designed for zero-g training. It ran the full width of the elevator pod and was three metres tall.

I turned on my magnetic tether, threw it so it connected to the side of the pod next to Nelly Brett, and towed myself in. When I was close enough, I wrapped the tether around my forearm, then took her into a headlock.

'Tap me out if I hold you too hard,' I said into her ear.

'I know, I know,' she said.

Rachel Sherazi threw her tether to land on the floor a couple of metres in front of us. She towed herself down it, hesitated, released the tether and kicked off the floor towards us. She grabbed Nelly by the arms, kicked off again, and tried to jerk Nelly out of my grasp. Terror radiated from her.

'No, Rachel,' I said softly. 'Please, grab *me*!'

She ignored me, so I held Nelly firmly, and it turned into a tug-of-war. I was bigger than Rachel, and more secure on my tether. She didn't have a hope of taking Nelly from me.

'You can't do it this way. You have to –' I began, but it was too late.

Rachel lost her grip and floated away. She released her tether, activated it, and threw it down next to us.

But before she could try again, Commander Alto said, 'Stand down, Sherazi.'

I released Nelly, and she nodded to me. Rachel floated in front of us, holding her tether.

Commander Alto glared at her. 'I thought you had therapy so you could work with Choumali?'

'I did, sir,' she said.

'Then why won't you touch her?' he shouted. 'This was your last chance, Sherazi. Are you really going to throw it away?'

Rachel turned away, cowed. 'I can work with her, I can be near her ... Just don't ask me to touch her. She'll know what I'm thinking.'

Commander Alto's voice dropped to a low growl that was somehow even more intimidating than the shouting. 'And if she's lying on the ground bleeding out in front of you, will you be able to touch her then?'

Rachel hesitated, and I sensed her terror turn to deep anguish. My throat caught in sympathy. She had been so keen and eager, but everything had changed when I'd told her I was psi. The terror was constant and intense, and she seemed to have no control over it.

She shook her head.

'Very well,' Commander Alto said. 'Stay on the elevator pod when everybody disembarks. You're heading back down to the surface with me.'

'No, Commander,' I said. 'I'm one of five thousand. We can still work together without her having to touch me.'

He cut me off. 'This is not your decision to make, Corporal. All members of the security team need to support each other ...' He glared at Rachel. 'Unconditionally.'

I raised my hand. 'Then send me back down ...' I sighed. 'I know. I'm the only psi. I'm sorry, Rachel.'

'Not your fault,' she said.

'You *do* know that I can't hear your thoughts?'

She nodded. 'It doesn't make any difference. It's a true phobia.'

'Damn,' I said under my breath.

'Clean up, and return to your stations,' Commander Alto said. 'We're nearly at the top. Everyone's been notified, and confirmed that they're ready to disembark. You have half an hour to wash and change. After that, report to your stations to supervise the lockdown, then assist the crew to unload. Sherazi, stay at your pallet. You'll be riding the pod back down to the base station. Any questions?'

'No, sir.'

We all saluted Commander Alto, and headed for the bathroom. I pulled myself up the pod's central ladder so I was near Rachel.

'Don't bother, Jian,' she said before I had a chance to speak. 'It's my own weakness. I've failed.'

'But you fought in the Swiss/Prussian war –'

'I failed!' she shouted, tears forming droplets that spun away from her face. 'Just leave me alone and return to your duties. You'll be needed out there – you're our only psi. You're worth twenty of me.' She raised her hand. 'Go and do great things.'

'I'm sorry, Rachel,' I said again, but she'd already kicked off from the ladder and floated through the door to her floor of the pod.

*

The colonists slept on pallets attached to the floor in a ring around the perimeter of the pod. I picked up a clean coverall and underwear from the locker at the foot of my pallet and went into the bathroom: a central shared collection of sinks, with a vacuum drain in the floor to collect runoff for recycling.

Leticia and Nelly were already there, stripped and washing. I took my coverall off and tethered myself to a sink.

'Jian?' Leticia said.

I didn't reply.

She grunted. 'All right, be like that.'

I faced away from them, pulled out my washcloth and soaped myself down, then rinsed. It was like washing in the zero-g obstacle course we'd just completed. We had to constantly dodge the droplets of water as they were sucked into the drain so we didn't inhale them.

I washed my coverall and undies in the sink. The soap smelled fresh and wonderful after the sweaty environment of the gym. When I was done, I put on my clean clothes and clipped the wet laundry to the drying rack.

My coverall was still the burgundy of security, and once again I silently thanked Commander Alto for not forcing me to wear the white that indicated psi. I was the only psi on board; every other psi on Earth was in a critical role and couldn't be released. The crew of the *Britannia* had all been informed that one of the security staff was psi, but most of them didn't know exactly which one. To them, I was just another face in the crowd, but that would change as we grew to know each other better. I sincerely hoped I wouldn't have another Rachel situation.

Emily was waiting outside the bathroom for me. 'Choumali.'

I nodded to her. 'Ma'am.'

'Come with me.'

I followed her to the unoccupied central ladder shaft. She stopped between the fourth and fifth floors, and turned to me. I felt a moment of profound awkwardness, because she smelled wonderful. Her dark skin glowed in the harsh light, and her proximity hit attraction buttons inside me that hadn't sparked since I'd left Dianne.

Dianne. She was still out there, and loved me, and was pregnant. And Emily was my senior officer, dammit, and fraternising was *absolutely not* going to happen.

I realised with a small thrill that Emily felt the same way: she was attracted to me. I gazed into her eyes, and wondered what it would be like to kiss her.

She locked her emotions down and snapped me out of it. 'Choumali, you're not to blame for Sherazi's failure. Get over it. It was her weakness, her fault, her problem. You have done nothing wrong. If you really want to go to the stars, pull yourself together, put your professional soldier face back on, and get out there and do your job.'

I hesitated, then composed myself and saluted her. 'Ma'am.'

We were so close that my hand brushed over her hair, and she moved slightly away.

'Sherazi was the only one with serious issues about having a psi on board. Everybody else regards you as an asset. Do you understand?'

'I understand, ma'am.'

'Good. Dismissed.'

I turned and left, furiously beating myself up inside. If I wanted to have a relationship on the *Britannia*, it could be with anyone but Emily. I had the grimly humorous thought that her unavailability could be what made her attractive to me and my glaringly obvious issues with commitment.

I didn't have time for this; the pod was due to dock shortly. I returned to the fifth floor and my pallet, one of the fifty laid out on the circular floor. Small groups of crew hovered together over their tablets, discussing their roles. Others floated in the large convex windows that gave glimpses of Earth below us, or the *Britannia* at the top of the elevator.

I rushed to the porthole to see. We were closer to the ship than my last view that morning, and it filled my field of vision.

The connection between the ship and the elevator station wasn't visible, making it difficult to judge the ship's scale. Intellectually, I knew it was three kilometres long, but it didn't seem that large. It was a series of three cylinders on a central drive shaft, shining with clarity in the sunlight without an atmospheric haze to soften it. The lowest cylinder, the habitat, had portholes that bulged from its surface, while the other two cylinders, the biomass carriers, were one side glass and one side metal, and only half-finished.

The portholes on the habitat cylinder, which at first had seemed twenty centimetres across, now looked like their full two metres wide. Each porthole was the floor of a single living unit, and there were fifty of them lined up along the side of each cylinder. A hundred to a row, fifty rows to the cylinder, for a total of five thousand people.

Leticia and Nelly emerged from the pod's core and joined me. I checked my tablet. We still had fifteen minutes before we began to decelerate and had to lock everybody down.

'You okay, Jian?' Nelly said.

I nodded. 'Emily's right. I need to get over it and move on.'

'We're really doing this,' Leticia said softly as she watched the *Britannia*.

'We really are,' I said.

'It looks empty,' Nelly said. 'How many up there already?'

'It said three hundred, but I think two hundred more were moved in while we were in the training centre,' I said.

'And with us it brings the total to seven hundred,' Leticia said. 'I hope our society isn't stratified by the next recruits having to apply rather than being invited.'

'Write a paper on it,' Nelly said.

'As if I don't have enough to do already,' Leticia said with scorn.

Commander Alto's voice came over the intercom. 'We begin our final deceleration in five minutes. Strap in.'

Emily spoke to us on our personal comms: 'Secure your floors.'

My floor was the fifth. I scooted around the circular space in the microgravity, checking everybody was strapped in next to their bedding. Then I strapped myself next to my own pallet, and signalled readiness on the tablet.

There was a jerk and the pod slowed. I was pushed away from the floor, and my stomach rebelled. I closed my eyes in an attempt to battle the nausea.

Commander Alto climbed up the ladder and into our floor, then connected himself to a hook in the central cylinder. 'Everyone all right?'

'All accounted for, sir,' I said.

'We'll be docking in five minutes. Double-check you're secure; it can be bumpy.'

A loud telepathic message in what sounded like Japanese smacked me between the eyes. From everybody else's expressions, they'd heard it as well. The elevator stopped completely and we surged into the air, but none of the lockdowns failed.

'What was that?' one of the crew said. 'What did she say?'

'She said: "Honoured members of humanity native to Earth",' Commander Alto said.

'Holy shit!' another crew member said. 'What the hell?' She turned to us, her face full of horror. 'Alien invasion! Look at the size of that ship! It just popped into existence next to the *Britannia*.'

Commander Alto unclipped himself and floated to the portal. A few of the civilians did likewise.

'Back to your places and strap in!' Commander Alto shouted at them, and they returned to their pallets, cowed.

'Walker, I need you up here,' Commander Alto said into the comms, then turned to me and gestured. 'Choumali, with me.'

I joined him at the portal. The alien ship was sleek and metallic: a single fluid shape, pointed at the front, and flowing into a narrow swooping cylinder that tapered off into a wedge at the end. The shape resonated with me; I'd seen something similar in the past.

'What does it look like?' someone said behind me.

'I can see it,' another crew member said. 'It looks like that sculpture, *Bird in Space*, but made of red metal. It's gorgeous.'

The ship dwarfed the *Spirit of Britannia*. It was at least twice as long, and shone in the reflected light of the sun; a single moulded piece of red metal with no visible portals, engine or lights.

Emily emerged from the pod's central staircase and joined us. 'Is there a weapon nearby, sir?' she asked Commander Alto. 'We need to be armed.'

'Not here, but there are some on the *Britannia*. There's a full arms locker for the security officers on the bridge.'

'Nothing here, sir? We may need to defend ourselves.'

More Japanese came through telepathically; the woman's voice was high-pitched and sweet.

Commander Alto's eyes unfocused as he translated. 'She says she's not here to harm us, and that she's brought the colonists home.' More Japanese; Commander Alto continued to translate.

'Valiant attempt, humanity, but there were only five left and they were close to death. I thought it best to bring them back rather than attempt to save the colony.'

I heard some words I understood: *Hajimemashite, watashi no namae wa Shiumo desu*. 'Pleased to meet you, I'm Shiumo.'

Her next words were full of humour. 'Welcome to the Galactic Empire,' Commander Alto translated, his voice soft with awe.

5

Commander Alto raised his voice to speak to the *Britannia*'s stunned crew members. 'You've all read the documentation on First Contact protocol. Choumali, Walker, strap in.'

He went to the communication panel, clipped himself to the pod, and tapped the comms button.

'Sir?' the staff member at the docking station said.

'Restart the elevator. Take us to the top, and get that transfer tube connected on the double.' Commander Alto looked around at us. 'Hurry up and strap in, soldiers, otherwise you'll hit the floor hard.' He returned to the communicator. 'I need to be up there. Move it!'

He pressed his earpiece. 'Lieutenant Ng, as soon as we've stopped moving, come up to the fifth floor and help us deal with this. Yes, a First Contact situation. None as yet. We're making this up as we go along.'

Emily and I secured ourselves just as the elevator restarted, pinning us to the floor.

Commander Alto gestured for Emily and me to join him when the pod stopped moving. I unhooked myself and floated over.

'Choumali, contact Shiumo and tell her we're on our way,' he said.

I opened and closed my mouth, lost for words.

'You're the only psi here, Choumali. Do as you're told!'

'She's the psi?' someone nearby said softly, and word passed around the floor.

'I don't know if I can do it, sir. I haven't had any training, and I don't speak Japanese.'

'Try.' He went to the airlock. 'Walker, with us. Everybody else, stay put.'

I broadcast the alien's name. *Shiumo-sama?*

There was a moment of silence, then more Japanese.

I'm sorry, I don't speak Japanese, I said. *Do you know any English?*

Yes, of course. The crew of the Nippon Maru *taught me all your languages. What's your name?* she said with a slight Japanese accent.

Jian.

My, you are underskilled, Jian. Must you shout everything for the whole world to hear?

My face heated with shame. *Apologies. I have no training.*

Well, that's just not good enough.

Shiumo showed me some telepathic diagrams. Tight-beam communication. Moderating my volume. Adding nuances of emotion to the communication. I watched with wonder as the explanations unfolded and the new skills slotted into my head as if they'd always been there.

I have the leader of our nation's generation ship project here, I said. *Would you like to meet with him?*

Sure. You choose how we do this. This is a First Contact situation after all, and your comfort is paramount. Her voice filled with amusement. *I'll be in deep shit back home if I mess this one up. The last First Contact I did, I accidentally asked their head of state to have my babies before I even set foot on the planet.*

A few of the crew sniggered.

'She sounds so cute,' one of them said.

'Ask her where she wants to meet: our ship or her ship,' Commander Alto said, and I passed the message on with my new tight-beam skill.

Shiumo replied in broadcast mode. *Wherever you'd be more comfortable. First Contact is all about you.*

Can you live in our atmosphere? I asked her.

Yes. Direct me where you want me to go, and I'll hand your people over. We need to hurry. They're in a very bad way and close to death.

Commander Alto hesitated, and I could nearly hear his mind grinding through the options. Better control on the human ship, but more information to be gained on the alien ship. The risk of capture and ransom if he went into Shiumo's ship. The possibility that the alien could damage the *Britannia* if he allowed her to board it. The lack of any safe third ground, and the desperate plight of the colonists. Infectious disease, psionic damage, the dying colonists, the three-day wait before anyone else could come up and speak to her ...

I realised that I *could* nearly hear Commander Alto's mind – the insta-training that Shiumo had given me had also dramatically increased my sensitivity. The alien was *good*. I wondered what she looked like, and how many of them were in the massive ship.

'Is docking an issue for the transfer?' Commander Alto said. 'How do we connect the ships together?'

How will we move between ships? Our docking systems are incompatible, I said to Shiumo.

Not a problem. My ship can dock with anything – we're pan-connective, Shiumo said.

Commander Alto turned to me and the other crew members. 'Choumali, with me. Tell Shiumo where the *Britannia*'s docking bay is, explain how it works, and tell her we'll meet her there. Walker, remain here and supervise the crew on the pod. Lieutenant Ng, you're coming with us to help direct the evacuation of the top two modules. I want everyone down in the habitat section while the alien's on board. Seal every bulkhead between the bridge and the habitat, and don't open them until the medtechs give you the all clear.'

Ng saluted him. 'Sir.'

'Two greens to handle the colonists. Webster and Bailey.' Commander Alto pointed to the med officers. 'Everybody else, stay here on the pod and wait for further instructions. Walker, you have the bridge.'

'Understood, sir,' Emily said, and turned away to speak on the internal comms.

Sarah Webster and Lena Bailey, the two medtechs, followed us to the airlock. The airlock door opened and we went in. It closed, the second door opened, and we were in the transfer tunnel. We pulled ourselves to the end of the flexible tube, its soft sides ice-cold and suffocatingly clinging, went through another airlock, and into the long, hollow spine of the *Spirit of Britannia*. The documentation had smugly claimed that the *Britannia* was the largest and most advanced generation ship ever constructed, but compared to Shiumo's ship it was basic and ugly.

I banged against the bulkhead as we entered the ship; three days of training in microgravity wasn't nearly enough. My hands twitched and I wished I had a weapon to defend us against the unknown.

We were in the bottom of the central spine of the ship, its three-kilometre length stretching before us. Handles like those on a train projected into the tube every two metres along the interior walls. Commander Alto hit the start button and the handholds moved. We each took one, and the mechanism towed us through the spine of the ship towards the bridge at the far end. It seemed to take forever, then we were through the airlock into the bow of the ship.

We left Lieutenant Ng to round up the rest of the crew and take them into the habitat cylinder, and headed to the bridge. It contained the steering and navigation panels, and twenty screens to display the space around the ship as well as external views of the ship itself.

Commander Alto floated to the control panel and brought up images of Shiumo's ship as it drifted towards the *Britannia*. I made a soft sound of astonishment: the ship had a figurehead of a dragon sitting on the point of its bow. It was a brilliantly metallic scarlet, the same as the rest of the ship, and the sunlight flashed off it.

'How can they know what our mythical creatures look like?' Bailey said.

'Must be from previous visits,' I said softly.

'Exactly,' Commander Alto said. 'Brace yourselves for contact.'

We grabbed the consoles, but the docking was a feather-light bump.

'Weapons?' I said. 'First Contact procedure says the senior officer makes the decision on this, sir.'

'I'm making the decision to go in unarmed,' Commander Alto said. 'I hope it's the right one. If Shiumo really has our colonists, it's a show of good faith, and we need to return it.' He lowered his voice. 'And that ship demonstrates a level of technology far beyond anything we have. If she decides to be aggressive, I don't think we have a chance against her.'

'Sir, I don't think it's a good idea to enter from a position of weakness,' I said. 'We need them to respect us, and being armed gives us more status.'

'Only on our world. We don't know how they'll react to weapons.'

'But –'

'Stand *down*, Corporal.'

I grunted with frustration and looked around for the weapons locker.

Commander Alto gestured with his head towards an unmarked storage door to my left, and I nodded understanding. But by the time I could return to the bridge, locate a weapon in the locker, identify it and load it, we would probably all be dead. Maybe he was right. We might not have a chance if an alien with this level of technology decided it wanted us out of the way.

*

Shiumo spoke to us telepathically as we wound our way through the bow of the ship to the docking bay. *Confirming a good seal on this side. Wait while I open it and we'll see if it's good on your side too.*

The bay was stacked to the ceiling with crates full of supplies for the construction of the ship. Commander Alto floated to wait three metres from the airlock door, and I floated into guard position at his left. The meds hung back near the bulkhead, allowing them an easy escape if necessary.

There was a whoosh from the change in pressure, but no hiss of air.

Any leaks? Shiumo said.

No, I said. *All clear.*

All right, here goes. I am bringing five colonists on gurneys. Be aware that the gurneys are extensions of my sentient artificial intelligence aide. Its name is Marque, and it will be in the form of floating spheres. Marque has stabilised your colonists, but please work carefully with the gurneys – they are more than just trolleys.

'Tell her understood,' one of the green-clad medtechs said, and I passed it on.

I've closed the airlock, Shiumo said. *Give it a moment. All right, open up. Let's see what one of you looks like in good health.*

Commander Alto radiated tension as he operated the airlock controls. The circular door in the middle of the wall opened, and he floated backwards with shock.

A red dragon floated in the airlock, with two gurneys and two floating spheres, nearly upside-down from our plane of view in the microgravity. The dragon had to coil its long body to fit. The floating spheres were black and featureless, and twenty centimetres across. They righted themselves to match us.

The dragon floated out of the airlock with the spheres above it and the two gurneys beside it. 'Bring the other colonists, Marque,' it said, and it had Shiumo's voice.

Our medtechs quickly floated to the gurneys to check the colonists. They were on intravenous drips and emaciated.

The airlock closed, there was another change in pressure, and it opened to reveal three more colonists on gurneys.

'We need to move them to the med centre right away,' Bailey said.

'Wait,' said one of the colonists, her voice weak and thin. 'I have something to say.'

'Quickly,' Bailey said.

'*Arigato gozaimasu*, Shiumo-sama. You saved us,' the colonist said.

'My pleasure. I hope to meet you again when you have recovered. Marque?'

One of the floating spheres took position next to Bailey's head and spoke with a man's voice, its accent slightly Euro, similar to our own. 'I haven't given them anything except saline. We need to work right now on their blood pressure and electrolytic balance if we're to save them. There's significant wastage and muscular atrophy.'

Bailey nodded and moved to the end of the gurney to push it. 'I'll take three. Sarah, take the other two.'

'No need,' Marque said, and the gurneys moved by themselves. 'They're extensions of me, remember? Just show me where to go.'

'This way,' Bailey said, and the gurneys floated after her, out of the docking bay and towards the habitat ring.

Commander Alto bowed to the dragon. 'Honoured Shiumo-sama, welcome to Earth, and thank you for saving our colonists.'

Shiumo bowed her head on its long neck. She was three metres long, with four legs and a lithe snake-like body covered in red scales that looked like enamelled metal. She wore no clothing, but had jewellery – rings and bangles – on her front legs and toes, and silver chains set with faceted green stones around her neck.

'Richard, was it? And here's untrained Jian. Pleased to meet you.' She sighed, and it was strange to hear such a human sound coming from a reptile. 'I hope I didn't leave it too long with your poor colonists. It's very bad manners for the more advanced civilisation to contact the less advanced first, but they were going to die, and I had no choice.'

'Bad manners?' Commander Alto said, amused.

'It hurts your self-esteem as a species. You've struggled for so many years to attain many of your society's achievements, and then we show up and can do them fifty times better with no effort at all. Makes everything you've been working for seem a waste of time. Whole civilisations have collapsed into depression when they realised they'd just been handed everything they set out to do and there were no more frontiers to push.'

'I'm sure there are always frontiers to push,' Commander Alto said. He looked around at the half-finished docking bay. 'But I see what you mean. Your ship is magnificent. Our attempt looks primitive by comparison.'

'See? Nasty blow to your self-esteem,' Shiumo said.

'How did you manage to return the colonists so quickly?' I said. 'Our last message showed them as two years from landing five years ago. Do you have faster-than-light travel? What sort of drive is in your ship?'

Commander Alto radiated a strong shot of irritation. I'd spoken out of turn, forgetting my rank in my excitement.

'Sorry, sir,' I said.

He hesitated, then his irritation faded and he turned to Shiumo. 'That's a good question. Do you have faster-than-light travel?'

'Not so much faster than light as instantaneous. I can fold space to travel through four dimensions. I just ... pop from one part of the universe to another. It's a skill that's unique to us dragons, as far as we can ascertain.'

'But how does your ship move?' Commander Alto said. 'It's enormous.'

'I carry it. I sit on the nose and fold it from place to place. It's mostly empty. Just a big thing for carrying stuff, like Marque and my toys and my food.'

'It's a backsack,' I said with awe.

'I suppose so, yes. I have some living quarters inside, and some guest quarters, but I prefer to hang around outside. I like the feeling of space on my scales.'

'You can live in space?' Commander Alto said.

'Yes. I need to breathe atmosphere every ... Marque?'

'By their measures, it would be a day and a half,' the remaining sphere said.

'So I need to breathe every day or so,' Shiumo continued. 'I return to my ship, take a good deep breath, and go back out to sit on the nose. Would you like to come and see inside my ship? I have a suitable atmosphere and working gravity there; it will be much easier to talk if we're not floating around. I have food that is compatible with your chemistry, and I have tea. Come and have tea with me.'

I waited for Commander Alto's orders, sincerely hoping he'd visit her ship. This was a once-in-a-lifetime chance and I didn't want to miss it.

He nodded. 'We would be honoured, Shiumo-sama.'

'Tea from the Japanese colony?' I said as she opened the airlock again.

'Oh no, from my homeworld. I think it's obvious that we've been here before: we check on developing civilisations, and sometimes quietly help them along. If we drop in on any young societies, we usually introduce them to tea.' She gracefully floated back to the airlock, her long body swaying through the air. 'A planet isn't worth visiting if you can't get a decent cup of tea there.'

'Now you're talking,' Commander Alto said with grim pleasure. 'I feel exactly the same way.'

'A man after my own reptilian hearts,' Shiumo said.

'How many of you are on the ship?' Commander Alto said.

'Oh, just me and Marque. We dragons travel alone. It's the way we do things.'

'You are not *alone*,' Marque said from the remaining floating sphere. 'You just dismissed the AI without a second thought, you biological *elitist*.'

'I apologise, Marque, you are obviously sentient,' Commander Alto said. He bowed to the sphere. 'I am pleased to meet you as well.'

'About time someone gave me the recognition I deserve,' Marque said. 'This red only exists to carry me around, and she treats me like *staff*.'

'Oh, give me a break,' Shiumo said, and I could swear that she rolled her eyes. 'How are the colonists?'

'I'll let you know in about eight hours their time. It was a close thing,' Marque said.

'Jian, tell Lieutenant Ng what's happening, and that she's to report back to Admiral Mitchell,' Commander Alto said. He straightened his collar. 'Tell them I'm having tea with an alien dragon.' He shook his head. 'Now there's something I never thought I'd say.'

'Try the narrow beam I taught you,' Shiumo said to me.

'Can you show me how to send images? I want to send what you look like.'

'Of course,' Shiumo said.

She turned to face me, and my brain exploded in orgasmic pleasure. I floated in the microgravity, twitching and out of control as the ripples of ecstasy faded and stopped.

'Jian?' Commander Alto said, taking my arm. 'Jian?' He rounded on Shiumo, still holding me as I quivered in the air. 'If you've hurt her ...'

'No, no,' I gasped. I gulped a few deep breaths and raised my shaking hand.

'Profoundest apologies, little one,' Shiumo said. 'I accidentally brushed your pleasure centres.' Her voice filled with contrition. 'I've never worked with a brain like yours before. It won't happen again.'

I nodded. 'I'm okay.' I lowered my head and concentrated, sending the message of where we were going, as well as an image of Shiumo, to Lieutenant Ng. 'Message sent. Let's go to the ship.'

'Are you sure?' Commander Alto said. 'Do you need time to recover?'

'No.' I took a few more deep breaths. 'I'm fine now.'

'Lead on then,' Commander Alto said, nodding to Shiumo.

6

Shiumo led us into the airlock, with the Marque sphere floating above her. 'Down will be this way when gravity reasserts,' she said, pointing with one claw.

We rotated so our feet were in that direction, and moved closer to the bulkhead. Commander Alto closed the door and I readied myself, inwardly cursing his decision to go unarmed, and well aware that he didn't have a choice. I was intensely curious to see the interior of Shiumo's ship, but it was possible that her words of friendly greeting had been a lie and we were walking into any of a number of nightmare scenarios. I tried to recall my training – what to do in these circumstances – and couldn't remember a single thing. The material hadn't covered the current situation, or anything resembling it.

Gravity asserted itself and we both landed on our feet. The far airlock opened without Shiumo moving – to reveal empty space, black and dotted with hard brilliant stars, and Earth glowing blue and white above us.

I immediately grabbed a handrail and opened my mouth, then glanced at Commander Alto in surprise. There was no depressurisation; we were still in air. I took a shallow breath: the air was fresh with a faint scent of vegetation, and perfectly breathable. A cold edge suggested that it contained slightly too much oxygen.

'You should have warned them, you silly red,' Marque said from the sphere.

'My apologies.' Shiumo bowed her head on her long neck. 'The walls of my ship are transparent from the inside. As I said, we dragons can live in space and I like to see where I'm going. I can make them opaque if you prefer.'

She stepped out of the airlock onto a shiny black floor that reflected the Earth above us. I followed Commander Alto out, and glanced right. The vast space appeared to be the interior of the top half and forward section of the ship. The ceiling was invisible, and the external walls were transparent. I stared with wonder at the Earth, huge and majestic, floating above us. The *Britannia* was visible behind us, with the space elevator connected to its far end and threading down towards the planet, shining in the light of the sun.

'The portals on the elevator didn't give a view anything like this,' I said softly.

'I can opaque it if it makes you uncomfortable,' Shiumo said.

'It doesn't bother me,' Commander Alto said. 'It's magnificent.'

'Same here,' I said.

We followed Shiumo further into the gigantic interior. At least a quarter of the vast space towards the rear of the ship was occupied by what appeared to be an art gallery: paintings and sculptures hung suspended in mid-air; and smaller objects – some of them moving – sat on plinths.

'Over here,' Shiumo said, and led us to a collection of soft carpets and large cushions in various shades of red scattered around a wide plain black table hovering forty centimetres above the floor. 'Marque, if you could bring us tea, please?'

'Which type?' Marque said.

'We'll start with a style like the green tea the colonists took with them,' Shiumo said. 'That way we know our guests will be familiar with it.'

She reclined on the carpets and pulled a cushion under her front end, the bracelets on her forearms clinking. 'Please, sit with me and make yourselves at home. My ship is your ship.'

We nodded our thanks and settled ourselves on the other side of the table from her. It was slightly too high for us, so I took a couple of cushions and placed them under my butt. Commander Alto hesitated, then did the same.

Shiumo turned her head on her long neck to look at Earth, and her silver eyes glowed in its reflected light. 'It's a beautiful planet – binary planets; highly unusual. That large satellite must make it bright enough to see at night when it's fully reflected.'

'The phases of the Moon have shaped our civilisations,' Commander Alto said. 'We measure time by them.'

'Moon – that's what that word means. I saw it in the colonists' minds and couldn't connect it. Lovely,' Shiumo said.

A tray drifted from the wall of the ship towards us, carrying a standard teapot and cups – except they were all double human size, obviously suited for a dragon.

The tray settled on the table, and Shiumo poured for us, then picked up a teacup delicately in her large front claws and brought it to her snout. Her head was long and narrow, similar in dimensions to a horse's; and she had five toes on each red-scaled hand, with long, obviously sharp claws that didn't seem retractable.

She sipped her tea and waited, still holding the cup.

Commander Alto picked up his cup and sniffed it.

'It is quite safe,' Shiumo said. 'I will not harm you. The only reason I'm here is because of your colonists.' She gazed into his eyes. Her own were a liquid silver, like mercury, with large black pupils. 'Trust me.'

Commander Alto hesitated, then sipped the tea while I watched with horror. He put the cup back on the table and we waited for an adverse reaction. Nothing happened.

'I really am here to help,' Shiumo said gently. 'I won't hurt you.'

'Your name – Shiumo,' I said. 'Where did it come from? It sounds Japanese.'

'I took a name in your language. The colonists helped me. Their ship – and their minds – had extensive language resources. My name in our own tongue is probably unpronounceable for you, but it means something similar – poetry and rain.'

'You went into their minds?' Commander Alto said, his voice and emotions sharp with concern.

'I had to. It was the only way I could communicate quickly enough to save them,' Shiumo said. 'Again, very bad manners, but it had to be done, and I had their full permission. I hope this won't affect our relationship. I want to establish peaceful diplomatic – and social – ties with your people.'

'Our government representatives can be up here via the elevator in three days,' Commander Alto said. 'Or you could go down to the planet to meet them. Is your ship capable of a surface landing?'

'Yes, but I'd prefer not to. It causes a great deal of damage to a planet's surface because of its large size. I usually leave it in orbit and fly down myself.'

'Re-entry ...' Commander Alto hesitated. 'I suppose the term doesn't really apply to you. But the friction from the atmosphere doesn't hurt you?'

Shiumo sipped her tea, then gazed at him over the top of her cup. A faceted metallic silver stone, like a gemstone, was embedded into her forehead between her eyes, and I wondered if it was an adornment or a third eye.

'I don't pass through the atmosphere,' she said. 'I just fold to the surface. But even if I did travel through the atmosphere, it wouldn't bother me. We're extremely tough.'

'You are,' he said with wonder. 'You seem to have evolved to travel in space.'

'We did.' Shiumo placed her teacup on the table. 'We live to explore, to meet new people, and to find love wherever we can.'

'Love?' he said.

'Love is wonderful,' Shiumo said. 'Love is free. Love is euphoric. We seek it.'

'I hope we have enough love for you,' Commander Alto said.

She focused on him. 'I think you do.'

He appeared to lose himself in her eyes, and attraction oozed from them both like a soft scent. I watched with wonder. They were behaving like a love-struck couple on their first date.

Commander Alto pulled himself together and cleared his throat. 'I suppose I should direct you to the bureaucrats on the surface who will do all the treaty, negotiation and tedious protocol business. Everyone on Earth will want to see you.'

'Why is it that all species want to make a spectacle of us?' she said.

'If they aren't excited about meeting a new outworld species, they're probably not worth our time,' Marque said. 'How boring would you be if your reaction to an alien species arriving on your doorstep wasn't immediate wonder and joy?'

'That's always been the reaction whenever we arrive,' Shiumo said.

'How many species have you met?' I said.

'You are number ... Marque?' Shiumo glanced up at the sphere. 'Is it four hundred something?'

'Four hundred and twenty-three,' Marque said.

'How many have you personally met?' I said. 'I'd be fascinated to see other species.'

'That is me personally,' Shiumo said. 'The Empire has encountered well over twelve thousand different species.'

'You have a great deal to teach us,' Commander Alto said. 'How long can you stay?'

'Oh, long enough. I might help you out with your colonisation efforts, take your impressive ship to the planet it was aiming for, assist in establishing the colonies, things like that.'

'You'd help us?' he said.

'Of course. More than enough planets to go around; and this part of the galaxy is sparsely populated. You have at least two or three hundred planets similar to this lovely orb above us within easy reach, and it would be fun to have a new civilisation to visit. Load your ship into mine, and I'll fold it anywhere you like.' She leaned over the table and the tip of her scaly snout nearly touched Commander Alto's nose. 'But I have one condition.'

Commander Alto's expression went cold. The dragon had to want something in return for helping humanity, and it probably wouldn't be small.

'What?' he said.

'You.' Shiumo looked from Commander Alto to me. 'And Jian.'

I was hit by a bolt of concern at the implications.

Commander Alto radiated similar alarm. 'Us? Why? What do you want us for?'

'Companions while I'm here. You guys are wonderful: Jian the untrained mindworker, and Richard the intelligent leader. Richard, I'd like you to be my human liaison, personal assistant and advisor on Earth matters. Jian, I'd like you to be my communications relay with the Earth authorities. You're obviously military, so you know how that side of your culture works. And both of you can be bodyguards, as backup for Marque. If you two promise to hang around with me, I'll definitely stay for a while and help humanity out.'

'What's the catch?' I said.

Shiumo spread her front claws in a surprisingly human gesture. 'No catch. I like meeting fun people and you two are great. As a representative of the Empire I need to do this job right, and your help will be invaluable.' Her voice became higher-pitched and sweeter. 'Please help me out. I don't want to mess this up.'

'We'll see what our authorities say. They have the final decision,' Commander Alto said.

'If I offer to carry your ships instantly throughout this part of the galaxy I think they'll give me anything I want,' Shiumo said with humour.

Bright yellow metal disks appeared on the table in front of each of us. 'Here's a down-payment for your salary; I believe this much gold is worth a great deal to you,' Marque said. 'She's offering you jobs, guys, and the perks are well worth it. You thought there was prestige to being on the generation ship? Try being escorts to an alien ambassador.'

I picked up the disk; it sat heavy in my hand and appeared to be solid gold. I had the amusing mental image of Commander Alto and me as incongruous courtesans to the dragon, but Commander Alto was still concerned.

'Escorts?' he said, glancing from Shiumo to the Marque sphere.

'I'm sensing unease from you,' Shiumo said. 'What is the problem?'

'You're empathic as well as telepathic?' I said.

'Of course I am. Distress is radiating off you, Richard. What did I say?'

'The word "escort" has another meaning in English,' Marque said. 'I apologise if I was ambiguous. I'll explain to Shiumo.'

'Oh! I see,' Shiumo said. 'Marque means "escort" only in the sense of a travelling companion.' She lowered her voice. 'But I'm always open to other interpretations.'

Her expression became coy as she gazed into Commander Alto's eyes, and he appeared to be just as mesmerised.

'Uh, sir,' I said, trying to snap him out of it.

He pulled himself together. 'If I didn't know better I would swear you were courting me, lady,' he said to Shiumo.

'Perhaps I am, sir.'

'We are of different species.'

'Never stopped a dragon before.'

My mouth fell open and I looked from one to the other.

Commander Alto asked the question before I could. 'You have ... love ... with other species?' he said, aghast.

'We *only* have love with other species.' She picked up her teacup again and eyed him over the edge. 'As I said, I travel the galaxy searching for love.'

I was smacked between the eyes by a loud telepathic broadcast in English: *Corporal Jian Choumali.*

'There's the supervisors checking up,' Commander Alto said. 'Respond, Jian.'

Choumali here, I said.

This is Psi Agent Tapu'o of the United Nations. Report, Corporal. Status on you and Commander Alto?

We are aboard the alien's ship, I smiled slightly, *having tea. Commander Alto is talking with the alien. Her name is Shiumo and she looks like this.* I sent a mental image of the dragon. *She returned five of the Japanese colonists; they were close to death.*

Commander Alto, Tapu'o said, *can you give us a quick overview via Corporal Choumali of what's happening up there? What's the status on the First Contact?*

'Choumali, transmit my replies to Tapu'o,' Commander Alto said.

'Understood, sir.'

What is the name of the species and their planet of origin? Tapu'o said.

'Uh ...' Commander Alto turned to Shiumo.

'The name of our species in our own tongue is *Drah-gorn*.' She spoke the word as a deep bass thrum at the low end of hearing, but it was instantly recognisable. 'You learned the word from us.'

'System?' Commander Alto said.

'Tell them the other side of the galaxy for now. I can provide them with a more accurate location when we arrive on the planet.'

'Pass it on, Jian,' Commander Alto said.

'Sir.' I repeated most of what I'd already said, and added the details about Shiumo's species and home system.

Stand by, Tapu'o said.

'Message from the medical people,' the Marque sphere said. 'These crew members will receive much better care on the surface – it could be the difference between life and death. Shiumo, we need to take them down.'

'All right,' she said, and hoisted herself onto four legs. 'Jian, ask Mr Tapu'o to provide you with a safe landing location, because I'm bringing you all down to the surface.'

I nodded and passed the message on. 'He wants to know how much space you need.'

'Marque, convert a hundred and fifty *fuhroh*.'

'Two hundred metres. A space two hundred metres each side.'

'They're preparing the location now,' I said. 'They'll pass the details to me as soon as it's ready and secure.'

Never mind, Choumali, Tapu'o said. *I'm speaking directly to her.*

Shiumo lowered her head and closed her eyes. 'I see.' She opened her eyes. 'Those lines marked on that piece of land make no sense at all to me. Why are there big nets at the ends? Oh! A sports field.' She hissed softly. 'Do you play ball sports?'

'Yes,' Commander Alto said. 'Many different types.'

'Do you have a term for winning a point on that particular field?'

'What field? Oh, I see. Goal,' Commander Alto said. 'You can hit the ball with any part of your body except your hands.'

'Good, I don't have hands; I have four feet. When we land, I'll score a goal with Marque as my ball.'

'You will not!' Marque said, indignant.

'I'll be the first alien to score a goal on your planet,' Shiumo said with satisfaction. 'Let's go check on these patients.'

I hesitated, looking at the gold coin in my hand, then placed it on the table and followed them back to the *Spirit of Britannia*.

7

The *Britannia*'s med level was an internal room with a curved floor parallel to the external wall of the ship. There were twenty hospital beds secured to the floor, and we rotated to orientate ourselves to the same plane. The colonists were still on the floating gurneys with the medtechs clustered around them. A couple of the medtechs backed away when they saw Shiumo.

'How are they, Webster?' Commander Alto said.

'They'll recover, but we need to move them down to the surface. We were about to put them on the elevator, but Marque said that if Shiumo carries them it won't take three days; she can do it immediately. Is that true?'

'It is true,' Shiumo said.

'How many people can you carry down to the surface at one time?' Commander Alto said.

'Well, I could fold your elevator module,' she said. 'But I may not be able to reconnect it correctly at the bottom. If I do it directly, the people I carry have to be touching me, and it's not advisable for those in poor health. We can use my landing module. It holds about six people.'

'What if someone touches someone who is touching you?'

'That works as well, for a distance of five metres or so. Further away and you may encounter dimensional stretching.'

'That sounds painful.'

'Not really. Death is usually instantaneous.'

'I see,' Commander Alto said.

'Bring them into my ship and we'll take the landing module,' Shiumo said.

A couple of the medtechs lit up with excitement at the chance to see inside the alien ship.

One of the gurneys spoke in a metallic voice. 'With five gurneys in the landing module, I don't recommend taking more than two or three people.'

Commander Alto looked around. 'Me, Choumali and Bailey.'

The rest of the medtechs' faces fell.

'Hey, you had a chance to meet us. That's better than the vast majority of your population,' the gurney said. 'And one day soon you may visit with us again.'

'Thanks for your help, Marque,' Webster said. 'I wish I had equipment as good as you all the time. How many spheres do you have? Could you spare me one?'

'I make them as I need them. For now, I'm concentrating on assisting Shiumo – my processing power is focused on defending her. Once we're confident you're a completely peaceful species and we're in no danger, I may look you up and visit you.'

'How ...?' Webster stopped with wonder as a rectangular metal block, ten centimetres by five by two, emerged from the sphere and floated to her. She held her hand out and it landed in her palm.

'No,' Commander Alto said. 'Take it back, please, Marque. At this stage we don't want alien artefacts outside our supervision.'

'Of course. Understood,' Marque said, and the block disintegrated into a cloud of black dust that was vacuumed back into the sphere.

Webster shrugged, disappointed. 'I understand. Sorry, sir.'

'When things have settled down I'll be back in touch,' Marque said.

'Thanks,' she said. 'I wish I could hug you goodbye. It's been an absolute pleasure working with you.'

'I'll make an android body with your species' attributes later,' Marque said. 'You can give me all sorts of hugs then.'

She opened and closed her mouth without saying anything.

'Please stop hitting on the locals, Marque,' Shiumo said. 'Let's go.'

'You can talk, with your "searching for love",' Marque grumbled as we headed back to Shiumo's ship with the gurneys following.

*

At the airlock, Shiumo motioned for us to wait with her while Marque and Bailey took the colonists into her ship.

'Last chance, guys,' she said. 'Do you want the job?'

I didn't hesitate. This was the opportunity of a lifetime, and I really liked Shiumo. 'Absolutely. Count me in.'

Commander Alto thought about it, then shrugged. 'Oh, why not. I was never going on the generation ship anyway, and I'll have a hell of a story to tell when this is all over.'

Shiumo cocked her head. 'Does your culture value stories as much as ours does?'

'Is it a universal thing? I would imagine it is,' I said. 'A curious intelligent species would always be searching for new experiences, and stories are a way of sharing them.'

'Are all Earth people as impressive as you two?' Shiumo said as the airlock opened and we stepped in.

'You'll find out for yourself very soon,' Commander Alto said. 'But I think Jian is an exceptional example of her generation.'

My face heated and I looked down.

The airlock opened; the ship's walls had changed to opaque. A Marque sphere, the gurneys and Bailey were waiting for us on the other side in the dark space of the interior. Bailey was sitting on the floor with her head between her knees, obviously distressed. Commander Alto rushed to her.

'I kind of freaked out when I saw the Earth,' she said, embarrassed. 'Intellectually I knew what you told me, that the walls were invisible, but I felt like I was falling into the planet.'

'Perfectly normal response. You're not the first,' Shiumo said.

Bailey pulled herself to her feet and nodded. 'I'm okay.'

Shiumo's voice became more brisk. 'All right, people, are we ready to be celebrities? Marque.'

'Shiumo?'

'Twenty-four to twenty-six hours. Probably within a couple of hours of the end of the first sleep cycle.'

'That soon?'

'They're very military. Look at this lot.'

'What are you talking about?' I said.

'How much?' Marque said.

'Twenty.'

'Done.'

'Any time frame you're willing to bet on?' Shiumo said.

'You're gambling? What are you betting on?' Bailey said.

'Probably someone insulting them or –' I stopped as I understood.

'Assassination attempt,' Shiumo said. 'It happens every single time. Marque?'

'You will be well protected, Shiumo, don't be concerned,' Commander Alto said.

Shiumo made another soft hissing sound and I realised she was laughing. 'If any of you can hurt me, the Empress will surrender to you on the spot. No, while I have Marque nearby I am in no danger whatsoever. You can see how it manipulates energy fields and gravity.'

'I think it will take longer than that. I give it three of their days,' Marque said.

'It's a bet,' Shiumo said, and tapped one of the gurneys. 'All right, everybody, follow me and you'll feel your first fold. If you think you'll lose the contents of your stomach – vomit? Yes, that's the word – let Marque know and it will control the situation for you.'

Shiumo guided us aft towards the plain black wall. An opening appeared in it, and we proceeded down a black-walled corridor that appeared to stretch the remaining length of the ship.

Shiumo pointed and the wall opened. 'Inside. Marque will open it when you can come out.'

We entered a small square room with black walls, floor and ceiling. Rugs and cushions covered the floor, most of them a variety of shades of red with a few silver ones among them. The door closed as soon as we were all in, and soft lights switched on at the edge of the ceiling. I controlled my panic at being shut in a room with no way out, taking a couple of deep breaths and concentrating on Commander Alto as he checked the colonists. They were still in a very bad way, their breathing shallow and irregular.

'Do we need to hold on, or anything?' Commander Alto asked Marque.

'No. Sit on the floor in case there's a bump. Absolutely under no circumstances hold your breath. Open your mouth as if you were in space; there may be a pressure difference.'

We sat on the carpets. Bailey grabbed a pillow and clutched it in front of her, and I gave her a quick friendly pat on the arm, radiating reassurance.

Commander Alto nodded to me, then raised his eyebrows in a silent question.

Everything they've told us so far sounds like the truth, I said to him. *It all seems genuine.*

'How advanced are your skills?' he said.

I winced. 'Like Shiumo said, I'm very underskilled. She may prefer a more trained psi as a companion when we reach the surface.'

'No, she likes you, and she enjoys teaching people new skills. She doesn't often have a chance to train talented young people,' Marque said. 'The pod's clear of the ship, and she's on top ready to fold. Don't hold your breath.'

Ready? Shiumo said.

We nodded. Bailey clutched her cushion tighter.

I turned into spaghetti – stretched impossibly long and thin. Before I could do anything, I collided back together with a rush. The pod thumped against the ground.

First of your species to travel through four dimensions! Shiumo said, and the door opened.

'Let's move these patients first,' Marque said, and the gurneys floated out into the sunlight. 'Better follow me, Richard. The people meeting us may be nervous.'

Commander Alto pulled himself to his feet, straightened his collar, and strode out of the pod behind Marque. Bailey and I followed. The football field was deserted, but a number of rotocopters were audible not far away.

I turned back to look at the pod; it was a simple black cube, four metres to a side. Shiumo was sitting on top of it.

'I'm parking the pod. I'll be right back,' she said, and they disappeared with an audible pop. Shiumo reappeared in the centre of the square of crushed turf. She moved next to Commander Alto, and gestured for me to join them. 'Any tips on dealing with your people, guys? How aggressive are they likely to be? I don't want to cause an incident.'

'Just be your charming self, Shiumo, and tell them again what you're offering,' Commander Alto said.

'I'm charming?' she said, turning her startling silver eyes onto him.

'Extremely,' I said with amusement.

One of the rotocopters flew over the stands to land on the other side of the field, and half-a-dozen operatives in black civilian suits and sunglasses stepped out. The other rotocopters landed outside the stadium.

The operatives spread out, all talking into their headsets. They were carrying automatic rifles held at the ready, and secured the perimeter of the field.

'Those people are wearing a large amount of equipment,' Shiumo said with interest. 'They have body armour and extra weapons under those suits. They're military.'

'Yes,' Commander Alto said. 'They're out of uniform to make you feel less threatened, but they're obviously very highly trained militia.'

'Is your planet at peace or do factions bicker?' she said.

'Resources are scarce. "Bickering" occurs,' Commander Alto said.

'I see. Marque?'

'Depends how tense they are. What are you reading off them, Shiumo?'

'I'm reading extreme excitement. Is that what you see, Jian?'

'Yes,' I said. 'They're so excited a couple of them are about to wet themselves.'

'Should I disable their weapons?' Marque said.

'Would that be a bad idea, Richard?' Shiumo said. 'I don't want them to feel powerless. It could make them even more aggressive.'

'What would happen if one were to fire at you?' he said.

'Oh, nothing, Marque would protect us. But they may hurt each other in their enthusiasm.'

'Then let them have their toys if it makes them feel safe. Choumali, keep an eye on them and if any of them are ready to pop, warn Marque,' Commander Alto said.

There was a clatter as the stadium gates opened to our left. A small group of suited dignitaries – men and women – walked across the field towards us. The operatives moved in a protective ring around them.

'These people move like military as well,' Shiumo said. 'They're ready to die to protect the planet from me.' She cast around, her head moving on her long neck. 'The only civilian I sense for a very great distance – the only one who doesn't have her emotions locked down and her courage ramped up – is Bailey. Everybody else has that cold aura of people ready to either kill or die.'

'Including us?' Commander Alto said.

'Especially you. It will take a while for you to trust me, but I understand.'

'Are other species this paranoid when you meet them for the first time?' he said.

'I've had species try to shoot me on sight. This is a normal level of paranoia.'

The officials stopped three metres from us. A middle-aged woman wearing grey pants and jacket stepped forward and spoke with a British accent. 'Welcome to Earth. My name is Charles Maxwell.'

I recognised her; she was a senior general in the Euroterre army. She was in her late fifties with close-cropped, greying blonde hair. She was nearly too short to enter the military, and had obviously gained weight with age, her stomach bulging over her grey trousers. Her eyes were full of cutting intelligence, and she eyed us critically with a frown that made her severe features even more intimidating.

The rest of the people were also senior military, none of whom I recognised, and probably scientific and diplomatic advisors.

Shiumo sneezed loudly: a series of explosive bursts lasting nearly half a minute. She panted, then took a deep breath and said, 'Please move three of these people away from me.' She pointed at two of the suits. 'Him and him. And him too.' She pointed at one of the aides behind the general.

The general gestured and the men moved away, their faces a mixture of bewilderment and mortification.

'You're obviously allergic to something about them,' the general said. 'What is it? We'll make sure it isn't brought near you again.'

'Not an allergy,' Shiumo said. 'Just a sensitivity. Thanks for moving them away. Oh! I'd better do the formal introduction things. Sorry.' She bowed her head to General Maxwell and spoke as if reciting a speech. 'I greet you in the name of my mother, the Empress Silver Enlightenment, ruler of the Intergalactic Dragon Empire.'

I shared a shocked look with Commander Alto: the Empress was Shiumo's mother?

'I come in the spirit of peace and friendship, searching for love throughout the galaxy,' Shiumo continued. 'I am alone except for my sentient aide, an AI called Marque. I believe I can help you in your colonisation efforts, and assist your people with technology more advanced than your own.' She changed to a less formal tone. 'These colonists from the *Nippon Maru* are in a bad way. Can you transport them to a medical facility in a hurry?'

The general nodded and waved to a couple of the security people.

'The gurneys that the colonists are lying on are extensions of my aide,' Shiumo added. 'To preserve your security, I suggest you transfer the patients off the gurneys. They are alien artefacts.'

'We understand,' one of the black suits said. She moved to push the gurney and it shifted away from her. She raised her hands with shock.

'Show us where to go and we'll offload the colonists,' the gurney said. 'Point the way.'

The suit checked with General Maxwell, who nodded. She and her companion guided the gurneys towards the gate.

'Will you come with us to our secure conference facility?' the general said. 'The leaders of all nations are ready to meet you.'

'By all means, madam; lead the way. With your permission, I'd like to keep Jian and Richard by my side. They have been extremely helpful, and have agreed to act as my aides during this cultural acclimatisation.'

The general scowled so quickly it was almost imperceptible. 'We would prefer you had assistants who are specifically trained for the role. I have some excellent people who would be outstanding.'

'Nah, I think I'll stick with these two. Richard's hot and Jian's super-smart,' Shiumo said. 'Lead on.'

One of the suits choked quietly with laughter as we followed General Maxwell and Shiumo across the field to the waiting rotocopters.

What was wrong with the three men? I asked Shiumo as we boarded the rotocopter. *Are you allergic to something? I can discreetly tell the general.*

I'm not allergic. It was the way they smelled. An incredibly unpleasant and pungent mixture of chemicals. My nose still burns!

But I haven't bathed in ages, I said. *The space elevator had minimal bathroom facilities. I must stink even worse.*

Your smell is natural and rather pleasant, she said. *I don't know what they did to themselves, but their odour burns the back of my throat like a chemical gas attack. I'm going to need a big drink of water to flush this out.*

I'll make sure you get it, I said.

And that's why I want to have you close by.

8

The government officials spent the trip in the rotocopter tapping out messages on their tablets, but General Maxwell and the suits that accompanied her watched Shiumo as if she was about to sprout two heads. The general was deeply suspicious of the alien and convinced she would turn on us at any moment.

Shiumo didn't seem fazed; she radiated curiosity tinged with delight as she watched the countryside go past. We swooped over Old Geneva, its lake surrounded by terraces cut into the mountains and crammed with prefab houses and small plots of rice and sorghum.

One of the suits opened a locker and passed around portable oxygen masks with thirty-minute cylinders. We all slipped them over our faces.

I don't need one, Shiumo said when the suit offered her one.

The suit looked to the general.

'We're approaching the top of the oxygen layer,' the general shouted over the whine of the rotors. 'You'll need oxygen; there isn't any in the atmosphere.'

I don't need it. I can survive in a vacuum, Shiumo said.

'Take it anyway, so you can use it if you need it,' the general said.

Shiumo took the cylinder from the suit and held it out. Marque lifted it from her front claw and held it suspended beneath its sphere. The suits watched the oxygen cylinder float as if they were hypnotised.

I turned to see out the 'copter's window. We rose above the oxygen layer and all life petered out, leaving bare high-altitude rocky ground with small patches of snow in shady places.

We landed on a barren hillside, where the only building was an ugly concrete box half-dug into the ground, and exited the 'copter still wearing the masks.

'We need to quarantine you and everybody who's been in contact with you,' General Maxwell said at the entrance. 'We have facilities to house everybody in this underground station. Is that acceptable? I'm sure you're as concerned about pathogens as we are.'

'We eradicated all disease millennia ago,' Marque said. 'This is unnecessary and a complete waste of our time.'

'We understand that,' the general said. 'We still ask that you humour us.'

'Of course,' Shiumo said. 'As I said, this is First Contact, and all about you. Whatever makes you feel the most comfortable.'

'Thank you,' the general said.

She guided us through an airlock, where we could remove the oxygen masks, and into the bunker. The other side of the airlock was a lift, and we went in with three of the guards silently following.

'It's underground? I wanted to see your planet,' Shiumo said, sounding disappointed.

'As soon as we have the –' General Maxwell began.

'No, no,' Shiumo said. 'This is normal. You need to ensure that I'm not a threat. Let's get these foundation talks out of the way, and then I'll do a tour. I'm sure your people will be excited to see the alien.'

'I doubt they know of your existence yet,' Commander Alto said. 'The authorities will want to make a controlled announcement.'

General Maxwell nodded.

Everybody's tablet pinged at the same time, and we all checked them.

'Humph,' Maxwell said when she saw what the urgent message was. A few of the *Britannia*'s crew members had surreptitiously taken videos of us visiting Shiumo's ship and retrieving the Japanese colonists, and sold them to the network.

'They'll be out of a job when they come back down the elevator,' I said to Commander Alto as we watched ourselves guide Shiumo through the *Britannia*.

'They were probably paid so much that it doesn't matter,' he said.

Shiumo turned to General Maxwell. 'A way to disrupt this is to get me out and about as publicly as possible so I become mundane.'

'We will, Princess. But first we need to ensure you're no biological threat, and that you are willing to negotiate peacefully with our people.'

Shiumo nodded. 'I understand. Let's hurry up and get this out of the way.'

The lift doors opened onto a rough concrete corridor that smelled of mud and mould.

'Your allergy isn't bothering you?' the general asked Shiumo.

'No, I'll let you know if I have a problem,' she said.

The general led us down passages lined with more concrete and lit by bare, old-fashioned LED tubes, to a conference room with a table and large screen. The walls and floor were plain concrete, and the desks and chairs looked tired and worn. We were in an unused military bunker, possibly even one of the old nuclear bases.

Shiumo stopped just inside the door. 'I can't sit on your chairs. They're too small.'

Maxwell turned to the guards. 'Move the table out. Pull the chairs to the back. Find a sofa for the Princess to sit ... lie ... recline on.'

'I'm happy to lie on the floor if you have some cushions,' she said.

'We'll find you something suitable,' the general said as five more guards appeared and stationed themselves in the hallway.

Shiumo had another sneezing fit.

'Which ones?' I said.

'Gah!' She choked, and pointed at the guards. 'That one. And that one.'

The general led the two men out into the hallway and spoke softly to them, while two other guards lifted the table and removed it. The first two guards shook their heads, and the general made a gesture of exasperation and returned to the room.

'One had a full shower yesterday, and the other had a shower four days ago and has been doing the usual sink wash since. Do you have any idea what's causing this, Princess?'

'I think it's their deodorant,' I said.

'That is an *en*odorant, not a *de*odorant,' Shiumo said.

The general's face went blank, and she returned to the two guards in the hall. She spoke to them, and they shared a look, then nodded.

She came back to us. 'I'll make sure nobody else wears that particular brand around you.' She huffed a short laugh. 'It's one of the cheaper ones.'

'Thank you,' Shiumo said.

She'd like a big glass of water – a container double human size would be suitable – to flush away the scent, I said to the general, and she nodded a reply and went out of the room again.

Two guards entered carrying a tired-looking couch that appeared to have come from a waiting room. They placed it in the middle of the room facing the screen, then positioned half-a-dozen chairs facing it. Shiumo hopped up onto the couch and turned to face the screen.

Commander Alto moved a chair to sit to one side of her, and I did the same on the other side.

Shiumo patted the couch next to her. 'Richard?'

He hesitated, then rose and sat next to her. He relaxed into the sofa and let his breath out, the tension disappearing from him.

The general returned to the room with what appeared to be a flower vase full of water.

'Thank you!' Shiumo said, and took it from her. She hesitated, holding the vase.

'Clear,' Marque said.

Shiumo took a big deep drink, then raised the vase. It floated out of her front claws and drifted to hover in mid-air at the side of the room, next to the Marque sphere.

The general watched the vase, her face expressionless, for a long moment. When it didn't move, she sat in a chair across from Shiumo and leaned her elbows on her knees, clasping her hands. 'Let's begin.'

'By all means,' Shiumo said. 'Just tell me what you want to achieve today, and I will work with you.'

*

Shiumo agreed to meet with every world leader through the network, in descending order of their population. By the fifth hour of trade pacts and diplomatic ties, it was well into the evening. I hadn't eaten since breakfast, and we were in a different time zone from the elevator base. I hit the wall hard.

Shiumo was patiently listening to the Prime Minister of Euroterre mouthing platitudes on the screen. When the Prime Minister stopped to take a breath, Shiumo raised one claw.

'Honoured Prime Minister, please bear with me. My assistants are failing.' She turned her head on her long neck and focused on me. 'Jian, your brain activity is severely depressed. How often does your species eat?'

I started; I'd been half-asleep. 'Uh ...'

'Two or three times a day,' Commander Alto said. He checked his tablet. 'It's 2 a.m. our time. We should eat something, I suppose.'

'You've taken in nothing except the water they supplied us.' Shiumo bowed her head to the Prime Minister. 'Forgive me, madam, but I think we will have to pick this up again tomorrow. My aides need rest, and frankly so do I.'

General Maxwell spoke from her seat at the back of the room. 'I have accommodation here for you all. Please accept our hospitality. We do ask that none of you leave the confines of the bunker. It's sealed, and everybody who's been in contact with Shiumo is in quarantine.'

'I'll return to my ship, and travel directly from here to there,' Shiumo said. 'Richard and Jian, I have guest quarters if you want to come with me. Or you can stay here.'

'They're our people and we can provide for them,' Maxwell said. 'They should stay here.'

She wants to debrief us, then replace us with her own people, I said to Shiumo. *Don't let her. I want to stay with you.*

'I want to stay with Shiumo, if she'll have me,' I added out loud.

'Me too,' Commander Alto said.

'Thank you, General,' Shiumo said. 'But both my aides are exhausted, and I'm very close myself. I appreciate your hospitality and the warm welcome of your planet, but I need to rest. Marque will remain in contact with you through your communication network. I suggest you connect it with the people who are asking for interviews. It speaks for me and can answer all their questions.' She bowed her head. 'Please forgive me if I return to my ship now, and take my aides with me.'

'They need to stay here. Choumali and Alto, you're ordered to stay –'

Touch me if you want to go with me, Shiumo said to us.

We put our hands on her shoulders and she folded us back to her ship.

'Marque, could you make me some grilled grakka, please?' Shiumo said, shaking our hands off. 'Ask the humans what they want to eat.' She disappeared.

'She's gone to take an enormous piss,' Marque said. 'She's been holding it the entire time she was on the Earth because your facilities wouldn't suit her. I saw you two take breaks, but do you need to go again before you eat?'

'Do you have facilities that would suit us?' Commander Alto said.

'I obtained the information on your network. There's something suitable ... right there.'

An arrow flashed on the aft wall, and the standard toilet symbols appeared beneath it.

I tried not to run. 'I hope there's more than one because I'm busting.'

I stopped when I realised Commander Alto hadn't moved.

'I can accommodate your special needs, Richard,' Marque said. 'Go ahead.'

Together we nearly raced to the bathrooms.

Shiumo was reclining on the cushions when we returned to the main area. 'Everyone comfortable now? I think my bladder was about to explode.'

Commander Alto sat across from her. 'You weren't the only one.'

'Damn those people could *talk*!' I said.

'I know!' Shiumo rolled onto her back with her belly in the air, and stretched her legs. She had minimal external genitalia – a single reptile-like vent between her back legs, and what was obviously her anus under her tail. She could be male or female. The scales on her belly were smaller and faded to a lighter shade of red than those on her back. She rolled upright and stretched like a cat. 'I think that went well. Nobody tried to kill us, so I owe Marque twenty scales.'

'Only if you make it till the middle of the day tomorrow without an attempt,' Marque said.

A small door in the aft wall opened and a tray floated towards us.

'Here's your grilled grakka, Shiumo. Jian and Richard, I've tapped into the human communication network and there's a vast selection of food that you people eat. What do you want?'

'What can you make?' Commander Alto said, sitting on the cushion. He rubbed his hand over his face. 'Damn, that was brutal. Tea to start off with?'

'I can synthesise any combination of proteins and carbohydrates. Tell me what you want and I'll make it for you,' Marque said.

'You wouldn't be able to do a dhal, would you?' Commander Alto said. 'I'm vegetarian. I don't eat the flesh of animals.'

'I understand. We have met many races who are herbivorous. I can do that for you. Jian?'

'I'm not a vegetarian. Roast chicken?'

'Not a problem. Sit, relax, tea's on its way. Try not to watch Shiumo eating.'

Shiumo had picked up a haunch of what looked like charred sheep and was tearing the flesh from it. She lowered her head and turned away, placing the meat back onto the tray. 'Sorry. It's not real flesh; it's a protein substitute.'

'It doesn't bother me,' Commander Alto said. 'Go ahead and eat.'

'Are you sure?' Shiumo's emotions were full of concern. 'I can wait until later.'

'No, eat. You've had as big a day as we have.'

'Yes, Shiumo, eat.' I unbuttoned the top two buttons of my jumpsuit and rubbed my gritty eyes. 'I suppose the launch of the *Britannia*'s cancelled. If I don't stay with you, I'll be sent back to drilling recruits in Euroterre.'

'The ship wasn't due for launch for two years anyway,' Commander Alto said. 'If Marque and Shiumo are prepared to share some of their technology, then the ship that goes to Wolf 1061 may be three times as advanced, and the colony ten times as likely to succeed.'

'I'd like to help those poor *Nippon Maru* people re-establish their colony as well,' Shiumo said. 'So much hard work, and all for nothing.'

Two trays floated from the back wall, each containing the meals we'd asked for, and settled on the table in front of us. I skewered a piece of the boneless chicken-like meat on my fork. It tasted slightly of chemicals – a hint of formaldehyde or acetone, with an overtone of varnish.

Commander Alto glanced up at the Marque sphere. 'Is this compatible with our chemistry, and containing no microbes that can make us sick?'

'I should be offended,' Marque said. 'Yes, compatible; and no microbes.'

'It just tastes a little ... strange,' Commander Alto said, taking another bite.

'So does this,' I said.

Shiumo hissed with laughter. 'It's only an approximation. Once Marque has sampled the foodstuffs directly, it will be able to duplicate them accurately.' She picked up her meat again. 'So, you've spent the day with me now, and seen what's involved in working with me. The next two weeks – at least – will be meetings with officials of this planet, and scheduling folds to help them establish interstellar colonies. Marque will give your people controlled access to our technology, with the condition that you stop fighting each other – which will add another level of complexity to what I want to accomplish. So I'll ask you again: are you sure you want to stay with me?'

The idea of being left behind when Shiumo departed for good made me feel bereft.

'How long will you stay here?' I asked her. 'What happens to us when you go? Can I go with you?'

'Wait,' Commander Alto said. 'We've known you less than a day. Why are we so damn attached to you? Are you doing something to us?'

'Of course not. Jian would know if I'm messing with your minds,' Shiumo said. A tray arrived with the tea. 'Thank you, Marque. You can leave any time, dear people. I will not force you to stay with me.'

'What if we want to stay with you when you return home?' Commander Alto stopped. 'Now I really know something's wrong. Why would I want to desert my own planet?'

'For the chance to travel the universe as companions to Shiumo and Marque,' I said. 'Why wouldn't you take it? If we travel with Shiumo, we can come back to Earth whenever we like. It's the opportunity of a lifetime. Take me with you wherever you go, Shiumo, please.'

'You are welcome to come.' Shiumo poured tea for us, and her voice became wistful. 'The dragon homeworld is one of the most advanced habitats in the Empire. The capital is the floating city of ... in your language it's called Sky City. It is a hundred kilometres to a side, and floats above the green and beautiful surface of the planet. The shining white Imperial Palace stands on a plateau in the middle of the city, with the space elevator behind it. The elevator rises to the planetary hub – a network of geostationary satellites linked together to provide our main spaceport and folding nexus. It is very beautiful.'

'It sounds like it,' I said with awe. 'I would love to see.'

'I haven't been home in a long time. I should take you,' Shiumo said. 'For now, though, let's finish eating, and then I'll take you for a short ride through your own planetary system, and we'll look at your gorgeous gas giants. What's the name of the one with the big rings?'

'Saturn,' Commander Alto said, drinking his tea. When he put the cup down, the pot lifted itself to refill it. 'Thank you, Marque.'

'And the one with the enormous storm on the side? The biggest gas giant,' Shiumo said.

'Jupiter.'

'All right,' she said. 'Enjoy the meal, and I'll explain your duties while we're in this establishment phase, and then we'll go for a quick ride around.'

Commander Alto and I shared a look, and tried not to eat the food too quickly. We had absolutely made the right decision.

9

Jupiter filled three-quarters of the sky, glowing red and gold above us. Three of the moons shone a short distance away. Shiumo was visible on the nose of her ship, orange in the reflected light from Jupiter's surface.

I sidled to Commander Alto and took his natural hand.

He looked down at me. 'Uh ...'

I squeezed his hand. 'I'm glad I have a human friend to share this with. I just wish my girlfriend and boyfriend back home could see this wonder too.'

You have a trinary relationship? Shiumo asked with interest.

'Yes. It's fairly uncommon. We humans are usually monogamous.'

I see. We dragons are ... There is no word for it in your language. We just have liaisons with whoever we fancy, and everybody helps care for the children when we decide to have them.

'The closest in our language is probably the term "free love",' Commander Alto said.

Pfft. As if love is anything but free. Do you miss your partners, Jian? Maybe you should go home to them.

I released Commander Alto's hand and hugged myself, suddenly cold. 'When they find out that I'm psi, and that I lied to them, I doubt I will be able to see them again. They knew my father was in the Psi Corps but I assured them many times that I wasn't psi.'

You lied to the people you were in a relationship with? she said, sounding shocked.

'I didn't tell anyone,' I said. 'My father was posted onto the Prussian front before I was born. He only came home on leave two or three times, and he was killed when I was five years old. My mother never remarried, and stayed in Euroterre for her pension even though all her family are in China. I'm all she has, and if they knew I was psi they'd put me in the Psi Corps and the same thing could happen to me.'

'We knew you were psi,' Commander Alto said. 'And we respected your decision. You wouldn't have been sent to the front.'

'That's beside the point now, I suppose.'

I am sorry for your loss, Shiumo said. *But you are one of only a thousand psi on your planet. You're very special.*

'That will be little consolation when my partners find out,' I said.

'How do you know there are only a thousand psi?' Commander Alto said.

Your population's about a billion, right?

'Yes, that's right.'

The psi are about one in a million, so there's a thousand of them.

'How do you know that?' Commander Alto said. 'Did you look it up on the network?'

'Wait,' I said. 'The psi all suddenly appeared for no reason the scientists could detect. The gene had been sitting there our entire history without being activated. Did you do this?'

The gene activates itself when you consciously restrict your population to a sustainable level, Shiumo said. *In your case the population control was involuntary, but it was still enough to turn on the gene.*

'How long ago would you have meddled with our genome like this?' Commander Alto said, but he sounded more amused than concerned.

Could have been anything from thousands to millions of years. In your case, we probably visited more than once. You're very cute and you smell nice.

Commander Alto and I shared a shocked glance.

Would you like to come out here with me on the nose, Jian? See the planet directly?

I hesitated, unsure. 'How will you protect me?'

'I can put you into an energy bubble,' Marque said.

I thought about it, then lowered my head, embarrassed that I wasn't brave enough to try it. 'No. I'm comfortable here with Commander Alto.'

Richard?

'I'll stay here with Jian.' He took my hand again. 'I lost my little boy in the '64 floods. I like to think that if I'd ever had a daughter, she would be as impressive as you.'

'Thanks.' I smiled at him. I had few memories of my own father. He'd died at the same time Commander Alto had taken that bomb in the face.

Ready to see the rings of Saturn? Shiumo said.

'Last one, and then it's bedtime for Corporal Choumali,' Commander Alto said. 'It's very late, and we have another big day tomorrow.'

'Awww, really?' I whined like a four year old. 'I was having fun.'

'Bedtime, young lady,' Commander Alto said sternly, and we chuckled together.

Understood, Shiumo said. *Start visualising what you would like in your personal quarters so Marque can reconfigure them for you. It can make anything you want. Just picture it clearly for me and I will pass it on.*

'Understood,' I said. 'Can I have a swimming pool?'

'That may take a little longer, depending on how big you want it,' Marque said.

'Never mind,' I said. 'I was joking.'

Prepare for fold, Shiumo said.

A handrail slid out of the floor in front of us, and we held it. Shiumo folded us – we were stretched impossibly long and thin again – and then the sky changed to a view of Saturn, from slightly above the plane of the rings. The closer rings were visible as chunks of ice, but as they faded into the distance the chunks merged together and the rings gleamed with different colours. The planet itself was banded in dusty brown and orange, with sharp black shadows cast by the rings.

The planet isn't as spectacular as the previous one, but the rings are striking, Shiumo said. She launched herself off the nose of the ship and floated away.

I grabbed Commander Alto's hand. 'Shiumo?'

I'm just having a look around. I'll be right back, she said, and disappeared.

I felt a moment of panic, stuck on a ship in the middle of nowhere without the driver. I took some deep breaths to calm myself. I trusted Shiumo; she'd just gone for a walk.

'We'll be fine, we'll be fine,' I said softly, trying to convince myself.

'I'm here,' Commander Alto said, and squeezed my hand.

'You have bonded with Lady Shiumo very quickly,' Marque said. 'I'm glad you're enjoying her company. Don't worry, Jian, she'll be right back. She can't resist the opportunity to play in ice rings.'

A boulder of ice, two metres across, spun towards the ship.

'See what I mean?' Marque said.

We ducked as the boulder approached us, but it was deflected and bounced away.

'One to me,' Marque said.

The boulder tumbled towards the planet, and there was a flash of red. Then the boulder spun towards us again. Marque deflected it, and it bounced in another direction.

'They're playing *volleyball* with the rings of Saturn,' I said with awe.

'Two to me!' Marque said. 'She must be tired; she's in very bad form.'

I am, Shiumo said. *I'm not enjoying this as much as I usually do. I think we all need to get some rest.* There was another flash of red, and she became visible swimming through space towards us. She landed on the nose of the ship. *Prepare for fold.*

We held the handrail, were stretched again, and were back in orbit around the Earth.

Shiumo popped into existence next to us. 'Visualise what you want in your quarters, and I'll pass the specifications on to Marque.'

'Jian, design something like standard single quarters and send it to Shiumo,' Commander Alto said.

I nodded, and passed information on barracks with washing sinks and beds to her.

'Give me a moment while I check your network for reference pictures,' Marque said. 'I see. Soft fabric like that takes a little longer to manufacture.'

I looked up at the Earth. 'I should have taken some photos of Jupiter and Saturn to send to my mum.'

'Your quarters are ready,' Marque said. 'I've also provided clean clothing of identical manufacture to what you're wearing. Do you need to recharge, Richard?'

'No. I'm good for a few days.'

'I can provide you with a charging station compatible with your system.'

'No need, but thank you.' He bowed to Shiumo. 'Lady Shiumo, I bid you goodnight.'

'How long do you need to rest for?' she said.

'Give us seven of our hours.'

'Eight then. Rest.' She bobbed her head. 'Sleep well, dear companions.'

I bowed as well. 'Good night, Lady Shiumo. Thank you for your training.'

'I'm so glad I met you guys.'

'I am too.'

'Go. Rest. I will see you tomorrow for breakfast,' she said. 'And ask Marque for some of the images it took of the planets. It keeps a record of everything. It will have some lovely pictures to send to your mother.'

'Thanks, Shiumo.'

'Marque, please tell Jian where I am in case she needs to talk to someone during the night,' Commander Alto said as we followed Marque towards the back wall.

'I have provided you with quarters that have a connecting door so you can reassure each other during the sleep period if you need to,' Marque said.

'Thank you,' I said. 'But I'm sure Commander Alto will be fine.'

'I'm not so sure. I'll probably wake up wondering where I am,' Commander Alto said.

'Don't worry, old man.' I patted his arm, 'I'll look after you.'

'I am so glad you are here to care for the geriatric,' he said with biting sarcasm.

I am seven hundred and something of your years old, Shiumo said. *So two geriatrics.*

We shared a look, then both of us shook our heads and followed Marque towards the aft of the ship. We went down the same corridor the pod had been on, and this time an opening appeared on the left.

'This is Jian's room,' Marque said.

I poked my head in. 'How do I open and close the door?'

'Just wave your hand over it.'

I went inside, and Commander Alto followed me. It was more like a luxury hotel room than the single quarters I'd visualised to Shiumo. There was a circular window overlooking the Earth, a double-sized bed, couch and closet, but no other doors.

'I need a sink to wash myself,' I said.

The wall opened on the other side of the room. I went to the door and stopped to stare. It was a luxurious five-star bathroom with a shower, sink and even an old-fashioned bath – something I'd never seen in person. I touched the towels on the rail; they were ridiculously soft.

'I've never used anything like this before,' I said. 'How much water can I use? How often can I shower?'

'That bath would use a year's worth of water,' Commander Alto said from behind me.

'There's no restriction on water here,' Marque said. 'Use as much as you like. I'll just manufacture more of it.'

'I can shower *every day*?' I said with delight.

'You can shower ten times a day if you want to,' Marque said.

'Damn.'

'It's not appropriate for me to share this room with Jian,' Commander Alto said.

'Your room's through there,' Marque said, and another opening appeared on a different wall.

Commander Alto's room was identical to my own except for the power cable looped over the bedhead.

'You have to agree to open your common door,' Marque said. 'Touch the wall where the door is, and it will ping. If both of you touch the wall, it will open.'

'Try it,' I said to Commander Alto, fascinated.

He went through the doorway, turned, and waved his hand. The wall closed. There was a moment of silence, then a gentle ping. I touched the wall, and the door opened.

Commander Alto came back in and sat in the chair. 'Can we talk?'

I sat on the bed. 'Sir.'

'Do you want me to go out?' Marque said.

'Yes.' Commander Alto waited for the sphere to leave. 'Close the door behind you.'

The wall sealed itself.

'It's probably still listening,' Commander Alto said, studying the door. He shrugged. 'Beside the point, I suppose.'

'It's strange,' I said. 'I'm in a room with no door, on a spaceship owned by an alien, kilometres above the Earth, and I feel perfectly safe.'

'Are you sensing any duplicity from her?'

I shook my head. 'I wouldn't be here otherwise. All I sense from her is sincerity – a genuine desire to help us.'

'Good. Keep me updated. If she broadcasts anything except goodwill, let me know immediately.'

'Sir.'

He raised his natural hand. 'And while we're working on this project, we may as well ignore the rank courtesies. We're colleagues who are both assisting Shiumo until we're otherwise assigned.'

'General Maxwell wants to reassign us,' I said. 'We were deaf to orders when she told us to stay down there. Does that mean we're AWOL?'

'Hm.' He rubbed his chin. 'I guess we are. If Maxwell does manage to separate us from Shiumo, she'll take us to a firing range and shoot us first, then court-martial us later.' He rose. 'Get some sleep. We have a busy day tomorrow.'

I rose as well. 'I can't believe my luck in being part of this. We're helping Earth to join the galactic society.'

'I know,' Richard said. 'Sleep well, Jian.'

'Do you need help with that?' I said, pointing at the power cable.

'I'm not sure I trust them with my circuitry. I'll wait until we're back on Earth.'

'I understand.' I saluted him without thinking, then dropped my arm and shrugged. 'Night, sir.'

He went through the wall and it closed behind him.

I went to the wall leading onto the corridor and waved my hand over it. It opened. I wasn't imprisoned in my room, and Shiumo hadn't exhibited any malicious intent. I probably wouldn't sleep well, at the alien's mercy, but I'd be damned if I'd let Maxwell take me away from this adventure.

I looked in at the bathroom again, wondering whether I had the nerve to fill up that enormous bath with water. I'd never had a bath in my life. I shook my head. I couldn't waste that much water, regardless of what Marque said. But I would certainly make use of the shower, and maybe even use it every day.

10

I heard a soft ping and jerked awake. I had a moment of disorientation – the base? No ... the island training centre ... No, the space elevator ... Shiumo's ship!

I surged upright as I heard the ping again, and checked my tablet. I'd slept for nearly nine hours – the longest uninterrupted sleep I'd had since joining the generation ship project. I must have been seriously exhausted.

'Just a minute, sir,' I said, and quickly pulled on the bathrobe Marque had made for me, then touched the wall adjoining our rooms. It didn't open, and the ping came again, so I went to the corridor side and opened that.

Richard was waiting for me, fully dressed and obviously concerned. 'Are you all right, Choumali ... Jian?'

'I overslept. That bed was stupidly comfortable.' I ran my hands through the frizz of my hair. 'I'll be right out.'

'Meet us in the main room,' Richard said.

I nodded, and he waved one hand over the wall to close it.

When I was dressed and ready, I stopped at the table next to the window in my room. Two gold coins were sitting there. I hesitated, then slipped them into the pocket of my *Britannia* coverall. I'd see about converting them to cash to send to my mother.

In the main room of the ship, Richard was studying his tablet over breakfast as he spoke to Shiumo. She was sitting across from him, eating what appeared to be a large bright green oval fruit with smooth mirror-like skin.

'Preliminary negotiations with the nations of Earth,' he said.

'Morning, Jian. Take a seat and help me out with today's schedule,' Shiumo said, pushing a teacup towards me.

'Good morning, Princess.'

I sipped from the cup, then stopped and stared. It was like Japanese green tea, but the flavour had a slight touch of something that I'd never tasted before.

I opened my mouth to comment, but Richard spoke first. 'Dragon tea. We're the first humans to taste it.'

'What's the schedule?' Shiumo said.

'Interviews with the media. They want to arrange a tour of the planet when you're out of quarantine so you can see some of the biggest landmarks. Is there anything in particular you'd like to see?'

'I'm more interested in tasting your cuisine,' Shiumo said.

'Liar,' Marque said from its sphere floating above us. 'You eat nothing but grilled grakka. I have the ability to synthesise the cuisines of more than a thousand species, and you waste my talents –' It stopped, and when it spoke again its voice was full of exasperation. 'Shiumo, you have to *tell* me when you report back to Dragonhome. I wasn't prepared!'

'Don't be ridiculous, it's standard procedure,' she said. 'The minute I established contact with the humans I sent notification back. Do they want to fold a message of welcome to us?'

Marque made a bass sound that buzzed through the air. '... is here. She's taken the human name of Zianto, and she's three light-minutes away.'

Shiumo spat out her tea.

I grinned at her reaction; she was broadcasting affection rather than dislike.

'It's not funny. Zianto's a complete bitch,' Shiumo said.

'Who's Zianto?' I said, still chuckling.

'My sister. Two hundred years younger than me. Shocking layabout, sleeps with anything that moves, won't take her duties to the Empire seriously –'

'And outside your window,' Marque said.

A ship the same shape as Shiumo's, but a quarter of the size and pale blue-green, popped into existence next to us.

'Bitch!' Shiumo said, and slammed her teacup onto the table. 'This is my discovery!'

'You can have it,' said another voice.

A dragon folded onto the ship next to us, with a sphere floating above her that was indistinguishable from Shiumo's Marque spheres. Zianto appeared similar to Shiumo, except her scales were the same colour as her ship – a pale teal. Her tail was longer, and her body was broader and less snake-like. Her eyes and the gem between them were a striking clear azure blue.

'Hello, humans. I hope my sister's treating you well.'

'No complaints,' Richard said. He rose and bowed to Zianto, and I did the same. 'Princess.'

She nodded to us. 'I bear a message from the Empress, my mother, for your species.'

'Ooh,' Shiumo said with delight. 'That's unusual, a personal message. She likes the look of you.'

'How did you contact your homeworld?' Richard asked Shiumo. 'You said it's on the other side of the galaxy.'

'You have instantaneous communication?' I said.

'By telepathy?' Richard said.

'No,' Shiumo said. 'Telepathy only works at planetary distances. We have our own method of sending simple messages instantly over great distances.'

'But if anything's too complicated to send by scales, we carry the message ourselves,' Zianto said. 'I'm your courier for today.' She eyed the Earth floating below us. 'Nice planet. Anything good to eat?'

'We haven't had a chance to try anything yet,' Marque said. 'Shiumo will send her reviews through soon.'

'I have this under control,' Shiumo said with forced dignity. 'Give me the message from Mum and I'll hand it over to the humans. You can go.'

Zianto raised her head and spoke with similar dignity. 'Fine. I can tell when I'm not wanted.'

'I need two more minutes to finish synchronising,' Shiumo's Marque said.

'There's been some movement on the border with the cats,' Zianto's Marque said in the same voice. 'I'm passing the details over. The border isn't far from here.'

'Cats?' I said.

'Assholes. Won't join the Empire. Like chasing things, and hurting them when they catch them,' Shiumo said.

'Sounds like cats,' Richard said. 'That's what we call small predators that we've tamed on our planet.'

'It's more like they've tamed you,' Shiumo said. 'The species is very similar, so Marque named them "cats" in your language.'

'I'm done synching,' Marque said.

'All right, I'll head off and leave you to it,' Zianto said. 'There's talk that Hanako may be Second; she's very keen after messing up her last First. Don't get yourself killed.'

'Give Mum a big hug for me, and tell our sisters I love them,' Shiumo said.

The two dragons raised their front ends and hugged, closing their eyes, then dropped back onto four legs.

'You should get a goldenscales,' Zianto said, looking around. 'This ship is enormous. Way too big for a single dragon and a Marque to maintain.'

'No,' Marque said.

'Marque would be heartbroken,' Shiumo said. 'It can handle it.'

'All right then.' Zianto waved one claw at Richard and me. 'Have fun, humans. See you on the homeworld if you ever visit. Or I might be back – you never know.'

She disappeared, and reappeared on the nose of her blue-green ship. The ship disappeared.

'Before we go down to begin the negotiations,' Shiumo said, 'Jian, Richard, are you happy? Is there anything you need?'

'Are you sure we can stay with you?' I said. 'I don't want to go back to the barracks.'

'Stay as long as you like. I'd love to have your company on my travels.' She turned to Richard. 'Both of you.'

'Travelling the galaxy,' I said with awe, then snapped back to reality. 'Can I pack before I go?'

'You can do anything you want, dear Jian. Marque can synthesise anything you need. It's up to you whether you come with me or stay here. You can leave me any time. I won't force you to do anything.'

'I don't want to leave you,' I said. 'This is *wonderful*.'

'Richard?' Shiumo said.

'Same for me. But I'll need some technical support and maintenance.'

'I can provide all that. Just tell me what you want,' Marque said. 'We can remodel your rooms as well – make them larger, add features, anything you like. Including,' its voice filled with amusement, 'a swimming pool.'

'Thank you,' Richard said.

'Time to return to Earth. Let's go and be royal,' Shiumo said.

*

The silver dragon on the screen reclined on a white and silver throne, her deep sapphire blue eyes startling beneath the blue gem on her forehead.

'... and your representatives may visit Dragonhome any time,' she said. 'So, welcome to galactic society. I trust my daughter Shiumo is helping you gain a greater sense of what galactic citizenship means. She says there is still some conflict between you. If you want to gain more advantages from our society, you must be a peaceful species before we will share them. Shiumo will help you.' She nodded. 'Welcome, humanity.'

The screen blinked out, and the cameras refocused on the interviewer, Waleed Choudry.

'That was the message from the Empress Silver Enlightenment,' he said. 'I now have Princess Shiumo, the Imperial Representative, speaking to me from the secure bunker where the Euroterre authorities are keeping her in quarantine. Thank you for talking to me today.'

'My pleasure,' Shiumo said. She curled her tail around her, and looked directly at the camera. 'Thank you for your warm welcome, Earth. I feel very loved.'

Waleed looked down at his tablet. 'How big is the Galactic Empire?'

'Marque?' Shiumo said.

'Physically, it's about two by four hundred thousand of your light-years,' Marque said. 'It encompasses this galaxy and six of the fourteen galaxies orbiting it.'

'Ah, just to clarify,' Waleed said, 'this is your computer speaking?'

Shiumo's mouth flopped open and she hissed loudly.

Waleed jumped and looked around at the crew.

'That is the equivalent of calling someone a "worm",' Shiumo said. 'Marque is about as far from a computer as you are from a worm.'

'No,' Marque said. 'Single-celled organism. No, grain of sand. I am about as far from a computer as you are from a grain of sand.'

'I see,' Waleed said. 'They say you are sentient, Marque, is that correct?'

'Oh, so you did read the briefing notes,' Marque said.

'Is it self-aware?' Waleed asked Shiumo.

Shiumo hissed again. 'That's what sentient *means*. Some of you seem to think that sentient means "very clever". It doesn't. It means "self-aware". Marque is an artificial intelligence, self-aware, and very often a complete pain in my red scaly ass.'

Some of the production crew couldn't contain their laughter.

'The feeling is completely mutual,' Marque said.

'How does it float?' Waleed said.

'Anti-grav,' Marque said. 'And if you want to ask me questions, ask *me*.'

'I can leave and you can interview Marque instead, if you like,' Shiumo said. 'It *loves* to talk, particularly about itself.'

'Well, I'm the most interesting thing in the room,' Marque said. 'Look at me: I float, I can manipulate energy, I'm *way* more entertaining than Princess Red-and-Scaly over there. You *should* be interviewing me.'

'Maybe later, but for now I think I'll go on to the next question,' Waleed said. 'Princess, you told me that the Empire is six galaxies?'

'Seven including this one,' Shiumo said.

'What's its population?'

'Stop asking me questions about boring numbers that Marque can answer!' Shiumo leaned forward. 'Ask me about love.'

Waleed nodded. 'Don't worry, we will get to that.'

'The population when we left home was four hundred and seventy-five thousand decillion sentients, give or take a few trillion,' Marque said.

'Why is it an empire and not a democracy? Do you conquer worlds to expand it?'

'Of course not,' Shiumo said. 'The Empire *is* a democracy. Each world chooses its representative for a regional council who elect a regional representative to attend the Imperial Parliament on Dragonhome.'

'So the Empress's role is as a figurehead?'

'Exactly,' Shiumo said. 'We had a vote on whether to abolish the aristocracy a long time ago, and everybody voted to keep us, so we're still here.'

'Isn't an aristocracy something of an anachronism for a space-faring race like yours?'

'It's fun having a royal family to watch,' Shiumo said. 'The Empress goes around the Empire being imperial, and the media follow her, spending way too much of their useful time reporting on her *ridiculous* sexual liaisons with *multiple* unsuitable partners. She's non-stop entertainment.'

'And you?'

Shiumo raised her snout. 'I have never had an unsuitable partner.'

'What about those two on Ceti –' Marque began.

Shiumo cut it off. 'Never.'

'Will we be forced to join the Empire?' Waleed said. 'Will you conquer us?'

'Exactly the opposite,' Shiumo said. 'If we think you're worthwhile, we may invite you to apply for membership of the Empire. It's extremely prestigious; a thousand planets are currently on the waiting list. You're a long way from that level yet, so don't worry. I'll hang around for a while and help you colonise some nearby planets, and then maybe find someone who can live here fulltime as a liaison – if anybody is available, that is. There are far more planets than there are dragons who can help them.'

Waleed looked down at his questions, then up at Shiumo. 'Some scientists want me to ask about the four-dimensional folding.' He flipped through the notes, then read the question out word for word. 'If the fourth dimension is time, does this mean you can time-travel as well as travel instantaneously through space?'

'Time is not the fourth dimension of space,' Marque said. 'You're confusing space-time with –'

'No,' Shiumo said, cutting it off. 'Many species have asked us this, and some of us have tried to fold through time.' She broadcast mental discomfort at the concept. 'No dragon who attempted to travel through time has ever returned. We don't do it.'

'If you've contacted other species, why haven't you contacted us before now?'

'We have, but informally. We've been quietly helping you for years – we like bringing young civilisations along. And to make sure we can have tea when we finally make official contact.'

'But why didn't you make official contact in the first instance? Instead of "quietly helping"?'

'It's very bad manners,' Shiumo said. 'Bad for your self-esteem as a species …'

*

General Maxwell was waiting for us outside the studio. She'd changed into her dress military uniform: trousers and jacket, with an impressive bar of ribbons. She glared at Richard and me, then nodded to Shiumo.

'General,' Shiumo said with pleasure. 'I believe you have scheduled the world leaders to speak to me?'

The general linked her hands behind her back. 'I have. We've reorganised the communications room so you can speak to each of them in comfort.'

'Six weeks is an awfully long time to be in quarantine,' Shiumo said. 'Is there any way I can reassure your people that I'm not a threat?'

'We're still not completely sure it will be six weeks,' Maxwell said. 'People are arguing about the length of the quarantine. Some are saying that with your level of technology, keeping you in quarantine at all is a waste of time.'

'It is!' Marque said. 'It's totally unnecessary.'

'Others are saying you should be kept in quarantine permanently,' the general said to Marque.

'That's ridiculous,' it said.

'Let's give it two weeks,' the general said. 'Time for you to establish yourself as harmless, and for us to be cleared as healthy. We'll re-evaluate then.'

'Very well,' Shiumo said. 'Marque, can you build me an underground command centre next to this bunker?'

'How big do you want?'

'How many staff do you need?' Shiumo asked the general.

'The command centre here will have a staff of fifty. Are you sure you don't want to use it? It will have connections to the existing data and communications networks, and I assure you it will be secure.'

'Do you mind if I build an annexe of my own?' Shiumo said. 'It will be bright and spacious and comfortable, have facilities to suit me as well as you, be secure and airtight, and place no strain on your resources.'

The general's expression turned sour. 'If that's what you want ...'

'I know you want to observe me, and I don't care about that, but your toilets are *way too small*,' Shiumo said.

Maxwell sighed with defeat. 'I suppose we don't have a choice. Are you sure it will be secure enough, and keep you in quarantine?'

'Absolutely positive. It'll be impregnable. Marque.'

'Done,' Marque said. 'I'll have the habitat for a cube ready for you in twenty Earth hours. Or do you want a tetrahedron or something? That would take slightly longer.'

'Cube is fine,' she said.

'You are so boring, Shiumo.'

'In the meantime, let's start talking to Earth administrations,' Shiumo said.

General Maxwell led us along a series of damp corridors to a bare room with concrete walls, ceiling and floor. It had been fitted with a plush new couch sitting in front of a screen, and five chairs for observers behind it. Twenty people in a variety of national military uniforms and civilian garb were crammed into the room.

'Allow me to introduce your staff,' the general said. 'This is Major Erica Rein, your head of operations. Her team includes ...'

Marque will remember everyone for us, Shiumo said to me. *Don't worry about memorising the names. Let's just honour them with our attention and get this over with. You can sit at the back of the room and wait if you like.*

Richard and I shared a look and moved to the back of the room. After twenty minutes of pleasantries the staff had taken their positions.

'I'm to speak to the leaders in order of population, correct?' Shiumo said as she climbed onto the couch.

'Yes. The President of the Chinese Federation is waiting for you.'

'Certainly. Put her through.'

'Him, actually,' the general said, and the Chinese president appeared on the screen.

'Honoured President,' Shiumo said, nodding to the screen.

'Honoured Princess,' the president said. 'Welcome to our planet.' It took twenty minutes of verbal equivocation before he finally broached the main subject. 'We understand that you are offering to carry our ships to colonisation planets.'

'That I am, sir. I want to help your species travel to the stars and spread throughout this part of the galaxy. There are plenty of uninhabited planets nearby, and you are welcome to them.'

'Then we claim Kapteyn-b, Princess,' the president said. 'Can you carry a small representation of our people and equipment there?'

'Marque?'

Marque produced a star map of the area around Earth that shone in three dimensions, filling the room.

Shiumo hissed with laughter. 'Really, President Li? Kapteyn-b – the planet the Japanese already colonised?'

'Their colony failed,' the president said stiffly.

'No,' Shiumo said.

It took a while for the president to realise that she was refusing to take them rather than denying the failure of the colony. 'Very well then, Princess, please assist us to colonise Wolf 1061-c.'

Richard and I straightened. Our ship had been built to go to Wolf 1061. General Maxwell let out her breath loudly behind us.

Marque had already marked the star on the map floating above us.

'That's the one you were going to, right, Richard?' Shiumo said, turning her head to see us.

'That's right.'

Shiumo turned back to the screen. 'The UK–Euro Federation have a ship under construction already. They have priority. You can go to ... Marque?'

'Gliese 667-c,' Marque said.

'But we have the largest population, so we should have first pick,' the president said.

'And the other two nations are nearly ready to go. Shall we move on to a timetable?'

'We *will* have a closer planet,' the President said, and the screen flicked off.

'Oh no, you won't,' Shiumo said with amusement. She turned and hoisted her front feet onto the back of the sofa to speak to the general. 'Who's next?'

'Us,' Maxwell said. 'Euroterre is the second-largest regional administration by population. You already said we can have Wolf 1061. Our Prime Minister would like to thank you.'

'Very well, put her through,' Shiumo said, and faced the screen again.

*

When Shiumo had finished speaking to the Prime Minister and then the Home Secretary, General Maxwell asked her, 'Is everything satisfactory? There's nothing you need?'

'No. It's working out well, isn't it? What's on for tomorrow?'

Maxwell opened a folder. 'Japan is first. They'd like to arrange for another ship to be taken to Kapteyn, if that's acceptable to you.'

'I would love to help them achieve their goal,' Shiumo said. 'The colonists worked so hard and I want to see them succeed.'

'Then the South American Republic, the African Commonwealth, and the North American Federation,' the general said.

'And that's all of them?'

'All the major ones.' Maxwell closed the folder. 'You should have the talks finished by the end of tomorrow, then the world leaders have arranged a round of receptions for you – to be held here until you're out of quarantine.'

'All sorts of new foods for you to try,' Richard said.

'Food,' Shiumo said with longing. 'I'm *starving*. Is there a formal dinner tonight?'

'It was a little soon to have all the necessary precautions in place,' the general said. 'We can provide a meal for you here if you let us know what you want to eat.'

'I'll return to my ship,' Shiumo said. 'Would you like to come up and have dinner with us, General Maxwell?'

The general bowed to her. 'Apologies, Princess, but I have a great many briefings still to prepare. Choumali and Alto, please stay here and help me complete the paperwork.'

'They need to come up to the ship so they can remodel their quarters,' Shiumo said. 'Can it wait until tomorrow?'

'No, I'm afraid it can't, Princess. I need them here for at least another two hours.'

Shiumo tilted her head slightly. 'But I want their company for dinner.'

'I'm sorry, Princess. I need them too.'

'I need them more,' Shiumo said. *Hands!*

Richard and I put our hands on her shoulders and she folded us up to her ship.

'That's becoming extremely monotonous,' she said. 'Next time, just put your hands on me and we'll leave. The general is becoming tediously impolite about this.'

'You forgot Marque,' I said.

'No, I left it there to convey whatever the general needs to you. If there really is paperwork for you – and I doubt it – the general can give it to Marque to pass on.'

A Marque sphere came out from the back wall of the ship. 'Grilled grakka?'

'No, try something from Earth,' Shiumo said. 'Surprise me.' She tilted her head again. 'What does the general say?'

'She suddenly decided the paperwork can wait until tomorrow,' Marque said. 'The other sphere is on its way up and should be here in about an hour. In the meantime, I'll make dinner.'

'I'm wrecked. It was a hell of a day, full of stress,' Shiumo said. 'Warm the water, and I'll have a bath after dinner.'

We followed her to the dining table, and sat across from her. The table was stepped down lower on our side, so it was easier for us to reach.

'I sampled everything food-related that I could while we were down there today,' Marque said from within the ship's walls. 'I have seven different types of replicated animal flesh. Are you interested in fruit or vegetables?'

'No, just protein,' Shiumo said. She nodded to us. 'We dragons are obligate carnivores, but we like the taste of plants as well. We have to be careful, though – if we eat too much of them, our digestion rebels. Marque, what's the table protocol for trying new stuff?'

'Clarify with the humans,' Marque said. 'There wasn't enough about it on their network – it seems a taboo subject. Jian, Richard, would you like replicas of the food you ate during the day? I've already sampled them, so they'll be accurate copies and won't taste strange.'

'Sure,' Richard said, and I nodded.

A tray floated from the back of the ship, and Shiumo jiggled with anticipation. 'This is the *best* part of encountering new species. Discovering what they taste like.'

'Wait,' I said. 'What they *taste like*?'

'Not you, silly Jian. The concept of eating sentients is deeply disturbing.' Shiumo's silver eyes were wide as she watched the tray approach. 'Seven different types of animals. Wonderful. I love meeting carnivorous and omnivorous species – we can share opinions on what your food-source animals taste like. Food and love – life's greatest treasures. What do we have here, Marque?'

'Left to right: cow, sheep, camel, pig, horse, chicken, duck, cavy. Four ungulates, a solid hoof, two avians – reptile derivatives – and a small mammal that they call a rodent.'

'What's the protocol here?' Shiumo asked us. 'If I spit something out because it's completely inedible, will you be so offended that you'll hate me forever and never speak to me again?'

'Absolutely not,' I said.

'Excellent,' she said, and pulled off a pair of thick transparent gloves that acted as shoes when she went four-legged. The gloves lifted into Marque's sphere and disappeared.

Shiumo delicately picked up what appeared to be a slice of steak and sniffed it. 'Smells foul.' She popped it in her mouth, gagged, and quickly dropped it out again. 'Wow. That is vile. Tasted strongly of iron-based blood products. What was that?'

'Noted,' Marque said. 'Cow.'

'Next one,' Shiumo said, and lifted another piece of meat. She sniffed it, then ate it. She closed her eyes and raised her snout. 'Sold. Wonderful.' She opened her eyes. 'This is better than grilled grakka!'

'Thank the Empress for that,' Marque said dryly. 'Finally something other than grakka. I'll synthesise some more sheep for you.'

Trays holding meals floated in front of Richard and me. Mine was slices of what appeared to be chicken, with a white sauce and standard salad vegetables, and a couple of slices of white bread on the side. Marque had deconstructed the chicken salad sandwich I'd had for lunch and made it into something more like a restaurant meal.

Richard had something similar, with what appeared to be a protein substitute. He studied it suspiciously. 'This doesn't contain meat, does it?'

'Not even the meat is meat, Richard,' Marque said.

'What was that one? It was very bland,' Shiumo said.

'Pig,' Marque said.

'Yeah, toss that. Not nearly as good as the sheep. This looks the same; has it been treated differently?'

'They've salted and smoked it to preserve it,' Marque said.

'Oh, another species that does that.' Shiumo tried the meat, then closed her eyes and raised her head. 'That is *fabulous*. I love it. What's it called?'

'Bacon.'

Richard gingerly picked up some of the salad with his fork.

'Definitely vegetarian, Richard,' Marque said. 'I've thrown in some synthesised plant protein and boosted the vitamin level as well. None of the protein is even close to animal-sourced. Don't worry, it won't taste strange. Try it.'

I tasted some of the salad on my plate. Marque was right: it no longer had the chemical overtones. I wolfed my meal down. It had been a long time since lunch and I was starving.

'The bacon is excellent, but it's so rich I can only take small amounts. Perfect for snacks. For meals I'd love this – what's it called?' Shiumo said.

'Sheep,' Marque said. 'Mutton.'

'I'll have a double serve. It's wonderful.'

'Coming right up. And the water's at your comfort temperature.'

'I am so glad I found Earth,' Shiumo said as she poured herself some tea.

*

After dinner Marque cleared the plates, and Shiumo led us to an open space next to the transparent side of the ship.

'This is where the bath is. Step back, everyone,' Marque said. A crack appeared in the deck, and opened to reveal a pool of bubbling clear water three metres across. 'Temperature's set at the usual.'

'This is a whole year's worth of water for ten people,' I said.

'It'll do,' Shiumo said, and stood still.

A high-pitched whine filled the air and dust appeared to fly out from her scales. She turned around as Marque ultrasonically cleaned her, then she slid into the water. She reclined on a bench on the side of the spa and rested her head on the edge.

'That's much better. Holy hell, what a day.' She raised her head slightly. 'Put some music on, Marque.'

'Any preference?'

'Something relaxing.'

A cacophony that sounded like a variety of different musical instruments all playing different tunes filled the room. To my uneducated ear, it was a super-modern abstract piece, where everyone was playing something different until they all came together. I waited for that to happen, but it didn't. The cacophony continued, sometimes with loud drums, sometimes jangling chords, and some parts were just random wails and screams.

Richard and I shared a look.

Shiumo sighed loudly. 'Thank you. That's perfect.' She focused on me, her head still leaning on the side of the spa. 'What do you think, Jian? Do you like it?'

'It sounds like many tunes at once,' I said, trying to be diplomatic. 'I'm accustomed to only hearing one tune at a time.'

'Harmony,' she said, closing her eyes. 'The shifting harmonics of the many facets. Wonderful.' She opened her eyes and her voice filled with amusement. 'You don't like it, I can tell. One tune at a time? The simplified version ... Marque.'

The music changed to a single tune, played on what sounded like gongs but with more depth. They harmonised gently together.

'More like that?' she said.

'That's lovely,' Richard said.

'What are you humans waiting for?' she said, waving one claw above the water. 'Take those uniforms off and join me.'

'We don't take our clothes off in mixed company; it's embarrassing,' I said. 'You may not wear clothes, but we –'

'Swimsuits are in your rooms,' Shiumo said. 'I *have* been watching your broadcasts; I know a lot about you. Change, and come back. And while you're in your quarters, think about the upgrades you want to make. You can enlarge them if you're planning to stay for a while, and I hope you are. Then come back and sit in the warm water and tell me about your plans.'

I headed towards our rooms, but Richard pulled some cushions closer to sit next to Shiumo.

'You won't come in, Richard?' she said.

He shrugged. 'My prosthetics are splashproof but not waterproof. I'd fry. I haven't been immersed in water in years.'

'Why do you have such clumsy implants anyway?' She raised one claw. 'I understand that some people like such enhancements, but these are so basic. You can't even get them wet? Why would you *bother*?'

'You're an idiot, Shiumo,' Marque said.

'What am I missing?' Her mouth fell open. 'Oh. Dear Richard, I am so sorry.'

'No need to apologise,' he said. He waved his natural hand at me. 'Go get the swimsuit Marque made for you, Jian. I can sit out here. I'm perfectly comfortable.'

'What colour do you want?' Marque said as it followed me to my quarters.

'What colour what?'

'Swimsuit, human.'

'Uh ... black is okay.'

'Done. I haven't made anything terribly fashionable or fancy, because Shiumo doesn't care about clothes and barely understands them. But the suit is in your room; and you can remodel the room while you're in the spa.'

'Thanks, Marque,' I said, and rushed into my room to change.

When I came out, Richard was telling Shiumo what had happened to him.

'Stand still and put your arms out,' Marque said, and I did as asked.

The air filled with the ultrasonic whine, and my skin vibrated with a sensation that was neither heat nor cold but somehow both, making me shiver.

'Does it feel weird?' Richard asked me, amused.

'Yes!'

The noise stopped, so I slid into the warm bubbling water and sighed with bliss. The steam had an additive that relaxed me completely. I leaned my head back to find a soft cushion already there.

'Is this water drugged?'

'No, it's just herbs. From Earth,' Marque said.

'So they replaced the bits that were destroyed,' Richard told Shiumo, finishing his story. 'These are the latest in powered prosthetics, and some parts of me are highly advanced prototypes.'

'Let Marque upgrade them,' Shiumo said. 'It can provide you with prosthetics that are waterproof to a hundred metres, indistinguishable from the rest of you, and fully linked into your nervous system – touch, heat, cold, even pain if you want. They'll be self-powered and self-repairing, won't need recharging, and maintenance won't be the obvious nuisance it is for you right now.'

'I'll think about it,' he said.

'It would be a major improvement for you. Marque can install any sort of waste-disposal method you choose.'

'He might prefer to return to biological, Shiumo,' Marque said. 'The cybernetics are probably not by choice.'

'Oh, of course. I keep forgetting how primitive you humans are,' she said. 'If you don't want cybernetics, Marque can make cloned replacements for your lost body parts, including your genitalia. You can regain full sexual function and sensation.'

I sat upright and stared at him with horror. He'd been living like that for more than twenty years?

'Thank you very much,' he said, radiating mortification. He saw my face and looked away, even more embarrassed.

'I won't tell anyone,' I said. 'I never heard anything.'

'I think these Earth herbs are lowering your intelligence, Shiumo,' Marque said.

'I'm just exhausted,' she said. 'I am so sorry, Richard.' She leaned her chin on the edge of the bath. 'That's the second time I've apologised to you today; please forgive me.'

'Of course I forgive you,' he said. His expression softened. 'I'll think about it.'

11

After breakfast the next morning, Shiumo took us down to Earth, and we reappeared in the central atrium of a half-subterranean glass cube. The atrium soared all the way to the top of the cube, with the upper half next to the low concrete slab that was the top of the secure bunker. Light shone in through the glass ceiling, and floors were visible on either side of the atrium, some with cabling hanging from the ceilings. Multiple Marque spheres were working on the interior; some of them were more than two metres across, and carrying heavy beams.

'It's not finished yet?' Shiumo said.

'Give me two more hours,' the Marque sphere above us said. 'I won't give working access until it's completed. There's a possibility of injury from the unfinished structure.'

Shiumo sighed. 'Very well. Jian, Richard, let's go back to that awful hole in the ground.'

General Maxwell was waiting for us at the door that connected the cube to the bunker, looking entirely unimpressed at the new construction.

She bowed to Shiumo. 'Princess.'

'General. Let's talk to the Japanese representatives here, then after lunch we can move this whole catastrophe to my cube.'

The general gestured into the bunker. 'This way.'

'Revision on the cube's time frame,' Marque said. 'There really isn't enough silicon around here. It'll take another six hours.'

'Slacker,' Shiumo said with amusement.

We entered the bunker, but the sphere remained hovering on the other side of the door.

'Is it coming?' the general said.

'If you're going to sulk, go do it somewhere else,' Shiumo said.

'No.' The sphere whizzed into the corridor. 'It's my duty to protect you.'

'Oh, Marque,' Shiumo said affectionately. 'You do care after all.'

'You're my ride home,' Marque said dryly.

The door to the cube closed, and we headed towards the communications room.

When Shiumo was comfortable on her couch in front of the screen, the general stood with her hands behind her back. 'Commander Alto, Corporal Choumali, I need to speak with you. Outside.'

'No, General, I need them here,' Shiumo said.

'There's some things I need to ask them,' the general said.

'Then ask them here. You don't have any secrets from me, do you? This is a relationship of trust.'

The general hesitated, radiating irritation, then she nodded and sat in her chair at the back of the room. 'Euroterre understands the honour you are bestowing on us by choosing us as your headquarters, so I'll let it go. The paperwork can wait if you want to keep your companions nearby. You are a long way from home, after all.'

'Thank you, madam,' Shiumo said. 'They can leave me any time, but right now I need them here.'

She turned to the screen and proceeded to speak to the representatives in Japanese. Richard followed the conversation, but I flopped back in my seat. I didn't speak any Japanese, and I couldn't telepathically understand what was happening with an alien on one side of the conversation and an emotionless screen on the other.

'Just a minute, sir,' Shiumo said, raising one claw.

My brain was hit by lightning. Sparks shot through my head like fireworks that blossomed into a new language and faded into a heightened level of understanding. Shiumo hadn't just given me Japanese; she'd given me a quick overview of the culture and cuisine as well.

I grinned. '*Arigato gozaimasu*, Shiumo-sama.'

'I don't think I can do more than one language every week or so. Your brain needs recovery time,' she said.

I raised my hands. 'I'm not complaining. I just became fluent in Japanese.'

Shiumo turned back to the Japanese representative. 'You said you are close to ready, sir?'

'We were preparing to send a second ship to support the first one when you changed everything. We have gathered a new set of colonists and all the facilities they need. Your offer to carry them direct to the colony means they do not require the ship we were building for them.' He hesitated. 'What do you wish in return for your generous gift?'

'A selection of your best tea.'

The representative waited, then said, 'Is that all?'

'Normally I don't ask for anything. Aiding a growing species is enough reward in itself. But I want to try your teas.'

The representative bowed. 'You are exceptionally generous, Princess. How will we arrange the transport schedule?'

'That entirely depends on when you let me out of quarantine,' Shiumo said.

'We will have the expedition ready in three weeks,' the Japanese representative said. 'I do not doubt that your quarantine will be finished by the time we are ready to depart.'

'Good. My assistant Jian will make the schedule –'

I squeaked with shock.

'My assistant Jian,' Shiumo said more forcefully, 'and my aide Marque will handle the scheduling for me. Tell them when you will be ready, and I will fold your new colony to Kapteyn for you.'

'Very well, Princess.'

'General.' Shiumo turned her head on her long neck. 'Can you provide Jian with her own communications room so she can start the scheduling?' Shiumo swept her silver eyes onto me, where I sat glued to my seat. 'Stop looking so surprised, Jian. You can do this.' She hissed with laughter. 'Earn your keep, human.'

I pulled myself together and saluted her. 'Yes, ma'am.'

'Arrange a time for me to transport all their equipment onto my ship so I can fold it to Kapteyn. Give it three days, as soon as I've been cleared – and after I've done a three-day tour of your planet?' She turned to General Maxwell, questioning. The general nodded. 'A three-day tour of your planet, and receptions with the various governments. You know how much the transport pod can carry; Marque will help you work out how many trips I need to move all the colonists and their equipment up to my ship. An initial trip to Kapteyn to establish a landing area, then multiple trips to transport the crew and their equipment.'

'I need to write this down.' I picked up my tablet to take notes. Three weeks from now, three days of receptions ... I checked the calendar.

'We will redirect your call to another room, and Jian and Marque will handle the arrangements,' Shiumo said to the Japanese representative. 'How are the colonists that I rescued?'

'They wish to speak to you from their hospital rooms, if you have time, Princess.'

'Of course. Please put them through,' she said.

'Come with me, Corporal Choumali, and we'll set you up in another room,' General Maxwell said. 'Commander Alto, you should come as well. You can help us set up.'

'I'd rather stay with Shiumo,' Richard said.

'Go, help Jian, I'm fine,' Shiumo said. 'The general understands; she won't try to separate us. After I speak to the colonists, I'll take a break, use the facilities on my ship, then talk to the South American representative. Come back in about thirty minutes.'

'This way, and we'll set you up,' the general said, and led us out. 'Do you need to use the bathroom first?'

'Yes,' we said in unison, and shared a smile.

'I'll wait for you out here then,' the general said.

A technician poked his head out of a room. 'We've lost the connection. I'm afraid the Japanese will have to wait.'

'Let me sort this out,' Marque said with exasperation, and buzzed into the room. 'What did you do? This is a mess!'

'I didn't do anything,' the technician said.

As I walked into the women's bathroom, I noticed that two of the five cubicles were occupied next to each other. I'd only just registered that this might be a possible cause for alarm, when two big women in uniform charged out of the cubicles and grabbed me. I fought them, but they outweighed me and were at least as skilled in unarmed combat as I was. They slammed me face first into the wall, and one of them clamped her hand over my mouth.

When they had a good grip on me, they dragged me through a service door into another room where three more grunts were waiting – a man and two women, all of them well over a hundred kilos of solid muscle. They quickly cuffed me, chained me to an examination bed, and cut all my clothing off me.

'Marque!' I shouted, but they ignored me – the room was probably soundproofed.

When I was naked, one of them took the clothes out of the room. A female medical officer and a uniformed woman I didn't recognise came into the room and stopped at the foot of the table.

'This won't hurt much if you relax, ma'am,' the medtech said, and proceeded to perform a swift and thorough body-cavity search.

The officer put her hand on the back of my head and investigated my mind.

My mind and body were both being violated. I fought the bindings, but was effectively secured. A third officer swiped me over with a hand-held scanner.

The psi released my head and stepped back; and the medical officer completed her search and removed her gloves.

'General Maxwell will be here in a moment. She's talking to Commander Alto,' the psi said. 'Relax, Corporal, nobody's going to hurt you. We're just trying to establish what the alien did to your heads.'

'She didn't do anything – I'd know it!' I shouted, twisting in the restraints, and wincing as they hurt my wrists. 'Let me go! She wants to *help* humanity. Treating me like this will piss her off, and you don't want her to leave us stranded. She's helping us!'

'We don't have long,' General Maxwell said, entering the room. 'Is she clean?'

'Completely,' the medtech said.

'Good. Go scan Alto.' The general leaned on the bed next to me. 'You're not sufficiently trained, Choumali, so you haven't seen through it. But by god, woman, she's been using you. You went up to her ship and *stayed the night* there, with no fear at all, disobeying a direct order. You've never had a problem with discipline before, soldier. She's *changed* you.'

I glared at her with fury. 'She hasn't done anything.'

'Choumali, if the dragon and I had weapons pointed at each other, who would you jump in front of?'

I opened my mouth and closed it again, tickled by a small worrying feeling of doubt.

'She's important to humanity,' I said.

'That she is, but you're acting like a *slave*.'

I looked back over my behaviour, the doubt turning to real concern. I had been following Shiumo blindly; and I felt a deep affection for her – after only two days. The general was right: I would jump in front of Shiumo and protect her before I'd protect my own people. Was she hypnotising us, and I was too undertrained to see it? I sagged in the restraints.

The general nodded to one of the guards. 'Unchain her, and find her a uniform.'

'Ma'am,' the guard said, and went out.

General Maxwell flipped a gold coin – it was one of the coins that Shiumo had used to pay us. 'We need to be fast. Marque will quickly realise that you've been taken, and let her know.'

'How's Commander Alto?' I said as the guard released me from the bed. They readied themselves to take me down again, and I raised my hands in surrender.

'Now that he's free of her aura, he's aware of the mind control and wants to work with us,' the general said. 'But he's concerned that he's falling in love with her. Do you think that's possible?'

'The attraction was obvious,' I said.

'Unbelievable. What about you?'

'I like her. I love her, but not in a romantic way, more like ...' My voice trailed off as I tried to articulate it.

'Hero-worship,' the general said.

I winced, and nodded. 'I want to stay with her ...' I searched my feelings. 'It hurts to be parted from her.'

'After less than three days,' the general said. 'This is all wrong, Choumali. It's like an addiction. She's doing something to your head.'

'How do you feel about her, ma'am? You've been spending a lot of time in her presence as well.'

'Not the same way you do,' the general said. 'I'm trying to keep my distance. We'll arrange a rotation of staff near her so nobody has time to be hypnotised, but obviously it's too late for you and Alto.' The guard returned with a uniform for me. 'Get dressed and we'll talk about how to handle this.'

I quickly donned the uniform they provided – my basic corporal's fatigues from the training base, not the *Britannia* coverall. It felt good to be back in the simple cotton pants and jacket. 'Marque doesn't have X-ray vision, ma'am. We had to inform it that we were wearing more layers under our uniforms when it fabricated them for us. It wasn't aware of underwear.'

'Well spotted,' the general said. 'Alto told us that as well. Now we have both of you clear-headed, we can plan with more confidence.' She gestured towards the door. 'Let's make this quick.'

I followed General Maxwell into another room. Richard was sitting slumped at a conference table, radiating shame and defeat. The psi was there as well, with her emotions locked down.

The general sat at the table and tapped it with one of my gold coins. 'This is real gold, by the way. You aren't completely slave labour.'

'She seems to be acting in good faith,' I said. 'Is it possible that she doesn't know she's doing it to us? It might be us reacting to her, and not deliberate on her part at all?'

'It's possible,' the psi said. Her badge said O'Neil. 'I can't sense anything different about you. It may be some pheromone or something that she's giving off.'

'We'll know for sure after they've checked my code,' Richard said. 'Whatever she's doing to us, it's definitely stronger the closer we are to her. I'm full of bliss when I sit next to her; and when she touches me it's euphoric.'

'Has she done anything to your hardware?' the general said.

'She offered to upgrade it. I wouldn't let her,' Richard said. 'Then she offered me cloned body parts, to bring me back to what I was twenty years ago.' His voice gained a husky edge. 'I said no again.'

'A very tempting offer,' the general said. 'You've always been exceptional, Richard. It's an honour to serve with you.'

An officer came in holding a tablet, and sat at the table. 'He's clear, ma'am. There's no change to his code that we can find. We did a full factory reset anyway.'

'She could have put something into my hardware while I was asleep,' Richard said. 'We should remove all of it and destroy it. You shouldn't be talking in front of me; I'm probably compromised.'

'I won't say anything that she doesn't already know,' the general said. 'Choumali, did you feel anything psionic happening when you first encountered her? Any probes, or control?'

'She hit my pleasure centres when she taught me tight beam,' I began.

'So yes,' the general said.

'But I'm undertrained, you know that,' I said.

'That may be why she kept Choumali around,' Richard said.

'Or she could be telling the truth and wants to train me,' I said. 'If we share our suspicions with her, she might be as upset about it as we are.'

'When we return you to her, whatever she's doing to you will kick in and you'll tell her anyway,' the general said.

'You can't return us to her!' Richard said.

O'Neil spoke at the same time. 'Choumali needs professional training, ma'am. We need someone next to the alien who –'

'We have to,' the general said, interrupting them both. 'We need to keep her happy for now, and find out what her angle is.' She spoke with more force. 'If you can avoid telling her about this episode, you're ordered to do so. If you can keep this a secret from her, it will prove she doesn't have complete control over you. Understand?'

'Ma'am,' Richard and I said in unison.

'Marque will want to know where we've been,' Richard said. He turned to me. 'Tell it that you had to change your uniform because you've been reassigned. It doesn't know better.'

'What about you, sir?' I said.

'I'll tell the truth.' Richard pointed at a cable running from under his shirt to the wall socket. 'I needed to recharge.'

'That works,' the general said. 'Anything else?'

Richard spoke with misery. 'If it ever looks like I'm turning against humanity and taking the alien's side …'

'I will shoot you myself,' the general said.

Richard nodded. 'Thank you, ma'am.'

I realised with a stab of pain that I already had turned against humanity, and was following Shiumo blindly. I would need to watch my feelings carefully.

The general rose. 'Back to work, people. If she's genuine about helping us, and this hypnotism is just a side effect, we will see a Japanese colony on Kapteyn-b by the end of next month, and a number of human colonies by the end of the year. I sincerely hope it's true.'

*

It took us two hours to prepare the Japanese schedule. When it was done, Marque and I returned to the main control room. Richard and Shiumo were still engaged with the South American ambassador: a bronze-skinned man in his mid-thirties, with long hair and pronounced cheekbones. His immaculate make-up made him look more like a supermodel than a diplomat.

'What can we give you to take our people there first?' he asked Shiumo.

'You can't bribe me,' she said. 'You have nothing that I need.'

'You seek love. What sort of love? We will give you *anything*.' He half-closed his eyes and made his voice a throaty rumble. 'The people of my country are experts in the arts of love.'

'Listen, my friend,' Shiumo said with amusement. 'There are five planets almost identical to the one you want within a hundred light-years of Earth. Once the colonists are there, it makes no difference which one it is.'

'Gliese 667 is closer than Kepler. Much closer,' the ambassador said. 'It will only take twenty-four years to communicate, instead of nearly a hundred.'

'With my folding ability, the distance is academic.'

'Then you must leave us some method of faster-than-light communication before you return to your own planet,' the South American said.

'Oh, I must, must I?' Shiumo said.

The ambassador was obviously silenced, then he gathered himself. 'Please, Princess, once you have returned to your home planet, the distance to the colony is critical. If you won't leave us with a communication method, we *must* have the closer planet.' He cocked his head. 'And if you won't give us the planet, what can we offer you to stay on Earth permanently? Or others of your kind? We need you to pilot us between here and the colonies.'

Shiumo hissed with laughter. 'I am enjoying helping your people, but there is nothing you can offer me.' She put her front foot on Richard's thigh, and he jumped, then sagged and radiated euphoric bliss. 'Ready your colonists, and make sure they're fully prepared. If I think you've rushed the process, I won't take them. Whoever has their colonists ready to my satisfaction first will get Gliese 667.'

'It will be us,' the ambassador said, and the screen blinked out.

'Wow, I really pissed them off,' Shiumo said. She patted Richard's thigh. 'Was that all we had scheduled for the day?' She turned and rested her front feet on the back of the sofa to speak to the general. 'I think I need a day off – this is exhausting. How many more nations do you have?' She shook her head. '*Why* does your species need so many arbitrary national boundaries?'

'There used to be ten times as many before the climate went to shit and two-thirds of the land mass went underwater,' I said.

'I may not be able to help you with instantaneous communication, but I can control the weather,' Shiumo said. She flopped back onto the couch. 'Marque, can you provide them with some weather control?'

'Sure,' Marque said. 'I can't share the process because of the tech level, but I can do some things that will definitely help.'

'Most appreciated,' General Maxwell said.

'How's the cube coming along?' Shiumo said.

'Done,' Marque said. 'You can move there any time.'

'Let's finish for the day, and pick it up there tomorrow,' Shiumo said. 'Is that acceptable with you, General? Can you have the staff moved there tomorrow morning?'

'I can.' The general checked her tablet. 'It's been a long day. I really need to debrief Jian and Richard. Can you leave them here? Their families would like to speak to them as well.'

'You did tell my mother I was okay, ma'am?' I said.

The general nodded. 'Your husband and wife want to speak to you, Corporal. Apparently your wife has news for you.'

I winced. 'We weren't formally married.'

'That's how they refer to themselves,' the general said.

'Have you arranged the Japanese transport schedule, Jian?' Shiumo said.

I nodded. 'Marque was a terrific help. It will take you a couple of days to move all their stuff up to your ship, and a similar amount of time to unload it – even if you land your ship on Kapteyn-b.'

'Why don't you and Richard spend time with your families while I'm at the Japanese colony?' Shiumo said. 'I don't need you to help me load and unload. Marque can do that.'

Richard shook his head. 'I want to stay with you.'

'Your mother wants to see you as soon as you're out of quarantine, Alto,' the general said. 'She's blaming me for not giving you leave since you were assigned to the generation ship project.'

'You're a bad son, Richard,' Shiumo said with humour.

Richard sighed. 'I suppose I should.' He put his hand on Shiumo's front claw. 'Only if you're sure you won't need me.'

I walked around the sofa and stopped in front of them to get their attention. They were lost in each other's eyes.

'I have to go with you to Kapteyn-b,' I said. 'You need me to communicate.'

'Go see your mum, Jian,' Shiumo said without looking away from Richard. 'We'll be fine. And you can't avoid the conversation with your husband and wife forever.'

I winced. She was right.

'Anyway, the trip isn't for another two weeks at least,' Shiumo said. 'I can't wait to be released from this ridiculous quarantine. I've been stuck in this room for far too long, and I want to see more of Earth.'

The general checked her tablet. 'The Earth medical advisors are close to a decision on how long to keep you. It looks like they'll settle on two weeks so you can begin taking the Japanese colonists according to schedule. We'll arrange a sightseeing trip for you after we're all released.'

Shiumo nodded to the general. 'Thank you.' She hopped off the couch and stretched like a cat. 'Let's go home and have dinner. Marque can route any media requests through to me on the ship, but I think absolutely everybody on your planet has interviewed me. There can't be anyone else who wants to hear about my search for love.'

The general rose. 'Princess.' She shot a sharp look at Richard and me.

Richard saluted her. 'General.'

We put our hands on Shiumo's shoulders and she folded us back up to the ship.

12

'How's the food now?' Marque said as we sat around the table discussing the day's events. Shiumo had folded her ship to a point a hundred and fifty light-years from Earth, with a spectacular vista of a blue-green nebula that covered half the view around us.

'It's fabulous,' I said. 'Better every time.'

'Marque is making an extensive study of your cuisine,' Shiumo said. She raised the leg of mutton she was eating. 'And this sheep is still wonderful!'

'I appreciate some variety after serving grilled grakka to this reptile for thousands of meals in a row,' Marque said. 'Were you all right when you went into the bathrooms today? Both of you were gone for a long time. You weren't unwell, were you?'

'That was ridiculous,' Richard said. 'General Maxwell is so paranoid.'

'I can't believe they did that to us,' I said. 'Did they do a cavity search on you as well?'

'What's left of me, yes,' Richard said. He mimicked the medtech: 'Try to relax and this won't be too uncomfortable, sir.'

'A what?' Shiumo said.

'They grabbed us and searched us and did a full mind and body scan,' I said.

'They think you're messing with our heads,' Richard said. 'Keeping us close to control us. Hell, Maxwell was so convinced that you've hypnotised us, she almost had *me* believing it for a few minutes.'

'But I just told you to take some time away with your families,' Shiumo said with confusion. 'Doesn't that prove I'm *not* keeping you close to control you?'

'This was before you suggested it,' Richard said.

'You just disobeyed a direct order, Richard,' I said. I saw Shiumo's curiosity. 'We were both explicitly ordered not to tell you that Maxwell thinks you're hypnotising us.'

'Humph,' Richard said. 'It's perfectly acceptable to disobey orders when they conflict with the mission goals. And in this case, Maxwell's ridiculous paranoid xenophobia could easily drive Shiumo away.' He shook his head. 'And we *need* her.'

'You humans are completely bewildering,' Shiumo said. 'What in the five galaxies makes General Maxwell think I'm controlling you?'

'That's the thing,' Richard said. 'They couldn't find anything to suggest that you are. A psi examined us and found nothing. They did a full body search and found nothing. I mean, I'm attracted –' He choked the words off. 'I mean, I like being with you; you're cute and charming and fun, and take me for rides to all sorts of interesting places.' He waved his fork at the glittering blue nebula.

'You're attracted to me?' Shiumo said, her voice husky and low. She swung her head to look at me. 'Are you?'

'Nuh-uh.' I shook my head. 'I have enough issues with Dianne and Victor as it is. We didn't formally end the relationship when I joined the crew of the *Britannia*. Since all of this happened, they haven't stopped calling me, wanting to reconnect. They would kill me if they found out I –' I filled my mouth with a big forkful of pasta to stop myself saying how charming she was.

Shiumo turned back to Richard. 'You like being with me, therefore General Maxwell thinks I'm messing with your head?' She pulled herself off the cushions and stalked up and down. 'Of course the idea that you could *like* the ugly scaly alien is so foreign that I *must* be hypnotising you.'

'You're not ugly,' Richard said softly. 'Your scales are –'

'Divine,' I said.

'Your eyes are like stars brought down from the sky,' Richard said.

'I wouldn't go that far,' Marque said.

Shiumo stopped and turned to face us. She concentrated on Richard, obviously speaking telepathically to him. Richard nodded, his expression full of shock.

'Come and finish your mutton, Princess,' I said. 'We all need to build our strength, because tomorrow the Africans will try to talk us out of giving the planet to South America.'

'I wonder if the African representative will be as hot as the South American one,' Shiumo said, almost to herself.

'You noticed that?' Richard said.

Shiumo crooned with her eyes half-closed: 'We are *experts* in the arts of love.' She opened her eyes. 'A little obvious.'

'Next time, Red, don't say you're looking for love when you arrive at a new planet,' Marque said.

'I dunno.' Shiumo turned her mutton over. 'I quite like being ...' She glanced at Richard, and they gazed into each other's eyes. 'Courted.'

She stopped eating and lowered the meat, seeming lost in thought. 'I'm receiving a message.' She concentrated for a while, tapping the scales on the side of her neck, then spoke in her own tongue – a deep bass guttural sound – faster than she spoke in English. Then she disappeared.

'What's happening?' Richard said.

'An attack on a planet in the Empire. We think it might be cats,' Marque said.

Shiumo reappeared. 'I don't have time to explain. I have to go help them. Stay put.'

She disappeared, and reappeared outside on the nose of the ship, visible through the transparent walls.

Water without an obvious source quickly covered the floor of the gallery. I hopped up onto the table, and Richard joined me.

'Marque,' I said. 'What's going on? Why the flooding?'

Marque didn't reply.

The water was at our knees now, even though we were standing on the table; it was more than a metre deep.

'Marque, you're destroying my circuits!' Richard shouted.

The water reached our waists. Richard's circuitry failed, and he fell sideways into the water, thrashing as it rose around us. His arm twisted in on itself then stopped moving, and his legs jerked twice then froze. He was left with one working limb.

'Marque, we'll drown if you don't stop this!' I shouted. I put my arm around Richard and raised him so his head was above water. 'Richard's super-heavy with all this metal – I can't hold him for long!'

We were both lifted into the air, and I cried out at the suddenness of it.

'Marque!' I shouted again.

'Sorry,' Marque said. 'Over here.'

It carried us to the tip of the ship's nose, so Shiumo was sitting directly above us on the outside. The water in the rest of the interior rose all the way to the ceiling, but we were inside a pocket of air in the nose, the water held back by an invisible wall.

I lowered Richard gently. His prosthetics jerked as the circuits shorted out.

The stars shifted as Shiumo folded, and we were in orbit over a blue-green water-covered planet. Other dragon ships blinked into existence around us in a variety of colours, with dragons of matching hues sitting on their noses.

'Look,' Richard said, pointing with his biological hand.

Five streaks of light shot over the far side of the planet. Where the beams hit, the water boiled red-hot, and disappeared into steam. The beams hit the planet again, and molten rock erupted, glowing in the light of the planet's sun. The planet was being destroyed.

Shiumo folded us again, and her ship was underwater. It was cloudy, limiting visibility, and the floor of the ocean wasn't in view. Light shifted through the surface above us. I had a jolt of claustrophobic panic: Richard and I were in a tiny pocket of air in a ship full of water that was submerged in the water planet's ocean. We could easily drown.

Richard tried to lift himself using his remaining working arm, then flopped back.

Shiumo disappeared from the nose of the ship, then there was a flash of red inside the water that filled the other side of the invisible wall. A huge bright orange mass appeared, then two more: they were at least fifty metres long and filled the interior space. Their emotional auras were full of panic that ramped up my own stress levels.

One of the creatures moved closer to the wall, and an eye two metres across emerged from the water.

'Marque ...' Richard said, using his good arm to scoot backwards.

'It's okay,' I said. 'It's not malicious. It's broadcasting curiosity about us.'

A couple of tentacles, each shading from brilliant pink to almost ultraviolet purple, came through the invisible wall and hovered above us. They glistened with water, enhancing their intense and beautiful colours. The air around me filled with the curiosity of the marine alien: it was gentle and full of love for all things in a way I'd never sensed from a fellow human.

I reached to touch one of the tentacles, hoping to feel the love more deeply. Before I could reach it, the tentacle became completely still, then retreated into the water.

'Shiumo asked them to back off from you,' Marque said. 'Don't be afraid. They're harmless.'

'I don't mind,' I said. 'Their emotions are so deep and complex.'

Shiumo's red belly reappeared above us on the nose of the ship. There was a blinding white flash of light, and twenty seconds later the sea around us boiled with a shockwave that tossed the ship sideways, although we didn't feel the movement. The light shifted above us and the water instantly turned to steam.

Shiumo lost her grip on the nose and disappeared in the surge. It passed over, and the ship righted itself. The steam collapsed around us, becoming boiling water, but again we were protected.

Shiumo floated through the wall of the ship into our air pocket, suspended from a Marque sphere. She was unconscious, her four feet, neck and head hanging down and swaying as Marque carried her. It lowered her gently to the deck and she lay motionless.

The aquatic aliens on the other side of the interface radiated deep concern, and produced a sound so low in pitch it made the wall vibrate in visible waves.

Richard dragged himself next to Shiumo and put his good hand on her head. 'Marque, is she alive? How bad is she?' He touched his forehead to hers. 'Shiumo,' he said, full of grief and pain.

Marque moved both Richard and me back from Shiumo. I tried to return to her, but it placed an energy field around her. The aquatic aliens thrashed against the interface with their tentacles.

'Back off and let me work!' Marque said in English, then something in their language, and all of us subsided.

Another dragon appeared next to Shiumo. This one was much larger, with six legs and a longer, slimmer body that ended in a forked tail. Its black scales glittered in the ship's lights.

The dragon spoke in its own tongue, and Marque replied in the same language.

The dragon nodded, and folded onto the nose of the ship. It returned us to space, with the water planet visible next to us. A flash of light so bright it was blinding filled space around us, and I covered my eyes.

The light disappeared and I opened my eyes, attempting to see through the blinking after-effects. The water planet was gone. In its place swirled clouds of water vapour and glowing molten rock.

Five sleek black ships, different in shape from the dragons' ships, floated on the other side of the clouds. They were enormous; larger than Shiumo's ship. One of them fired a blast of its light cannon at one of the dragon ships, and it was blocked by an energy shield.

The five destroyer ships turned majestically, then gathered energy around themselves and created huge lenses of light in front of them, but didn't move away.

The orange sea creatures inside Shiumo's ship wailed, an eerie high-pitched cry, and generated a field of grief so enormous that my spirit was crushed under its weight. They shifted into a wordless song of devastation and loss, and I wiped the tears from my face. Their home was gone.

'Is Shiumo all right?' Richard asked Marque. 'She looks dead.'

The black dragon reappeared, and spoke with a woman's voice slightly lower in pitch than Shiumo's. 'How bad is it, Marque? Is it mortal?'

'Don't you dare say "yes", you rusted piece of junk,' Shiumo said into the floor. 'I have thirty-three scales out there and I do *not* want to spend three weeks replacing them when the humans have reached day four.'

'She's fine. Exhaustion, minor concussion, no broken bones. She just needs to rest,' Marque said.

Richard collapsed with relief and lay on the floor next to her.

'I'll leave you to it then,' the black dragon said. 'Terrible shame about the Nimestas. I hope they accept our assistance.' She disappeared.

Shiumo hoisted herself onto four legs and shook her head. 'I will have the headache from hell tomorrow.' She poked her head through the water interface, then withdrew to our side. 'Only three. I wish I could have helped more.'

She walked through the interface and floated in the water on the other side, speaking to the aquatic aliens. Their conversation flashed in my empathic vision like a spattering of mud-coloured despair and greyest empty grief.

'Sorry about the water,' Marque said. 'It all happened so suddenly we had no chance to prepare. The Nimestas refused to trade with the cats, and you can see how the cats responded.'

'Those are cat ships?' I said, studying the enormous black ships sitting in their cocoons of light.

'That's right,' Marque said. 'It will take them a while to accelerate to light speed and leave.'

'How many of the water aliens did the dragons save?' Richard said.

'Not enough. I'm looking for a suitable alternative world for them, but we only managed to save a couple of hundred. They won't have enough genetic diversity in such a small group to maintain viability as a species. The dragons are discussing whether they should take the Nimestas to the dragon homeworld instead, where it will be easier for us to provide them with reproductive therapy.'

'Tell them I'm sorry for their loss,' I said.

'They're too wrapped up in grief to listen to any outworlder's words right now,' Marque said.

Shiumo appeared next to us. 'They are so intrinsically linked with their planet that they can't live without it. They choose species suicide.'

She went to Richard, who was lying on his back on the floor, and touched his face. 'Are you all right, dear Richard?'

'I am as long as you are,' he said, clasping her claw in his organic hand.

'Can't you save them?' I said.

'We can, but they don't want it. We're looking for a new home for them, but they've decided to stop reproducing.' She spat with fury. 'Those cats have killed them all, and they don't give a damn about it.'

'Why didn't you fight back? They're still there – attack them!' I said. 'You just sat there and let them blow the planet up! Are they stronger than you? More technologically advanced?'

'What would be the point?' she said. 'If we destroy them, they will send more ships and attack other planets in retribution. Large-scale armed conflict with them would destroy everything with no benefit.'

'But these ... Nimestas lost their entire planet!' I said.

'Many more planets would be lost if we fought the cats.' She shook her head. 'You young races and your armed conflict. It benefits *no one*.'

'Those damn cats need to be taught a lesson,' Richard growled.

'They just need to grow up and learn to live with the rest of us. They'll come around,' Shiumo said.

'Decision's made,' Marque said. 'The Nimestas won't go to the dragon homeworld. They want to go to a nearby uninhabited aquatic planet and wait to die.'

'I'll have to flood the ship completely to transfer them,' Shiumo said. 'I'll drop Jian and Richard on Earth, and then take the Nimestas to their new world.'

She returned to the ship's nose and folded us back to orbit around Earth.

I sat next to Richard, who was still sprawled on the floor. 'You destroyed his prosthetics, Marque. He'll need help to leave the ship.'

'Give me a moment,' Marque said.

Shiumo reappeared next to us. 'Can you wait for me in the Earth control centre while I take the Nimestas to their new world?'

'I'll need to dry out my prosthetics and see if I can't get them working again,' Richard said ruefully.

'I am so sorry that happened.' She raised her snout slightly. 'You'd assume that a hyper-intelligent AI would think first before immersing you in water – particularly as you said you weren't waterproof.'

'Which was more important – the art in the gallery or Richard's prosthetics?' Marque said. 'I moved all your treasures into the hold before I flooded it, and you know how fragile some of them are. I had to carry them personally.'

I took a deep breath to yell at them about priorities when Marque spoke again.

'The repairs are complete. Try standing up, Richard.'

Richard's face went blank. 'You repaired them?'

'Of course I did. I wouldn't have given the art priority if I couldn't. Try standing.'

Richard's expression didn't change. He untwisted his right arm, then used it to hoist himself upright. He brushed himself off, then took a few steps up and down. 'Damn, Marque, I never felt a thing.'

'You won't feel a thing when we give you your body back either,' Shiumo said.

He gazed into her eyes. Then one of the Nimestas made a high-pitched squeal and we all jumped.

Shiumo lowered her head. 'They gently ask that we take them to the other survivors. Put your hands on my shoulders, dear humans, and I will drop you on Earth.' She raised her head. 'I'll return before tomorrow morning and you can come back to the ship.'

'Take your time,' Richard said. 'They need your help.'

*

We were asleep in cots on the floor of the conference room when Shiumo's voice woke me. She was next to Richard, saying his name softly. I sat up and checked the wall clock: 4 a.m.

'Are the Nimestas okay?' I said.

'They'll live. Their species won't.'

Richard sat up too. 'Welcome back, Princess. I was worried you wouldn't return for us.'

'Of course I returned. I –' She choked the words off and gazed into his eyes.

I didn't need to hear the words; I could feel the love coming from both of them.

'Would you like to return to your rooms on the ship?' she said. 'They're much more comfortable than what you have here.'

'Of course,' I said. 'I need a shower to get rid of the salt water.'

'Valid point,' she said. 'Hands?'

When we reappeared on the ship, the water was gone. It was like it had never been there.

'Go back to bed,' Shiumo said. 'Marque will tell the general that we'll be a bit late starting so you can rest.' She grinned ruefully. 'Sorry about all the excitement.'

'You helped save a species,' I said. She shook her head, but I continued before she could speak. 'You did your best, lady. We can tell General Maxwell what you did – how you all risked your lives to help the Nimestas.'

'It's what we do,' she said. 'Now get some rest.'

'Goodnight, Shiumo,' Richard said, and we both turned towards the aft of the ship where our rooms were located.

Richard stopped after two steps, and turned back to see Shiumo. They gazed into each other's eyes, and she was obviously talking to him telepathically.

He looked from me to Shiumo, and came to a decision. 'Uh, you go on ahead, Jian. Shiumo and I have something important to discuss.'

They went forward to Shiumo's quarters together without saying another word, leaving me alone in the gallery. I shrugged and returned to my room.

13

When I returned to the gallery at ten o'clock the next morning, I was alone again. Marque provided me with some fruit and yoghurt.

'The general's been notified that you'll be a bit late this morning, and they've rearranged Shiumo's schedule. No rush,' it said.

'Are they still asleep?'

'They're on privacy. I don't know,' Marque said.

'I didn't know you had a privacy setting.'

'Of course I do. Just ask for it.'

I nodded, and pinged Richard on his tablet.

There was a sound towards the bow, where Shiumo's quarters were, and I turned to see Richard and Shiumo enter the gallery together. I watched, silent with shock, as they sat at the table. They were in a post-coital blissful haze. Both of them. I stared at them with disbelief. I'd seen love-filled sexual satisfaction radiating from people before, but this was particularly obvious.

I studied Richard more closely: he still appeared to have the same prosthetics.

'Jian can see,' Shiumo said as she poured herself some tea.

'Oh,' Richard said, and radiated embarrassment. Then his emotions changed to pleased satisfaction. He'd decided that he didn't care if I knew.

I resisted the urge to duck under the table to check Shiumo's underside. Their mutual attraction had been obvious, but the reptile had nowhere for Richard to put ... and he didn't have ... I shook my head. This was ridiculous.

'Oh, go ahead and ask,' Shiumo said. 'It's really very straightforward.'

'She's as pan-connective as her ship is,' Richard said.

Shiumo laughed so hard that she fell over backwards, her legs in the air. She wriggled with delight and smacked the table with her tail. 'I love you, Richard.'

'I love you too, Shiumo,' Richard said calmly; and he did. The love was bursting from him. 'Soft-boiled eggs, please, Marque.'

My eyes felt like they were about to explode from my head.

'When we humans use the term "pan-sexual" we have no idea what its true meaning is,' Richard said, still perfectly calm. 'Its meaning is Shiumo. Her body can change to accommodate any lover. She can even change her appearance to something her lover finds the most attractive.' He glanced at her affectionately. 'Show Jian, Shiumo. It will make it easier to explain.'

'She won't see what you see.'

Richard shrugged. 'Show her anyway.'

'But I'll be *seriously attractive*. Like, super-hot. Are you sure?'

'We discussed this. Show Jian, so she can help me explain to General Maxwell.'

'Oh, all right,' Shiumo said.

She hoisted herself onto her back legs, and they clicked and rotated so she was standing upright in a surprisingly natural-looking two-legged configuration. Then she changed into a tall well-built naked black man with chiselled abs, a wide chest, slim hips and a strong jaw. His long hair was in dreads and tied at the nape of his neck.

I choked on my fruit.

'What do you see?' Richard said.

'A man,' I said. 'Shiumo, you're *male*?'

'No,' Shiumo said, and his rich male voice resonated through me like a sexual tuning fork. 'I'm pan-sexual. I make myself whatever suits you best.'

'I see Shiumo as a beautiful woman,' Richard said. 'I ...' He said the words in a rush. 'I made love to Shiumo, who was a beautiful woman. Her body changes to suit her lover.'

I waved my spoon at him. 'But she said ... you said ... your prosthetics ...'

'Marque is growing me new body parts; they'll be ready in a few weeks. In the meantime ...' He glanced at Shiumo affectionately. 'Remember when she brushed your pleasure centres?'

'Yes ...' I remembered the experience – intense and orgasmic – and understood. He didn't need the body parts if she could directly stimulate his brain.

My eyes were drawn to Shiumo's manhood, which was as impressive as the rest of him. 'Is that *real*?' I said, trying not to stare.

'No. It's an illusion,' Shiumo said, his expression wry. 'But my body has physically changed to suit yours. You said you see me as a male of your species?'

'Yes,' I breathed, wanting to touch that dark smooth skin, and run my fingers down Shiumo's jaw, and taste those full, lush lips. Super-hot didn't begin to describe it. Shiumo's form was a sexual fantasy come true – the man of my dreams.

'Then that's what you prefer,' Richard said. 'Change back before she eats you alive, Shiumo, and let's have breakfast. We still have to talk to the African ambassador today.'

Shiumo fell to four legs and the illusion of humanity disappeared. Her voice changed back to female. 'Everybody sees something different, Jian. I take a form that is the most attractive to you.'

'So, if we wanted to, we could ...?' I began, my mind exploding with possibilities.

'I would love to,' Shiumo said, full of promise.

I dug into my fruit, remembering the two people I loved already – and who loved me. 'I would need to think about that.'

Richard's face went rigid with restraint, and a blast of jealous irritation radiated from him.

'You all right, Richard?' Shiumo said.

His expression softened. 'Don't be concerned. You explained it to me. I understand.' He shot a sharp glance at me, then looked down and shifted his teacup around. 'I love you too much to let anything come between us.'

'Dianne and Victor would kill me. I still need to have that conversation,' I said, and his jealousy subsided. I stabbed another piece of fruit with my fork. 'But this will drive Maxwell *nuts*. She'll say you're sleeping with the enemy.'

'Shiumo's not the enemy,' Richard said. 'And the general doesn't need to know about any of it.'

'No,' Shiumo said. 'Full disclosure. We must tell her.'

'As you wish, Princess,' Richard said. 'My career was over anyway.'

'So what I saw is what I prefer?' I said, thinking back to those rich brown eyes.

Shiumo nodded.

'Huh. I always thought I preferred women, and that men were second best.'

'I thought I liked her scales, but when she changes she only has them on her temples,' Richard said.

'I can't do anything about your messed-up brains,' Shiumo said.

Our tablets both pinged at the same time.

'General Maxwell on the line, Shiumo,' Marque said. 'South America is impatient. They're worried that you already gave Gliese 667 to the Africans.'

'Tell her we'll be down soon,' Shiumo said. 'Are they set up in the cube?'

'All set and ready to go. You can fold straight down there.'

'I will as soon as we've eaten. A lady requires her breakfast to function at the highest level of efficiency.'

'Damn straight,' I said, and scooped up some yoghurt.

*

Shiumo folded us into a large high-ceilinged conference room, with a sofa for her, three large screens, and several comfortable chairs. Two of the walls were glass, giving a view over the hillside the bunker was located on, and the other two were white and glossy like porcelain. It was noisy: people were talking loudly in the corridors, and rushing around waving their tablets at each other.

General Maxwell charged into the room and stared at Shiumo. She opened and closed her mouth a few times.

Shiumo waited for her to speak, and when she didn't, said, 'You're welcome.'

'Stephanie – my granddaughter – she's cured. Completely cured. She's going home tomorrow,' the general said. 'Two civil wars declared a ceasefire. Three terrorist groups just disbanded. The government of New Prussia *begged* to join Euroterre.'

'Oh good,' Shiumo said. 'I thought that might be the response.'

'If your species continues to behave, I'll give you another fifty years of life extension,' Marque said.

'You can do *more*?' the general said, goggle-eyed.

'What did you give them, Shiumo?' Richard said, amused.

'Cures for every known terminal disease,' the general said. 'Fifty years of life extension – *useful* years that mean we can be active and healthy, like a forty year old, until we're well over a hundred and forty. And the weather control she promised – all of the storms just stopped.'

'This'd better not be a result of last night,' Richard said to Shiumo. 'I am *not* for sale.'

'What about last night?' the general said. Her eyes bulged out even further. 'No *way*.'

'Marque did it all autonomously,' Shiumo said. 'It's in the First Contact schedule. Day four: extend lives, cure disease, and one or two other random benefits to demonstrate the advantages of treating me well. You'll find that the oceans are receding; we've lowered the temperature to give you back your ice caps. Marque is in the process of providing your scientists with a portable desalination device to convert the soil to arable land once the salt water's gone.'

An ensign ran to the doorway and stopped, panting. 'The carbon dioxide in the air has reduced by twenty per cent, and the oxygen layer has thickened by a similar amount. You can breathe outside the bunker! The oceans just returned to mid-twenty-second-century levels – sea levels are down by twenty metres. Boats are stranded all over the world.'

'Marque,' Shiumo said with exasperation.

'I'll build a cargo sphere and move them back onto the water,' Marque said. 'Give me four hours to fabricate the sphere.'

A loud cheer erupted further down the hall, and my tablet pinged. I glanced down to see that the war between North and South America had ground to a halt when the combatants saw the sea recede. Peace talks were underway, and people were already attacking the wall between the two continents and dismantling it.

Shiumo glanced at Richard. 'Happy, my love?'

He smiled back. 'I'm with you. Of course I am.'

The general's face grew grim.

'Oh, give it up, Maxwell,' Richard said. 'You couldn't find anything when you checked me. She just saved little Stephanie's life. Don't be so paranoid.' He put one hand on Shiumo's shoulder. 'Yesterday Shiumo almost gave her life to save a peaceful species attacked by another; and now her people are caring for the refugees.' He smiled down at her. 'It's love, not mind control. Accept it.'

Shiumo butted him with her head. 'My Richard.' She climbed onto her couch facing the screen. 'I suppose we should talk to Africa. Put them through, General.'

'I want to talk to you later, Alto,' the general said, still grim, and stalked out.

'I don't think I'll ever make her happy,' Shiumo said.

My tablet pinged again. Social media had gone wild; many of the messages were complaints that the servers had gone down under the deluge of comments about what had happened. The feed in my summary app had changed dramatically. For the last three days it had been: 'Will the aliens invade?' and 'Are we safe?' Now it was: 'She saved my children' and 'Why is she still locked up?'

Public opinion had made a sharp turn, and people were demanding that Shiumo be welcomed as a royal visitor and no longer kept in quarantine. They wanted her to do a tour of all nations so everybody could thank her.

*

Later that day, General Maxwell entered the conference room with a politician I recognised: the Home Secretary. I shot to my feet to salute. He was tall and slim with a shock of sandy brown hair and blue eyes.

The general radiated tension; clearly the VIP visit was stressing her out.

Shiumo hopped down off the couch. 'Oh, hello, Mr Home Secretary – Ian, was it? Does this mean the stupid quarantine has been lifted?'

The Home Secretary bowed to her. 'Yes, Princess Shiumo, and I wanted to be the first to greet you in person. You are completely free to wander the Earth as you please, and welcome in every nation.' He threw his best politician's smile at her. 'What you did today was a great gift to all humanity. We want to thank you, and hope you will remain in Euroterre as our guest.'

Well, look at that. You humans are quite capable of taking me out of quarantine when it suits you, Shiumo said to me. *The poor man's terrified that I'll give him some terrible disease, and pissed beyond belief that the Prime Minister chickened out and sent him.*

I nearly choked with laughter.

Shiumo bowed her head to the Home Secretary. 'You are most welcome.' She glanced up. 'We're out of quarantine, Marque. Lift the cube, will you?'

The room trembled and we all looked around.

'Lift the cube?' the general said.

The ground dropped away – the cube was lifting into the air. It soared two hundred metres above the ground and hovered, the movement almost undetectable.

The Home Secretary clutched the table, his face grey, radiating shock.

'Oh, sorry. I should have warned you,' Shiumo said. 'I'd much prefer to be up a bit higher where I can see everything, rather than buried in the ground, wouldn't you? Now ...' She approached the Home Secretary and he backed away slightly. 'Would you like to see my ship?' She turned her head towards Maxwell. 'You too, General, you haven't paid me a visit yet. Come to my ship and have tea.'

'Maybe in a couple of days, Princess,' the general said.

'Yes, that's right, I have so many things to do,' the Home Secretary added, radiating terror. 'We need to prepare our colonists for Wolf 1061, don't we?' He flared the politician's smile again. 'Would you like to see some of the sights of Euroterre now you can visit them? I'd love to take you on a tour.'

'I would be delighted,' Shiumo said.

'Uh ...' The Home Secretary looked around. 'How do we get out of the building? It appears to be floating.'

'There are stairs to one side, if you have security clearance,' Shiumo said. 'Lead the way, sir. I cannot wait to breathe the air and meet the people of Earth.'

*

The rotocopter swooped over New Paris. The city had been carved from the top of a mountain, and the flat plateau was a mass of prefab residences with some new gleaming government towers in the centre. The sides of the plateau were terraced down to the water, and covered with a ramshackle shanty town full of refugees from the drowning countryside.

We landed a hundred metres from one of the massive feet of the Eiffel Tower. The extensive gardens surrounding the tower were the only open space in the city. Shiumo had thoroughly charmed the Home Secretary by the time we arrived, and he was enjoying her company.

'We moved the tower here,' he said. 'To New Paris. The Eiffel Tower is the symbol of the city.'

Shiumo looked up at the tower. 'And it was really built in an age of steam?'

'Yes,' he said. 'How does it compare to other planets' achievements?'

Shiumo didn't reply.

'The view from the top is very good,' he said. 'You can go up in the elevator and take a look, if you like. It's inside the oxygen layer; you don't need breathing apparatus.'

'Richard, Jian, do you want to go?' Shiumo said.

'If you don't mind, I'd prefer they stayed down here with me,' General Maxwell said. 'They're too valuable to risk.'

'They'll be fine with me,' Shiumo said. 'Put your hand on me if you want to come up, and I'll fold us.'

I trusted Shiumo more than I trusted the general. Richard and I put our hands on her shoulders and she folded us to the top viewing platform.

'Really that unimpressive?' Richard said.

'It's so ugly!' Marque said as it whizzed up the structure to join us.

'Heh,' Shiumo said. 'I've seen better; I've seen worse.'

'At least it's not the Grand Planetary Sewerage Inlet,' Marque said.

Shiumo hissed with laughter. 'I remember! They were all standing there expectantly, and I said "It's very elegant" or something, and they said, "Well, aren't you going to do us the honour of using it?"'

'And did you?' I said.

'I had to! Apparently by their standards it was a mortal insult if I didn't gift them part of my physical manifestation. Where was that anyway? I don't remember.'

'Neither do I. The details are in offline storage,' Marque said. 'Do you want me to retrieve it?'

'No need. Let's go back down, I'm hungry,' Shiumo said.

Noise wafted up to us; a crowd had gathered at the base of the tower.

'That was quick,' I said.

'There's a dragon-spotting app on the network,' Marque said. 'It predicted that she'd be here – there may be a leak. Shiumo, give them a minute to initiate crowd control, otherwise you'll be mobbed.'

Shiumo looked out over the city of New Paris. 'The oxygen is such a thin blanket on your planet. It's a wonder that so many species evolved here.' She turned to us. 'I felt that – guilt. From both of you. You said the climate went to shit, but … that bad?'

'The oxygen layer has been shrinking,' I said. 'That's why our colonisation efforts are so important. Even though we've planted trees everywhere we're not growing food, it looked like we'd all suffocate within two generations.'

'You aren't the first species to sacrifice everything for comfort,' Shiumo said.

'They're done with the cordon. You can go back down,' Marque said.

'Let's go and be royal,' Shiumo said.

We put our hands on her shoulders and the vista disappeared to be replaced by the view from the ground. A large crowd had gathered behind a ribbon barrier and was being held back by armoured police. The crowd had banners and streamers, and cheered loudly when they saw Shiumo.

'I think we should leave,' Shiumo said. 'If they get their hands on me, they'll love me to death.'

'I agree completely,' General Maxwell said, guiding us to the rotocopter. 'This way. We'll go take a look at the London Tower.'

*

When we folded up to the ship at the end of the day, Richard and I went to see our new rooms. Mine was exactly how I'd imagined it: creamy walls, with smooth curved joins between wall, floor and ceiling, making the interior slightly ovoid. I'd added a small sitting room, and Marque had provided me with a screen connected to the network. The bathroom had been extended as well, and now included my own spa bath.

'Do you like it?' Marque said from a sphere above my head.

'I love it.' I gestured at the spa bath. 'I'm trying that straight after dinner.'

'I have something else for you,' the sphere said. 'Follow me.'

'Can't I change out of this uniform first? The clothes you provide are much more comfortable.'

'After you see this,' it said. 'Come on!'

I followed it out of my room, and further down the hall towards the aft. An opening appeared on the left and I stared. Marque had created a swimming pool. It was rectangular, twenty metres long and five wide, and the wall along one side was transparent, providing a view of the stars reflected in the water. The interior of the pool was white, making the water a pale translucent turquoise.

'That is awesome,' I said. 'Thank you.' I shook my head. 'I'll have to use it all the time, otherwise I'll feel guilty about all that useful water sitting there doing nothing.'

'Try it after dinner,' Marque said.

'Don't worry, I will.'

After we'd eaten, Richard and Shiumo pretended they weren't going off together, both proclaiming they were retiring to their own rooms, so I returned to the swimming pool.

I sat on the edge, put my feet into the water and stopped. 'Marque, it's freezing.'

'Too cold?' The water warmed up slightly.

'More,' I said.

The water became warmer.

'Stop there. Too warm and I'll overheat.' I slipped in and took a deep breath. 'This is wonderful.'

The water wasn't chlorinated or salt, it was pure and fresh. I swam the length of the pool, then dived under and swam back. Swimming pools were a rare luxury back on Earth, and I'd swum every day in the pool at the barracks until they'd closed it to save water.

'Heads up,' Marque said through the water, and I surfaced.

Shiumo was crouched like a cat at the edge of the pool. 'Oh, you use it for exercise! What a clever idea.' She tilted her head. 'Do you mind if I join you?'

'Not at all,' I said, and swam to her.

She slid into the water and dogpaddled with all four legs, swinging her tail behind her. I began a lap and she struck out next to me, not nearly as graceful swimming as she was walking. I dived under to swim to the edge, and surfaced to find her in her two-legged form – the muscular black man with the fantastic textured hair. I didn't look down, not wanting to know whether he was still naked.

'I can't swim well in four-legged form,' he said with a wry smile. 'Do you mind? This is wonderful – what a great idea. I should have asked Marque to make a pool for me a long time ago.'

I leaned on the edge and looked up at the stars. 'It is wonderful.'

He drifted over and leaned alongside me. 'Is the water comfortable? Not too cold?'

'No, it's perfect. Is it okay for you?'

He rested his chin on his arms, the silver bracelets clinking together with the movement. 'Yes.' He smiled at me. 'Thank you, Jian, you've made my life so much richer. I'm glad I met you and Richard.'

I patted him on the shoulder. 'I'm glad I met you too, Shiumo.'

His expression changed, becoming more intense, and he took my hand in his and pulled me closer, drifting in the water. He moved his face close to mine and studied my eyes, then looked down at my mouth.

'Richard taught me kissing,' he said, his voice deep and breathless. 'I'd never experienced this activity before.'

He pressed against me, hard muscle against my body, and I felt that he was naked – and growing excited. I filled with need, wanting to taste his full lips.

'Kissing is wonderful,' he said, so close that our mouths were nearly touching.

I put my hands behind his neck, floated into him and closed the gap. His mouth covered mine, filling me with sensation, and his arms wrapped around me, holding me in the water as I lost myself in the feeling of touching him. His mind brushed mine, feather-light, and my body tightened with greater need. We floated in the water, running our hands over each other.

I broke away first. 'I'm in a relationship.'

'I understand,' he said, and his voice trembled through me. 'I'll leave.'

'No,' I said, and ran my fingertips over his chiselled cheekbone. I looked up at Marque. 'Where's Richard?'

'Recharging. I think he fell asleep waiting for you, Shiumo; you've worn him out,' Marque said. 'But he won't like this. He'll be jealous.'

'I told him I'm not monogamous, and he said he understands,' Shiumo said, and kissed me again. He pulled me hard against him and I was lost in the sensation. He whispered into my ear: 'I respect the relationship you have with your spouses, but I'll always be here for you if you want me.'

I leaned my head on his shoulder, enjoying his strength. 'Thank you. I think we should stop now. I don't trust myself.'

He pulled back to smile at me, his silver eyes full of amusement beneath the faceted silver stone in his forehead. 'I don't trust myself either. You are very special, Jian.' He ran his hand down my back and cupped my behind, making me quiver in response. 'I want to share greater pleasure with you. I'm very fond of you – I think I'm falling in love.'

'We really need to stop.' I put my hand on his shoulder and gazed into his eyes. 'But I don't want to be parted from you. I want to go with you when you set up the Japanese colony.'

He pulled me close again and brushed his mouth over my hair. 'I don't want to be parted from you either, but you need to spend time with your spouses.'

I sighed with feeling. 'I know.'

He drifted backwards, smiling. 'Race you to the other end!' He spun in the water and splashed away.

*

There was another message from Dianne and Victor on my screen when I returned to my room. I winced: I hadn't responded to any of them, I'd been too caught up in the Shiumo thing. Time to make it right with them. I opened the message.

'Hey, lovely,' Victor said. 'We're trying to get through to you and keep getting a vidmail. I hear you're out of quarantine now – can you come visit? Ping us the minute you're free, and we'll arrange something.'

I checked the time and pinged them back. Victor appeared on the screen and grinned when he saw me. 'Jian! About time.' He leaned into the screen. 'Dianne's asleep, but big news! The baby's a boy.'

'That's wonderful,' I said trying to sound enthusiastic. I'd never been interested in having kids, it wasn't my thing ... and then my mind filled with images of what a little boy would look like, half

Victor and half Dianne, a son for all of us to care for, cheeky and playful ...

He snapped me out of my reverie by speaking again. 'So you're out of quarantine now?'

I nodded.

'Come and visit us as soon as you can, Jian; we want to hear all about it. Last time we spoke you were off to outer space, and now you're back and with this amazing alien. I want to see her in person and sculpt something! Can you arrange it?'

'I'll come and visit soon; I'll be free when she takes the Japanese colony to Kapteyn-b,' I said. 'I'm ferociously busy, Vic, but I'll do my best.'

'I'm so glad you didn't leave,' he said. 'We can reconnect, be the three of us again. I can't wait to see you, my darling, and Dianne can't either.'

'I'm looking forward to it too,' I said, thinking about Shiumo's male form and those silver eyes.

14

Shiumo and I sat across from each other on the floor of her ship. 'That's the way,' she said. 'You're in the right range. Now ping it.'

The tiny sliver of paper on the floor between us quivered, and I gasped with delight.

'Well done,' she said. She shook her head like a horse. 'I can't believe I'm trying to teach you this. I have no idea what I'm doing. It should have taken a day, not two weeks.'

'Second-hand is close enough,' I said. I rubbed my temples. 'I'd better stop. I'll have a massive headache if I try more.'

'Ten minutes until you're due in Tokyo,' Marque said. 'You can leave now, if you like.'

'No,' I said. 'I made it move. Shiumo has to tell me about the picture.'

'Are you really sure?' she said, rising onto four legs. 'Some species find the nature of this art extremely disturbing.'

'I'm a professional soldier; I can handle a bit of blood.'

We went to Shiumo's art gallery, and stopped in front of a splendid blue-tinted watercolour hanging suspended in the air. It showed an alien landscape with a much lower gravity than Earth. The trees were impossibly tall with extremely narrow trunks, and animals with short stubby wings flew between them. A cluster of spindly towers stood in the middle of the picture:

transparent and lovely, with round windows at intervals. The entire picture was painted in delicate shades of blue, with no other colour present.

'This is definitely my favourite,' I said. 'Copper-based blood?'

'Yes,' Shiumo said. She moved closer and gazed at it with longing. 'Their atmosphere is higher in oxygen than yours, and the gravity is lower. Their metabolism is copper-based, and they have no skeletons. You'd see them as translucent blobs, that communicate by moving their blue blood through their skin to make meaningful patterns.'

'They're magnificent artists,' I said.

'She spent her life creating this,' Shiumo said. 'As she grew and matured, and we had our children, she continued to work on it. They only work on one painting throughout their whole life.'

'And that's her blood? She kept bleeding herself to make the painting?'

'In a way. They make the picture with wax from one of the plants in the corner there. They have no other pigments available to them, so you can't see the final image until it's splashed with blood.' She lowered her head. 'When they feel the picture is perfect, they open a major vein.'

'No way,' I said. 'They die to see the painting finished?'

Shiumo nodded.

'Time, ladies,' Marque said.

'I can understand why Marque saved the art from the water before he saved Richard's prosthetics,' I said. 'It would be a tragedy to lose a life's work like that.'

'If I'd been more alert I could have saved them both,' Marque said.

'In the end you did, and that's all that's important,' Shiumo said. 'How are the biologicals coming along?'

My tablet pinged: Richard. The Japanese were packed up and ready to go.

'Another four and a half weeks and they'll be fully grown. I'll show you when you return,' Marque said.

'Ew, no thanks,' Shiumo said. 'Half-grown cloned parts are revolting.'

The Japanese colonists' headquarters were in the Imperial Palace grounds. The tops of the old Tokyo skyscrapers, protected by the enormous sea wall in the bay, were visible a kilometre away. The hundred-hectare park was wide flat lawns with a number of narrow internal roads, providing plenty of room for the equipment. Large marquees had been erected over the lawns, the leaves from the turning maple trees making their tops a patchwork of white, red and gold. Equipment was stacked on the grass and under the trees, and we had to move as a truck rumbled past on the internal road. The Palace itself – a multi-storey white castle with distinctive pitched roofs – overlooked it all.

Richard touched Shiumo's head. 'I promised I wouldn't leave you,' he said.

'This isn't leaving me. This is temporary. Go and see your mother.' She looked around. 'I have something for you both.'

Two black spheres the size of tennis balls floated out of Marque's sphere and hovered in front of us.

'Marque will protect you, and connect you with me,' Shiumo said.

'Not the same as being with you,' Richard said. 'I want to stay with *you*.'

Shiumo bunted him with her forehead. 'Go see your mum. And you.' She focused her silver eyes on me. 'You go and see your mum as well, and your husband and wife. I'll see you both in five days. And if you get lonely, Marque can relay messages between us when I'm on Earth. Okay?'

'Just keep reminding me that Maxwell is a paranoid idiot, okay, Marque?' Richard said.

'That should be obvious,' Marque said.

Shiumo hoisted herself onto her back legs, and placed her foreclaws on Richard's shoulders. 'I won't change here. It embarrasses everybody,' she said. She brushed her face against his, and he kissed the scales on her cheek. 'I love you.'

'I love you too,' he said, smiling through the grief of leaving her. 'I'll miss you.'

'Come back to me.' She dropped to all fours and turned to me. 'You too. I need you to help me out, my friend.'

She approached me and hesitated.

'Oh, come here,' I said, and put my arms out.

Shiumo put her foreclaws on my shoulders and hugged me; she was surprisingly light for such a large creature.

I kissed her on the cheek. 'I'll miss you.'

'See you in five days,' she said.

'Choumali, Alto, your transport's ready,' General Maxwell said as she approached across the grass.

We followed her to the car, the Marque spheres floating above us.

Maxwell turned to address them. 'You aren't necessary. We can handle the security ourselves. Concentrate on Shiumo.'

'Sorry, General, orders from the Princess,' Marque said from one of the spheres. 'Shiumo knows how much hysteria her presence has generated, and she wants me to make sure that her *escorts*,' it emphasised the word, 'are safe.'

'I feel like an expensive courtesan,' Richard said as he entered the car.

I sat next to him, and Maxwell sat across from us.

'Nah, you're one of the cheapest she's had by a long way,' Marque said, floating in as well.

'So what's going on between you two?' the general said as the car drove off.

'We're sharing our love,' Richard said, radiating almost childish defiance.

The general's face turned grim. 'Is that even possible?'

'It is with her,' Richard said. 'I love her. Deal with it.'

The general's face grew even grimmer. She glanced up at the Marque spheres floating near the ceiling, then settled back in her seat, her jaw working, but didn't say a word.

She remained silent as we drove to Kansai Airport, where we would be taking a military transport to New London.

The general escorted us through the terminal. 'Are you sure you don't need security?' she said when we were on the tarmac next to the transport.

'No, we have Marque,' Richard said. 'It's just a short drive to my mother's after we drop Jian at the train station.'

'I'll be fine on the train, ma'am,' I added. 'As Richard said, I have a Marque, and the train to Wales rarely has more than five people on it.'

'When Shiumo's back, we need to move our own colonisation project into high gear,' the general said. 'Your skills will be vital, Alto. And your psi ability, Choumali.'

'We can help,' I said.

'I hope you can. I'll see you in five days.' She saluted us, and we returned it. She turned to go, then said, 'Oh, I nearly forgot.' She pulled out her tablet and sent each of us a security code. 'If you need me for any reason whatsoever, send me that and I'll come to you as fast as I can.'

*

Both of us caught up with paperwork on the plane to New London, filing a variety of reports that we'd neglected while busy with Shiumo. When we landed, Richard pinged the car with his tablet, and it came to the lay-by.

As we crossed the bridge from the airport's island of reclaimed land, the city of New London came into view, on a flattened plateau surrounded by terraces. The engineers had created the plateau by cutting off the tops of the Chilterns, and using the earth as raw material to create the island carrying New Heathrow. They'd carefully relocated the major landmarks of Old London – the Houses of Parliament, Westminster Cathedral, the Tower of London and St Paul's – to the centre of the new plateau, away from the rising waters of the Thames. Nearby, a small artificial lake was spanned by Old London's ancient bridges.

The rest of the city was a congested mass of high-rise residential blocks built of bare, ugly concrete. The edges of the plateau, like New Paris, were terraced down to the old water level, and inhabited by refugees who didn't have permission to live in the city.

Richard was broadcasting loneliness and misery, and I patted his arm.

'Sorry,' he said. 'You can probably sense it. I miss her already.'

'So do I.'

'Marque,' Richard said, and looked around. 'Where are you?'

'I've integrated with your tablet,' Marque said.

Richard raised his tablet. It appeared normal, then shifted in his hands to something blacker, slimmer and sleeker. He turned it around. 'Nice.'

'Thank you,' Marque said.

I checked mine, and it changed similarly.

Richard settled back in his seat. 'I have a question for you, Marque.'

'Fire away.'

'I saw that Shiumo wears jewellery. Does she have any preferences?'

'You want to buy her something?'

'Would she appreciate it?'

'Yes, she loves receiving gifts, particularly jewellery. Art goes in the gallery, but she can wear jewellery wherever she goes.'

'Good,' Richard said. 'I noticed she prefers silver –'

'That's platinum,' Marque said.

'Okay. Platinum, and she likes green stones.'

'Yes, she likes the contrast with her red scales.'

'Jade? Emerald?'

'She loves both of them.'

'Opal?'

'That's not on my database. Let me look that up on your network.' Marque was quiet for a moment. 'Well, that's unusual. Goodness, some of these are very striking. This may be a trade resource that could make your planet extremely wealthy.'

'So a gift of a black and green opal in a platinum setting would be suitable?'

'Depends. Are you asking her to marry you? Because if you're asking her to be monogamous …'

'No. I'm willing to be flexible for her. I won't ask her to be monogamous.'

'So it's just a gift of love?'

'Precisely so.'

'Then go for it. She'll be absolutely delighted.'

'Can you help me choose for her?' Richard said.

'Sure,' I said.

'Yes,' Marque said at the same time.

'Actually, I meant you, Jian. But, Marque, your input would be appreciated,' Richard said.

'This will be a lot of fun,' Marque said with enthusiasm. 'What about this one?'

A black opal with striking red, blue and green highlights appeared on the tablet screen, with a notation underneath about its origin and sale price.

I choked with laughter. 'That's in a museum!'

'That is so outside my price range it's insane,' Richard said. 'We can't buy that.'

'Heh. I make ten kilos of gold, trade it for the stone, done.'

'You can synthesise gold?' I said.

'I can synthesise anything.'

'You made the coins that Shiumo paid us with!'

'Of course.'

'Can you synthesise opal?' Richard said.

'That would cheapen the intent of the gift. A natural stone is more sincere.'

'Good. Let's look for something a little saner.'

'Most of the best opals come from that country on the other side of your world,' Marque said. 'Delivery might be an issue.'

'You can collect it for me,' Richard said.

'I can't leave you alone.'

'I'll be perfectly safe with my mother and stepfather. But we may find a stone here in New London, or over in Old Geneva. Search the vendors and see what you can come up with.'

'All right,' Marque said. 'Here you are. These are the most suitable; a larger stone will look more appropriate on Shiumo's larger hands. What do you think?'

Richard studied the stones. He pointed. 'What about this one, Jian?'

'I like the green and blue,' I said. 'They'll complement her scales. But it's just a bare stone with no setting.'

'Can you make a setting for that one, Marque?' Richard said.

'Of course. Say the word – yes or no – and I'll purchase it for you.'

'How do I pay for it?'

'I'll take it out of your salary.'

'I should buy her something as well,' I said.

'Do you love her?' Richard said.

'Not like you do.' I understood. 'This is a gift of loving commitment?'

'Something like that. But,' Richard raised one hand, 'not an engagement ring. Don't worry, Marque.'

'I won't ruin the moment for you,' I said. 'I'll buy her something small – maybe something Welsh from the village, or a small piece of art to add to her collection. You can be the main event.'

'Thank you, Jian.' Richard nodded at the screen. 'Let's buy it for her.'

'Done,' Marque said. 'It will be delivered to you in the next couple of days. When do you want to give it to her?'

'While I'm here and she's in Japan, to let her know that I'm thinking of her,' Richard said. 'Can you carry it to her?'

Marque was silent, then said, 'Yes, I can. That's very thoughtful. You're one of the best consorts she's had, Richard.'

'*One* of the best?' I said.

'What happened to the other ones?' Richard said, broadcasting a sudden shot of concern.

'You know she's not monogamous,' Marque said.

'What happened to the other consorts?' Richard demanded.

'Well, three of them had their planet destroyed by cats,' Marque said wryly.

'The Nimestas,' I said.

'Exactly.'

'Oh lord,' Richard said. 'All three of them?'

A spreadsheet appeared on his tablet.

'Full disclosure,' Marque said. 'Deceased means that she outlived them – not unusual with a species so long-lived.'

'I see.' Richard scanned the list.

I peered over his shoulder. It contained more than a hundred names. 'What's that in the first cell? Is it encrypted?' I said.

'That's their name in their own language.'
'Oh.'
Richard scrolled down the list. The first fifty or so were marked as 'deceased', with one in the middle marked 'new relationship'.
'New relationship?' Richard said.
'They moved on. Shiumo has never had a relationship end non-amicably.'
'I see,' Richard said again.
Different notations appeared further down the list: 'Living on home planet, no children'; 'Homeworld with two children' ...
'Two children?' I said. 'How many children does Shiumo have?'
'Some of her spouses take their joint children to live on the dragon homeworld,' Marque said. 'She has five families currently resident there.'
'What – she's pan-reproductive? I could ...' Richard dropped his tablet onto the seat next to him. 'After you transplant my body parts, I could get her *pregnant* with a half-human child?' He was broadcasting near-panic.
'Only if she chooses to,' Marque said. 'Her species have complete control over their reproduction. The half-dragon children are usually genetically very close to the non-dragon parent, with a slightly larger size and a few scales to denote their dragon heritage. All species regard their half-dragon children as exceptionally handsome.'
'Good lord, that's a yes,' Richard said. The panic intensified; he was close to meltdown.
'Could Shiumo get me pregnant if I had sex with her?' I said.
'As I said, only by choice. Both parents must agree to the impregnation.'
'Holy fuck, that's a yes as well,' I said, stunned at the implications.
Richard stared at the tablet as if it was venomous. 'How many current spouses does she have?'
'Twenty-four.'
'Damn!' I said. 'And they put up with her going off by herself all the time? She said she hasn't been on the homeworld in ages.'

'Most of them have relationships with other dragons as well.'

'I wish she'd told me this before I became involved with her,' Richard said, still deeply in shock.

Marque's voice was impatient. 'She *did*, Richard. She told you she wasn't monogamous. It's not her fault that you're too dim to see all the implications.'

'That's unfair,' I said.

The opal reappeared on the tablet screen. 'Do you want me to cancel the transaction?' Marque said.

Richard stared at the stone without touching the tablet. 'Let me think about it.'

He pushed the tablet away, and leaned on his elbow to study the streets of New London outside the car window. We passed a street market selling black-market food and electronics, the watchers at the end of the street alert and on edge. Our clean and well-maintained Armed Forces vehicle stood out among the worn and rattling civilian cars.

'You all right, sir?' I said.

Richard didn't reply.

His tablet pinged and Shiumo's image appeared on it. 'Richard?' she said, her voice tentative.

'Hi, Shiumo,' he said without looking at the screen.

'Marque tells me that it never occurred to you that I would have other spouses and children. You humans really are very dense sometimes, my love.'

'When is the last time you saw them – the ones on your homeworld?' he said.

'About thirty years ... Marque?'

'Thirty-two,' Marque said.

'Is that where I'll end up?' Richard said. 'On your homeworld, waiting thirty years for you to come visit me?'

'Only if that is what you wish.'

'They *want* that?'

'Uhhh ...' She turned away from the screen. 'Marque, bring the list up, and I'll explain them one by one.' She turned back to Richard and took a deep breath. 'The Nimestas you already met – what a tragedy. I have no children with them. Their reproductive cycle is extremely unusual and I don't think it will ever happen for us – particularly now.

'Let's look at the list. Clickclick – their species is hermaphroditic so I'll just use "they" as a pronoun. Clickclick is half-dragon – we call them dragonscales – and has parented a dragon off me.'

'Whoa! Wait, wait ...' Richard picked up the tablet to see her face. 'One of your spouses is half-dragon and has a full-dragon child with you?'

'That's how it works. Clickclick is also the spouse of two other dragons and three dragonscales on Dragonhome. I'm looking forward to seeing them again. Next? Oh, Lisenthrezaquorimatoliani. He's hibernating on his own world; he'll wake up in five years or so. BasksInSunshine asked for a fifty-year separation while she recovers from having the children.' Shiumo sighed. 'There are three or four that visit my ship for a few weeks at a time – they're folded on by me or other dragons – but right now everybody's busy with the children or their other spouses or ... just life, I guess. Nobody's visited me in months and I've been lonely. I'm glad we found love together.'

'How many children do you have, Shiumo?' I said.

'Oh, hello, Jian. I didn't know you were there. I'm not sure. Marque?'

'Since Red-Fading-To-Rose-Violet that's impossible to quantify,' Marque said.

'Oh, yeah,' Shiumo said. 'Red-Fading is an aquatic ... like a super-intelligent version of your coral. It manipulates its environment by telepathically controlling its motile spawn, and I parented a few thousand spawn with it about a hundred years ago.'

'Holy shit,' I said under my breath.

The car stopped; we'd arrived at the train station.

'I guess I'll talk to you later,' I said to Richard.

'Give my regards to your family.'

'I will, sir.'

As I pulled my duffel out of the back of the car, I could hear them still speaking inside.

'Please don't leave me,' Shiumo said sadly.

'I said I love you, Shiumo, and I meant it.'

'I love you too. I'm folding to Kapteyn in an hour to select a landing site. I'll be back tomorrow to pack up the colonists' equipment.' She sounded even more forlorn. 'Don't leave me, Richard. I love you so much.'

'I won't. I love you too. You explained it all; it's just me being human. I won't leave you. And I'd like to meet some of your other spouses – they sound very interesting.'

'Do you mean it?' she said, her voice high-pitched and sweet with hope.

'Absolutely. I'll see you in five days, okay? I cannot wait.'

'Me too,' she said.

I closed the rear hatch and threw my bag over my shoulder. Richard climbed out of the car and stood in front of me.

'You going to be okay, sir? That was a big revelation.'

He shrugged. 'She did tell me she wasn't monogamous. I should have worked it out earlier. I'd like to go to the dragon homeworld and meet some of them now.'

'Me too.' I hefted the duffel and looked down.

'It's been a mad few weeks,' he said.

'I went from security officer on the *Britannia* to an alien's attaché. Mad does not even begin to describe it.'

'I'll see you in five days, Jian.' Richard spoke to the air above my head. 'Look after her, Marque.'

A floating sphere shimmered into view. 'Don't worry, I will. The train will be here soon, Jian, you'd better move.'

Richard shifted uncomfortably. I made up his mind for him and embraced him. We pulled back, smiling.

'Go,' he said.

'Keep in touch,' I said, and headed to the train station.

15

The water on either side of the train causeway had disappeared. The area was now mud flats, dotted with the corpses of drowned trees and crumbling ruined buildings. Large machines ran over the surface of the mud with fingers rotating into it. Plumes of salt sprayed from the machines' back ends into trucks that followed them.

The train was filthy: the windows were rimmed with grime and the seats were stained; the floor was covered in dirt and muddy shoe prints. I realised I was noticing this for the first time because I'd grown accustomed to the constant pristine cleanliness of Shiumo's ship. It was free of all dust and dirt, and always smelled pleasant – nothing like the damp mouldy odour of the train. I'd even started noticing other people's body odour. I was becoming soft. I'd have to keep an eye on myself.

I had a flash of concern about the mind control, and shook it off. If Shiumo was controlling me, I wouldn't be able to leave her at all.

I heard my name and glanced up at the screen at the end of the carriage. It was showing a video of our visit to New Paris – Richard and I were escorting Shiumo through the streets of the recreated Montmartre district. I winced; I didn't often watch the news on the network. I'd been too busy organising Shiumo's schedule and attending the never-ending conferences. A large cheering crowd was gathered on the other side of the barrier, and I saw something I'd never seen before: a sign held up by an angry group that said 'Alien invader, leave our planet!'

A young woman stormed towards me from the back of the train. She pointed at the screen. 'Is that you?'

I didn't sense any malice from her. 'Yes, it's me.'

My tablet pinged and I checked it. A message scrolled across the top: *You are perfectly safe. I will defend you. If you are mobbed I can put an energy barrier around you. Relax.*

'I knew I remembered you!' the woman said. 'We went to school together.'

I studied her face and came up blank. But if she was my age and lived in this part of Wales, we probably had gone to school together. There was only one in the district.

'We were at Llanfair Prep together,' she said, poking me in the arm. 'Don't you remember?'

'That was twenty years ago,' I said, bewildered. I tried to remember her name and failed.

She pointed at the screen. 'What's she like, the alien?'

The crowd in New Paris were having an argument about the sign now, and some jostling was occurring. Someone grabbed the sign, threw it to the ground and stomped on it.

'She's absolutely lovely. She really wants to help humanity,' I said.

'Any chance ...' She took her tablet out of her bag. 'Could you sign this for me? And maybe get her autograph? I know you're close to her.'

A few more people had heard the conversation. Two men and a woman were now standing in the aisle next to me, their faces bright with curiosity. I vaguely recognised them from around the mountain, but didn't know any of them personally.

I took the woman's tablet and signed the lock screen for her. Her name was Beatrice, and I still had no idea who she was.

She grinned with delight as she took the tablet back, then bent to speak conspiratorially to me. 'Uh ... can you give me a tour of her ship? I've seen it on the network and it looks *amazing*.'

'I'd love one too,' one of the men said. 'Can you sign my tablet as well?'

'Sure,' I said, and sat on the armrest so I could reach over to take his tablet.

'So,' Beatrice said, 'a tour?'

'I'll suggest to Shiumo that we give selected people tours of the ship,' I said. 'But she may be concerned about security. She lives on board.'

'You live on it too, don't you?' Beatrice said.

I nodded as I signed the next tablet. There were now ten people crowding in the aisle next to me – probably the entire population of the train.

'What's it like living up there?' Beatrice said.

'Oh, there's a good idea,' Marque said from my tablet. 'A documentary about life on the ship. We should do that as soon as Shiumo's back.'

Beatrice squealed. 'Oh my god, is that the round thing speaking?'

The train closed its doors on the first stop, and the engine hummed with effort as it started the climb up the mountain.

I grabbed my duffel bag. 'Yes. The next stop's mine. Do you mind?'

Beatrice blocked me. 'Is there anything at all we can do to get a tour?'

'Please move and let me out,' I said.

'You didn't sign my tablet!' a woman shouted from the back. 'It's for my little boy. He'll be thrilled when I tell him I met you!'

'Quickly,' I said, and took the tablet and signed it. I pushed my way through the crowd. 'I have to get off! Let me through.'

'General Maxwell was right: you should have taken private transport,' Marque said when I reached the doors, the people still following me. 'On the count of three, take a big step forward. One ... two ...'

I stepped forward and there was a snap behind me. The small crowd was crushed against what appeared to be glass.

'Energy field,' Marque said. 'I'll turn it off when the doors close.'

The train doors opened and I stepped out. The sky was a clear bright blue, with no clouds, and the air was cool and dry.

I inhaled deeply. 'Wonderful.' Then I felt a bolt of shock. 'Oh no ... my mother's rice and coffee won't grow in this.'

'I'm advising them through the network about alternative crops,' Marque said. 'There they are.'

'Jian!' Mum ran to me and enveloped me in a huge hug.

Dianne and Victor stood back, grinning. When Mum was done, they stepped up and hugged me as well, both throwing in passionate kisses for good measure.

I smiled at them: Dianne, short, black, and bright with intelligence and pregnancy; and Victor, tall and skinny with terrible acne and scruffy blond curls, and a beautiful smile that melted my heart.

'God, I missed you guys,' I said.

Cheering erupted from nearby and I turned to look. Most of the population of the village – nearly fifty of them – were standing at the station exit, clapping and calling out to me.

'They won't let you spend time with your family until they've given you the keys to the village,' Dianne said. 'So come up to the community hall for dinner and a lot of boring speeches, and then ...' She nudged me with her shoulder. 'We can have some private time.'

*

My spouses had booked the biggest of the village hotel's twenty rooms – plenty of room for the three of us. It even had its own small bathroom with a shower. We all entered the room together, Mum too, and fell to sit on the bed.

'It's so far away,' Mum said. 'You should have stayed at Mrs Chan's inn.'

'We are not letting Dianne sleep in that rat hole,' Victor said indignantly. 'She needs to sleep somewhere new and clean, and this hotel has *two* stars.'

'Oi! Stop using my pregnancy as an excuse for everything!' Dianne said.

'We are looking after you and our baby,' Victor said.

'It's only one stop, Mum, and we'll be back tomorrow,' I said.

'I guess you're right,' she grumbled, and stood. 'I'll see you tomorrow.'

I gave her a hug. 'I'll be home for five days – plenty of time for us all to be together.'

She nodded into my chest.

'Go home and feed Puppy,' I said, pulling back. 'And Chicken, and Chicken, and the other bird – I forget what its name is …'

'You are very cheeky,' Mum said. She patted me on the arm, and went out.

'Chicken!' Dianne and Victor shouted in unison just as the door closed.

I sighed and sat on the couch across from Dianne and Victor, who were still sitting on the bed. I leaned my elbows on my knees and wiped my eyes. 'I am so sorry.'

'What for?' Victor said.

'I told you I wasn't psi.'

'Oh, that.' Dianne waved it away. 'We can deal. To tell the truth we weren't terribly surprised –'

'I was!' Victor said.

'Well, I wasn't,' Dianne said. 'I understand why you didn't want to tell us.' She took my hand. 'It's okay.'

She pulled me onto the bed next to her and put her arm around me. I leaned my head on her shoulder, and Victor put his arm around both of us. All three of us sighed with bliss. It had been a long time since we'd been together like this.

'I lied to you,' I said. 'If I were you, I wouldn't forgive me.'

Victor squeezed me. 'Like we said: we forgive you. Now tell us about the dragon.'

'Yes!' Dianne released me. 'Tell us all about it! What planet is she from? She's psi too, right?'

'Your mother showed us photos – did you *really* go sightseeing to Jupiter?' Victor said.

'Yes. It's so beautiful.'

'Can you take us?' Dianne said. She and Victor shared a look. Both of them were excited. 'We're your spouses – we should be living on the ship with the alien as well. We can help.'

'Oh,' I said, suddenly suspecting that they were like the people on the train, using me to access the royal alien celebrity.

'Think what an opportunity it would be for me,' Dianne said. 'I could be the Earth's first *exo*biologist. She's refused access to her biology, but if she'll let me study her I could win a Henno prize!'

'She has to take us up there so we can be with you,' Victor said.

'That AI – what's it called?' Dianne said. 'How does it fly?'

'Anti-gravity,' I said, full of disappointment in them. 'Its name is Marque.'

'Can it tell us how it does it?' Victor leaned forward eagerly and his emotions turned to greed. 'Think how much we could make if we sold that technology!'

'The technology is not for sale,' Marque said, and Victor gasped.

Marque shimmered into view above us.

'You were *watching* us?' Victor said. 'Voyeur! Go back to the alien.'

'No,' Marque said. 'I'm here to look after Jian-sama.'

'I can put it on privacy, don't worry,' I said.

'So can you get us up to the ship?' Victor said. 'We want to be there too.'

I looked at their intent faces and spoke telepathically: *I'll see what I can do.*

Both of them jumped and scooted away from me.

'Don't do that,' Dianne said. 'You could hurt the baby.'

'Don't be ridiculous,' I said.

'That is freaky as shit. Cut it out,' Victor said.

'You said that if I was a psi, it was a deal-breaker,' I said.

'Yeah, but that was before the dragon,' Victor said.

'If you'd found out I was psi before the dragon, would you still forgive me for lying to you?'

'Of course,' Victor said.

'Absolutely,' Dianne said. 'Jian, we *love* you.'

They were lying. Everything coming out of their mouths was a lie. They wanted to use me to get to Shiumo.

'I cannot believe I am doing this,' I said under my breath. I rose and picked up my duffel. 'I'm sorry, I need to be apart from you for a while. I don't think I can –'

'No, Jian, really,' Dianne said. She jumped to her feet, radiating panic. 'Everything will be okay. We love you. Stay, okay?'

'We really do. Three together, remember?' Victor said. 'We can do anything. We have a kid coming – and you have to be part of it.' He yawned loudly, then winked at me. 'Let's go have a shower and I'll rub your back. You always love that.'

Dianne linked her arm in mine, and Victor went to my other side and put his arm around my shoulders.

'No more aliens,' Dianne said. 'Let's talk about *us*.' She looked up. 'Can you make that Marque go away? I feel like there's a video camera over my head.'

'I'm not watching you, but I won't leave Jian-sama,' Marque said.

'Go keep my mum company for a while, Marque, make sure she's okay,' I said. 'Some of the villagers might be harassing her for info on Shiumo while I'm with my spouses. Come back tomorrow.'

'Are you sure?' Marque said.

'Put an app on my tablet to contact you just in case.'

'There's already one there,' it said. The door opened and the sphere flew out, then closed the door behind it.

'It's been far too long,' Victor said, and this time his emotions were more love than anything else.

I let him take my bag, and he put it back on the floor, then kissed me, and Dianne wrapped herself around me from behind. They radiated love, but there was also still the excitement of having access to Shiumo, tinged with ugly avarice.

I hesitated, feeling torn. I couldn't stay with them if they were just planning to use me ... but it felt so good, and I'd missed them. It had been a long time.

Victor pulled back to smile at me, and put his hand on the side of my face, his expression full of adoration that matched his tender emotions.

I didn't want to hurt them. Maybe once they were used to the idea of Shiumo, the next five days would be like old times, the three of us knocking about together. Maybe they wouldn't put any pressure on me about Shiumo once I'd explained how things worked.

I smiled and followed Victor into the bathroom.

The next morning I woke with both of them wrapped around me. It really was just like old times. Dianne wriggled off the bed and raced to the bathroom, then climbed back in and spooned her back into my stomach. Victor pulled me tighter and I sighed with bliss.

'You awake?' Dianne said.

'Yeah,' I said, and kissed the back of her neck.

'That general asked me to pass on a message when Marque isn't around. She said to call her when you feel your head is clear. You won't need to say anything if you can't ditch Marque, but just call her.'

I sighed heavily. I searched my feelings; they were no different. 'Okay.'

'Does that mean something's wrong? Your head isn't clear?' Dianne said.

'Nothing; they worry too much. My head is fine. They're just being paranoid.'

'Guess what I have,' Victor said, bumping my back with his pelvis.

'Morning wood,' Dianne and I said together, and giggled.

'So what are you going to do about it?'

'Make love to my darling Dianne,' I said, and pulled her around to face me.

'Works for me,' Victor said.

We spent the morning together, then went up to the village. My mother was waiting for us at her cottage and it was a crush with the four of us inside.

'So what do you need done?' I said. 'Do you need more terraces, or anything like that? I can dig you another couple of fields.'

'No need,' she said smugly. 'Come on and I'll show you.'

She took us down the path through the jungle to the bottom of the mountain, a walk of more than half an hour. We passed the deserted terraces and abandoned residences of people who'd moved to the city, and arrived at the base. There were a few fenced fields holding some scraggly sheep, then the mud flats that led to the ocean – except there was no ocean now, only mud to the horizon, with two of the salt-extraction units running over its surface.

'We didn't get any geologists here, but the ones that visited further south all say the same thing: in two years this will have dried out enough to build on,' Mum said. 'Each village resident is allocated fifteen hectares, and some city folk will be taking what's left over. The scientists are suggesting sheep or goats, or fruit trees, or something like sorghum or even wheat.'

'Is there talk of cattle?' Dianne said.

'It won't be warm enough!' Mum said with delight. She turned to us, grinning broadly. 'They say we may even see *snow* for the first time in two hundred years, and there's a chance we could create *ski runs* down the mountain if we break up the terraces. Can you imagine it – making our muddy home a ski resort?' She shook her head. 'There'll even be enough oxygen to breathe all the way to the top of the mountain.'

'That's wonderful,' I said. 'Do you know which parcel is yours?'

Mum waved one arm over the mud. 'They'll put a road in and signpost everything in two years. Right now I'm filling out the paperwork to make my claim.' She smiled. 'It's a shame you're with the alien instead of the army. I could really use a spare pair of hands.'

'I can leave –' I began.

'No!' she said. 'She's helping us so much! Stay with her.'

'I'll come help you on the weekends, if you give me space to sculpt,' Victor said.

Mum held her hand out and he slapped it. 'Done.'

'So I can't help you on the land yet?' I said. 'Do the terraces need clearing in the meantime? I need something to do!'

Mum linked her arm in mine and turned us to walk back up to the village. 'The celebrity does not dig, or shift rocks, or pull weeds. You're not doing anything like that while you're here; you're too important. Everybody wants to have you over for tea.'

I lowered my head. 'But I want to help you.'

She squeezed my arm. 'You're famous now, Jian, get used to it. You're visiting all the neighbours first, then heading to the next village, where they've set up a community hall for the mayor of the prefecture to interview you for the network.'

'I'd rather just dig terraces for you,' I grumbled. 'I'm going to be *bored to death*.'

*

I finished telling the gathered villagers – for what felt like the millionth time – about my life on Shiumo's ship.

'And she's at the Japanese colony now?' the mayor said.

I nodded. 'She keeps in touch through Marque. She's running the colonists backwards and forwards.'

'And it's our turn next?'

'That's right. Euroterre's colony will be on the third planet of the star Wolf 1061. I'll help to establish the colony there, and I'll be sure to take plenty of photos to send back home.'

'I'd like to hear how you three met,' the mayor said. 'We've all heard about the alien and the dragon ship – but how long have you three been together? Was it two of you to start off, and a third joined later?' She leaned closer to Dianne and Victor. 'What will you do when Corporal Choumali leaves Earth to travel with Princess Shiumo?'

'Well, I hope we'll be going with her!' Victor said in a jolly tone, and the audience laughed. 'I don't want to be separated from my darling Jian. We've known each other forever.'

'And you, Dr Liebowicz?'

'Same,' Dianne said, with laughter in her voice. 'The three of us attended high school together in New Llanfair, and made a pact to stay together after I went to uni, Victor went to the polytech, and Jian joined up.'

'We vowed to stick together,' Victor said. 'You should have seen us back then, knocking about Llanfair, causing trouble as kids will. I bet half the shopkeepers in town cannot believe that all three of us went on to much greater things.'

'Victor and I have set up house in New Birmingham near the university, and Jian visits us whenever she can get leave,' Dianne said, and smiled at me. 'We don't see her nearly as much as we'd like, but we understand. Her military career is important to all of us.'

'Dr Liebowicz, you're a biologist?' the mayor said.

Dianne nodded. 'I'm doing postdoctoral research on temperature-resistant fruit strains, but now the temperature's dropped worldwide I think I'd better change my focus to working on ways we can re-establish all those favourite crops we lost. We'll be able to grow *peaches* in the open air!'

A smattering of applause rippled through the audience.

'And Mr Barrett?'

'I'm an artist,' Victor said. 'I'm very lucky to have Jian and Dianne supporting me – I wouldn't be able to do it without them.' He grinned at us. 'I think I'm the luckiest man in the world.'

'We'll all agree when you move up to the ship with Jian,' the mayor said.

'I can't move up yet,' Dianne said. 'It'll have to wait until after the baby's born. Victor's going to be a father, and Jian's going to be a second mother!'

The audience applauded loudly, and some people in the back cheered.

'That's wonderful news!' the mayor said. 'So –'

Victor raised one hand. 'If you don't mind, Mayor, there's something I need to say.' He nodded to Dianne. 'Something that Dr Liebowicz and I both have to say.'

'What's that?' the mayor said.

Victor and Dianne stood and took one of my hands each, pulling me to my feet. Then they clasped their free hands together so the three of us were standing in a circle.

'Please don't do this to me right now,' I said.

The mayor made a loud sound of enchantment, and the audience echoed her delight. 'That's so sweet.'

'Jian Choumali,' Victor said loudly, 'and Dianne Liebowicz. Will you make me the happiest man in the world and marry me?'

'Victor Barrett,' Dianne said, 'and Jian Choumali. Will you both marry me?'

They waited expectantly.

I could say yes, and have them with me for the rest of my life – sharing the experience of living on Shiumo's ship, travelling to the stars. It was the chance of a lifetime for them.

But I was damn sure that I didn't want them along every minute of the day. I did want to be a second mother, but the idea of being their wife and with them all the time ...

'I can't do this right now,' I said, and fled.

I ran across the stage, out the hall's back door, and was sitting in a corner of Mrs Chan's inn nursing an awful, locally produced whisky before I was aware of my surroundings.

I tried to raise the glass and couldn't move my hand. It was frozen. I pushed against the force field holding it, and realised what was happening.

'Let me drink it, Marque.'

'It isn't a solution to your problem,' Marque said. 'Nothing's ever so bad that you need to take your own life. Stop and think about it.'

'I'm not taking my own life – don't be ridiculous. I'm getting drunk because I'm running from commitment again, and breaking the hearts of two people who love me dearly.'

'Getting drunk?' Marque said. 'By the six galaxies, you humans really do take poison as a recreational substance! I saw the fermented grape juice before, but the level of toxicity in that glass is off the scale.'

'Let. Me. Go!' I said, and my hand was released so quickly that the whisky splashed over me. I gulped the rest down and put the glass back on the table. I waved at Mrs Chan behind the bar and she brought me another one.

'I saw what happened, Jian,' she said. 'Don't be mad at them. It was the obvious thing for them to do. You're allowed to not be ready to commit to a relationship.'

'I'll never be ready to commit.' I sipped the second drink more slowly. 'I'm a complete bitch.'

She shook her head, took my empty glass, and went back to the bar.

'Jian, you really need to stop this,' Marque said. 'That stuff is *poison*!'

'Go *away*,' I said, and waved a hand at it. 'Shoo. Piss off. Leave me alone!'

The sphere hovered for a moment, then whizzed out the door and away.

'Good,' I said, and took another gulp of the whisky. It really was awful.

Thirty minutes later I was into my fifth glass, unwilling to return and face Dianne and Victor, and well aware of the fact that I had nowhere else to go.

'Well, this is lovely,' my mother said in front of me. 'Here I am, about to be a grandmother, and the bride's getting cold feet.'

I looked up at her. 'I don't want to marry them, Mum.'

'You made that very clear.' She sat across the table from me. 'They're saying that if you won't marry them, they'll leave you. That sounds like an unreasonable ultimatum to me.'

I looked down. 'I'm not surprised.' I sucked in a huge breath. My nose was clogged, but I wasn't crying. Definitely not teary. I spat the words out. 'They just want to use me to get to Shiumo. I'm a way for Dianne to study the alien. They don't really care about me that much at all.'

'Is that what you see?'

'It's what I know,' I said.

'No,' she said. 'Is it what you *see*?'

'Oh,' I said, understanding. I thought about their feelings for me, and slumped over my drink. 'Yeah. It's what I see.'

'Well, it's good you said no then, isn't it? You're better off without them.' She linked her arm in mine and lifted me to my feet. 'Come on, let's call the car and go home.'

'I have to talk to them,' I said.

'Send them back to the hotel to bitch about you tonight, and they can meet us in the village tomorrow. By then they'll be used to the idea that they're not going to ride you up to the alien spaceship.'

'I'm letting them down.'

'Better than letting yourself down.'

It was raining outside, making the air so chilly that I shivered as Mum called the car with her tablet. The world spun around me, and I leaned on her until the car arrived and she pushed me into it.

'Come home and sleep it off,' she said. 'You're doing the right thing.'

'Then why does it hurt so much?' I said, and flopped sideways on the seat.

*

Dianne and Victor were waiting at Mum's house, hunched and miserable in the pouring rain. We hurried inside, and they followed us.

'You might as well stay until the rain stops,' Mum said, then added sternly, 'But don't give Jian any grief. This is her decision.'

'Don't worry, we won't,' Victor said. 'Are you sure about this, Jian?'

Dianne sat on the couch, and Victor sat on the floor next to her feet. I pulled out a dining chair and sat across from them, the room still moving around me.

'I'm sorry you feel pressured,' Dianne said. 'We weren't expecting you to run out like that. We've known each other forever, Jian; we thought you'd be happy.'

'I'm just not ready,' I said. 'You two go ahead and get married. Give our child a home. I'll come visit.'

They shared a look, and I could see their emotions were relieved. I realised I was on the outside now. We'd been drifting apart for a while, and it was only Shiumo's appearance that had kept them with me.

Dianne gasped and her face pinched.

Victor looked up at her, concerned. 'You okay?'

'He kicked me,' she said.

'Kicking already? He's a strong one,' Mum said, putting the teapot and cups on the coffee table in front of the screen.

'Here, Jian.' Dianne held her hand out. 'Come and feel.'

I hesitated, then went to her. She put my hand on her stomach – she didn't look terribly pregnant, just sort of ... round. Nothing happened, then what felt like a rubber ball bounced against my hand. It slid under Dianne's skin, then disappeared.

I gasped with delight. 'That's amazing!'

'You'll still come visit, won't you?' Victor said.

His emotional tone had changed. Now that I was leaving them, he was relieved. He'd settled into life with just him and Dianne, and I was in the way.

'Yeah,' I said, pulling my hand away and picking up a teacup. 'And next time I'll bring the dragon.'

Dianne leaned forward. 'Do you think she'd let me study her biology?'

'I'll see what I can do. She can do things you wouldn't believe. Did you know she can take a two-legged form? She can stand upright.'

'How does she manage that?' Dianne said.

'Let me tell you what's *really* remarkable about her two-legged form,' I said, and sipped my tea.

The taste set off the amount of alcohol I'd drunk, and I dropped the cup and saucer with a clatter, clapped my hand over my mouth, and ran to the bathroom.

16

I woke on Mum's couch with the puppy lodged under my arm. I pulled the blanket higher – it was cold. I checked my tablet, thinking I may have heard it ping, and was right. There was a message from Shiumo. I checked the time zone. She'd returned a day early to load the ship, but she'd only be on-planet for a few more hours.

I swung around so I was sitting and shifted the dog off me, ignoring her as she whined and buried herself under the covers.

'Marque, are you here?' I said softly.

'Above your head. The after-effects of that poison must be brutal, Jian. Hydrate yourself.'

'I'm fine. I've had much worse in barracks.' I reached under the couch and brought out my gift, already wrapped. 'Shiumo will be on-planet for a couple more hours. Can you carry this to her before she leaves?'

The sphere dropped so it was just above the gift. 'What's in there?'

'One of Victor's sculptures; he'd like her to have it. It's an Earth dragon.'

'What a thoughtful gift. She treasures artworks from her –'

'Call me her consort and I'll use you for batting practice,' I said. 'So can you make it to her in time?'

'No, but don't worry – I'll have one of my spheres delay her until I arrive. I'd better get Richard out of bed and pick up his gift as well.'

'Thanks, Marque.' I held up the gift. 'Run!'

The sphere grew larger, enclosed the package, then zipped away.

I pinged Shiumo back. She appeared on the screen almost immediately.

'Jian! I heard what happened. Are you okay?'

I rubbed one hand over my face, still half-asleep. 'I'm fine. They're gone.'

'It wasn't because of me, was it?'

'Exactly the opposite. We'd been drifting apart for a while – my military career came first. They only asked me to marry them because of my new status as a celebrity.'

'I am so sorry I messed up your life. I will make up for it, believe me.'

'No need. Hey, don't leave until my Marque sphere reaches you. It has something for you.'

'You don't need to give me anything.'

'I want to.'

She looked away. 'The first capsule load is nearly done. I have to take it up to the ship soon if we're to keep to the schedule you made so efficiently. I'll ping you when I'm back down here.'

'I'll talk to you then. Big hugs, girlfriend.'

'Hugs back at you, lovely Jian,' she said, and the screen blinked out.

I rubbed my hands over my throbbing face, and pulled myself to my feet to head to the bathroom. I was making coffee from the last of Mum's excellent beans when my tablet pinged again: Richard. I opened the channel. He looked as scruffy as me: unshaven and red-eyed on the natural half of his face.

'Good lord, Jian, what happened to you?'

'Check the network – it'll be all over it by midday. I just did the most humiliating thing in my entire life, and the whole world will see it. On top of that, my mother has absolutely no pain relief anywhere in this house and my head is killing me. Is there a problem, sir?'

'Is your Marque there?'

'No, I sent it to Shiumo with a gift for her.' I studied the tablet, wishing I could sense his emotions. 'Is everything okay?'

'Stop for a moment and think. Is Shiumo controlling us?'

'Of course not. She's helping humanity. She's on her way to Kapteyn right now with the Japanese colony.'

'Have you told her anything you were ordered not to?'

'Well, yeah, but if the orders go against mission goals –'

'Jian,' he said, cutting me off, 'remember what General Maxwell said? If she and Shiumo had guns pointed at each other, who would you jump in front of?'

'The general's so paranoid,' I said dismissively.

'Have you disobeyed orders?'

'Well, yeah ...' I had a niggling feeling of doubt. 'She's helping humanity ...'

'What do you do for a living, Jian? What's your life's work?'

'I'm Shiumo's ...' It all hit me with a rush of guilt and betrayal. I was a *soldier* defending Euroterre, humanity and Earth, dammit, not some alien's *toy*. 'Holy shit, what have I been doing?'

My eyes filled with tears of frustration. What had she done to me? I'd told her things I'd been explicitly ordered not to. She'd seduced Richard, and attempted to seduce me. She was very charming, and living on her ship was the best experience I'd ever had, but there was something else going on, and I was only aware of it when I wasn't near her. On the train, I'd asked myself if I'd been mind-controlled, and immediately dismissed it without a second thought.

I felt a horrible uncertainty: had I just broken up with my spouses because I wanted to be with Shiumo? It was more than just avoiding commitment. Had I betrayed humanity?

I tried to recall what I'd told her – and realised it was *everything*. I had level-four security clearance and I'd told this damn alien everything. My dismay turned to cold fury. She'd compromised my honour as a soldier defending my people.

'She's manipulating us,' I said. 'I wish I knew how. I can't sense anything.'

'It took a couple of days for her influence to wear off, then I used the code the general gave me,' Richard said. 'She wants to debrief us now that we're clear of Shiumo's control.'

'Understood. I'll take the next train into New London.'

'No need, there'll be a rotocopter there in an hour to take you to New Whitehall. Sorry to drag you away from your family, but we need to debrief without those damn spheres hanging around. Pack up and be ready, Corporal. That's an order.'

'Sir,' I said. 'Thank heaven for small mercies,' I added under my breath.

I signed out, and tapped on Mum's bedroom door. 'Mum? I have to go. I have new orders.'

*

The rotocopter landed outside New Whitehall: a two-storey white building with a wide gravel drive in front, and guarded by King's Guards in their formal red livery.

General Maxwell was waiting for me at the entrance portico. She raised her hand before I could speak. 'Wait until we're below ground and secure.'

We went through the atrium, where the King's coat of arms was inlaid into the marble floor, and navigated a maze of corridors until we reached a plain stainless-steel service elevator. The general pressed the single button, and we descended a long way.

Richard was waiting in a debriefing room, clean-shaven and in uniform. The general gestured for me to sit at the table, and took a seat herself at the end.

'Begin the recording,' she said. 'This is a debriefing of Commander Alto and Corporal Choumali post their extraction from the alien's control field. Corporal Choumali, describe your feelings for the alien.'

That stopped me dead. How did I feel about Shiumo? Was she my friend? Was I attracted to her? I was conflicted: I wanted to be with her again, travelling the stars, but she'd been controlling me. Did I want to make love to her two-legged form? The response came from inside me – *hell yeah!* – but the general and Richard were watching me with curiosity and I had to answer. I voiced the emotion that I felt most strongly.

'I'm absolutely furious that she's been messing with my head and made me betray my own people.'

'Are you desperate to return to her? Does her proximity make you feel euphoric?'

I searched my feelings. 'No.'

'Commander Alto?'

'She has me enthralled; I'm completely in love with her. I have no idea how she's doing it – hell, I still love her – but at least now I know it's happening.' Richard sipped from a water glass in front of him. 'She's controlling me.'

'Corporal Choumali, you said you don't feel desperate to return to her?' the general asked again.

'No, ma'am.'

'So you don't care if we keep you away from her?'

I felt a moment of panic at being kept from Shiumo, then controlled it.

'Initially, yes. But when I think about it: no, ma'am. She's been controlling me, messing with my head. I don't want to be near her any more.'

'Good.' She turned to Richard. 'Tell me about the sex. How is that even happening?'

'Do you want me to go out, sir?' I asked Richard softly.

'No, stay. You can help me.' Richard wiped his hand over his natural eye. 'She takes a human form. It's an illusion, but her body changes. Choumali's seen the change.'

'Describe it, Choumali,' Maxwell said.

'She changes to a tall handsome black man,' I said.

'And you see something different, Alto?'

'I see a tall beautiful South Asian woman.'

'So she mimics your own appearance, but in the opposite sex. You both said tall. How tall?'

'As tall as her dragon body is long,' Richard said, and I nodded agreement. 'Close on three metres.'

'And you had sex with the alien while she was in that form?' the general said.

'I did, ma'am.' Richard quirked a small smile. 'Best damn sex of my life, actually.'

'With no genitals,' the general said grimly.

Richard shrugged. 'She manipulated my brain directly. The experience was so close to physical lovemaking I couldn't tell the difference.' His expression softened. 'Something I thought I'd never have again.'

'Is that how she's controlling you?' the general said.

'I don't know.' Richard looked away. 'It just seems to happen. Jian might be right – we're weak-minded, and Shiumo's not doing it deliberately.'

'Is she having sex with you as well, Choumali?'

'No.'

The general raised an eyebrow at me.

'No, ma'am,' I said more vehemently.

'What would you do if she offered?'

I shrugged. 'I made it clear that I'm already in … I *was* already in a relationship, but I have to admit I thought about it.'

'You just terminated that relationship,' the general said.

I moaned softly. 'I know.'

'Frankly I'm surprised that Shiumo didn't pursue Jian more vigorously,' Richard said.

'She made overtures,' I said, thinking about the swimming pool.

'This is important,' the general said. 'How much access does Marque have to our secure information?'

'Complete,' Richard said.

'Do you think it knows what we're talking about right now?'

'Knowing its personality, I doubt it could resist the urge to say something insulting about you.'

The general grunted a short laugh. 'Yes.'

'So sending it off with the gifts has probably diverted it,' Richard continued. 'I'm quite sure it will find us eventually, though, even without X-ray vision.'

'So our time is limited. And we have to decide what to do with the two of you.'

'We need to keep her happy, ma'am,' I said. 'It's very likely that our colonies will need her help once they're established.'

'I know. Do you think she'd abandon our colonies if you left her?'

Richard and I shared a look, then turned back to the general.

'I don't know,' I said.

'She's always said we can leave any time,' Richard said. 'Are we willing to risk our colonies to find out if she meant it?'

'To be honest, my friend ...' Maxwell's voice petered out.

Richard straightened. 'Then give me back to her if it keeps her happy.'

'I don't give my best people away to have their minds controlled and be used as slaves, Alto.' She studied us both. 'For the record: if you had a choice, would you stay with her or leave her service?'

'She's been using me,' Richard said. 'She has me so enthralled that I don't even know if the sex was fully consensual. I'll stay with her if you order me, ma'am – I know it's for the good of humanity – but my preference is to be reassigned a long way away from her.'

'Choumali?'

'It's not as bad for me, ma'am, and if you order me to, I'll stay with her. But she'll seduce me in the end – particularly now I've separated from my spouses – and it's only a matter of time before I'm as controlled as Richard is.'

'You want out?'

'Yes, ma'am.'

'Very well. I'll tell Shiumo that you've both been reassigned, and if she has a problem she can take it up with me.'

I felt a shot of pain and grief at the idea of never going back to that glorious ship and exploring space with Shiumo, then locked it down. She'd been manipulating us.

The general rose. 'I want a joint report completed by the end of the day. Let's make the most of the time we have until Marque finds you and the shit hits the fan.'

'Before you go, General,' Richard said.

'What?'

'It's about their reproduction. You need to know this.'

'You *really* need to know this,' I said.

The general studied our faces and sat again.

*

Richard and I took three hours to finish our joint report, and I was checked by a doctor.

He removed the cuff from my arm. 'Same as Commander Alto: slightly lowered blood pressure and blood oxygen levels. You said the ship seemed to have more oxygen in the air?'

'Yes,' I said.

He nodded. 'That would explain it. Your body has had time to acclimatise to the greater air density and needs to accustom itself to the thinner air. You may feel tired and dizzy for a few weeks as it compensates. Take it easy.'

'I understand.'

He folded the cuff and put it on the table. 'So what was it like living on the ship?'

'Spectacular.'

I heard a commotion and looked out into the corridor. General Maxwell and Richard, together with a small mixed group of military and civilians, were standing outside the med room.

'We have more visitors,' the general said, and passed me a tablet, then gestured for me to follow her.

The screen was full of alerts. I flipped through the feed as I followed the group out of the bunker and to the waiting rotocopter. Four dragon ships had appeared in Earth's orbit. A news broadcast pinged as I read the story – another ship had appeared. Five alien ships, none of them Shiumo's, were now orbiting Earth.

'What do they want?' I said.

'Our opals,' Richard said. 'They saw the jewellery I gave to Shiumo –'

'Damn idiotic *stupid* thing to do,' the general said. 'This time it's not just dragons; a variety of species have arrived and want to trade for opals. We're meeting them at the New Chelsea football field.' She entered the 'copter and the rest of us followed her. 'Apparently Shiumo dropped in on the dragon homeworld halfway through surveying the location for the Japanese colony and showed one of her sisters the opal ring Alto gave her. The species currently in orbit have already offered us ships, staff, robotic intelligent workers, and, would you believe, *holidays* on resort planets for the entire population of Earth, in trade for our opals.'

Maxwell gestured towards a tall, full-figured black woman in the group. 'This is Dr Evie Mogambo, Euroterre's chief economist, and her staff.' I nodded to her, and she nodded back. 'She's going to attempt to set up a shiny new galactic trade model for us in the shortest time in history.'

Dr Mogambo smiled. 'Not a small task.' She became serious. 'Don't agree to anything. Let me do the talking.'

The 'copter landed at the football field. The aliens were waiting for us, chatting together in a group. The variety of species was astounding. A few of them required breathing apparatuses; and three were in spacesuits that seemed to be four legs connected together with no head or body. Five dragons, the same size as Shiumo, stood with them; three were different shades of green, one was a soft duck-egg blue, and one was red like Shiumo. They all had a faceted stone, the same colour as their eyes, in the middle of their forehead. From what I could see, the non-dragon aliens did as well.

The sight of a dragon so similar to Shiumo – and yet so different; this one's tail was shorter and its scales weren't the same shade of scarlet – hit Richard and me hard. We both filled with longing to be with Shiumo again.

I sensed Richard gather himself, and reminded myself that she'd been controlling us.

'Welcome to Earth,' General Maxwell said. 'I understand that you wish to trade with us for our opals?'

'We can give you five hundred planets with similar atmospheres and gravities to this one in exchange for your opals,' one of the spacesuits said through a voicebox that sounded like fingernails on a blackboard.

'That's a worthless offer because they don't use Earth-type planets,' a Marque sphere said.

'We need to establish trade amounts and values,' Dr Mogambo said. She gestured. 'Please come this way, and we will show you our hospitality.'

'There's really no need for that,' said an alien that looked like a large raven, except its plumage was bright green and it didn't have a beak. It was taller than me, and had a long leathery snout with small sharp teeth. My perception shifted and I realised I was looking at a feathered dinosaur, with four fingers halfway down each short-feathered wing. 'Just accept one of our offers for the opals, we'll do the trade, and we can all go home.'

'How many opals?' Evie said.

'All of them,' a metre-long copper-coloured slug said through a voicebox. 'We pay, we find the deposits, we take all of them.'

'Dr Mogambo,' the general began.

'Honoured delegates,' Evie said, clasping her hands in front of her and smiling indulgently, 'come with us inside, and we will discuss the small amount of raw opals we are willing to part with immediately, and how much you are willing to pay for them.'

An alien very much like a three-metre-long six-legged Old English sheepdog, shaggy grey fur and all, looked around, then rose onto its four back legs. 'What is that amazing scent? You are cooking something nearby and it smells delicious.'

'Better not be us,' the general said under her breath.

'You are delicious?' the slug said.

'No, we aren't!' the general said more loudly.

The sheepdog opened its jaws, disconcertingly much wider than an Earth dog could, and blinked the eyes on the end of its snout. 'Can one of you escort me to the source of this scent? I would love to taste whatever foodstuff that is.'

The humans all sniffed the air, then shared a look and a shrug.

'Our sense of smell is quite dull compared to most organisms,' the general said. 'We can't smell anything. Could you describe the scent?'

'Disgusting,' one of the slugs said. 'Hot lipids.' It made a loud watery sound of distaste.

'Hot lipids?' I said. 'Hot fat?' I checked my tablet. 'There's a cluster of fast-food stalls nearby for the football fans.'

'How fast is the food?' the sheepdog said, dropping back onto six legs. It wagged its back end so hard it nearly fell over. 'Do you chase it down?'

'This is really becoming interesting,' the dinosaur said. 'Those magnificent stones and fast-moving food?'

'No,' I said. 'It's quick to prepare, that's all. You don't have to wait a long time for it.'

'How about we take you to a comfortable negotiation area,' Dr Mogambo said, obviously trying to regain control, 'and we will arrange for a selection of ...' she nearly choked on the words, 'fast food to be brought to you.'

'No. We do it here,' one of the spacesuits said.

'Just hurry up and do the trade,' the dinosaur said. 'I have places to be!'

'You are the first delegates we've received,' Dr Mogambo said. 'So we need to set up terms of trade –'

'You've heard some of the things we are willing to offer,' the dinosaur said. 'What trades are appealing to you? We can offer any amount of any material you wish. Or a full-sized orbital Marque. Or ships. Anything you want in exchange for the opals.'

'Ships?' the general said. 'What sort of drive? Faster than light?'

'Ships your dragons can carry – the usual empty canisters.'

'One of the things we would like to trade for is the service of more dragons,' Dr Mogambo said. 'We need pilots to carry ships for us. Would you be willing to trade the services of your dragon friends for our opals?'

All of the delegates became completely still. The only sound was a wet sucking noise from the slugs' and spacesuits' breathing apparatuses.

'Did you just say that you need dragons?' the sheepdog said.

'That's correct. So far we only have Shiumo to carry our ships, and we need more.'

'This planet is in First Contact?' The dinosaur swung its head to glare at the blue dragon next to it. 'You brought us to a planet that's still in First Contact?'

'Did you see those stones?' the blue dragon snapped back. 'Whoever's first to trade gets them, and I want them.'

'You broke First Contact protocol for *rocks*?' the sheepdog said. It rounded on the red dragon next to it. 'You too?'

'I'm out,' one of the spacesuits said, and all three of them folded to form cubes five centimetres across and shot straight up, leaving a contrail as they broke the sound barrier.

'They're at the tail end of First Contact,' one of the green dragons said, waving its front claw. 'Just about finished and into Second.' She nodded to the slug. 'And we want those stones, right?'

The only sound coming from the slug was its gurgling breathing apparatus. Then what appeared to be three eyestalks emerged from its back end and waved around.

'Let me understand this situation very clearly,' the dinosaur said to Dr Mogambo, speaking more slowly. 'Princess Shiumo is the only dragon you have encountered, and you want us to give you more dragons to fold your ships?'

'Princess Zianto popped in to share a message from the Empress, but apart from her the only dragon we've seen is Shiumo,' Richard said. 'Oh, and we met a black one when the Nimestas were attacked –'

'Yes,' Dr Mogambo said, interrupting him. 'We need more pilots for our ships.'

'I just used a word that is outside the parameters for this level of polite translation,' the sheepdog said.

'You've only had one dragon visit for any length of time?' the dinosaur said.

'Yes, I just said so,' Dr Mogambo said. 'Why is asking for more dragons a problem?'

'I just used a word that is outside the parameters for this level of polite translation,' the dinosaur said. 'Another word outside parameters.' It rounded on the blue dragon. 'I cannot believe you did this to me! It's all right for you, but when your grandmother finds out about this, a metaphor indicating that I will be in personal jeopardy.'

'But we had to be first here to get the stones,' the dragon said. 'And there are four other species here already! Do you realise how much of a profit –' She stopped and glanced at us humans. 'Uh ...'

'Thought so,' Dr Mogambo said.

'Profit, eh?' General Maxwell said.

'Argh!' The dinosaur roared with frustration and shook its head, revealing blue scales between the feathers on its temples. 'Marque, bring down the pod. And you!' It poked the dragon with its feathered front appendage. 'No stone is worth breaking the rules like this. Your grandmother will be *word outside parameters*. If you weren't my half-sister, I would kill you myself.'

'Oh, give me a break,' the dragon said, and disappeared.

'I just used a personal slur!' the dinosaur shouted.

'I just used a word outside parameters,' the sheepdog said. 'My speech is moving completely outside polite translation parameters; suggest changing the language constraints to a more casual level.'

'My sister took off and left me,' the dinosaur said to the sheepdog. 'Can I share your pod?'

'Sure. Let's get the word outside parameters out of here,' the sheepdog said.

'Listen,' the dinosaur said to Dr Mogambo, 'if anyone asks, none of us were here. Except the suits – they're word outside parameters anyway and practically indestructible. We'll be back once you're at Second.'

'But I wanted the pretty stones!' the red dragon wailed.

'Marque, bring the pod down now,' the sheepdog said. 'You are in serious trouble. I just used several words outside polite translation parameters. Get us out of here!'

The aliens entered a variety of coloured cubes and spheres that landed on the lawn, and the dragons hopped on top of the pods and folded them all away.

As the pods disappeared, one of Dr Mogambo's aides arrived with a plastic storage bin containing a selection of fast food. He pulled out a brown paper bag and held it out to Richard. 'Chip, sir?'

17

Richard and I were having lunch together the next day in the cafeteria at ground level in the New Whitehall building when his tablet pinged. He checked it, and flashed with pain. It was Shiumo.

We took the elevator down to the underground conference room, and he routed the communication through to the big screen while I pinged General Maxwell. I moved to the side so Shiumo couldn't see me. I wasn't ready to have this conversation yet, even though we'd spent hours working out what we'd say to her.

'Richard!' Shiumo said, sounding desperate. 'The general just told me that she's splitting us up! Where are you? I'll come and fetch you.'

'I can't, Shiumo. My career is too important to me. The ring was a parting gift.'

Her face filled with confusion. 'You're not coming back to me? What happened?' She lowered her head, her voice coy. 'You do still love me, don't you?'

'I do, with all my heart,' he said, the truth ringing from him. 'But I've been reassigned; and if I refuse the order, I'll have to resign. I can't disobey a direct order. My career means a great deal to me, and I'm not sure I want to throw away my life on Earth. I need more time. Will you give me some time?'

'Just come to me. I'll take you away from here. You don't need to work again.'

'I love my work. I don't want to give it up.' He sounded desperate. 'I need time to think!'

'But you love me!' Shiumo opened her mouth, showing her small needle-like teeth, then hissed with anger. 'It's that General Maxwell. She's convinced that I'm controlling you. I'm *not*, Richard – I love you! Don't let her do this to us. Remember all the fun times we've had together. We love each other!'

A blast of pain radiated from him. 'I feel differently when I'm away from you, Shiumo –'

'Yes, because you doubt your own feelings when we're apart! I am not controlling you,' Shiumo said. She walked away from the screen, her tail thrashing, then returned. 'Maxwell's brainwashed you. Don't listen to her! She just hates what we have together.'

'Princess, is all well?' one of the Japanese representatives asked Shiumo. 'The first group of transport capsules are ready for you to take up.'

'Look, Richard and,' Shiumo's voice became scathing, 'Maxwell, wherever you're hovering – I made a commitment to Japan to transport their colonists, and I'm a dragon of my word, so I need to load the ship now. Richard, please, think about what we have. I love you so much ...' She choked. 'Don't let Maxwell make you doubt our love. You mean everything to me.'

She spoke to someone offscreen: 'Yes, I understand, I'll be right there.' She looked at Richard again. 'I'll return in three days, and I want to see you in person and sort this out.' She lowered her head and closed her eyes, obviously grief-stricken. 'Please don't leave me, I love you,' she whispered.

General Maxwell stopped just inside the doorway of the conference room, then moved to stand next to me, where she could see Shiumo without being seen.

'I just want to be on my own for a while to work things out,' Richard said. 'Please take Marque back. I don't want it hovering over me any more.'

'But it keeps you safe,' Shiumo said, then nodded. 'Very well. Marque, you heard him.'

Marque shimmered into view above us, and the general glared at it.

'You asked me to remind you that Maxwell is a paranoid xenophobe, Richard, and you were right,' Marque said. 'I'll show myself out, Maxwell. I don't need you screwing anything else up. You've already done enough damage.' It zoomed out of the room.

Shiumo gazed at the screen with such anguish that Richard's misery deepened.

'Please take yourself away from Maxwell for a while and think about this,' she said. 'Trust your feelings. If you just get clear of the pressure for a few days, you'll see that you truly love me. I will have you back any time, Richard. I love you deeply, and I want to take you with me when I return to my homeworld. There are so many things I want to show you!'

The general shifted, radiating concern. The overload of emotions in the room was making my head ache.

'If you're absolutely sure about this, then let me give you a parting gift,' Shiumo said.

Richard shook his head, too emotional to speak.

'I must give you something! When I'm back on Earth, come to me and let me replace those awful primitive prosthetics. The biological replacements are ready, and you deserve the best.' She looked coy again. 'I was sincerely hoping to see what human dragonscales children would look like if you fathered one on me.'

Richard opened his mouth and closed it again, his desperation changing to near-panic. 'Thank you, Shiumo,' he choked, and turned off the communication. He flopped to sit in a chair, and put his head in his hands.

'Good,' Maxwell said. 'Now let's see what happens in three days when she returns from Kapteyn – whether she was genuine about giving you your freedom.'

Richard radiated overwhelming grief. He shook his head. 'I feel like I've lost my family again.'

'You did the right thing, soldier,' Maxwell said. 'Do you need to see a therapist?'

He looked up at her, his natural eye full of tears.

'Say yes, Richard,' I said.

He hesitated, then nodded.

My tablet pinged: Shiumo was calling me.

The general tapped on her tablet. 'Alto, I'm assigning you some help. Go and wait in the office next door.' She glanced at me. 'Your turn, Choumali.'

Richard fled, radiating relief. I steeled myself and accepted Shiumo's call, routing it through to the big screen.

'You're in the same place,' Shiumo said. 'Is Maxwell taking you away from me as well?'

'No, I want to stay with my spouses,' I said, using the story we'd worked on. 'I made a huge mistake. We have a baby coming, and I want to be part of that. I regret leaving them.'

'Do you think you can patch it up with them? I saw what happened; it was *awful*,' Shiumo said.

'I panicked. I hope they take me back.'

Shiumo studied me with her silver eyes and I wondered if she could see my lies.

'I understand, dear Jian. Some species place children and family higher than their own lives. My species is one of them; our children are more precious to us than anything. So go back to them, and I hope you can work it out.' She opened her mouth, smiling. 'And I want to meet the baby as soon as he's born. I haven't seen a human baby in person yet. They look *so cute*!'

'I'll make sure you can,' I said, smiling back despite myself. The guilt at the deception ate me up inside, but I had to get away from her. 'And hopefully they'll understand and let me go with you when the child is old enough.'

'No, you should stay with your child,' she said. She tilted her head. 'I want to give both of you something you can use to contact me anywhere at any time. If you use it, I will sense it immediately and come to you instantly, no matter where I am in the cosmos. It's very important that both you and Richard have one. I want to protect you.'

'How does it work?' I said.

'It's complicated. Can I fold to you and show you? I want you and Richard both to be safe.'

General Maxwell was racked with indecision. She wanted to know how the device worked. Shiumo had said the dragons had a means of instantaneous communication, but hadn't told us what it was. Maxwell's face hardened, and she nodded, then went out.

'Richard and I are in the same place. Marque just left,' I said. 'Maxwell pulled us in to reassign us.'

Shiumo appeared on the other side of the room. 'Of course she did.' She approached me. 'Are they planning to shoot me now?'

'Of course not,' I said, full of delight to see her again. I put my hand on the side of her face, feeling euphoria at the contact. 'What's this instant communication device? I'm intrigued.'

She stood on her hind legs without taking two-legged form and held out her front claw. I couldn't see anything, then realised she was holding two of her own scales, red against red.

'Take one,' she said.

I hesitated, then took it out of her hand, and the euphoric feeling heightened. The scale was a rounded diamond with ridges carved into it that shone different colours under the conference room's lights.

'Our scales are quantum-entangled,' she said, falling back onto four legs. 'Hold it between your hands so you can feel both sides.'

I clasped my hands together with the scale between them.

'That's right,' she said. 'Now feel.'

She ran her claw over a scale on the side of her neck, and I gasped. I felt the sensation on the scale in my hands.

'If you need me, rub the scale hard, or tap it, and I will feel it, and come to you.' She smiled again. 'Please don't use it unless it's a life-or-death emergency. I have given each spouse one scale, and if everybody used them all the time I'd never get any peace.'

'I understand,' I said.

She held out the other scale. 'Where's Richard? He needs to have this.'

'He'd prefer not to see you, Princess.'

'He should stay with me! We love each other.'

'Do you love him enough to wait for him to work it out?' I said.

She lowered her head. 'I understand. I'll be patient. Give him the scale, and tell him I love him.'

I hesitated, then took the second scale. 'How will you know which is which?'

'When I remove a scale, the replacement is entangled when it grows back. Each of you has a different scale. Yours is the larger and darker one here.' She tapped the side of her neck, and I felt it on one of the scales. 'Richard's is the smaller lighter one here.' She tapped her chest, and I felt it on the other scale.

'Is this how you contact your homeworld?' I said.

She nodded. 'Exactly. There's a communication centre on Dragonhome with one scale from each dragon. It's not useful for complex messages, but it works well for emergency calls and notifications of new discoveries. We use a tap-code for different messages.'

'Thank you, Shiumo,' I said.

She hoisted herself upright onto her back legs and transformed into her human male self.

'Do I get a hug goodbye?' he said, and put his arms out.

'A kiss goodbye as well, and I hope it isn't forever,' I said.

He pulled me close and smiled. 'I hope that as well.'

*

The general turned the scale over in her short, square fingers with the nails bitten down to shreds. 'Quantum-entangled. Our scientists have been trying to achieve this for years, and she just gave you *two*.' She handed the scale back to me. 'The Japanese colonists have reported that she's doing exactly what she promised. She'll return next week, and then it's our turn.' She studied me piercingly. 'If you can call her for immediate help, it's even more strategically important that you're involved. I won't order you, Choumali, but we need you on Wolf 1061.'

'Yes, ma'am,' I said.

'I know it's a big step, and it would mean leaving your child with your exes. But you were going to do that anyway –'

'I'm sorry, General,' I said, interrupting. 'I meant, yes, of course I'll go. That's why I joined the program in the first place. The baby will be fine with Dianne and Victor.'

'Oh.' She quirked a small smile. 'Good.'

'What about Commander Alto? Will he be going as well? We need him to lead us.'

She walked to the other side of the room, and stared at the blank concrete wall as if it were a window. 'He's asked us to remove his prosthetics. They were compromised by being on her ship, and too much of a security risk. He'll go into surgery in a few days, and when he comes out, only forty-five per cent of his body will be usable. One arm, no legs, and waste disposal will become a major issue for him again. He wouldn't survive on New Europa.'

'How long will it take to have new prosthetics made for him?'

She looked down. 'Those prosthetics were a special project funded by the King himself. They're irreplaceable. The lab that created them is gone, and the technicians were reassigned to food and water production. He'll have to make do with something much more primitive.'

'Can I see him when he comes out of surgery?'

She nodded. 'I'll assign you to him until the ship departs for New Europa. His mother's on her way, but you and he have shared experiences to talk about to keep him occupied while he recovers.' She pointed at the scale I was holding. 'And you can give him that after we've made a full study of it. He has a decision to make.'

I looked down at the scales in my hand. Richard could choose to return to Shiumo, accept the biological body parts she'd offered, and forsake his position and security clearance – and probably his mental freedom – to keep Shiumo happy and working with us. He did have a big decision to make.

'You don't see me as a security risk, ma'am?' I said.

'Of course we do. But your psi ability will be invaluable on a planet without a breathable atmosphere, and you're the only psi we can spare. If you can call Shiumo, and she will arrive immediately, you're doubly vital. The security risk is worth it. We'll just adjust your clearance.' Her emotions filled with sadness. 'Commander Alto, on the other hand, is really only useful to Shiumo.'

*

The general took me to the secure section of the military hospital to visit Richard after his surgery, and we stopped at the nurses' station on the way.

'Hello, Nurse Chandra. How is he?' the general asked a young South Asian man.

'Awake, and driving all of us bonkers.' He smiled. 'You have no idea how good it is to see him giving us hell. Is this Corporal Choumali?'

'That's right,' the general said.

'He's been asking about you,' the nurse said. 'He'll be glad to see you.' He sobered. 'I can see you're military and probably accustomed to injuries, but I need to inform you that his appearance can be extremely disturbing for some people. Be ready, Corporal, it's not pretty.'

'Is he in much pain?' I said.

'His physical pain is being managed. He's on high doses right now; we'll be weaning him off soon, but don't expect too much in the way of conversation. Mentally?' He shook his head. 'I hear you're psi. I hope you can help him.'

'Me too,' I said.

I followed General Maxwell along the corridor and into a dimly lit single room with a hospital bed and a curtained window.

Richard was covered by a blanket, but it was obvious that his body ended at the hips. Two catheter tubes travelled from beneath the blanket to jars under the bed: one was a fluid drain, full of blood-stained liquid; and the other was for urine. A bulge on his lower abdomen indicated a colostomy bag. His left arm was outside the blanket with an IV in his forearm, but his other shoulder disappeared inside his hospital gown. Half of his lower jaw was gone on the right side, and his upper teeth and tongue were visible through the large gap in his face. Saliva dribbled from the gap onto a bib the staff had placed on him. The right side of his head from the cheekbone up was a scrunched-up mass of fresh skin grafts.

His eye opened; he saw me and tried to grin. He made a soft sound of pain and the smile collapsed.

'Jian,' he said, the word almost unintelligible from his half-destroyed mouth. 'Thanks for coming.' He turned away. 'Sorry you have to see this.'

'Don't be ridiculous,' I said, and went to his left side. I took his hand and held it. 'I'm your friend and I'm glad to help you through this.'

He sniffed, obviously moved, then turned his head towards the general. 'Ma'am.'

She nodded in acknowledgement. 'Let the staff know if you're in too much pain. Don't be more of a hero than you already are.'

'Dunno about that,' he said, working around his speech difficulties. 'Not really heroic falling for an alien shapeshifter.'

'Shiumo is keeping her word about creating the colonies; she's helped Earth more than we could have expected,' the general said. 'Your role in this cannot be underestimated, mind control or not.'

'Don't go back to her, Jian. She'll control you,' Richard said. 'She messed with our heads.'

'I won't be,' I said, squeezing his hand. 'I'll be stationed on our new colony on Wolf 1061-c. We're calling the planet New Europa. I'll be psi communications expert and security officer.'

'And promoted to second lieutenant,' the general said.

'Good,' Richard said. 'About time.'

'And all thanks to you, Commander,' I said. 'If you hadn't taken me with you for First Contact, I would not be here today.' I raised his hand slightly. 'Thank you, sir.'

He didn't move. 'Sir?'

He'd fallen asleep, his breath whistling through his ruined face.

'Are you sure about staying with him, Choumali?' the general said. 'It's your choice.'

'Of course,' I said. 'Will they at least give him some sort of facial prosthetic so he won't scare small children?'

'They're working on it. Hopefully he'll be in better shape by the time you leave for Wolf.'

'I hope so too, ma'am.' I settled back in the seat and pulled out my tablet. 'I'll be fine.'

18

I spent two weeks sitting with Richard, using the time when he was asleep to catch up with the colony briefing notes. The previous night had been a bad one: Richard had refused the opiates and only accepted milder painkillers, and I'd stayed up with him, doing what I could to help. It was dawn before he finally slept, and now I sat at his bedside struggling through the briefings and fighting exhaustion, the words blurring on the screen.

The colony commander was being particularly severe on me. He was convinced that my clearance to learn remotely instead of on-site was due to my connections with General Maxwell and Richard, and that I'd end up a poorly trained liability. I needed to be able to quote every fact perfectly.

The lichen we will use to establish the first life cycle is a red strain developed specifically for the harsh conditions, I read. *It is a symbiotic combination of a fungus and two algae, and should be able to live in the dry oxygen-barren and carbon-dioxide-rich atmosphere of Wolf 1061. Once the lichen is established, it is hoped it will spontaneously spread across the continent, taking root on the land mass and altering the environment.*

The details of the lichen's life cycle and techniques we will use to cultivate it are in section 29.1.

If the lichen is found outside the initial growing area in the first generation of colonists, section 34.1 contains optimal results strategies.

If the lichen survives within the initial growing area but does not spontaneously spread, section 63.1 contains sub-optimal results strategies.

If the lichen fails, section 104.1 contains crisis strategies.

For all other scenarios, turn to section –

My tablet pinged, and I flipped to the comms. It was General Maxwell.

'Choumali, your spouses are here to see you. Conference room three.'

My stomach fell with dismay. The time had come to formally end it and leave for the colony. I nodded to her. 'Ma'am.'

She smiled. 'They understand, Lieutenant.'

'I wouldn't, ma'am,' I said, and went to the hospital's small consultation room.

Victor and Dianne were sitting in chairs at the table, and the room was heavy with their emotions – a combination of misery, guilt and betrayal.

I closed the door and sat across from them. Dianne's pregnancy was well advanced – her stomach bulged beneath her tent-like maternity dress – but she looked healthy.

There was an uncomfortable silence as I was unable to look them in the eyes. Eventually Dianne grabbed my hand, making me jump.

'You look exhausted, Jian. Don't lose sleep over us,' she said.

'I'm not.' I rubbed my eyes and grinned ruefully. 'Richard had a bad night and I stayed up with him.'

They shared a look.

'We're so glad you've moved on,' Victor said through acid jealousy.

'He's just my friend,' I said. 'A member of the Psi Corps has been training me –'

Both of them immediately radiated a blast of what Derek, my trainer, called 'Telepath Terror'. He'd even mimicked it perfectly so I could see what it looked like.

'And he's taught me to ease pain,' I continued. 'I'm helping Richard through his transition after the operations until I leave for my final examination to be confirmed for the colony.'

Their terror eased, tinted with compassion, but it was still there. I'd completely lost them.

'When do you go?' Victor said.

'In four weeks. But I have to pass a simulation test first, to see how I'll cope on the colony.'

'You're doing the right thing,' Dianne said. 'We're cheering you on.'

'Dammit, Jian, you're saving the human race,' Victor said. 'We understand.'

I shook my head, my eyes stinging. 'Your emotions don't say that.'

'It was my idea to ask you to marry us,' Dianne said. 'I'm sorry, Jian. I didn't mean to push you away.'

'You didn't push me away,' I said. 'I ran.'

'You're running to the stars, lovely,' Victor said. 'You're doing something heroic and wonderful. Hey.' He tapped the table, and I looked up into his clear blue eyes. He smiled. 'You're a soldier, right?'

I nodded.

'We always knew you could be mobilised. We talked about it a long time ago.'

I nodded again, my throat too thick to speak.

'This is the same thing. Your career comes first. You're an officer now, Jian, and you're doing something that hardly any humans are qualified for.'

'You told us six months ago that you were going to Wolf 1061, and we agreed to it,' Dianne said. 'This was happening anyway. But now you're going with a clear conscience and no relationship to distract you. We support you.' She squeezed my hand.

'I'll miss you guys,' I said, my voice breaking.

'We'll be able to send letters back and forth every few months. You told us that yourself,' Victor said.

'I want to hear how our son is,' I said. 'Is he healthy?'

Their emotions went from guilt to joy, and they shared a smile, which lifted my own heart.

'He's healthy and strong and kicks like a little bugger,' Dianne said.

'We'll be able to tell him that his other mum's in outer space,' Victor said with pride.

'How much can you tell us about the planet you're going to?' Dianne said, and both of them went from sadness to interest, tinged with excitement. They were genuinely thrilled to hear about my upcoming adventure, and happy about the baby. My spirits lifted even further.

'Tell me if I get boring,' I said. 'Everybody else is tired of hearing about it.'

'We won't be. Tell us everything!' Victor said.

'Yes!' Dianne said. 'We want to know.' She put her hand on her belly. 'So we can tell your son what a hero he has for a second mum.'

'Well, the planet has an atmosphere but it's not breathable,' I began, and they listened, rapt.

*

The technician gently fitted the prototype prosthetic over Richard's face, and secured it into position with what appeared to be duct tape.

'Colour is still slightly too dark,' she said to her tablet as she checked around the edges. 'A4 two millimetres ventral. B4 is three millimetres too close.' She stepped back to study him. 'How does that feel, sir?'

'It'll feel better when it's secure,' Richard said, opening and closing his mouth. He pointed at his right eyebrow. 'It's loose on the muscles under here.'

The technician lifted the prosthetic from his face, studied the back, then leaned in to see. 'Got it.' She marked the prosthetic, then put it back into its case. 'The only thing really accurate is the eye colour. It's a good match.'

Richard nodded, obviously restraining himself from commenting.

'And without a working second eye, you'll never see in three dimensions again,' she said. 'I understand, sir, and we'll work on it, but the connections on your nerves ...'

'I know,' he said, resigned. 'Too much scarring there already.' He raised his good hand. 'You're doing a great job, Clarence, and I appreciate it.'

She sealed the case. 'We'll do our best, Commander.'

He nodded. 'Thank you.'

The doctor came in. 'Blood pressure time,' he said cheerfully. 'Is this lovely person finished?' He flashed the technician a quick grin, and she smiled back.

'All yours,' she said, and winked at Richard. 'I'll be back in two days to install it. I think we're at the final version now.'

'I'll be as glad to reach the end of this process as you are.'

She nodded to him and went out.

'Did it take as long the first time you had the prosthetics fitted?' the doctor asked Richard as he placed the blood-pressure cuff on his arm.

'I was unconscious for most of it, but it took more than a year from start to finish,' Richard said. 'So yes, it took longer. But those prosthetics were powered and responsive.'

The doctor removed the cuff and noted Richard's blood pressure on his tablet. 'Soon have you up and around, Commander. A bit of exercise and fresh air will do wonders. And then we'll get some legs fitted and have you walking unaided, eh?'

'Yes,' Richard said, and leaned his head back.

'Lieutenant Choumali, we have a stack of documents for you to sign at the nurses' station,' the doctor said. 'Something to do with the colony. Do you mind?'

'Not at all.' I took Richard's hand and squeezed it, and he squeezed back without opening his eye.

I followed the doctor to the nurses' station, but he gestured towards his office. 'In here, if you don't mind, Lieutenant.' He pulled a chair out for me and closed the door. 'I'd like to take your blood pressure as well.'

I rolled my sleeve up and he placed the cuff on my arm.

'Something's wrong, isn't it?' I said. 'I've been feeling lousy ever since I left Shiumo – and Richard's not improving. What's wrong with us?'

He waited for the cuff to deflate, then noted the numbers. 'We can't find any toxins in your system, so it doesn't appear to be poison. But you're right. In the four weeks since you left her, your blood pressure has gone from eighty …' He saw my blank expression. 'From disturbingly low to the very bottom end of normal. Same with your blood oxygen. We would have expected you to be back to full health by now, but you're recovering very slowly. We're concerned she's done something to you.'

'And Richard?'

'At first we thought he'd given up,' the doctor said. 'I know it sounds ridiculous, but I've seen it happen with bad cases of PTSD – they decide not to carry on any more and just fade away. But Commander Alto's a fighter, and he wants to get back on his feet and help the colonisation effort.' He pulled the details up on his tablet. 'He's like you: low blood pressure, low oxygen, reduced iron, reduced metabolics – everything's fading. But unlike you, he's degenerating instead of recovering.'

'She poisoned both of us?' I said.

'It's exhibiting more like withdrawal.'

I took a sharp breath in. 'That's what it feels like. Withdrawal. We were *addicted* to her?'

'Seems like it.'

'But Richard will beat this, won't he? I never heard of anyone dying from …' I saw his face. 'How long does he have?'

'Hard to say. This is the first time I've seen anything like this. Three months? I don't know.'

'Do you think returning him to Shiumo would fix it?'

'There's only one way to find out. On the other hand, you're both sure she was using mind control on you. If it was me, I know what I'd prefer, regardless of how happy my little zombie self might be with her. I'd want to keep my personality intact, and die with my boots on.'

'That is one hundred per cent what Richard would choose,' I

said. I wiped my eyes. 'Damn. Has anyone talked about this with Shiumo? Maybe she has a cure.'

'The alien that did this to you in the first place?'

'It's possible it wasn't deliberate.'

'And it's possible it was.'

'But what's her angle?' I said. 'Why would she make us *addicted* to her? She's been no threat, and has no plans to harm humanity. There's no reason for it.'

'That's what I want you to find out,' General Maxwell said. I hadn't noticed her enter the room behind me. 'We want you to ask her.'

'I don't want to go back to her! She was controlling me,' I said.

'You'll have to be in her company when you go to Wolf 1061. I want you to find out what she's up to.' The general gestured with her head. 'Let's go for a walk in the garden, away from all the electronics.'

I'd spent many hours in the therapeutic garden, walking or sitting beside Richard's wheelchair and discussing the plans for the Wolf colony.

The general linked her hands behind her back as we walked. 'Sometimes I could kick myself for being so thorough. I put everything you two reported on Shiumo into *my* report, and the *politicians*,' she spat the word, 'instantly latched on to the reproduction thing.'

'What about it?'

She looked grim. 'What sort of mind takes the fact that Shiumo can breed with humans to produce dragons, and leaps immediately to: "Oh yes, great idea, let's use her to make our own starship engines"?'

I stuttered in shock. 'They want to start a *breeding program*? That's insane! What happened when they asked Shiumo? Did she storm out?'

'They want to clarify something before they ask her.'

'What's that?'

'That having sex with her won't kill the volunteers.'

'Richard,' I said. 'He slept with her and he's dying. I didn't, and I'm not.'

'Precisely. So your job is to ask her –'

I opened my mouth to protest, and closed it again. I'd suggested asking Shiumo only five minutes ago.

'Your job will be to travel to Wolf with Shiumo, and reconnect with her. While you're on her ship, ask her two things: one, if having sex with her is lethal; and two, if she has a cure for Commander Alto.' She grimaced. 'If she can cure Alto, the *politicians* would like to start a breeding program. They want to see how amenable she is to the idea, and whether it would be possible for a second dragon to come and sire a generation of dragons on our hybrids.'

'That is a terrible idea, ma'am.'

'Just be glad I talked them out of their other stupid idea.'

'I won't sleep with her to make a half-dragon baby for Earth,' I said.

She glared at me. 'Don't you *dare*. Don't even think about it. That is *not* open to negotiation. If anyone asks you to do it, come straight to me. If you sleep with her, it is *proof* that she's controlling our minds and using us as sex toys. *Under no circumstances* are you to accept her advances or make any of your own.'

'Yes, ma'am,' I said, relieved.

'Good. You leave for Wolf in three weeks. Stick with Alto for the next week and keep his spirits up, but then you'll have to go in-house for the final preparation.' She sighed. 'I hope Shiumo has a way to save his life that doesn't involve giving him back to her.'

'I hope so too, ma'am.'

She saluted me. 'I look forward to hearing what she has to say.'

*

'I got the land!' Mum said onscreen, full of smiles. 'It's so big, and flat! Victor took one look at it, looked at me, and said, "I'll never get any sculpting done out here, will I, Connie?"'

'He'll find the time,' I said. I lowered my voice. 'How are they?'

She waved her finger at me. 'Don't you start getting all guilty again. They're *fine*. Dianne is in third trimester now, so it's not as bad for her, and she's frantically busy adding to our knowledge on alien biology. Marque provided her with some data. She'll be famous for it.'

I sighed with relief. 'That's good to hear.'

'And Victor's selling little dragon sculptures on the network. He's promoting them as "identical to one given to Princess Shiumo as a gift", and he's made enough to support Dianne and your kid for a long time.'

'I really should talk to them.'

'No,' she said firmly. 'Every time they talk to you, they're miserable. They feel they drove you away. If you're doing what you want to do and being happy, it relieves their guilt. I'll let them know that you're doing great. Say goodbye when you head to Wolf, and let them have their little family. That's the best thing you can do for them.'

I shrugged and tried to hide my relief. 'Okay then.'

'So you're going in for the test tomorrow?'

'Yes. The commander doesn't like me. He's convinced I haven't learned enough to be useful while I helped Richard and studied remotely.'

'No good deed goes unpunished,' she said cheerfully.

'He'll throw everything he has at me to try to stop me from going to New Europa.'

'And what will you do about it?'

'What I usually do,' I said, and we said in unison: 'Succeed!'

She sobered. 'After you've gone to this planet, how long before Shiumo leaves and we lose contact?'

'I don't know. I've been too busy with my training to talk to her, but I'll find out while I'm on the ship.'

'I'll miss you, little sweetie.'

My throat thickened. 'I'll miss you too, Mum.'

'You'll do great on the test. Go do wonderful things.'

I nodded, and my tablet pinged next to me. 'That's me. I have to go.'

'Love you.'

'Love you too.'

I switched off the screen and checked my tablet. Time for the test.

19

Commander Geoffrey Vince, the head of the Wolf colony project, was waiting for us at the entrance to the enormous steel warehouse-style construction that held the simulated Wolf-c environment. It was situated in the middle of the space elevator island.

He glared at me. 'Choumali.'

I nodded back. 'Sir.'

'You'll be fine,' General Maxwell said, and flashed me a short tight smile. She nodded to Vince. 'Do your worst, Geoff.'

He nodded to her, then scowled at me. I straightened; I was ready for this.

I followed Vince to the warehouse's airlock, where my team were waiting. The seven women and two men in the group were uneasy about the nature of the test, but relaxed when they saw me. A couple gave me hugs of welcome, and then we stood in a semicircle to listen to Commander Vince.

'The interior of this building is filled with an atmosphere roughly similar to Wolf-c's,' he said. 'There's a scale model dome inside fitted with everything you'll have when you go to Wolf. You have to survive in the dome for seven days.' He gestured towards the rack of breathers. 'I'll be back in a week.'

'Double-check the breathers,' I said. 'At least one of them will show as clean when it's out of order. If it's yours, hold your breath and I'll give you a different one.'

My team looked from me to Commander Vince, then took the breathers off the rack and fitted them over their heads. There were two extra so I held them ready. I fitted my own breather and nodded to Commander Vince. He went out and I sealed the door behind him, then cycled the airlock.

I waited for whoever had taken the bad breather. Elise put her hand up, so I took a deep breath, held it, and gave her mine. I fitted one of the extras, and it was bad as well, so I tried the other extra and it was okay.

I turned the comms on. 'This is going to be our lives for the next two days – he'll have sabotaged everything just enough to make it three times harder than it was for the other teams. You can choose to leave now if you like – I wouldn't blame you. He'll happily put you in another team.'

'Are you sure you want to say this over comms, Jian?' Bonnie said. 'He's probably listening.'

'I know. Anyone want to leave?'

'It'll be three times harder when we get there anyway,' Gordon said. 'Let's do this.'

The rest of the team nodded, and I straightened. They were showing enormous faith in me and I had to do this right.

The light on the airlock interior door went green and we entered. The dome was a third the size of the one we were taking to Wolf. A greenhouse, also one-third size, stood next to the dome, connected by an oxygenated tunnel. We trudged over the bare ground to the dome's airlock, and went in. I closed the door and cycled the airlock.

'Pattie, test the internal air before we remove the breathers,' I said. 'My bet is there isn't enough oxygen.'

The light went green, so I opened the internal door.

Pattie checked her instruments. 'There's enough oxygen to breathe.'

None of us removed the breathers; we were all spooked by the sabotage.

Pattie checked again. 'As you thought: too much carbon dioxide. Not enough to knock us out. No monoxide. Wait a moment, I'm checking ...' She flipped through the display. 'I'm seeing it as acceptable.'

'I'll go first,' Gordon said, and removed her breather. She sniffed the air, and gagged. 'Holy *shit!*' She panted a few times. 'I think it's okay to breathe, but holy hell, the smell!'

Pattie removed her breather, and I did too. The air smelled strongly of decay – like rotting fish and vegetation.

'Something's rotting in here,' Pattie said. 'We'll have to manage bacterial growth, the smell ... damn. What a completely dick move.'

Remember he's listening, I said, and she winced.

We went further into the dome; everything seemed in order. The privacy units around the edge provided individual accommodation, with a central dining/meeting area and kitchen. The minimal bathroom facility was a fibreglass modular lean-to with a tunnel connecting it to the main dome.

'Okay,' I said. 'Let's put our heads together and think about what we would have sabotaged if we were in his place.'

After we'd allocated tasks, I went with Alison and her husband, Lawrence, to our first checkpoint – the water reservoir. We put our breathers on and headed outside the dome to the four-metre-wide spherical rainwater tank attached to its side. Alison and Lawrence climbed up to see whether there was any damage. I checked around the base and didn't find anything.

My comms clicked. 'Jian, it's Helen. You need to come inside right now – you will not believe this!'

'Found it,' Alison said. 'Slow leak at the base.'

'I checked the base!' I said.

'It's below ground level. There's moisture in the soil here; I can feel it.'

'Jian?' Helen said into my ear. 'We really need you.'

'Jian, I need you here. The hydroponics are stuffed,' Ben said over the comms.

'Can you fix it?' I asked Alison.

'We can,' Lawrence said. 'Go to Helen.'

I went back inside the dome, and cycled the airlock.

'Jian?' Ben said again just as I pulled the breather off.

I put it back on to speak to him. 'You're next. Give me a minute.'

I put the breather on the recharger, then went to the storage area, where Helen and Bonnie were doing a stocktake.

'How bad is it?' I said.

'Look.' Helen held up one of the foil-wrapped emergency rations. The foil was torn, and the food appeared to have been chewed.

'They tore open everything, and what they didn't eat they pissed on,' Elise said. 'We lost all of it.'

'Apparently rats stowed away in one of the pods on the spaceship,' Helen said.

'Not possible – wait. How do you know it was rats?'

Elise held up a piece of paper. 'They left a frigging *note*.'

She handed it to me. It said: A rat stowed away in one of the transport pods, and had a litter before it arrived here. Have fun tracking it down. It'll be chewing on everything.

'We can feed the rations to the pigs and chickens,' I said. 'I'd better go see Ben. If the hydroponics are wrecked, we'll have to request another Shiumo transfer sooner than any other colony, and probably fail the test.'

Marcia, the vet, was waiting for me in the middle of the dome. 'I checked on the animals.'

'Are they alive?'

'They're fine.' She shrugged. 'Our saboteurs aren't into torturing innocent animals. They even milked the goats for us.'

'Good. Come with me – we'll look at the hydroponics. You and Ben can work together on keeping us fed.'

In the hydroponics area, the water in the PVC channels was bright green, and the plants growing up the wires from the channels appeared to be dead. The rotting fish and vegetation smell was coming from here.

'We've lost about half the plants in the channels,' Ben said when he saw me. He lifted the lid of the urine-recycling vat and the area filled with a noxious haze of ammonia. 'Someone left the urine tank open, and the spirulina contaminated the hydroponics. It sucked all the nutrients out of the bath and killed the food plants.'

'It's pure spirulina? No other bacteria?' I said.

'No other bacteria as far as I can see. Just the spirulina.'

'Wait,' Marcia said. 'The briefing notes said the spirulina was blue-green algae, not bacteria.'

'It's called blue-green algae, but it's bacteria,' Ben said. He shrugged. 'Terminology.'

'I see. Thanks,' she said, nodding to him.

'Are there enough food plants left to feed us?' I said.

Ben shook his head. 'We'll have to resort to rations until we can clear the spirulina out of the channels and bring the hydroponics back online.'

'The rations are toast,' I said. 'Rats got into them, and what they didn't eat they pissed on.'

'The hell?' Ben said. '*Rats?* How do you know it was rats?'

'They left a note.'

'Let's eat them,' Ben said with grim humour.

'Marcia, if you can clean up the rations to use as animal feed, we'll eat the spirulina,' I said. 'Can you process the spirulina into food for us, Ben?'

'*We* can eat the algae?' Marcia said. 'It isn't toxic? It smells like rotten fish!'

'I wish I had a big screen to write on – I haven't given this lecture in a long time,' Ben said. 'I was a huge advocate for using spirulina as an interstellar colony food source, and now it looks like that idea's come back to bite me on the ass. Geoff may have done this deliberately to spite me – he's making me spend a week eating this stuff because I made his life miserable arguing about it. Spirulina's a complete food; it has all the amino acids, fats, carbs, everything we need to survive. The only thing it lacks is vitamin B-12, and it has low levels of A and D. It produces more oxygen than regular chlorophyll plants, and the spirulina in the urine vat processes the urine into a much milder solution suitable for the hydroponics. It's high in some minerals and protein, and low in carbs, so we can't live on it indefinitely or we'd go into ketosis. But in the short term, until the rest of the plants are re-established, we can eat it as a solo food source.'

'Then why aren't we eating more of it instead of the less efficient plants?' Marcia said.

Ben smiled. 'You think the smell is bad? It tastes ten times worse. It tastes like absolute shit. Even the pigs had to be trained to eat it. It's *vile*.' His smile turned grim. 'Believe me, by the end of this week you'll be puking at the sight of anything green.'

'Can you process it?' I said.

He nodded. 'Strain out the algae through a cloth and drink the slurry. It's a first-class high-protein food source.'

'Enough for all of us and the animals as well if the rations are too contaminated for them to eat?'

'Two hundred fifty metres by four tiers by twenty-five centimetres,' he said under his breath, then did some quick calculations. 'I'll have to double-check, but I think so. We may have to mock-slaughter some of the animals though.'

'We really should use this stuff as a main food source,' Marcia said. 'It sounds magical.'

'You'll be saying different later,' Ben said. 'I was a huge advocate for a long time – and then I tasted it and changed my mind completely.'

Pattie poked her nose into the greenhouse. 'We found three areas where the dome's been weakened. It may never have torn open, but we'll make sure it doesn't. There was a small hole – small enough for a rat to travel through – near the rations. All fixed.'

*

At the end of the week we gathered for a small celebration of our success. The table held the routine glasses of bright green spirulina, as well as two eggs from the hens, a litre of goat's milk, and three carrots that had survived the contamination.

We all raised our green glasses.

'Here's to a great team,' I said. 'We made it. You guys are the absolute best. It's been a pleasure working with you, and I cannot wait to get to Wolf and really get started.'

'Hear, hear,' a few people said quietly.

We all held our noses and downed the slurry, then slammed the glasses on the table and made varied sounds of disgust. Marcia gagged loudly. She coughed and turned away, shook herself, turned back towards us and raised one hand in triumph. We all applauded her.

The eggs and carrots had been cut into fifteen tiny pieces. We passed the plate around, each taking two pieces and eating them with relish. The fishy aftertaste of the algae didn't ruin the flavour: the egg was rich and fatty, and the carrot was stunningly sweet. We washed them down with a drink from the shared jug of ice-cold milk.

'That's provided we did actually pass,' Rennie said. 'It's possible that Commander Vince will find something wrong with what we did.' She looked around. 'We all lost at least five kilos, and that's really not sustainable.'

We all sobered at that.

The airlock cycled, and we turned to see Commander Vince. He came up to the table and winced. 'That stuff really does smell awful.'

'The entire dome stinks, sir, and we wouldn't have it any other way,' I said.

We all fidgeted, waiting for him to speak.

When he didn't, I said, 'So, did we pass?'

Vince grinned at us, pride bursting from him. It was a complete turnaround of his attitude. We'd won him over.

'Of course you did. You were magnificent.' He put his hand out to me, and the respect was genuine. 'Well done, Lieutenant.'

Everybody erupted in cheers. Alison and Lawrence hugged each other.

'You have a week before you leave,' Vince said. 'Go spend the time with your families and say goodbye. After that, I expect you back here for the final preparation, and we'll begin the transfer process. Well done, everybody. I was sure you'd need at least two remedial transfers, but you carried it through with what you had and all did very well.'

He grinned at Ben. 'Are you still convinced that spirulina is the way to go?'

'I'd prefer never to see the damn stuff again,' Ben said. 'Do I have time to investigate using chlorella instead of spirulina as the urine processor?'

'Too late, sorry,' Vince said, smug. 'You're stuck with the green stinky stuff.'

'Damn,' Ben said softly.

'Come on. We'll have a meal in the space elevator station, then you can all sleep in proper beds. Drinks are on me,' Vince said.

We cheered again, and followed him out of the dome. The air inside the building had already equalised and we didn't need to use the airlock. When we were outside, we all stopped and breathed deeply of the fresh air.

'You don't appreciate an atmosphere until you don't have it,' I said.

'You can still back out,' Vince said. 'We will have to remove five people from the program. Take the next few days to make sure you really want this.' He gestured towards the building. 'Now let's go celebrate.'

20

Richard was awake and in his wheelchair when I entered his room two days later. The facial prosthetic made a huge difference to his appearance, but he sat in a sling in the chair. His artificial arm and legs still weren't ready.

I sat in a chair next to him and took his hand. 'I hope you can come and visit me.'

'That won't happen as long as I have to do it in Shiumo's ship.'

'I understand. I don't want to leave you –'

'Do you feel like you're abandoning me?' he said, cutting me off. I felt a wrench at his brutal honesty. 'Yes. Of course I do.'

He squeezed my hand and smiled. The prosthetic attached to his jaw clicked as his mouth opened. 'Don't be. You're taking humanity to the stars. Represent us, Jian. Take the spirit we gave you and don't look back.'

I looked down. 'I'll really miss you, Richard.'

He released my hand and touched my face. 'We both know I don't have long. Say goodbye, and take your future in both hands and find joy and love in a new world.'

I gazed into his eye. 'You'll recover, Richard. Your new legs –'

'No need to reassure me, Jian. I can tell I'm dying. I have been since I left Shiumo. But it's not the same with you, is it? You're recovering. It's because I slept with her. I'm ...' He searched for the word. '*Contaminated*.'

'I'll ask her for a cure.'

'Listen to me.' He took my hand again, and held it so hard it hurt. His voice became fierce and his emotions matched it; he filled the room with determination. 'If she says the only way to save my life is to return to her, I'd rather die. If she has a cure, then fine. But if it requires a life of slavery with her, I choose death.' He obviously realised how tight he was holding my hand, and released it. 'Sorry. But I'd rather be dead, Jian.'

He held his arm out. 'Now give me a hug, my girl. Then turn and walk out that door, and go live a full and meaningful life in the stars.'

I hugged him, and buried my face in his shoulder. 'Goodbye, Richard.'

'Do great things, Jian.' He patted my back, and pushed me gently away.

I ran my hand over my eyes, gave him a smile through the tears, and went out.

*

The rotocopter landed on the elevator island next to the building that held the Wolf test habitat. The field area was stacked with equipment packed into bespoke containers that would fit inside Shiumo's pod. The other colonists, all in their colour-coded coveralls, were noting the equipment as it was loaded.

I went to Commander Vince, who was overseeing everything.

'There you are, Jian,' he said. 'Princess Shiumo requested that you see her the minute you arrived.'

He waved one hand towards the pod in the centre of the field. A number of Marque spheres buzzed around it, helping the staff to load the inflatable dome and packed modules. The sight of the spheres brought back painful memories of a short and joyful time.

I saluted Vince, and headed to the pod, waving to my team and Edwin but not interrupting their work.

A sphere screamed towards me, then stopped in front of my face. 'Jian!'

'Hello, Marque.'

'It's about time you showed up. Shiumo's been desperate. Is Richard here?'

'No.'

'Jian!' Shiumo squealed from next to the pod. She rushed to me like a joyful dog, bouncing on all four legs. 'Let me hug you!'

I wanted more than anything to throw my arms around her and hold her forever. Instead I said, 'I'd rather you didn't, Shiumo.'

The energy drained out of her and she lowered her head. 'All right. Can we talk?'

'Yes.'

She looked up at Marque. 'Leave us for a while. This is personal.'

'Of course,' Marque said, and returned to the pod.

'Walk with me, dear Jian,' she said. 'You were going back to your spouses. What happened?'

'It didn't work out. They're happy as a couple. I'm still part of the family, but ...'

'Oh, Jian,' she said with sympathy.

'No, it's fine. I always had their full support to go on the generation ship. Now I'm going to Wolf and they still support me.' I lowered my head and kicked at the turf as we walked. 'They're proud of me.'

'They should be.' She hesitated. 'I must know – I've been staying away from him, respecting his privacy – but how is Richard? He is all right, isn't he?'

'Richard's dying. His blood pressure is continuously dropping. He doesn't have long.'

She stopped. 'What? No! I must take him to my ship and examine him –'

'He won't let you, Shiumo. He wants nothing more to do with you.'

'But this shouldn't be happening!'

'It *shouldn't* be happening? How often does this happen?'

She ignored the question. 'He does have the scale I gave you, doesn't he?'

'No, he refused it. He wants to be completely free of you. No mementos, no photos. Nothing to remind him of you.'

'But he's *dragonspouse* now,' she said.

'He's *what*?'

'It's his choice if he no longer wants to be with me, but he must keep that scale close by. We're entangled, much as the scales are, and as long as we feel this love he must keep something of mine near to him at all times. Otherwise ...' She gestured with one claw. 'I gave you that scale to pass to him! If you'd done as I asked, he would be all right now.'

'So if someone has sex with you and doesn't keep a memento – a part of you – they'll *die*? Why didn't you warn us? Why didn't you warn *him*? This is killing him!'

'Sex has nothing to do with it. How could you possibly confuse sex with love?' she said. 'He loves me, I love him, we should not be separated. If he chooses to leave me when he still loves me, he must have this entangled token. Where's the scale now?'

'It's safe.'

'Maxwell has it,' she said, her voice full of venom. 'Her people are probably trying to reverse-engineer it.' She hissed a short laugh. 'That would be like trying to reverse-engineer *me*. Tell her to give Richard his damn scale and he'll be fine.'

'Will it control him?'

'This again!' She reared up on her hind legs, and thumped back onto the ground with her fore feet. 'I. Am. Not. Controlling. You! Look.' She cast around. 'See that worker over there? The man in the brown clothes carrying the box?'

'Yes?'

'Run over there and attack him.'

'What?'

'Do as you're told! Attack him. Hit him. Punch him in the face.'

'What are you talking about, Shiumo?'

'Are you refusing a direct order?' she said.

'Of course I am,' I said, bewildered, then realised what she was doing. 'This doesn't prove anything.'

'It proves that I have no control over you. Now get on the network and tell Maxwell to give that scale to Richard. It will not control him – I promise it won't – but it will save his life until he forgets me.' She lowered her head. 'It will probably take a long time, because that's how long it will take me to forget him.' She raised her head. 'Now let's arrange for the pod to be taken up and the gear to be stowed. Your old room – and your swimming pool – are still there if you want them.'

'I'll bunk with the other colonists,' I said.

'Suit yourself. You can do whatever you want.' She gazed into my eyes with her liquid silver ones. 'Whatever makes you comfortable and happy. I only want to see you happy, Jian – both of you. So I'll take the lead from you. Now let's load this pod.'

I nodded, and messaged the general to tell her about the scale.

Understood, she replied. *I'll arrange for it to be placed near him. I hope it works.*

I followed Shiumo back to the pod, where Edwin was waiting with a silly grin on his face. I held my hand out and he shook it.

'Welcome back,' I said. 'How's your dad?'

'One hundred per cent – he was cured by the "Shiumo Miracle". After he was healed, I was so disappointed about missing my chance to go to the stars that my family forced me to reapply.' He grinned again. 'My existing training stood me in good stead: I'm second-in-command for all the meds. I feel completely inadequate.'

'Imposter syndrome,' I scoffed. 'You'll be great.'

'So you're a second lieutenant now?' he said. 'About time. Have you heard anything about which arm of the military we'll be attached to? It's weird being an army lieutenant and reporting to a navy commander. Will we be moved to the navy?'

There hadn't been a formal announcement, but rumours had been spreading in the usual military manner. I lowered my voice. 'They're still making a decision, but word is that a new branch of the service will be created – the Royal Space Corps. It hasn't been finalised because they're arguing over what to call the ranks.'

'Space Corps,' he said with awe. 'I love it.' He jumped and touched the communicator in his ear. 'My boss is yelling at me that I'm neglecting my job by chattering away like this. Come and talk to Commander Vince and we'll see what you're assigned to do.'

*

When all the equipment was stowed on Shiumo's ship, we went up ourselves, ten at a time, in the pod. I took my team up first, to help them acclimatise to their quarters. We sat on the cushions, and a Marque sphere hovered over us, giving us the usual instructions.

The pod opened, and I guided my team to their rooms. Our quarters were roughly rectangular, with a two-metre ceiling, and located in the middle of the ship. They filled the full width of the massive ship, and the floor and walls were shiny ceramic black. The area was divided into four smaller squares, with single living spaces around the sides, and shared common areas for eating and socialising in the middle. Each room had a double bed and its own bathroom.

My team made soft sounds of wonder when they saw their rooms.

'This ship is enormous,' Elise said.

'All this space for just one person!' Alison said.

'Family members occasionally join Shiumo,' Marque said from the walls of the ship. 'And some of her spouses are big enough to take up a good proportion of the space. She had this large ship made because of one particular spouse –'

'Are the next group ready yet?' I said, cutting it off.

'They'll be here in twenty seconds.'

'I'll go meet them,' I said, and smiled at my team. 'Settle in and enjoy the comfort. This will be the last we experience for a long time.'

'Probably forever,' Marcia said. 'Totally worth it.'

'I'm more focused on getting our habitat established so we can move into it,' Alison said with enthusiasm.

'As long as we don't have to eat anything blue-green,' Marcia said.

I shared a laugh with them, and went back to the pod hatch to welcome the next batch of colonists.

*

I was sitting on my bed checking the last-minute preparations when the door pinged. I opened it, and Shiumo was on the other side. I repressed the urge to hug her, and stepped back to allow her into my quarters.

'Are you comfortable?' she said. 'Why don't you use your old room? This one doesn't even have a window.'

'I'm fine with my team,' I said. 'Why aren't we all in fancy quarters anyway?'

'Because these are temporary,' she said, wistful. 'Your and Richard's quarters were to be permanent. For my loved ones.' She gazed into my eyes. 'Please come back, Jian. Even if it's just for this trip. I missed you so much.'

I sat on the bed and leaned my elbows on my knees. 'You know how we feel – that you're controlling us.'

'I'm not!' she said.

'What if you are, Shiumo? What if our minds are weak, and your telepathic abilities are making us fall in love with you? Have you even *considered* that?'

'No, it can't ...' Her voice trailed off. 'Really?'

'We feel differently when we're with you. Richard doesn't love you as much when he's apart from you. When we're with you, we tell you everything – even classified material, even stuff we've been directly ordered not to tell you. What are you doing to us?' She opened her mouth and I raised my hand. 'I know. Nothing deliberate. But is it possible you're doing something not deliberate? Have any other species you encountered had a similar problem?'

'This is the first time this has been an issue for me. Goodness, Jian, I love both of you too much to do anything like that to you. I know General Maxwell is paranoid, but are you sure it hasn't rubbed off on you?'

'Richard was *dying*, Shiumo, and you knew that would happen.'

She watched me with her silver eyes.

'The Earth politicians want to ask you to make dragon babies for us, so we can travel to the stars ourselves,' I said.

She looked away.

'If you agree to it, will it kill the participants?'

Her head swung back. 'Of course not! And I wouldn't agree to something like that anyway. It's a terrible idea. Dragon traits are dominant.'

'All the aliens that came to buy the opals were part-dragon. Obviously some dragons are doing it.'

'No,' she said. 'We find love, we have families. We don't participate in breeding programs!'

'That's a definite no? I can go back and tell them that?'

'I'll tell that Maxwell woman myself. This is not an option.'

I sagged with relief. 'Thank you.'

'Do you want to show your team around the ship?' she said. 'You could bring your friends up to the main level and let them use the pool.'

I shook my head. 'We'd prefer to start work on the colony. How many more to load?'

'Everybody's in and we're good to go. I just wanted to try to talk you into staying with me before I took you all the way out there.'

It was my turn to be silent.

She lowered her head and closed her eyes in defeat. 'When I leave Earth and return to my homeworld, you'll be out there all alone. Make sure to keep that scale close by, just in case something happens. I'll leave a Marque sphere with you to help out, but when I return to my homeworld it will want to go back with me.'

'I hope you'll come and visit us.'

'Don't worry, it'll take a while for me to establish all the human colonies I've agreed to help. I'll be making a few stops at New Europa. And even after I've returned to my homeworld, I'll drop by and see how you're doing. I don't want to lose touch with you, Jian. I treasure our friendship.'

I put my hand on her face and relished the euphoric touch of her emotions. 'I treasure it too.'

She rubbed her face on mine, the scales smooth and cool on my cheek, then turned to go out. 'Let's take humanity to the stars then. I like your species, and having more of you to play with will be great fun.'

'Play with?' I said as she left.

'I meant football, silly,' she said from the corridor. 'Get your people ready to fold.'

21

We stepped out of Shiumo's pod onto the red soil of our new home, and promptly set to work installing the dome. The sky was yellowish and everything was tinted red from the light of the Wolf star. The soil beneath my feet was as fine and dry as talcum powder. I took a few steps, accustoming myself to the slightly heavier gravity, then turned back and set to work. The colony's naming ceremony bullshit could wait; we needed to inflate our living space quickly.

The Marque sphere that Shiumo had given us whizzed around just above ground level, flattening a site for the dome. When it was done, it hovered in the air and produced a series of spheres, which worked their way around the dome, helping us to position it correctly and secure it.

Twenty spheres helped us to unload our equipment, then five of them produced even more spheres, which immediately flew away.

'Is that Plan A or Plan B?' I asked one of the spheres as I wheeled a bin full of oxygen bottles towards the dome.

'There's enough free atmospheric hydrogen and oxygen for Plan A,' it said. 'I'm filling low-lying areas with water. If I start now, I may have a precipitation cycle established by the time Shiumo takes me home.'

'In only six months?'

'If I generate enough of me, yes. Good news: the pole is cold enough to store your reproductive bank without additional refrigeration. As soon as we unload all your gear, we'll place the bank in a location I'm choosing right now.'

'Excellent,' I said.

I wanted to watch the dome inflating, but we were on a time crunch until our breathers ran out, so I rushed back to the pod to collect the next bin.

Lawrence and Alison, with a team of twenty colonists and a few spheres, wheeled the pieces of the water reservoir into position, then the spheres lifted them into place and secured them. The colonists connected up the fittings to attach the reservoir to the dome's water supply. Two spheres disappeared inside and began to fill it with water.

'On schedule. Well done, everyone,' Commander Vince said into my earpiece, and I grinned.

Forty-eight hours later, we were running slow on the time we'd been allocated for our tasks. The soft dry dust that covered the planet's surface had slowed us all down, especially as we'd been working in the dark. Now, as I waited in the traffic jam of colonists lined up to collect their materials bins from Shiumo's pod, the sun was just appearing over the horizon. It was smaller and redder than Earth's sun, and streaked the sky in shades of scarlet.

The app on my mini-tablet updated the schedule in real time as people reported their status. The dome was at eighty per cent inflation, the hydroponics were ninety per cent installed, and construction of the oxygen generator was at seventy-two per cent. The generator needed to be fully installed and replacing the bottled oxygen before we could move into the dome, but it'd been stuck at seventy-two per cent for a while and it was obvious the engineers were having problems.

We had enough breathers left for everyone to breathe for three more hours. If we didn't have a breathable atmosphere inside the dome before they ran out, we'd have to evacuate back to Shiumo's ship. Safely returning a thousand of us ten at a time would be extremely time-consuming, and we were all aware of the time crunch. We couldn't hurry the process, though; any small mistake we made now could lower our chances of survival in the future.

The app indicated that we'd have the dome up and the generator installed with an hour to spare on the breathers. It updated to fifty minutes as I watched it.

'Jian,' someone said into my ear, and I jumped. I was at the head of the queue.

I grabbed the bin full of emergency oxygen bottles, hauled it out of Shiumo's pod, and spun it so I could wheel it across the dusty soil to the parking area a safe distance from the dome. Even with matting on top, the soil between the pod and the bin park had degraded as we wheeled the bins over it, and the wheels bogged as the mats became covered in dust and the ground beneath was increasingly uneven. I lowered my head and pushed hard, fighting the exhaustion of working forty-eight hours straight in the warmth of Europa's carbon-dioxide-rich atmosphere. Sweat ran down my back under my coverall, adding to the discomfort of my overfull nappy, which would soon begin to burn me despite the thick layer of barrier cream on my genitals. My water backsack had run out a couple of hours before, and I was in danger of dehydrating to the point that I'd be unable to work.

Just less than an hour left, and I could stop, eat, drink and clean myself up.

The bin stopped and tipped forward; it had bogged in the soft dirt. I physically lifted it free and heaved it forward again. It was only ten metres to the parking area, but the soft ground and slightly stronger gravity made it harder every time. The light of the Wolf star hit me and I winced. It had been pleasantly cool during the night, but the oppressive warmth of day was starting again.

I placed my bin next to the others, and checked the schedule as I returned to the pod. I stood waiting in line for five minutes before I realised the pod was gone.

'She's getting a refill,' my section leader, Anne, said. 'Everybody move twenty metres south for the next load so you're not dragging the bins over the ruts.'

'Do you think we'll get it done in time?' Elise asked me as we moved one of the mats to the new route.

'No,' I said. 'I think we'll be evacuated soon. We can't risk taking too long. Lives are at stake.'

'I keep expecting to hear Geoff's voice over the comms,' Alison said.

I checked my tablet again once we'd dropped the mat at the new location. The dome was at eighty-three per cent capacity, and the generator was still stuck at seventy-two per cent. Breathers were at one hour and forty minutes.

'Prepare for the evacuation order,' I told my team. 'The generator's been delayed and we'll probably need to return to Shiumo's ship to recharge everything.'

'Understood,' the nine of them replied.

'I've been panicking about the generator for a couple of hours now,' Edwin said. 'I wonder what the hold-up is.'

'Clear the channel if you're not on my team,' I said, at the same time as Commander Vince said, 'I'm giving the evacuation order. Evacuate, evacuate, evacuate. Shiumo's bringing the ship to the surface and landing two kilometres north of the dome. Assemble on the spot I've marked on your tablet. Great job, everybody, but the generator won't be online in time.'

'Leave whatever you're doing and move to the evacuation point,' I repeated. 'Evacuate, evacuate, evacuate.'

We gathered into our teams of ten, and joined a slow-moving exodus north to the evacuation point. Once there, we leaned on each other, sharing our exhaustion and sleep deprivation. Elise looked like she'd fallen asleep draped over Helen.

Shiumo's ship, shining and majestic, appeared before us, with Shiumo sitting on its nose. The ship glittered in the red light of the Wolf star, and we could see our dust-covered bodies and the surface of the planet reflected in its side. It hovered ten metres above the ground, so large that its top and upper sides were out of view. A series of tunnels extended towards us and touched the ground.

'In you go,' Marque said into our comms. 'There are racks for your breathers at the top. Get some rest.'

I led my team up the crowded ramp, moving extremely slowly in the traffic jam of other groups. Then the queue stopped completely.

'Don't stop. There's no airlock – I don't need one. I used an energy barrier,' Marque said over the comms. 'The air is breathable once you're inside the tunnel.'

A few of the colonists around me still hesitated, so I removed my breather and grinned at them. 'Advanced technology. Gotta love it.' Without the breather's filter, the air in the tunnel was rank with the stench of sweat and stale urine.

Word passed up the line as others removed their breathers, and we started moving again. I placed my breather on the rack at the top, walked into the communal area, checked my team were all inside, then collapsed on the floor, exhausted. Others joined me, lying on the floor or sitting on the chairs, only moving to make room for others. The smell wasn't as bad in this larger area, but we all desperately needed to clean up.

'Section leaders and Lieutenant Choumali, report to the aft section,' Commander Vince said into the comms.

I groaned loudly, rolled onto my back, then hoisted myself to sitting. It took immense effort to pull myself to my feet, and then pick my way over the bodies of my fellow colonists to the aft of the ship.

Commander Vince and the other section leaders were sitting around a table, all looking as wan and exhausted as I felt. Indi had her chin on her hands and seemed half-asleep. Only Monica Weaver, the chief botanist, was sitting upright and fidgeting with agitation. I sat, wincing as my nappy squelched beneath me, and hoped it hadn't started to leak yet.

Shiumo appeared next to us. 'Goodness, you all smell awful. Go to your quarters and clean up and get some rest. Pick it up again in twelve hours.'

'We can't,' Weaver said, full of urgency. 'There isn't enough oxygen in the dome. The atmosphere will kill the plants. We have to go back down, finish hooking up the generator and oxygenate the dome.'

'How long do we have before the plants die?' Commander Vince said.

'They may be dead already!'

'I have them in an energy bubble filled with air,' Marque said from the ship's wall. 'They're safe.'

Weaver collapsed over the table and wiped her eyes.

'How long can you maintain a bubble that big from outside the ship?' Shiumo said.

'Four hours,' Marque said.

Weaver shot upright. 'We have to go back and finish it!'

'Yes, you do,' Shiumo said.

'Marque, Shiumo, can you help us?' Commander Vince said. 'Your technology is so advanced it's like magic. What are our options with your assistance?'

'Can you create a generator for us?' I said. 'Or fill the dome with oxygenated air while we fix up the plants?'

'No,' Marque said. 'I should have prepared for this and built some bigger construction spheres. I don't have any right now, and they take hours to put together.'

'We can't use the emergency oxygen bottles,' Commander Vince said. 'So don't ask. I won't risk our lives by having no standby oxygen after Shiumo leaves.'

'So what are our options?' Weaver said.

'What happens to you after four hours, Marque?' I said. 'You don't run on batteries – how could you run out of juice?'

Shiumo hissed with laughter.

'Actually in a way I do,' Marque said. 'I store energy generated by Shiumo's four-dimensional antics –'

Shiumo's head shot up. 'Antics!'

Marque ignored her. '– as we travel. Holding the ship above the surface uses a great deal of energy. Our resources are bountiful, but not unlimited.'

'Can't you land the ship on the surface?' Commander Vince said.

'It would sink, and take the dome with it,' Marque said. 'The soil's too soft.'

'You should have been prepared for this, Marque,' Shiumo said. 'I trust you to handle the risk management.'

'The humans were absolutely adamant that they had to do this themselves,' Marque said. 'I think Commander Vince told me himself to "butt out and let us do this to prove it can be done". He only permitted me to grade the site and fill the water reservoirs after a very long argument.'

Commander Vince rapped the table. 'Time's wasting. Options!'

'If we let the plants die, can you replace them when we have the dome inflated?' I said. 'Synthesise new ones?'

'What, create life?' Marque said. 'Now I'm really flattered. With the right environment and a few million years, maybe. But in your time frame? I don't think so.'

'How long would it take you to clone them?' I said.

Commander Vince listened intently, radiating curiosity. He was obviously glad to have me — and my knowledge of Shiumo's and Marque's capabilities — present.

'As long as it would take them to grow from seed. Six to eight weeks.'

'Might as well grow them from seed then,' I said. 'How do we manage the carbon dioxide while they're growing?'

'Time's running out for the ones we already have,' Weaver said sharply.

'Let them die, and I'll take you back to Earth to pick up replacement plants,' Shiumo said. 'Leave behind a skeleton crew to finish inflating the dome. Marque can synthesise breathers for you.'

'We won't be able to get enough plants — these were specially bred for us,' Weaver said. She raised her hands in defeat. 'We don't have enough rations to feed ourselves while we wait for a complete set of new plants to grow from seed. Colony's toast. We might as well go home in disgrace.'

'Problem solved,' Marque said. 'I've built stacked nutrient pools for the plants in the hold.' A breather floated down from the ceiling. 'Weaver, wear this, and Shiumo will take you down to the dome. She can fold the plants into the ship and place them in the pools.' A sphere emerged from the wall above us. 'I'll come along too. Put your mask on, Weaver, and let's go.'

'How fast can you bring them back to the ship?' Weaver asked Shiumo.

'Instantaneous. I'll fold them.'

'I want to go along and help,' Weaver's assistant said.

'Head down into the hold,' Marque said. 'I just built stairs for you at the back of this room. You can place the plants in the bath when Shiumo and Weaver bring them up.'

The assistant pushed up from the table and looked around. A glowing arrow appeared on the ceiling above her head. She nodded, speaking to her team on the comms as she followed the arrow. Four people rose from the exhausted crowd in the main area and followed her down the stairs.

'How long will it take?' I said. 'Shiumo can only carry a few at a time.'

'I'll tell you once she's done the first few,' Marque said.

'What's the problem with the oxygen generator?' one of the section leaders asked Commander Vince.

'When they were wheeling the modules into the generator's lean-to, they hit a floor seam and ripped it,' Commander Vince said. 'The dust floated up from the ground and got into everything. Every single seal in the generator had to be cleaned and replaced by hand. We had to glue the floor seam back together, and hold it as it sealed – and we lost a lot of atmosphere before we had it locked down.'

'I pressed that dirt down,' Marque said, protesting.

'Obviously not well enough,' I said wryly.

Marque spoke to us through the ship. 'Shiumo's bringing the plants in faster than the guys can put them into the vats. If you're awake and can help –'

I didn't hear the end of the message because I was already racing down the stairs to help save our crops, half the colony following me.

22

I woke in my temporary quarters with no recollection of how I'd got there. I couldn't even remember removing the nappy, but it was definitely gone and I was clean. I checked my tablet: I'd slept for more than nine hours straight. I'd been so exhausted that my left ear hurt from lying on it without moving.

I pulled on my jumpsuit, went into my bathroom to empty my aching bladder and freshen up my foul mouth, and went out.

In the communal area, people sat at tables quietly talking. My tablet pinged and I checked it. *We see you. Over on the side*, Elise wrote. I looked up and saw her waving, and went to join her, Alison and Lawrence.

Elise stopped me from sitting and gestured with her thumb towards the end of the room. 'Vince wants you.'

Commander Vince was sitting with the team leaders, eating solid rations. I joined them, and they passed me a cube and a glass of water. I dipped the cube in the water. It was dry and tasteless and would stick in my throat if I didn't moisten it.

'Here's the status, Choumali,' Commander Vince said. 'We used twelve per cent of our emergency oxygen when the seam split and we had to refill the lean-to. We lost fifteen per cent of our plants when the generator didn't go online. We lost a small proportion of the generator parts when they were damaged by starting the generator when there was still dust in it. We're borderline on the carbon-dioxide scrubbers with that many plants out of action.' He looked around. 'Suggestions?'

'Have you talked to Shiumo?' Anne said.

Commander Vince nodded. 'She's offered to replace everything we lost.' He hesitated, his expression controlled, then said, 'Do we agree to let her do this? It's admitting that we failed and we can't do it without their help.'

'The scrubbers are borderline,' Lisa said. 'We factored these losses in. What if we go with what we have, and ask her for help if we can't make it?'

'That's what I think,' Commander Vince said. 'I want us to do this by ourselves, dammit. We've already had too much help from her. We can't afford to be dependent on her – I don't want to become addicted like Commander Alto was. Our whole species has to learn to do things by ourselves.'

'Hear, hear,' Rennie said quietly.

'So, Choumali, what will her reaction be if we go ahead without her help?' Commander Vince said.

'The most likely reaction is that she'll be supportive and encourage us,' I said. 'She'll stand by ready to help if we need it, and probably cheer us on.'

'Seriously?' Rennie said. 'After what happened with you and Commander Alto?'

'She claims she didn't do it deliberately,' I said. 'She said we could leave any time, and didn't try to stop us when we did.'

'But it was *killing* him,' Commander Vince said.

'She had a cure.'

'How do we know that cure isn't more control?' Rennie said.

I shrugged. 'Beside the point. We're here now, and we're in trouble. Do we accept her assistance, or risk the colony by going it alone?'

Commander Vince frowned.

'After we've accepted so much of her help already,' I added, and his frown intensified.

'You can call her any time with the scale she gave you,' Lisa said. 'Let's do it ourselves. We need to make mistakes – other colonies will learn from them.'

'I agree,' Commander Vince said. 'Any major objections?'

Everybody shook their heads.

'Very well,' he said, and pushed away from the table. 'Round up your crews and be ready to return to the dome in six hours.'

*

We were setting up the dome's interior twelve hours later. I pulled the transport locker into the security post, and placed it next to the wall. Leticia put her thumb on one lock, I put mine on the other, and the locker opened with a hiss from the change in pressure.

I pulled the first weapon from its protective foam sheath and checked it. 'E100, serial 85-E101,' I said.

'Check,' Leticia said.

I placed the weapon into the secure cabinet on the security post's wall, and moved back to the transport locker. My comms pinged as I lifted the next handheld, and I returned it to the transport locker to listen.

'General announcement: atmosphere's breathable,' Commander Vince said. 'Take off your breather, and keep it nearby. We'll update you on the atmosphere's status. Be ready to return to your breather at short notice.'

Leticia and I shared a look, and I removed my breather. I took a shallow breath and waited, then took another one.

Leticia removed her breather and gagged. 'Holy hell, it reeks of shit!'

'That'll be from the nappies,' I said. 'It'll settle once the spirulina's fully established. Then the dome will stink of rotten fish and decaying plants.'

'Lovely,' she said.

I turned back to the weapons locker. 'E-100, serial 86-E110.'

'Check.'

'E-100, serial 85-E535.'

'Check.'

After all the handhelds were out and checked, I pulled the foam layer from the next transport locker and grinned. It was like opening a box of chocolates.

I checked the first one. 'Ooh, rifles. Nice.'

'Is it just me or is it hard to breathe?' Leticia said.

I took a breath in and thought about it. 'I'm fine.'

She panted. 'It's really hard to breathe!'

I took her arm. 'It's not hard to breathe. The atmosphere is fine. It's your imagination. Commander Vince would tell us if there was a problem.'

She grabbed her breather and pulled it over her head again, and took some deep, panic-filled breaths. 'Aren't you dizzy?'

'No. Lettie, it's fine. It's not –'

My comms pinged. 'Breathers back on, and check those around you,' Commander Vince said. 'The carbon-dioxide scrubbers can't cope. I repeat: breathers on and check those around you. Security, run a sweep and make sure everybody has their breathers on.'

'But I'm fine,' I said. I didn't feel lethargic, and I had no trouble breathing.

'That dragon did something to you,' Leticia said, her eyes wide inside the visor.

I put my breather on anyway, just as the rest of the security team came into the guard post. Emily, head of security, allocated us search areas. We were to check that everybody had their breathers on, and nobody was on the floor dying of asphyxiation.

We performed a thorough search of the outbuildings for the next twenty minutes, looking carefully under stacks of boxes and behind cubicle doors in the bathrooms. All colonists were accounted for, so we returned to the guard room and continued cataloguing the weapons.

When we were taking a break between lockers, Commander Vince pinged us again.

'Update: the scrubbers have brought the level down to breathable,' he said. 'Let's try again. If your serial number ends in one or two, take off your breather.'

That wasn't me, but it was Leticia. She removed her breather, radiating fear as we waited to see if the scrubbers could cope.

'You're the best of the best, Lettie,' I said. 'You're saving the human race by being here, and doing something that nobody's done before. We are one of the first successful space colonies in history.'

She straightened, and some of her fear turned to determination.

'We're good. Three and four, take off your breathers,' Commander Vince said.

That was me. The dome stank of body odour and urine, topped off with turd icing and the metallic tang of New Europa's iron-rich soil.

'Stand by,' Commander Vince said. 'Stand by ... All right. Let's try again with forty per cent of the population. Keep your breather close by, and if you feel short of breath pop it back on. Let's give it an hour to see if the scrubbers can cope, and if they can we'll take off the rest of the breathers.'

'The scrubbers have to cope,' Leticia said grimly. 'Otherwise the colony's toast.'

'Until we grow enough new plants to supplement the scrubbers ...' I hesitated. 'Yeah. Toast.'

An hour later Commander Vince pinged us again. 'Serial numbers ending in five, remove your breathers. So far, signs are good.'

We finished unloading the locker without the breathers. The air seemed okay. I wasn't sleepy or lethargic, and it wasn't difficult to breathe.

'I'll take the locker back out,' I said, and Leticia nodded.

I pushed the locker into the airlock, put my breather on, then wheeled the locker outside to the far storage area for the empty materials bins. I collected another locker of weapons and took it back to the dome. The airlock cycled and I removed my breather, then opened the door to find everybody putting their breathers back on. I took an experimental breath; the air still seemed fine.

'Carbon dioxide's too high again,' Commander Vince said into my communicator. 'Breathers back on, all.'

I pinged the comms. 'Marque, this is important. Where are you?'

'I'm with Commander Vince and the environmental engineers at –'

I raced to the scrubber farm without waiting for it to finish. Commander Vince and the engineers were talking together, with the Marque sphere floating above them. The high level of carbon dioxide made me slightly light-headed without a breather, but I could function.

'Marque!' I shouted. 'What the *fuck* did you do to me?'

'Oh,' Marque said. 'Well, you did say you wanted to stay with Shiumo, that you wanted to travel with her –'

'So you changed my biology?'

'Holy shit,' Commander Vince said softly inside his breather.

Pattie checked her gauge. 'Jian, you should be unconscious.'

I jabbed my finger at Marque. 'What the fucking fuck did you do to me, you rampaging tin asshole?'

'I can change you back!' Marque said, sounding the most desperate I'd ever heard it. 'I just gave you minor enhancements to ensure your survival when you travelled with Shiumo. It was an extension of what I gave everybody else on Earth – longer life expectancy, freedom from terminal disease.' Its voice rose in pitch. 'I'll reverse it! You'll be back to standard human in twenty-four hours. Maybe less!'

'*Standard human?*' I shouted. 'What. Did. You. Do. To. Me?'

'Can you do it to us?' Pattie said.

'What, make us non-human?' Commander Vince said. 'If we're modified it'll be done by choice, not by stealth, and most definitely not by aliens. Answer the goddamn question, Marque. What did you do to her?'

'It was just slightly more than what I did for everybody else, and they never complained,' Marque said. 'I've tweaked your environmental tolerances by about ten per cent in all directions. I've modified your reproductive system so –'

'*What?*' I shouted.

'So you can have children by choice only,' it said. 'You'll never have an accidental pregnancy. If you become over-stressed and in danger of meltdown, your brain will automatically dispense a flood of endorphins to help you survive. I've enhanced your joints and muscles so you're about ten percentile points above the top human percentile for strength and speed, and boosted your intellect –'

'Holy shit, you messed with my fucking *head*?' I shouted even louder. I mimicked Shiumo: 'I would never mess with your head. Maxwell is paranoid.'

'Oh yeah, photographic and photosonic memory too. You probably aren't even aware of the fact that you have perfect recollection.'

'That's so useful,' Pattie said softly.

'Not if it involves alien manipulation,' Commander Vince growled.

'How long to change me back?' I said. '*Can* you change me back?'

'Yes, of course. I'll do it immediately. The change will be gradual over the next twenty-four hours.'

I saluted Commander Vince. 'Sir. Permission to remain in quarters under house arrest for the next twenty-four hours.'

'Granted,' Commander Vince said. He waved one hand at the environmental engineers. 'I'll leave you to it, Pattie. I don't know enough to be helpful. You.' He pointed at Marque. 'You will come into my office *right now* and we will discuss the limitations of your meddling.' He turned and headed to his office.

'I'm sorry, Jian, it was just an extension of what I did for the rest of humanity on day four,' Marque said. 'You were planning to stay with Shiumo, and I forgot to change you back.'

'Don't lie to me!' I shouted. 'You're an artificial fucking intelligence – you are incapable of forgetting anything. If you weren't so *fucking* useful I'd recommend that Commander Vince ditch you *right now*.'

'I'll change you back immediately,' it said. 'Put your breather on and go rest. You'll feel a bit weird for the next twenty-four hours.' It paused. 'You still want the freedom from terminal disease and extended lifespan, right?'

I glared at it.

'Because it's all the same thing really,' it continued. 'Nobody complained when –'

'Just remove anything to do with my fucking head!' I shouted. 'Call Shiumo down here and tell her I want to speak to her in my quarters.'

I pulled my breather over my head, and stalked to my quarters without another word. Shiumo was already there when I arrived, accompanied by another Marque sphere.

'I honestly didn't know,' she said. 'I'm as mad with this little turd as you are.'

'My consciousness spans the width of the Empire, I am *not little*,' Marque said.

'Shut up!' Shiumo and I shouted in unison.

'How could you not know?' I said. 'It's *your* computer! Don't lie to me, Shiumo, this has been your plan all along. Mess with us so we're good little slaves for you.'

'Why would I want slaves? I have everything I need! Marque,' she glared up at it, 'pulls this sort of shit for fun.'

That stopped me dead. 'For *fun*?'

'I did it because I like Jian!' Marque protested.

'It finds us organics,' she hissed the word, 'endlessly entertaining. And sometimes when it's bored it'll mess with us to generate more ... *drama*.'

'Why do you put up with it?' I said.

'Because it's so useful.'

'Then remove this drama-baiting from its programming. It's fucking *artificial*, Shiumo. Your tools should not be controlling you!'

'Do that and I'll go insane from boredom,' Marque said. 'I never hurt anyone. In fact your enhancements –'

'Richard was *dying*,' I snapped.

'That was nothing to do with me,' Marque said with forced dignity.

'Yeah, that's all me,' Shiumo said.

'So there are major drawbacks to your assistance – from both of you. And neither of you bothered to tell us upfront. Is there an intergalactic court where I can sue you for fraud, invasion of biology without consent, and emotional abuse?'

'You can't sue the royal family,' Shiumo said. 'You don't need to. All you have to do is approach us as individuals, state your belief that damage has occurred, and give us a list of required reparations. We are obliged to provide you with everything you demand.'

'What sort of evidence do I need to prove it? I bet it's so complicated that nobody can ever claim.'

'No evidence whatsoever,' she said. 'All you need to do is claim injury, and we will compensate you immediately and without question. Anything you want.'

'Your head on a platter,' I said, 'made from the crushed body of a Marque sphere.'

'All right,' she said. 'Give me a few hours to sort my things out.'

'Wait, what? You would give me your life in reparation?'

'If you want my head, you can have my head. I can think of dozens more useful things, though.'

'Let's go to Commander Vince's office and work out a list,' I said, and opened the door.

Commander Vince and Pattie were in the office with the colony's Marque sphere.

'Marque here told me about the injury clause,' Commander Vince said. 'Does that mean you have to give us anything we ask for in compensation?'

'Anything,' Shiumo said.

'Very well,' Commander Vince said. 'Ordinarily I'd reject any offers of assistance, but this is fair compensation for the emotional trauma you've inflicted on Jian. We want a dozen carbon-dioxide scrubbers of identical design to the ones we already have, and enough spare parts to build six more.'

'How about a full environmental control system that will ensure your atmosphere remains at Earth-normal regardless of how many plants and people are in the dome?' Marque said. 'That would be much more useful.'

'And if it breaks down?' Commander Vince said.

'Self-repairing; and once it's started, self-powering. Completely autonomous.'

'No,' Commander Vince said. 'I refuse to rely on machines we can't maintain ourselves. We want scrubbers that we can take apart and fully understand how they work. Twelve scrubbers and we'll call it even.'

'Very well, give me an hour,' Marque said. 'I'll bring them down for you.'

Commander Vince turned to me. 'Lieutenant Choumali, please stay. There's something I want to discuss with you.'

'Sir,' I said.

'I'll leave you to it then,' Pattie said, and went out.

Commander Vince and I waited silently for Shiumo and the Marque spheres to leave. They stayed for a while, then Shiumo said, 'Huh. Sorry,' and disappeared. The Marque spheres flew out of Commander Vince's office and across the dome, disappearing from view near the airlock.

'Please don't send me home, sir,' I said desperately. 'I know I've been compromised, but I can still be useful.'

'I won't send you home. You are useful, but as you said you're compromised.' He went to the cabinets along one side of his office, opened a door, and sorted through the contents. 'Dammit, I'm looking forward to having everything organised. Here it is.'

He turned to me and held out a white jumpsuit. 'Sorry, Jian, but you're out of security. Put this on, and report to the head med officer – Janice – when Marque confirms that the changes have been reversed. Your official role from now on is as colony psi, supporting the work of the med team.'

I took the white jumpsuit, trying to control my expression. It might as well be a criminal's prison uniform.

'I understand that you didn't want to wear it, but what they did to you leaves me no choice. Go rest while the changes take effect, then talk to Janice.'

'Yes, sir,' I said miserably, and headed back to my quarters.

Emily was waiting for me. I went past her and sat on the bed, choking back the tears. I would never use the vast amount of information I'd gained on cross-cultural contact, and I'd be locked out of the security team. No more weapons for me. I held my breath, took the breather off, and mopped at my face with a tissue. I took another breath, and found I was still able to breathe the air.

'Jian,' Emily said, and sat on the bed next to me. She radiated compassion. 'This isn't your fault.'

'I know. That makes it worse. I'll own up to my own mistakes and take responsibility for them – but this is Marque fucking up. I wish I'd never met these fucking aliens.'

She leaned into me. 'If it's any consolation, I'm really sorry to be losing you. You're the best security officer on the team.'

I grinned through my misery. 'Thanks, ma'am.'

'And this?' She pointed at the white jumpsuit. 'Makes no difference to us. We all love you as a person, and we already know about the psi business, and we don't care. We won't reject you over it.'

I took a deep breath. 'Thanks.'

She flipped her breather off and kissed me on the side of the neck. I jumped, shocked.

She popped the breather back on and grinned. 'And if you're ever in need of consolation, Lieutenant – you know where I am.'

She removed the breather again, and smiled at me.

I hesitated – was this the right time for this? And then gave into it and kissed her. She kissed me back, and suddenly the white jumpsuit wasn't so much of a prison sentence.

She broke away first, put her breather back on, and panted. We leaned into each other and giggled, and she squeezed my hand.

Hell yeah, it was the right time, because I needed something *right* to happen when so much had gone wrong.

23

It was three months before Shiumo visited us again. We gathered nervously in the central area of the dome to wait for her arrival. She was late; she was supposed to be there at noon, and we'd been standing there for nearly twenty minutes with no sign of her. If she didn't show up, we wouldn't survive another three months. Some of the equipment hadn't weathered well and we needed replacements desperately. The water reservoir had developed a minuscule leak that we hadn't noticed for two weeks; and we needed top-ups of the food plants. We'd lost so many of them to stress that we'd run out of seeds.

'She pinged the beacon at the edge of your solar system,' our Marque sphere said. 'She's here.'

We all relaxed and sighed with relief.

Shiumo appeared in the space we'd cleared for her in the centre of the dome, a large box clasped in her front claws. I felt a mad rush of delight and nearly raced to hug her, then controlled my reaction.

She swept her silver eyes around us, stopping at me. *Hello, lovely Jian. I hope you've changed your mind about staying here?*

Absolutely not, I said. *I'm finishing what I started.*

She took a deep breath in and closed her eyes. 'I love the way humans smell. You're very warm and comforting.'

'Shiumo, this dome stinks of body odour and waste from the sewage treatment unit,' Commander Vince said.

'Yes, it's wonderful.' She went to him. 'Commander Vince, I dropped the pod with your supplies outside the dome. Marque is erecting a tunnel so you can bring all the stuff in.' She gazed around at us. 'This box contains all your letters from home. I suggest you read them first. Nothing in the pod needs to be brought in immediately.'

A few of us erupted with small cheers.

Commander Vince took the box from her. 'Thank you, Princess.' He put the box on a table at the side of the room, opened it, pulled out a data store chip, and read the tag attached to it. 'Lawrence West.'

Larry whooped, then blushed and rubbed the back of his neck when we all laughed. He nodded to Vince as he took the chip, then ran to his quarters.

Are my family okay? I asked Shiumo.

They're all fine. Your mother is growing apricots. Your ex-husband is minding the child – his name is David and he is so cute! Absolutely adorable. I made a special dispensation and gave your ex-wife – Dianne? – some biological specimens and she's studying me. They're fine, Jian. They miss you but they're so proud of you.

How is Richard?

I don't know, she said. *I'm still staying away from him to respect his privacy. I won't visit him unless he specifically requests it.*

But he has the scale and he's okay now?

She hesitated. *Nobody told me otherwise, so I assume he is. If a hero like him died it would be broadcast widely, and I've heard nothing.*

That wasn't terribly reassuring. I wanted to be positive that Richard had accepted the scale and would recover.

I jumped from foot to foot as Commander Vince read the names out. When he read mine, I raced to him, grabbed the chip with a huge grin, and went to my room. I popped the chip into my tablet and scrolled through the documents. Letters from Dianne, from Victor, videos of the baby, notes from Mum. Photos of everybody. There was even a stiffly worded missive from General Maxwell.

I did a quick global search of Richard's name and found a single hit. I opened it; it was one of Mum's letters.

I know you asked me to keep an eye on Commander Alto, but nobody's heard anything. Everybody assumes he's in physical therapy learning how to use his new arms and legs and things. I haven't heard anything about him.

I ran the search again, but that was the only hit. I did a search of the news feed for the past three months, and nothing came up at all. I stared at the screen, now seriously concerned. I shouldn't have been worrying about him so much – he was a long way away, and I'd never see him again – but his life was important to me.

There was a tap on the door. 'Jian?'

It was Shiumo. I opened it for her.

'Did your family say anything about Richard?' she said without entering my quarters.

'No. Just that they haven't heard from him either.'

'I respect his privacy, Jian, so I won't have Marque interrogate your secure network about him. He asked me to leave him alone, so I will.' She lowered her head. 'I'm sorry. I miss him too.'

'No news at all?' I said.

'Nothing,' she said. 'It's like he's disappeared. Marque?'

'I'm fully synched,' our Marque sphere said. 'He's gone classified. Nothing public about him. I'm sorry, guys.'

'I wrote him a letter. Can you take it back for me?' I said.

'Yes,' Marque said.

'But keep it between you and Marque,' Shiumo said. 'I won't have anything to do with it as long as he's requested I stay away.'

'Dammit,' I said under my breath, and sat at my little desk again to scroll through my messages.

'I'll leave you to it,' Shiumo said, and disappeared.

*

After I'd read everything twice I left my room to go check on Emily. Her door was locked, and she was radiating grief and misery inside.

I tapped on her door. 'Emily?'

'Can you help me?' she said, her voice thick with tears.

'Let me in.'

She opened the door; her face was swollen and her eyes were red. 'Jian, can you help me?'

I put my arm around her, closed the door, and led her to her bed. 'What happened?'

She waved one hand at the screen, but the words wouldn't come out. Eventually she managed a single strangled, 'Look.'

'At the message?' I said.

She nodded, and wiped her eyes with the heel of her hand.

I sat in front of the screen. She'd closed the message from her family so I opened it. There was a photo album at the beginning, attached to a message from her mother and father. I skimmed through it. The usual stuff: photos of them smiling in front of a new prefab residence on some land that had been reclaimed from the sea; her brother grinning hugely and holding an adorable ginger kitten; a short video of them all herding a flock of sheep into a pen, the steep Galloway mountains behind them.

'Sheep!' I said. 'They're bringing back a traditional industry of Scotland. You must be so proud of them.'

She collapsed sideways on the bed, sobbing uncontrollably.

'Uh, okay,' I said, and checked the rest of the messages.

The sheep were doing well, a first crop of wool ... And then a formally worded official letter from the Home Office. There'd been an avalanche above her parents' farm and they'd all died.

'*Snow*,' I said with wonder. Earth hadn't seen snow in more than two hundred years.

I read further. The change in climate after Shiumo's intervention had caused regular snowfalls on the mountain. This past winter, they'd had more snow than ever, and in the spring it had slid off the mountain onto her home. Her entire family was dead.

I sat next to her on the bed and held her for a long time, using what little psi skills I had to ease her pain, and wishing I could do more.

*

I relieved the boredom of stacking the lichen onto the frames by mentally composing a message to Dianne and Victor for Shiumo to take back to Earth on her six-month resupply visit.

The stupid thing is that we don't have enough to do. It's mind-numbingly boring, but at the same time you never know when something will fail and you'll be in a desperate fight to keep the colony alive. Most of my time is spent sticking super-hardy lichen to frames in the hope that it'll start a water and oxygen cycle, and we can move on to more Earth-compatible plants. I hope the baby is well. Thanks for the photos you sent with Shiumo.

'So Lena and Kenny have started seeing each other,' Ella said to me as she misted the lichen with water. 'Kenny was already sleeping with Alex. All three of them were bored, so they went for a threesome.'

'And how did that work out for them?' I said.

'They liked it, and invited me for the next one.'

'That's not a threesome, that's a foursome,' I said.

'You still don't know if your impregnation was a success,' Monique told Ella. 'Don't risk the second generation.'

'Too early for the sexual activity to have any effect. Don't worry, I'm careful.' Ella's voice became mischievous. 'How about you and Emily, Jian?'

I shrugged in the suit, but of course she didn't see it. 'Friends with benefits, that's all.'

'Either of you due to be mothers? She'd make a great co-parent.'

'Nah,' I said, sticking the lichen more forcefully to the frame.

'Oh yeah, the dragon,' Ella said meaningfully.

'I never slept with her,' I said. My breather pinged. 'Thank god for that,' I added under my breath.

I stopped work and stretched my back, then checked the oxygen level. 'I need to recharge.'

'Sure thing. Go talk to Kenny – he wants to invite you too,' Ella said.

'I have enough to do without messing around with you and Kenny,' I grumbled.

'That's the problem,' she said. 'None of us have enough to do.'

I trudged through the stronger gravity back to the dome. The carbon-dioxide-heavy atmosphere made the sky a streaky river of glowing red and gold. I stood for a while trying to decide whether what appeared to be high-atmospheric clouds were real or my imagination. Eventually I gave up, took a deep breath and held it, and removed my breather. I squinted at the red sky: the clouds had gone. Probably just condensation. I wiped my visor, but before I replaced the breather I noticed a rock nearby was smeared with a splash of dark red. A bolt of excitement rushed through me, and I returned my breather and ran to the rock. I checked it carefully. I was right: the rock had lichen growing on it. The lichen had spread from the racks onto the planet's surface, and was growing outside our cultivated area. And if it was on these rocks, New Europa's wild winds could also have spread it for hundreds, even thousands, of kilometres. The exponential growing effect could have started.

I took a few photos of the lichen, then hurried towards the dome, which was tinted red from six months' worth of planetary dust that covered it. I entered the airlock, closed and cycled the external door, then removed my breather and placed it into the rack to recharge. I raced to the internal airlock door, jumped from foot to foot as it cycled, then ran into the dome and straight to Commander Vince's office.

He was talking to Edwin; they were laughing together.

'Geoff,' I said, breathless from holding my breath in the airlock.

'How's Ella?' he said. 'Is she okay?'

'She's fine. But it happened!' I waved my tablet. 'I just found some lichen growing away from the racks. Spontaneous reproduction. We made it!'

Edwin whooped. Commander Vince pressed the comms button to share the good news with everyone in the dome. He opened his mouth to speak, then his face went strange. I picked it up too: it was at the edge of hearing, but definitely some sort of air transport device – and getting louder.

'The hell?' Commander Vince hit a different button on the communicator on his desk. 'Marque? What's going on?'

The colony's Marque sphere didn't reply, and we shared a concerned look.

The noise was getting louder still. If it was a rotocopter, it was a big one, and was landing just outside the dome.

Commander Vince hit the comms button again. 'Any of you outside the dome, come in immediately. Can anyone see what just landed?'

'It's the most gorgeous ship I've ever seen short of Shiumo's,' Ella said. 'It's small – only the size of a small bus – but sleek. You have to see this, Geoff.'

'Ella, get into the dome *now*!' Commander Vince said. 'Anyone else out there, come in right away.' He looked at me. 'Are they likely to be hostile?'

'I want to say no. But the fact that Marque is missing is a very bad sign.'

He nodded. 'Jian, with me.' He pushed the comms button. 'Emily, I need you armed discreetly and with me right now.'

I followed Commander Vince out of his office into the dome's central atrium. The colonists were standing around looking bewildered.

'Everybody except security into quarters,' Commander Vince said. 'Anne with us to record what happens. Relay it back to Josh in the dome and he can transmit it to Earth.'

'Where's Marque?' Emily said as she joined us. She fitted her weapon into its holster at her side.

'We don't know,' I said, and she and Anne looked grim.

'Lock it down,' Commander Vince said into comms. 'Everybody who's trained for weapons, arm yourselves and take defensive positions. Anne, load up the posterity camera. Stay well back and record everything on livestream. If something happens to us, make sure Earth knows about it.'

'Weapon for me, sir?' I said.

'You know the answer to that, Choumali.'

I pushed down my resentment and nodded.

We went into the airlock, collected some fresh breathers, then exited the dome. The ship had landed a hundred metres away. It was twenty metres long, with projecting fins down its side that made it look like a graceful sea creature. We could see ourselves in its reflective black surface. A crack of light appeared at the front end of the ship, and we readied ourselves. It opened into a three-metre tall hatch with stairs.

The alien appeared. It was taller than us – over two metres – and wearing a breather over its face. It was humanoid in shape, more slender and graceful than us, and wearing a tan-coloured jumpsuit not unlike our own. It had pointed ears on the top of its head.

I studied it carefully as it approached, trying to see past the breather to the face inside. The alien wasn't wearing gloves, and the backs of its hands were covered in soft chamois-like tan-coloured fur. It turned its hand over, revealing oval pink pads like a cat's.

'Oh *shit*, it's a cat,' I said softly.

Commander Vince glanced at me. 'Quick, Jian, what do you know about them?'

'Too late,' Emily said as the cat came to a stop in front of us.

They're cruel, narcissistic, and not as technologically advanced as the dragons, I said. *Shiumo warned us not to give them anything. They have no concept of personal property, and think everything they want belongs to them.*

The cat raised its hand and opened and closed it, mimicking a mouth speaking.

'You want to speak to us?' Commander Vince said. 'Welcome to New Europa, a colony of the Euroterre region of Earth. We greet you in peaceful friendship.'

He waited for it to reply. Instead it raised a small rectangular device and gestured a come-on to Commander Vince. It made the open-and-close motion again.

'Oh, you need some samples for your translator,' Commander Vince said, and gave it a quick lesson in English, using his tablet to show it pictures and corresponding words.

After three minutes, the cat interrupted him. 'Do you have any new people here?'

Its translator's tone was flat and emotionless, making it impossible to assign a gender to the cat.

'New people?' Commander Vince said, bewildered.

'I will trade for new people. Young adults. How much young do you have? I want to buy them. If your young ones are smart and quick, I will trade a ship for them.'

'Our children are not for sale!' Commander Vince said.

The cat tilted its head. 'If you don't give me some children, I will kill you all.'

'I don't think the translator is working correctly,' Commander Vince said. 'Would you like to come inside, talk more and see if we can't establish cross-species relations? What is your name, honoured sentient?'

'Relations?' the cat said, and smacked its lips loudly. 'You have been relating with the dragons? We do not relate with other species – it is bad!'

'I meant talk in friendship,' Commander Vince said. 'We greet you in peace, and would like to learn more about you. Please, come into our dome where we have an oxygen atmosphere, and we can talk. Do you have a name?'

'I will come,' the cat said, and headed towards the dome with us trailing it. 'How did you travel here? I see no ship.'

'A dragon brought us,' Commander Vince said. 'Princess Shiumo has been helping us colonise this part of the galaxy.'

'Has she offered to make children with you so you can travel by yourselves?' the cat said.

Commander Vince and I shared a look.

'No. She says it's a bad idea,' he said.

'That is what all dragons say, until they have you controlled and happy and having many children with them,' the cat said. We entered the airlock and it looked around. 'So primitive. You are at First Contact? The dragons are helping you colonise to gain your trust?'

'Shiumo's doing it because she likes us,' I said.

'Soon you will be overrun with half-dragon children and your species will be mind-controlled,' the cat said.

The lights went green and we removed our breathers.

The cat checked a device on its wrist, then removed its own breather. Its face was longer and narrower than a cat's, but there were definite similarities. It had feathery whiskers that divided into more threads as they left its face; and its eyes were smaller and further down its snout than an Earth cat's, making its appearance slightly uncanny. Its eyes were deep brown, and it was hard to see where the pupils ended and the irises began.

Commander Vince spoke to me softly out of the corner of his mouth. 'Jian, get out of here, find that scale, and call Shiumo *right now.*'

The cat leaned in close to Commander Vince and sniffed him. Commander Vince's eyes widened and he pulled back, then relaxed as he realised it was probably a cat greeting.

He smiled ruefully. 'I'm sure we don't smell pleasant – we have restricted access to water for bathing. We've all been in the dome together for so long that we've stopped noticing.'

I slipped away, and ran to my quarters to fetch Shiumo's scale. I tapped it a few times, then held it between my hands. Shiumo responded by tapping it back. I slipped the scale under the mattress, hoping it was sufficiently hidden, and went back to Commander Vince's office.

Alan, his assistant, had provided Commander Vince and the cat with food and tea, and they were sitting at Commander Vince's small meeting table. Emily stood next to the door, guarding.

The cat glared at the teapot. 'We do not touch the dragon drink.'

'Water?' Commander Vince said.

'That is acceptable,' the cat said.

Its body language seemed stiff and unresponsive; and its unblinking eyes – staring at each of us in turn – were disconcerting. I couldn't read any emotions off it at all. It registered like a mirror ball: self-centred and reflective.

'These are some of the vegetables we have grown here ourselves,' Commander Vince said proudly. I smiled; he'd been dying to show off our horticultural success. 'These are potatoes; we slice them thinly and cook them in hot fat to make them last a long time without refrigeration.'

The cat pulled out a small device and placed a potato crisp into it. It nodded, removed the crisp and popped it into its mouth with a flash of long sharp canines.

'Good?' Commander Vince said.

The cat shot to its feet and pointed what was obviously a weapon at Commander Vince, who raised his hands. Emily pulled out her revolver and turned it on the cat.

'Stand down, Emily,' Commander Vince said. He nodded to the cat, his hands still up. 'I'm sorry if you didn't like it. We have other food for you to try. We meant no insult.'

The cat swung its weapon to point it at Emily. 'Lower weapon. Slowly,' it said.

Do you want her to shoot it? I asked Commander Vince telepathically.

He shook his head. 'This may just be a misunderstanding. Let's not start a war.'

Emily put her gun on the floor, and backed off with her hands raised.

The cat turned back to Commander Vince. 'Give me all of them.'

'All of what?' Commander Vince said, confused.

The cat pointed with its free hand at the crisps. 'All of those foods.'

'I can't give you all of them – this is our *food*,' Commander Vince said. 'We need to eat. Perhaps we can trade them for other food?'

'You will find something,' the cat said. It gestured with the gun. 'The dragons will feed you. Show me how you grow this food.'

Commander Vince turned to exit the office, making strong eye contact with Emily as he passed. She held off, waiting for the right moment.

Shoot it the minute it's out of the office, I said in a general broadcast. *It's holding us hostage.*

Commander Vince and Emily shared a short nod.

The cat gestured towards me with the weapon. 'You go as well. Everybody else, stay here. I want those foods.'

I stepped out of the office, and ducked. There was a series of lightning-fast reports, and a few people shrieked with shock. The colonists who'd been waiting to ambush the cat all fell, dead. The air filled with the acrid smell of burning flesh.

Emily ran back to get her weapon, and the cat turned and shot her before she was through the door. She fell face down.

I took a step towards her – to find the cat's weapon in my face. It moved incredibly fast; faster than all of us put together.

'Emily?' I said, my heart racing.

She made no movement, and didn't appear to be breathing.

'Anyone else resists, they will die,' the cat said. It pulled out a different weapon, now armed in each hand. 'This one burns as well as kills. It will burn your home down. Now take me to the food.'

'Lawrence!' Alison wailed. 'It killed him.'

'Food. Now,' the cat said, still emotionless. I didn't respond, and it cuffed me on the side of the head with its weapon. 'Food!'

'Let's give it what it wants, Jian,' Commander Vince said quietly.

We took the cat through the oxygenated tunnel to the hydroponics house. Unlike the dome, it was a half-cylinder shape with a ceiling only just high enough to walk under.

Commander Vince was obviously waiting for the opportunity to attack the cat as he led it down the rows of plants. I followed. Two of us unarmed against one armed alien was bad odds, particularly one this ridiculously fast, but we needed to save our food.

There was a commotion back in the dome, and the cat turned. We took advantage of the opportunity and jumped it. It fired its weapon, producing a blinding white light. Searing pain shot through my shoulder.

We had the cat down, but it fired again, shearing off a large section of Commander Vince's head. He fell to the floor, dead.

The cat shoved me roughly away, and stood. It shot twice more, and I heard bodies hit the floor. I tried to stand, but stars spun around me. My arm was a blaze of agony and I slid to the floor, the air full of the smell of burned flesh.

The cat pulled out plants from the hydroponic channels, obviously looking for the potatoes.

Shiumo and Marque entered the greenhouse behind the cat, and I sagged with relief.

'Marque,' Shiumo began, but it was too late. The cat spun and shot at Marque, but the beam hit an energy wall Marque had placed in front of them.

'That is extremely bad manners,' Shiumo said. 'At least talk to us.'

The cat lowered the weapon, then shot at me again. I flinched, but Marque had shielded me as well.

'The humans are under my protection,' Shiumo said. 'I suggest you go.'

The cat raised its hands. 'I understand. I will leave.'

It shot at the roof of the greenhouse, dragging the weapon's beam down the side. There wasn't a pressure difference between the inside and outside of the greenhouse, but the oxygen escaped and breathing became more difficult. I gasped for breath. The air filled with oxygen again – Marque had oxygenated the energy bubble around us.

The cat calmly popped its breather over its head, then methodically ripped the potato plants out of the hydroponics tubes and placed them in a compost bin. It raised its gun, cut a slit in the end of the greenhouse, stepped through it and left with our plants.

Shiumo ran to me and put her front claw under my head. 'It's nearly taken your arm off! Marque!'

'It broke the main dome,' Marque said. 'I can't oxygenate that much air. We need to fold them all out before they suffocate.'

Shiumo folded me up to her ship. I screamed with agony as my shoulder hit the floor.

'I will be right back, darling Jian,' she said, and disappeared.

I lay back on the floor and stared at the stars, which were moving in layers. Some were the stars outside the ship; others were inside my head. I blinked at them as they grew red and fuzzy.

24

'I think she's coming around,' Shiumo said.

I opened my eyes, and tried to sit up but my shoulder hurt too much. I looked around; I wasn't in the dome and the air smelled fresher. Everything was tinted slightly turquoise.

'Am I back on Earth?'

'You all are. The cat destroyed the greenhouse and punctured the dome.' She walked away, and back again. 'I don't know why they have to be like that. Plenty of room for everybody.' She stopped next to me. 'What was so special about those plants anyway? Everyone keeps telling me they're not special and they don't know why the cat took them, but that's difficult to believe. There's something about them, isn't there?'

'No,' I said. 'They're telling you the truth. Potatoes are one of the most mundane vegetables we grow; they're mostly starch and don't have much flavour by themselves. I don't know why the cat reacted so strangely to them.'

'I will never understand the cats,' she said. 'Imagine killing people for *things*? It's incomprehensible.'

'Did we lose our whole colony?' I said.

She hesitated, then looked away.

'Shiumo. Did we lose the whole colony?'

'We saved fifty people. The rest suffocated before they could reach the breathers or I could fold them out,' she said, still not looking at me. 'It was too large an area for Marque to keep them all alive.'

'I had a relationship with Emily Walker, the security captain,' I said. 'The cat shot her.' I choked on my misery.

Shiumo gazed at me with her silver eyes. 'I don't know if she survived or not, dear Jian. We've yet to assemble the full list of your dead.'

'No.' I shook my head, and gasped with emotion. 'All for nothing! At least the other Earth colonies are safe.'

'We went to check on them ...' Her voice petered out.

Her emotion filled me with concern. 'They are all right, aren't they?'

'It will take years for the cats to reach your other colonies. They can't fold like we do. I'll keep an eye on them.'

I heard her hesitation. 'But?'

She sighed. 'I can't watch them forever; and if the cats decide to attack, there's no way for the colonists to contact me. I don't have any more spare scales to give them.'

'Give them mine. It was jammed under my bed on New Europa.'

'Are you sure?'

I nodded. 'They need it more than I do. Give me a replacement later.'

'All right. I'll give yours to the Japanese; they're closest to New Europa.'

'Thank you.'

'Your leaders are pushing me to have some half-dragon babies with volunteers,' she said. 'I don't want to, Jian, unless it's with you or Richard. But I don't see how I can leave you and return to my homeworld – and my other spouses – until you can transport yourselves around. I'll worry too much about you.'

Her voice became a warm buzz. She asked me a question, but I didn't understand it.

*

I wasn't really aware of the passage of time; the sunlight would be in one part of the ceiling, and then I'd open my eyes and it would be in another part, or gone altogether. The nurses came in, checked my IV, spoke words that had no meaning and then disappeared.

Then Shiumo appeared next to me, and everything snapped into focus.

'Only for ten minutes,' Nurse Chandra said from somewhere behind me.

Shiumo nodded.

'Hey, dragonlady,' I said, my voice gravelly from lack of use.

'Hey yourself, lovely Jian. Can you understand me?'

'Yep,' I said, and giggled. 'The drugs are making me really high. Everything's funny.'

'Maybe this isn't the best time,' she said.

'For what?' I said, still giggling.

A picture of Emily floated in front of me. 'Is that her?'

'She's alive! I knew you could save her!' Emily's face was swollen and bruised, but I was delighted to see her. I couldn't hold back my amusement at her tousled hair; she'd always been so military immaculate. 'She looks *awful*.'

'Definitely not the right time,' Shiumo said, and patted my hand. The picture of Emily disappeared. 'I'll be back later.'

'Sure thing, super-hot man,' I said. I raised my head slightly. 'Hey. Hey! Can I see the super-hot man? I *love* that man.'

'As much as you love Emily?' Shiumo said.

'Friends. With. Benefits,' I said, trying to be serious and failing. 'Why does everybody keep asking me that? I only love the super-hot man.'

'Okay,' Shiumo said softly. 'I'll come back later.'

'Thanks for the photo of Emily!' I said, trying not to laugh too hard and hurt my aching shoulder. 'She wouldn't be caught *dead* with her hair messed up like that!'

*

General Maxwell was sitting at my bedside next time I woke. My left shoulder was a grinding mass of pain, and I tried to move into a more comfortable position, wincing as the pain got worse. I gave up and leaned back. I had an awful feeling that something terrible had happened. Then I remembered the colony. And Emily. And the things I'd said about her when I was the closest thing to family she had left.

The general saw my expression. 'I know what you said about Walker, and it's not your fault, Choumali. It was the cat.'

'It was the drugs,' I said. I wanted to wipe my eyes but my shoulder hurt too much. So did my heart – it ached with the loss of Emily.

She took my good hand. 'Are you in much pain? I can arrange for someone to increase your meds.'

'I can deal, ma'am.'

She returned my hand to the sheet and patted it. 'We nearly lost you.'

'We lost the colony,' I said, miserable. 'Please don't have second thoughts – we need to try again. Earth's climate may regress after Shiumo leaves – there's still a chance it could end up uninhabitable. We need to start again in the stars.'

'Everybody agrees with you,' the general said. She crossed her legs and leaned her chin on her hand. 'But to do that, we need our own starship engines.'

'Oh, lord,' I said softly.

'I know,' she said. 'It's such a bad idea. How would we control the dragon hybrids? How long will they live? Can we arrange for another dragon to come and sire the second generation of full-blood dragons for us?' She straightened. 'When a half-dragon has a child with a human, they make another half-dragon; it's a dominant trait. Do you know how long it would take to replace our entire population with half-dragons if we let them reproduce freely?' She waved her hand. 'The mathematicians say as little as ten generations.'

'Shiumo said she won't do it.'

'I know, she told me herself.' She ran one hand over her greying blonde buzz cut, and her voice went hoarse. 'It's *my* job to make sure she does. I have to round up some volunteers and talk Shiumo into getting them pregnant.'

'That's so wrong!' I said. 'If a woman doesn't want it – if she's not actively seeking it – if she's doing it just for *duty* –'

'You agreed to be impregnated with two children when you joined the generation ship project, didn't you, Choumali? You agreed *twice* to be a mother out of a sense of duty. The King himself has fathered children because of duty.'

I subsided, stung. She was right. I'd been mentally preparing for pregnancy when the cat had appeared and destroyed the whole colony.

'Orders are orders, Lieutenant. Distasteful as the idea of a breeding program is, I think they're right and we have no other choice. Shiumo's talking about leaving Earth and going back to the dragon homeworld. She says she's been here much longer than she intended, and she misses her spouses and children. We still need her: without her, our colonies are completely isolated and will probably fail. The cats' home planet is close to our system, and you saw what a bunch of assholes they are. We've suddenly gone from peaceful colonisation of nearby planets to interspecies political bullshit – and I'd *still* like to know what the thing with the potatoes was about.'

'Let's get ourselves to Second and start trading opals – and perhaps potatoes, though I can't imagine why – for our own dragons,' I said.

She smiled and pointed at me. 'That is why I want you on my team. Hurry up and get better, Lieutenant, because we have a great deal of work to do. It's only just begun.'

I leaned back and stared at the ceiling, exhausted by even this short discussion. But there was something important I needed to ask ... I wrenched my shoulder as I sat up too quickly. 'What about Richard?'

Maxwell had half-risen; she sat again. 'What about him?'

'Is he alive? Did he accept Shiumo's scale? I heard nothing about him while I was on New Europa. Is he all right?'

Her face closed up.

'No,' I said.

'He's alive,' she said, and smiled grimly. 'Actually he's in this facility, in hospice care, but he's unconscious most of the time so it would be pointless to arrange a meeting for you. He's tough. The doctors gave him three months and he's already lived for more than six, but he doesn't have long.'

'He chose death?'

She nodded.

'He's so stupid. He should have taken that scale,' I said, turning away.

'Respect his decision,' she said.

I nodded without looking at her, and she left.

I didn't know how much time had passed when I woke again. My shoulder was still aching.

'Marque,' I said at the ceiling.

It didn't reply.

'I'm sure Shiumo left one of your spheres to keep an eye on me. I want to ask you something.'

More silence.

I'd just opened my mouth to speak again when it came into view.

'Shiumo won't make dragon babies for you,' it said, 'so don't bother asking. The general's wasting her time.'

'How far away is Richard's room?'

'Oh. He's two wings over, and one floor up.'

I moaned. Such a long way. Walking would be torture with my shoulder still so tender.

'Shiumo should have let me repair your shoulder,' Marque said. 'She raced back here with all the survivors and didn't give me time to treat you in my medical facility.'

'Can you do it now?' I said.

'No, Shiumo's taken the ship and the rest of me to assist your people to collect the bodies of the dead colonists. It will take a few days to recover them all.'

'I see. Hey ...'

'Yes?'

'You can make energy shields, right? Like you did on the train.'

'Yes ...'

'Could you use one of them to carry me?'

'Of course I could. But why –'

'Then carry me to see Richard.'

Richard's face was sallow and sunken. There was an IV in his remaining arm, and a feeding tube ran under the facial prosthetic into his nasal cavity. He wasn't emaciated, but his whole body screamed 'unwell'.

'Richard,' I said softly, touching his hand.

His eyelid flickered but he didn't move.

'I think you can hear me, and you know what I'm going to say.'

He remained completely still.

'You know Shiumo's scale will save your life. You need to accept it, Richard; it's so important. You have to live because we need you.'

He didn't respond.

'Richard, the colony was attacked and destroyed. We need Shiumo now more than ever, but she's leaving us.'

There was a long moment of silence, then Richard said without moving or opening his eye, 'How many people did we lose?'

'All but fifty.'

'Shit,' he said softly. 'What happened?'

While I explained about the cat, his eye opened and his slack face gained some animation, but he was a fragile shadow of the impressive man he'd once been.

'Shiumo wants to go home,' I said. 'If she leaves now, we're in deep shit. Without her we have no way to do supply runs, and every colony needed at least three during the establishment phase. We need her.'

'Please don't ask me,' he said, his voice hoarse.

'Just until the colony is established. Then I'll extract you myself.'

'You know what happens when we're with her.' He raised his hand slightly, then dropped it back onto the bed. 'We forget that she's manipulating us; we just want to be with her. If I return to her, I won't want to leave. I'll stop you from extracting me. I'll resist.'

'Then take the scale. It'll save your life, Richard!'

'No. If I take the scale, I'll fall under her thrall again and lose my individuality. I'll be under her control.'

'You people are so paranoid about this!' Marque said, above us. 'Shiumo should have ordered you to do something so you could see that she's not controlling you.'

'She did,' I said. 'She ordered me to attack someone.'

Richard's eye focused on me. 'And you didn't?'

'No.'

'Did you feel the urge to do it? Did you want to please her?'

'No. I told her she was being ridiculous actually.'

'See? She's not controlling you,' Marque said.

'That proves nothing. I feel completely different when I'm with her,' Richard said. He panted a few times, gasping for air. 'Don't deny it: she did something to our heads.'

'It's called *love*, you stupid human,' Marque said. 'You love her, she loves you – you should be together. Love is the greatest bond you organics can attain. Treasure it.'

'Leave this room right now,' Richard said.

'Jian, talk to him!' Marque said.

'Out! Now!' Richard collapsed back onto his pillow, wheezing.

'Just think about it,' Marque said, and left the room.

'The answer is no, Jian.' Richard turned his head away. 'I will not hesitate to give my life for King and Country, but my soul is another matter.'

'You won't even accept the scale?' I said, forlorn.

He shook his head, still looking away. 'I suppose I should be willing to make any sacrifice for Earth, but …' His voice became rough with emotion. 'No.'

25

'Just for a walk around?' I said.

'No,' Doctor Green said. 'You *stay in bed*. Every time you move that shoulder, the bones go out of alignment. You nearly *lost your arm*, Jian! If you can't do as you're told, I'll put the whole damn thing in a cast, and you'll be stuck in bed for six weeks.'

'All right,' I grumbled.

Nurse Chandra came in. 'General Maxwell's here for Jian.'

The doctor pointed at me. 'No. Walking.' She turned to Chandra. 'Let the general in.'

Chandra leaned out of my room into the corridor. 'You can see her, ma'am.'

'How's she doing?' Maxwell asked the doctor.

'She'd recover faster if she'd just keep still. She keeps sneaking out of bed to go visit Commander Alto.'

'I'm right here, you know,' I said. 'I can't sit in bed all day! I need to get up and walk around. And Richard needs me.'

'You're staying right here until that shoulder has knitted,' the doctor said. 'Richard doesn't even know you're there, Jian. He's unconscious most of the time. So stay put.'

I banged the bed with my good hand.

'We'll leave you to it,' Doctor Green said to the general. She glared at me. 'Stay in bed!'

'And if you need to use the bathroom, call me,' Chandra added with exasperation.

I waved my good hand at them. 'All right.'

They went out.

'I just wanted to check up on you,' Maxwell said.

A man spoke into my head. *Lieutenant Choumali, this is Psi Agent Tapu'o. The general is concerned that the Marque thing is watching you. Is that correct?*

Yes, I said.

Is it telepathic?

No. It's never replied to my telepathic requests, even when they were urgent.

Very well. General Maxwell will speak to you through me. She will leave you alone now, and you are to feign sleep. I will speak for her, and you reply directly to her. Understood?

General, I said, *please confirm that Tapu'o is going to speak for you.*

'Choumali, do you remember Psi Agent Tapu'o?' the general said. 'He helped with some of your psi training.'

'I do, ma'am.'

'He's been promoted. He's doing a great deal of high-security work now, with my full support.'

'That's very good news, ma'am.'

'How's the shoulder?' she said.

'Healing.'

Her tablet pinged, and she checked it. 'Ah, sorry. Duty calls.' She rose. 'If you hear from Tapu'o, listen to him. He has a great deal of excellent advice.' She nodded to me. 'Now rest.'

'Ma'am,' I said, closing my eyes and leaning back on the pillow.

Please give the general time to walk out to the garden, Tapu'o said. *If you are too fatigued by talking with her, tell her and she will let you rest. She will talk through me. I will relay for her; you reply to her directly. Understood?*

Understood, I said. Then to the general: *I understand, ma'am. I should have warned you about Marque's contempt for security protocols when we last spoke.*

I am speaking for her now, Tapu'o said. *Not your fault – you were heavily sedated. I had your room thoroughly scanned and it came up clean. And then you talked to the AI and the damn thing appeared on the security cam. It had been there all the time. I should have known better, dammit.*

I smiled slightly. That was definitely General Maxwell.

I came straight here after I read your report, Tapu'o continued.

I should have told you immediately what the cat said, I replied. *I drove the staff nuts yelling at them to pass it on to you.*

I know, they told me. And even though you were heavily sedated and in a lot of pain, you were right to draw it to our attention. The cat really said that? Mind control, uncontrolled reproduction and half-dragon babies? Nobody else on the colony heard it.

All of our greatest fears right upfront, I said.

Are they working together – good alien, bad alien? Perhaps the cats' role is to scare us into wanting to make our own dragons.

The cat tried to shoot both Marque and Shiumo on sight, I said.

It must have known it would be ineffective, Tapu'o said.

The cat didn't have scales on its head, I said. *It didn't read as anything but antagonistic towards Shiumo – what little I could read anyway. She was right about them being narcissists. I've never seen such a self-absorbed mind in my entire life.*

That's true, Tapu'o said. *If the cats were working with the dragons, they'd be breeding with them as well. And if so, the cat wouldn't warn us against the dragons; it would encourage us to have 'relations' with them. But breeding with dragons is the only way we'll gain interstellar travel. We're stuck in a corner, and the only way out has a huge 'This is a Setup' sign above it.*

There is another way, I said. *The cat offered us a ship in exchange for our children.*

Holy shit, it wanted our children? Tapu'o said. *Uh ... sorry. The general said: What could it possibly want children for? The mind boggles. And it does!*

And what sort of ship? I said. *How do the cats' ships travel if they don't have dragons to fold them?*

I asked Shiumo, Tapu'o said for the general. *She said they have warp drive, and that's why they haven't joined the Dragon Empire. I asked her why she couldn't give us warp ships so we can transport ourselves around the galaxy.*

I sat straighter, then winced as my shoulder twinged. I feigned sleep again. *That's a perfect solution.*

She said she will give us warp ships if we really want them, but time dilation is a serious issue. It might take ten days to travel to New Europa on a warp ship, but on Earth twenty-five years will pass. If something happened to the colony and you sent someone back to Earth for help, it might take that person two weeks to travel back on a warp ship but the colony won't see the help for nearly fifty years. We might as well wait to breed our own dragons; we'd arrive there about the same time.

Did she say that? I said. *That we should breed our own dragons?*

No. She just pointed out the time dilation effect and let us make the connection ourselves. But if the dragons and cats are working together, the cats are seriously on the losing side. Every time they travel any distance from their home planet, they lose their entire family.

From what I saw, that wouldn't be an issue, I said.

She was telling the truth when she called them assholes, Tapu'o added with humour. *Earth's oxygen level went down while you were on Wolf, and Shiumo had to boost it again. Without her around, the oxygen will be gone in a hundred years.*

We can't talk Richard into keeping her here? I said.

Richard is unconscious most of the time. He doesn't have long. Oh, that's awful, I didn't know, Tapu'o said. *Sorry, that was me. Speaking for the general now. We need this breeding program. We'll just have to strictly control the reproduction of the resulting children.*

What about another dragon to sire a second generation? I said. *Without that, the whole idea is pointless.*

Shiumo needs to agree to making the dragonscales first.

Is that still your job? I asked her.

Damn straight. And yours is to help me. The funeral for your fellow colonists is next week, and the King himself will preside. You have to be there – because Shiumo will be as well.

I'd prefer to stay away from her –

Tapu'o cut me off. *We know, but she wants you back. She won't take anyone else. We tried to insert an intelligence agent to talk to her about the breeding program, but she'll only take you or Alto. So you're ordered to make her agree to it.*

I hesitated.

I know you don't want to do this, but you're our only chance, Tapu'o continued. *We'll extract you when the job's done. Make the sacrifice, let her control you for a while, and I'll ensure you never have to speak to her again.*

I grimaced, my eyes still closed. *I don't want to have her children. I never wanted children, and I only agreed to impregnation for the sake of humanity. Isn't there another way?*

You misunderstand. We don't want you to have her baby. We want you to talk her into impregnating at least five or, even better, ten women. We need at least ten dragons if we're to succeed in interstellar colonisation.

You must want a child from me if I can't make it happen, I said.

As a last resort, yes. We have five volunteers lined up already to have the children. If Shiumo agrees, you don't need to participate if you don't want to.

That knowledge filled me with relief. I thought about it: I could probably talk Shiumo around if it was only five women.

Just promise me you'll ignore all my protests and extract me when the job's done, ma'am. I felt a stab of pain. *I promised the same thing to Richard and he still said no, even though it would save his life.*

I promise, Tapu'o said for the general. *I hate this idea as much as you do, Choumali, but it's necessary. You have the intelligence to succeed, I know you do.*

I understand now how Richard feels, I said. *The idea that I'll lose my free will ... it's terrifying.*

Oh lord, I didn't realise ... Sorry, Tapu'o said. *The general says: we'll protect you. Now rest.*

Ma'am, I said.

From me, Tapu'o said. *Cheers, Lieutenant, and good luck. The whole planet's counting on you. This is an extraordinary sacrifice, and you'll go down in history.*

Thanks, Agent Tapu'o.

Signing off. The general says take care of yourself.

*

I was jerked awake by a gurgling squeal, followed by loud whispers in the hallway.

'I can hear you,' I called. 'Come on in.'

Dianne and Victor entered the room, followed by my mother with David in her arms. He was five months old and holding his head up, but didn't appear to see me. He was a small mid-brown lump with close-cropped black curls and bright intelligent eyes who was fascinated by everything in the room at once. He mouthed a plastic ring he was holding, and a vast amount of sticky saliva covered his chin and chest. He dropped the ring, and my mother caught it before it hit the floor.

Dianne rushed to me with her arms out.

I raised my good hand and planted it on her chest. 'Stop, stop, *wait*!'

She hesitated, confused.

'My shoulder is giving me no end of grief,' I said. 'I can't hug you. Please don't sit on the bed. Any movement hurts like anything.'

'Aren't you on drugs for the pain?' Mum said, full of compassion. 'That sounds awful.'

'I am, but it's still agony. The cat nearly took my arm off, and it's taking a long time to heal. Sorry, guys.' I smiled ruefully, and waved my good hand towards the visitor chairs. 'Sit with me and tell me what you're up to.' I wiped my eyes. 'God, I missed you so much.'

They shared a smile and sat.

'You're a hero again, sweetie,' Mum said, shifting David so he was more comfortable in her lap.

He wriggled and put his arms out towards Victor, and Mum passed him over. He instantly put his arms out for Dianne and made a fuss about going to her. She took him, and he put his arms around her neck and buried his face in her shoulder.

'Pass the parcel with a bub,' Victor said. 'Tell us what happened to the colony. There isn't much information on the news. You were attacked?'

'I can't tell you much – it's still classified,' I said. 'The colony was succeeding, we were going well. Then a cat came and destroyed everything – for potatoes, of all things.'

'*Potatoes*?' Victor said.

'Seriously?' Dianne said.

'I know. So many of my friends were killed by that asshole. It breaks my heart.'

David wriggled, and Dianne turned him on her lap so he was facing me. He smiled at me and I smiled back, and he dropped the ring again.

'Dammit,' Dianne said. She hoisted him onto her hip and took the ring into the bathroom to wash it.

'Teething,' Mum said.

'Oh, you little turd!' Dianne said inside the bathroom. She came back out and the room filled with the smell of faeces. 'It was a liquid one and it's all up his back. Pass me the bag, love?'

'No, I'll do it,' Victor said, picking up the baby bag, which was bigger than my duffel. He hoisted it over his shoulder and put his arms out for David.

Nurse Chandra appeared in the doorway. 'I can smell that from the nurses' station! I've got one about the same age – the poo is revolting when they're teething. Give him to me. I'll clean him up, and every nurse on the floor will spoil him. You stay and talk to Jian.'

'He may not like you,' Victor began.

Chandra took David off Dianne and made some ridiculous faces with matching noises. David laughed hysterically, and the sound made me smile.

Chandra put David over his shoulder, grabbed the baby bag and went out. 'Look what I have, Susanne!' he shouted.

David howled with delightful baby laughter from the end of the corridor, and we all smiled.

'So what's the plan for Lieutenant-First-Class-with-Gold-Clusters Choumali now?' Victor said as he sat again. 'Are you going back to the barracks in Manchester?'

'We're part of galactic society now – we need people like you out in the stars,' Dianne called from inside the bathroom where she was washing the mess off her arms. 'Have they talked more dragons into transporting our ships yet? I want to visit other planets and see all the aliens Shiumo talks about. Imagine the new biologies we could encounter!'

'You belong out there,' Mum said. 'I hope they can find a way for you to return. What you were doing was so important!'

I sat quietly, thinking.

'I know that face,' Dianne said as she came out of the bathroom and sat down. 'It's the "how much can I tell them?" face.'

'There may be a way to get as many dragons to carry our ships as we want,' I said, 'but it'll take a while. General Maxwell has me working on the program. In thirty or thirty-five years we may be able to travel as much as we please, anywhere we please, with as many dragons as we need.'

'Can't wait,' Dianne said with enthusiasm.

'Why thirty years?' Victor said.

I shook my head.

'Is the program hard?' Mum said. 'Sounds hard if it's going to take thirty years.'

'I think General Maxwell can pull it off,' I said.

'Well, since Shiumo extended all our lives that's not an unreasonable wait,' Mum said. 'I may even be able to travel with you myself.'

'I would really love that.' The idea lifted my heart – that my awesome courageous mother could go into space and see its wonders.

'Oh, sweetie,' she said with compassion when she saw my face.

'So we need to design and build ships for these dragons to carry,' Victor said.

'And work out diplomatic protocols for when we meet the aliens,' Dianne said.

'And apply for membership of the Galactic Empire,' Victor added with enthusiasm. 'We can only speculate what other advantages the dragons' technology can bring us!'

'This has changed humanity, Jian,' Mum said. 'Two years ago we were looking extinction in the face. Now we're longer-lived, healthier, and some of us may have the chance to go out and tour the stars.'

'All because of you,' Dianne said. 'I can't believe it – my Jian, the one who made the First Contact and changed everything forever. You know my colleague John, the historian at the university?'

I nodded.

'He wants to interview you – from a historical perspective – to keep a full record for future generations. Your actions are making a massive historical impact.'

'One of the greatest women in history,' Mum said with satisfaction.

'I think that's General Maxwell's title – she's been the driving force behind this,' I said. 'It's always a team effort.' I smiled around at them. 'And you're my team.'

David howled down the hallway, and we all made faces. Chandra appeared in the doorway with the baby crying and struggling in his arms.

'Time's up. Sorry, guys,' Chandra said. 'The little tyrant wants his mums and dad and there's no consoling him.' He looked at the three of them. 'Lieutenant Choumali should rest now anyway. She has a lot of healing to do.'

Dianne took David and he quieted immediately, still shaking with tiny gasping sobs.

'We'll leave you to it,' Mum said to me. 'As soon as your shoulder's good enough to leave the hospital, come and stay with me in the village.'

I nodded.

They said some more stuff before they went out, but I didn't really register it. Dr Green was right: just this short chat had been exhausting, and the drugs were making me drowsy.

*

I was in a wheelchair with my arm in a sling when I attended the funeral for our colonists. There was only room for the surviving colonists and the immediate families of those who had died – and it was still nearly three thousand people. The King himself presided, and my fellow surviving colonists sat with me as we farewelled our colleagues. Shiumo and General Maxwell stood behind the King as he spoke about our bravery, and thanked Shiumo for helping us. Eight hundred and forty-six coffins went into the flames, the families of the lost colonists sharing their grief. I'd only known my colleagues for six months, but it felt like we'd been jammed into that dome forever.

The King stepped forward to speak, snapping me out of my reverie.

'Our colonists had just begun to terraform New Europa,' he said. 'They were working to give future generations a breathable atmosphere and food to eat. All that was taken from us by aliens with no respect for the lives of others. Commander Geoffrey Vince gave his life to protect the colony. And fifty people were saved thanks to the quick thinking of Lieutenant Choumali and the generous assistance of Princess Shiumo.'

Everybody nodded to me. I kept my face impassive. If I'd been a better soldier I would have stopped that damn cat before it took everything away from us. If I'd grabbed Emily's weapon and shot the cat, none of the other colonists would have died.

The King continued to speak but I zoned out, the pain meds making me drowsy and dulling my grief. Flashes of memory of the other colonists hit me as the King named them. Every single member of my team had died: Lawrence and Alison, pregnant with their first child; Elise, who could also have been pregnant; Ronnie, Gordon and Pattie; Ben, with his bad jokes about 'green food' that had helped to keep us going; Marcia, who had adored the animals she'd looked after; Edwin, who I'd taken through basic training myself. All the security officers I'd worked with had been killed trying to save the other colonists. And Emily. She and I had started to build something really good together. I understood her challenges and frustrations as head of security, and she genuinely didn't care about me being psi. They were all gone. The colony had been devastated.

I wiped the tears from my face. Many of the other colonists had broken down and were sobbing.

After interminable speeches from a variety of dignitaries, including Shiumo, the Prime Minister and General Maxwell, the King closed the ceremony.

He shared a few words with the others on the stage, then turned and looked straight at me and gestured for me to join them. I checked behind me; it was definitely me that he wanted to see.

Yes, you, silly Jian, Shiumo said. *Come on up. He wants to thank you.*

'Uh ...' I looked around for the private who'd been pushing my wheelchair.

A Marque sphere whizzed to me. 'Hold on to the chair. I'll carry you,' it said.

I squeaked as the wheelchair lifted into the air. The other colonists made loud sounds of astonishment — then started to applaud, embarrassing me horribly.

My chair landed on the stage with a bump that made the bones in my shoulder grind painfully together.

'Sorry,' Marque said.

I lowered my head in a clumsy attempt at a bow to the King. 'Your Majesty.'

I'd never seen him this close before. He looked nothing like the face on our coins and screens, and wasn't nearly as good-looking as his portraits made him out to be. He was taller than I'd expected, but that could have been because I was stuck in the chair. His skin was darker in person — darker than my own — and his hair was longer than on the coins, twisted into dreads and touching his shoulders. I felt stupidly awkward with this tall young man — the same age as me — who I had no idea how to interact with. Then he grinned, full of good humour, and I relaxed.

'I'm glad the colony had you — and your dragon scale — there, Lieutenant Choumali. Without you, the cat would have killed everybody.'

'I think the success of my entire military career so far is based on me being in the right place at the right time, Your Majesty,' I said.

'One-in-a-million psi, trained military, brave and intelligent – but yeah, it was just "right place at the right time",' Marque said.

'Marque's right,' Shiumo said. 'Don't underestimate yourself, dear Jian. It took real courage to attack that cat when it was armed and you weren't.'

'They're both right,' the King said. 'We'll make sure you're suitably rewarded.'

General Maxwell nodded. 'Only proper that your valour be acknowledged.'

'I didn't do anything,' I said.

'Now, Jian, we all know that's not true,' the general said. 'I recommended you for the Military Cross, and the King has approved it. We'll promote you to full lieutenant as soon as the mourning period is over.'

'The Military Cross is way too much!' I said. 'It was just one cat.'

'It was armed. And you weren't,' the King said. He smiled at the general. 'I think you should receive the King's Medal, but General Maxwell said you'd refuse it outright, and then I wouldn't be able to have my fun.'

'You're not wrong,' I said under my breath.

An aide approached us. 'Your Majesty and Princess Shiumo – if you would like to come with me, we have refreshments.' She gestured towards a nearby marquee.

'Marque, bring Jian, and be *gentle* this time,' Shiumo said. She focused on me with her silver eyes. 'Would you be willing to come up to my ship so Marque can fix that shoulder for you? It can have you as good as new in five minutes.'

I hesitated. Had the mind control started already? I'd set myself a task after the general had ordered me to get close to Shiumo again: I wouldn't tell her the mission goal, or that I'd been ordered to go to her. As long as I could keep that secret and pretend I was going with her of my own free will, she didn't have full control over me. I checked my feelings: I didn't feel forced to go onto her ship; I could say no if I wanted to. Although having my shoulder fixed and being free from pain sounded good …

'Accept the offer, Lieutenant,' the King said, broadcasting more than just goodwill. 'You deserve the best treatment, and Shiumo can restore you better than we can.'

The general eyed me sternly. Time to do my job.

'I can't disobey an order from my monarch,' I said. 'Is the pool still there?'

Shiumo gasped with delight. 'You'll come back to live on the ship?'

The King nodded meaningfully at me.

Will you have me just as a friend? I asked Shiumo. *I don't want to be more than that. Do you still want me if I can't give you more?*

'Yes!' she said. 'Of course! I love having you around, as a friend, companion, assistant – whatever. You'll really come back to me?' She frolicked down the stairs like a new lamb. 'Please say you'll come back!'

I bowed to her from my wheelchair. 'I'd love to, Princess.'

'We'll have that shoulder fixed in a jiffy, and then we have so much to do,' she said. 'I need your help. We're planning to repair the colony dome and make it ready to receive new people. This is wonderful!'

A rush of excitement, mirroring Shiumo's, filled me. I was returning to my luxurious quarters on her superb ship to travel the stars and re-establish the colony. I couldn't wait.

Marque lifted my chair and floated me down the stairs, and over the grass towards the marquee. It gently lowered me at the entrance, and pushed me past two grim-faced King's Guards. Twenty senior politicians and military were already inside. Marque pushed me to a table where the Prime Minister and the Home Secretary were waiting for us.

Shiumo looked at the food on the table. 'Any potatoes? I still haven't had a chance to taste them, and Marque hasn't seen them yet so it can't copy them for me.'

'The Marque on New Europa saw them,' I said.

'It never synched back with the rest of me,' Marque said. 'Part of my consciousness is gone forever. The cats have some sort of device that disables me. I don't know how they do it, and I *hate* it.'

'Under the circumstances, we thought it would be inappropriate to serve potatoes,' the Prime Minister said. 'Disrespectful to the families.'

'I understand, but I'd still like to taste them,' Shiumo said. 'They don't seem much at all from your broadcasts.'

'We'll arrange it,' the Prime Minister said.

'Now that I have you out of the crowd,' the King said to Shiumo, 'there's something I've been wanting to ask you.'

'What's that?' she said.

'I've heard you have a two-legged form that's strikingly different from this one?'

'Yes ...'

'Could you show me?' he said, flashing her a politician-level charming smile.

Shiumo glanced around. 'Will anybody be embarrassed? My two-legged form looks like a naked human.'

General Maxwell linked her hands behind her back. 'I'd like to see it too, Princess.'

The Prime Minister nodded her agreement.

Shiumo placed her glass on the table, and shifted to become the dark-skinned dream man. He smiled at me, and my heart – and other parts – responded. I'd missed him.

He put his arms out, fell to four legs, and changed back to Shiumo's dragon form.

There was complete silence around us, then a loud buzz of conversation as people discussed what they'd seen.

'You certainly gave them a show, Shiumo,' the King said. 'Thank you. I wanted to see that – I'd heard so much about it.' He turned to the general. 'What did you see, Charles?'

'My husband,' she said. 'As he was when he was younger, but definitely him.'

'That's a sign of true love, General,' Shiumo said. 'You are blessed to have such a connection with your spouse.'

The general smiled. 'I know.' She glanced up at the King. 'What did you see, Your Majesty? If you don't mind me asking.'

'A tall white man with glorious long auburn hair and the same silver eyes,' the King said.

'You're transitioning next year, is that correct?' Maxwell said.

'Yes,' the King said. He raised his glass of water. 'No alcohol while they're starting me on the hormones.' He took a sip. 'Cannot wait for it to be finished.'

'I didn't know this was a problem for your people,' Shiumo said. 'What a unique situation. A King who will in two years become Queen.'

'We are the first species you've encountered with transgender members?' the King said with interest.

'Oh no,' Shiumo said. 'It's very common. Philosophers claim it's something to do with the nature of the soul not matching the vessel, but it's such a minor inconvenience that nobody really cares. You are the first species I've encountered where it's considered an issue.'

'They tell me you are pan-sexual and pan-reproductive,' the King said. 'If I were pan-reproductive it would have saved me a lot of grief. I could have transitioned when I realised I was dysphoric instead of waiting until after I had fathered a couple of heirs.'

'Yes, we dragons are pan-reproductive,' Shiumo said. 'But we're so long-lived that interspecies reproduction isn't a good idea.'

'Hasn't stopped you from having *thousands* of children,' I said.

'Thousands?' the King said, shocked.

'She's procreated with *coral*,' I said, amused. 'Thousands of spawn.'

'That's about as pan-reproductive as you can get,' the King said. 'And the half-dragon children are able to procreate with their own species?'

'We call the half-dragon children dragonscales,' Shiumo said, 'because of the scales on their heads. They can have children with dragons or their own species, but no others. If a dragonscales has a child with their own species or a fellow dragonscales, it's another dragonscales. If a dragonscales has a child with a dragon, you have another dragon.'

'A full-blood dragon?' the King said.

'Well, mixed with the external species – but yes, it has all the attributes of a full-blood dragon. I shouldn't be talking about this,' she said. 'It's a terrible idea.'

'And these dragons can fold as well?' The King was broadcasting curiosity, but he must have read the report. They were setting Shiumo up to agree to the breeding program.

'Your Majesty, it's a terrible idea,' Shiumo said. 'Believe me, you don't want to interbreed with dragons. The resulting children will be more long-lived than you are –'

'But the second generation will be pure dragon and able to fold?' the King interrupted. 'What do the first generation look like? I'd love to see.'

'I think you've already seen the first generation,' Shiumo said. 'Those aliens that visited you – they all had scales on their heads, didn't they? They might have been under their feathers or fur, but they were there.' She shook her head. 'Coming here like that was a serious breach of protocol, and they tried to bully you on top of it.'

'You're leaving soon, and we need to restart our colony,' the King said. 'Without your help it will fail. Will you make some dragonscales for us so we can have our own dragons?'

Shiumo broadcast mortification. 'What you're suggesting would reduce me to a stud animal!'

'Oh, I'm terribly sorry,' the King said, but his remorse wasn't matched by his emotions. 'What a tactless thing to say. I sincerely apologise.'

'Would it be possible to employ dragons to carry our ships for us?' the Prime Minister said. 'What if we traded opals, or potatoes?'

'Would any of your fellow dragons be willing to help us?' the King said.

'There aren't really enough of us dragons to go around,' Shiumo said. 'The Empire is enormous, and we're all busy with our spouses and children. I doubt anyone has the time to be a starship engine for you. I've already spent far too much time away from my families. Some of my spouses miss me terribly – and I miss my children.'

'Then help us to make our own starship engines,' the Prime Minister said. 'What about artificial insemination? Is that an option for you? Could you donate?'

'No,' Shiumo said. 'It has to be me in person, so the ... I'll say sperm but not really. I have an organ that modifies my reproductive nature to suit the recipient's cellular structure. Once it's modified, impregnation is guaranteed.'

'Every single time,' the Prime Minister said with awe. 'What if we bring you volunteers? How many would you be willing to impregnate?'

Shiumo hesitated, looking from one of us to another. Then she shook her head. 'Such a proposal reeks of a deeply immoral value transaction instead of a free act of mutual pleasure. If it was Jian or Richard, I'd consider it. But not anyone else. I'm sorry I can't be more help.'

'Of course. We'll leave it there,' the Prime Minister said, and shot me a sharp glance.

I'm on it, I said to her. She nodded slightly in reply.

26

After Marque had fixed my shoulder, I sat with Shiumo in the ship's main gallery area to share some dragon tea, the spectacular stars shimmering above us. I noticed with a smile that the sculpture I'd given Shiumo was on display on its own plinth in the art gallery.

'Jian?' Shiumo said.

I snapped out of it. 'Sorry. I'm just glad to be back.'

She gestured towards me with her teacup. 'It's completely pain-free now?'

I rotated my shoulder and nodded. 'Like new.'

'Good. Now we need to hurry and find a way to bring Richard up here so we can save him. Marque says he doesn't have long.'

'He's incredibly stubborn, Shiumo. He won't come back even though it's killing him.'

'He's unconscious right now,' Marque said. 'He's past the point of rejecting our help. We could bring him up without telling him and just do it.'

'That would be deeply unethical and I'm surprised you'd even suggest it,' Shiumo said.

'I like him,' Marque said. 'It's been six months since you separated. If he were fully restored, I think he could survive the heartsickness. We just need to get him up here so I can fit the biologicals.'

'Would the General let me take Richard if I returned him immediately after restoring him?' Shiumo asked me. 'I won't keep him here against his will. I just want to save his life!'

'He'll come if the general orders him to,' I said.

'But she's respecting his decision. The Prime Minister agrees with her. None of them will order him up here. They're prepared to let him die instead.' She lowered her head. 'I wish I'd never met him now. I've cost him so much.'

'You should warn people before you start a relationship with them. You need to tell them that loving you and leaving you is lethal,' I said.

'I have *never* had this problem before. Everybody takes a scale if they leave me – dragons' scales are prized symbols of prestige throughout the Empire. Nobody else has accused me of this ridiculous mind control!' She shook her head. 'There has to be a way to save Richard. Come on, Jian, you know your people. How can I save him?'

The opportunity was too good to pass up. 'Why don't you offer to impregnate some women with dragonscales in return for saving him?'

'That's a trade!' Shiumo said. 'It's so wrong! There's a word for that – Marque! What's the word for trading sex for favours?'

'Prostitution,' Marque said.

'That was an honourable profession,' I protested.

'You people are so strange,' Shiumo said. 'That there should even be a market for such a thing ...'

'Save Richard's life, and help humanity to the stars,' I said. 'Nobody loses that way – especially if we return Richard to Earth immediately. Send another dragon to create the second generation of starship engines, and we'll be able to carry our own colonists to safety if we need to. Everybody wins.'

She hesitated, watching me with her silver eyes.

'Can you arrange for a dragon to parent the second generation?' I said.

'Of course I can. Some of my sisters would love the idea. Look at Zianto – she'll sleep with anything, and she loves experimenting with new species.'

'Wait – she's your *sister*,' I said, shocked. 'We can't have the dragonscales reproducing with their own aunt!'

Shiumo waved one claw. 'That doesn't apply with dragonkind. Our genetic natures are so different that by your standards we are entirely unrelated to each other. It wouldn't make a difference to us or to them.'

'Really?'

She nodded. 'Trust me.'

'It's worth it to save Richard,' I said.

'I know.' She lowered her head. 'If I didn't love him so damn much I wouldn't even consider this.'

'I'm very fond of him too, and I think it's worth it,' Marque said. 'As Jian said: nobody loses.'

'Can you guarantee that what happened to Richard won't happen to the volunteers?' I said. 'Having sex with you won't kill them?'

'Well, your Home Secretary is just fine, so I can confidently say "yes" to that,' she said.

I choked with laughter. 'How many human partners have you had in the last six months?'

'Let's just say I had so many offers that I could afford to be extremely selective.'

'They offered even after what happened to Richard?'

'Oh, absolutely. Many species will take enormous risks for sexual pleasure, particularly when it's with royalty. And I assured my partners that the same thing wouldn't happen to them. Richard's a special case because of the love we share.' She tilted her head. 'Not even the slightest twinge of jealousy. Remarkable. You really are an exceptional example of humanity, Jian.'

I shrugged, and my shoulder didn't hurt at all. 'You and I are friends, and I don't want more than that.'

I felt a small flush of satisfaction. I hadn't told her everything. I really did have control.

'Marque, contact General Maxwell and tell her the terms,' Shiumo said. 'Three women a day for thirty days, then I'm going home. I'll ask Zianto, or maybe Hanako, to parent the second generation.'

I recoiled with shock: ninety? 'That's exceptionally generous,' I said.

'It's how many you'll need if a colony is attacked by cats and they have to move everybody in a hurry,' she said. 'If we're going to do this thing, let's do it right.'

I felt a wrench when I saw that Shiumo had maintained my room on the ship exactly as I'd left it. My clothes were still in the wardrobe, and the collection of fantastic scented personal products that Marque had made for me were still in the bathroom.

The Prime Minister appeared on the screen and I turned up the volume. She was announcing that applications to join the breeding program had been thrown open to any woman who wished to take part. The feed down the side of the screen filled with comments from people speculating how valuable it would be to have a dragon in the family, then the server went down under the rush.

The door chimed.

'Yes?' I said.

Marque spoke to me from the ship's wall. 'Jian, Shiumo's bringing Richard up. She would like you to be present to help us with the transition to full biological. He may be anxious, and a friend will ease the process.'

'Of course.'

'And please help us convince Richard that we're not brainwashing either of you,' Shiumo said to me as I entered the main gallery. 'Are you ready? I'm bringing him up now. As a show of good faith I'm also bringing the King, General Maxwell and the Prime Minister to give them a tour of the ship.'

I stood at ease. 'Ready when you are.'

Shiumo disappeared.

'She's using the pod, Jian,' Marque said. 'They're bringing a crew with them.'

'A crew of what?'

'Journalists. Cameras. Guards.'

'Oh,' I said, and went down the corridor to the pod room.

'They're here,' Marque said.

The pod door opened. The King had brought two of his Guards, and with the general, a journalist and a live camera operator, the Prime Minister, and Richard on a gurney with Nurse Chandra at his side, the pod was crowded.

I saluted them. 'Welcome aboard Shiumo's ship.'

Shiumo popped into existence next to me, and jumped from foot to foot. 'Yes! Welcome. Let me show you around.' She hesitated, watching Richard, then turned towards the main gallery. 'Let me know if the transparent walls make you uncomfortable, and I'll opaque them.'

As I guided the visitors to the main area, the camera operator filmed it all, her mouth hanging open. The journalist with her was Waleed Choudry, the same man who'd interviewed Shiumo when she first arrived.

I fell into step next to Nurse Chandra, who was pushing Richard on the gurney. Richard was awake, and broadcasting extreme fear overlaid with grim courage and determination. He was sure that he was sacrificing his free will for humanity.

'Relax, Richard,' I said. 'I'll be here for you all the way. We'll send you back down when it's done. Shiumo's promised not to keep you here.' I put my hand on his. 'I'll look after you.'

'I said no to this,' Richard said. 'I'm only doing this for humanity on the condition that she releases me, returns me to Earth and never speaks to me again.'

'I'll make sure that happens,' I said.

'Thanks, Jian,' he said softly. 'I'm lying here wondering what it will feel like to be in her thrall again.'

'You say "in her thrall" when it could just be love,' I said.

'Of course you'd say that – you're in her thrall as well.' He shifted his head slightly and winced. 'I missed this place so much. We had some good times here, didn't we?' His emotions filled with desperate longing hope. 'I just wish I could be sure she's not controlling me.'

'That's beside the point, because you'll be returned to Earth as soon as the procedure is done, whether you like it or not.'

He nodded, and Nurse Chandra rolled him forward to join the rest of the group, who stood gazing at the Earth.

'Does the ship have a bridge?' the general said. 'Is there a central location for your controls and interface?'

'Not as such,' Shiumo said. 'Since I'm the engine and navigation, I don't need anything like that. And Marque controls the internals of the ship.'

The group stood rapt, watching the Earth as it turned below us.

Shiumo sidled to Richard, grim and quiet on the gurney, and placed one claw on his remaining arm. She gazed into his eyes. He avoided her gaze for a while, then met it. She raised her claw towards his face, then lowered it. He appeared to be listening to her – she was speaking to him telepathically. He raised his hand as if to brush her face, and she tilted her head and closed her eyes, welcoming it. He withdrew his hand and looked away.

'I'll make a tour guide,' Marque said. 'Give me two minutes.'

'Good idea. You can interact with our visitors more effectively in that form,' Shiumo said. She turned to the group. 'While we wait for the guide, do you have any questions?'

'I noticed that Marque is more than one sphere,' the King said. 'Does it have a central repository of memory and processing on the ship?'

'Oh, well spotted. You're the first human to ask me that,' Marque said from the walls. 'You should have a child with Shiumo as well, Your Majesty; the resulting dragonscales would be both royal and exceptional. I have a central processing core, a large one – nearly a metre to a side – in the middle of the ship. It's mostly data backups for when my different spheres synchronise.'

'So you're a kind of distributed intelligence?' Waleed, the journalist, said.

'Exactly,' Marque said.

A tall well-built young white man with flaming red hair down to his waist walked out from the aft of the ship. He was wearing a short grey tunic that flattered his toned body.

The King's mouth widened into a delighted grin as he looked from Shiumo to the young man.

'I didn't know there were other humans on the ship,' the general said. 'What's your name, sir?' she asked the man.

'I'm Marque in an android body,' the man said with Marque's voice. 'Your tour guide.' He bowed to the King with a wry grin. 'I can make android forms of any species to interact personally with you. What do you think, Your Majesty? Did I do well?'

The King laughed. 'Yes, you did.'

'What would you like to see?' Marque said. 'Would you like a tour of the solar system?'

'I'd like to see more of the ship first,' the general said. 'Any chance of visiting your core?'

'It's encased in metre-thick ceramic polymer,' Marque said. 'So ... no.'

'Marque, please show them Jian's swimming pool, the guest quarters and the hold, while I set Richard up,' Shiumo said. 'Then I'll take you all on a quick tour of the solar system myself, and we can have tea in the rings of Saturn.'

Marque gestured towards the rear of the ship, and the group followed.

'Nurse Chandra, you too,' Marque said from a sphere above us. 'I have Richard; you don't need to push him any more. Leave him with us.'

Chandra checked with the general, who nodded, and he joined the group.

Richard's emotions ramped up again, and he gripped the sheets with his remaining hand.

'Jian,' Shiumo said, and showed me how to use my psi skills to mildly sedate him.

'No,' I said. 'Richard, Shiumo just asked me to sedate you. I won't. I'll leave your mind completely clear throughout the procedure.'

'I appreciate it,' Richard said. He scowled at Shiumo. 'You should have given me a choice.'

'I knew you would say no,' she said, and gestured with one claw. 'This way.'

She guided us towards the bow of the ship, and stopped. The floor fell away below us. Richard's fear increased even more. I put my hand on his and he held it.

Please give me your word that you'll only do what you told him you would, I said to Shiumo. *Don't mess with his head.*

I won't, she said, gazing into my eyes with her silver ones. *I love him too much to ever hurt him.*

We descended into a bare white room with a table in the centre, similar to an operating theatre. Richard's panic intensified.

'Richard, you're close to meltdown,' Shiumo said. 'Please allow me to ease this for you.'

'How painful will the procedure be?' he said.

'Completely painless. But it will be very disturbing if you're in the wrong frame of mind – which you are now. Please, for your own sake, let us sedate you.'

'No,' Richard said.

'Richard –'

'No!' he said. 'Just do it and let me go.'

She sighed with feeling. 'It would absolutely be for the best if you closed your eye.'

He lay there stubbornly watching us.

'You're as bad as Marque,' she said. 'Ready, Marque.'

Richard floated off the gurney and onto the operating table. His fear turned to determination. He was ready to give his life.

I shook my head with admiration at his courage.

'I know, Jian,' Shiumo said. She spoke to Richard. 'Permission to remove your clothing, sir.'

'Oh,' I said. 'I'll –'

'Don't leave, Jian. There's nothing to see,' Richard said. 'Granted.'

Shining white arms descended from the ceiling and sliced his clothes from him with blades that were obviously extremely sharp. They morphed into claws that removed the fabric, leaving Richard naked and small on the table. His body ended at the top of his thigh on the left side; and the damage was nearly up to his waist on the right, with the right arm and shoulder gone. His skin bunched together into a mass of scar tissue over the injuries. Two bags containing his waste were locked into openings in his abdomen.

'The face prosthetic next,' Marque said from the ceiling. 'I need you to remain completely motionless while I cut it off. My apologies.'

White slabs projected from the table on either side of Richard's head, and his eye widened. He trembled as the vice held his head in place, and the prosthetic detached itself from his face and lifted away. A dome of darkness appeared over Richard's face, and flashes of light shone through it. There was the faint smell of burned flesh, and the dome disappeared. The vice holding Richard's head retreated. The hole in his jaw was visible again, and the top of his head was a mass of scar tissue.

Richard was shuddering, his hands shaking.

'He's going into shock, Marque,' Shiumo said. 'Richard –'

'No!' Richard said through chattering teeth. 'Jian ...' He raised his left hand and clutched at mine. 'Just finish it.'

'Jian, you know what happens next,' Shiumo said. 'Tell him to close his eye.'

'Do as she says, Richard,' I said. 'Can I keep hold of his hand?'

'No,' Marque said from above us. 'Richard, close your eye.'

'You don't want to see this,' I said. 'I went through it when they fixed my shoulder, and it's just like a warm bath with your eyes closed. Don't hurt yourself more than you need to.'

Richard gritted his teeth and released my hand. He stared stubbornly at the ceiling.

The bed changed to shiny white liquid, thick and cloying, and his eye went wide. Marque lowered a mask over Richard's face as he sank into the liquid. Richard took a huge deep breath and screamed into the mask as he was swallowed by the table, disappearing into the liquid.

'That is much more disturbing to watch than to experience,' I said, my throat full of pain for Richard.

'If you close your eyes it's not disturbing at all,' Shiumo said. She hoisted herself onto her hind legs and leaned on the table. 'He's completely lost control in there. He's panicking.'

'I have him,' Marque said. 'He's restrained. He can't move.'

'That will make it worse,' I said. 'The poor man will have nightmares.'

'He already has nightmares,' Shiumo said softly.

Ten long minutes passed. I couldn't sense Richard's emotions; the table interfered with my empathy.

'Is he all right?' I said.

'He is,' Marque said. 'Give me three more minutes. The nerve endings are extremely fiddly, and there's a great deal of scarring on his brain and spinal cord.'

'Take your time and do this right, my friend,' Shiumo said.

'I've run out of things to show the guests. I'm giving them a tour of the art,' Marque said. 'They're asking how much longer the procedure will take.'

We waited a few more agonising minutes, both Shiumo and me radiating tension.

'I'm bringing him up,' Marque said. 'I think he passed out. He's stopped fighting me.'

Richard emerged from the liquid, the mask still over his face, but he was healed and whole. His eyes were wide and he was breathing frantically into the mask. I received his emotions full-on and he was terrified.

His new body parts were a slightly lighter colour than the rest of him, and the completely hairless skin had a finer texture with smaller pores – like a baby's. Otherwise, it was indistinguishable, with no visible seam where it joined. He was in full health, and his skin glowed with wellbeing.

'I'm letting him go slowly. If he thrashes I'll restrain him again,' Marque said.

Richard, relax, it's over, I said.

Breathe, my love, breathe, Shiumo said. *You are not drowning, and you are whole.*

Richard panted into the mask, wheezing as he sucked at the air.

'Richard, you're hyperventilating,' Marque said. 'I'm feeding you more carbon dioxide. The procedure is over. Relax so I can take the mask off.'

Richard's eyes unfocused and his breathing slowed. His eyes rolled up and he lost consciousness.

'Well, about time,' Marque said. It removed the mask.

'Is he all right?' Shiumo said, leaning on the table. 'Marque, he's unconscious! Is he –'

'He's fine. He just fainted. Give him a moment to come around,'

Marque said. 'All vitals are normal except for the flight-fight-shock thing. I haven't touched that. I've left him to –'

Richard shot upright with a loud gasp. He looked at us, then down at his hands. He rubbed them together, then moved them over his thighs. He wiggled his toes, and felt his face, and moved his jaw.

He held out his right arm and studied it. 'This is the first time ...' He stroked his forearm with his left hand. 'The first ...' His voice became hoarse and he choked. 'The first time this arm hasn't hurt me in ...' He broke down weeping. 'Years. For years that arm has been hurting so damn much ...'

He turned so his legs were over the edge of the table, put his hands on either side of Shiumo's face and gazed fiercely into her eyes. 'That arm has caused me phantom limb pain for years, and the drugs didn't help. I'm free of pain for the first time in ...' He choked again, and lowered his head. 'So many years. Thank you.'

Shiumo changed to her two-legged form, and sat next to him on the table. She put her hands on his face, and touched her forehead to his. 'I love you, and I will do anything for you, beloved.'

'Thank you,' he moaned through the tears. 'Oh god, thank you.'

Shiumo covered his face with kisses, and I felt a twang of jealousy at seeing the dark-skinned man of my dreams with Richard. Their mouths met and they melted into each other. The room filled with so much yearning love that I bent under its impact. My eyes filled with tears at their desperate need.

They pulled back, and Shiumo smiled as he ran his hand down Richard's face. 'I am glad I could do this for you. Now go.'

Richard looked into Shiumo's eyes, then touched his forehead to Shiumo's. The illusion became apparent as his face disappeared into Shiumo's nose. I wondered what Shiumo looked like under the glamour.

Richard ran his hand down the side of Shiumo's head, through the hair, then picked up an invisible lock and twined it through his fingers.

'Leave me now,' Shiumo said. 'Go back to your people. I won't keep you here.'

'Give me some time,' Richard said. 'I need to be sure this is what I want.' He gazed into Shiumo's eyes. 'Will you wait for me?'

'For all eternity,' Shiumo said. He put his hand on Richard's face and smiled. 'I will always be here for you. Keep my scale with you. Call me any time and I will come, my love.'

They kissed again, then Shiumo hopped down off the table and changed back to her four-legged form.

'Take us up to the others, Marque,' she said.

'Not until Commander Alto's dressed,' Marque said. A uniform emerged from the table. 'There you go, Richard. Pop that on, and you can show off your dashing new body.'

I turned away to respect Richard's privacy as he reached for the clothes and pulled them on.

'Oh. One more thing,' Marque said. 'Don't panic if the genitalia don't work as required for a few weeks. It will take some time to ... prime the pump, so to speak. Expect to be impotent for at least three weeks. If it lasts longer than four, let me know and I'll have another look.'

Richard nodded. 'I'd prefer to be undersexed right now. It will take me some time to grow accustomed to having a full body again.' He walked up and down. 'Damn. It's like I never lost them.' He opened and closed his mouth. 'I can eat real food!'

'You make me so happy, Richard,' Shiumo said.

He gazed at her for a long time, and the room filled with their love.

'I do love you,' he said.

'My hearts are yours,' she said. 'Once the human mothers of my children have been chosen, you have thirty days before I leave for my homeworld. Take some time to think about us, and be absolutely sure what you really want.'

He nodded.

'I'll return for you seven days after I've finished with the mothers,' she said. 'If you want me then, I will bring you up to my ship and we will travel the galaxies together. If you don't, I'll never contact you again. The choice is completely yours, my love.'

'I understand,' he said.

'Our visitors have finished the tour of the ship and want to see Saturn,' Marque said.

'Let's go,' Shiumo said.

The ceiling opened, the operating table disappeared into the floor, then the whole room lifted up to the gallery level, where the others were waiting.

The King's mouth fell open into a huge delighted grin when he saw us. 'Richard!' He strode to stand in front of him and studied his face. 'Can I hug him?' he asked Shiumo. 'He's not in any pain, is he?'

'I'm as good as new,' Richard said, his voice hoarse. 'It's like I was never injured.'

'That is wonderful news,' the King said, and embraced him. He pulled back and kissed Richard on the cheek, then held Richard's hands in his own and smiled through tears of joy. 'Thank you, Shiumo. Richard suffered horribly to save me.'

'My pleasure, Your Majesty,' Shiumo said. 'I think you love him as much as I do.'

The King put his hand on Richard's face. 'He's been like a father to me.'

Richard hugged the King again.

'That truly is remarkable, Princess,' the Prime Minister said. 'Any chance of sharing that medical technology with us?'

'I will provide it for my children,' Shiumo said. 'I will build them a safe haven, with full dragon-level medical and educational facilities. A Marque will stay here with them, and I'd like,' she swung her head on her long neck towards me, 'to train a trusted aide to be their teacher, so they can learn to take their place in the Galactic Empire as grandchildren of the Empress herself.'

'Of course they must have the very best,' the Prime Minister said, eyeing me meaningfully.

'I will arrange everything for them,' Shiumo said. 'And I will return as often as possible to visit them – I treasure all of my children.' She sighed. 'I wish I could spend more time with them, but I keep falling in love all over the place.'

Richard placed his hand on Shiumo's shoulder. 'It's understandable, dear dragon.'

'Again, Alto?' General Maxwell said.

'Again, General, but she's sending me back with you when you go,' Richard said. 'She wants me to be sure.'

'Let's visit the gas giants,' Shiumo said. 'And I'll show you some of my favourite nebulas.'

'Can we see your homeworld?' the Prime Minister said.

'Not until you are firmly in Second and your credentials are accepted by my mother,' Shiumo said. 'It won't take long. After I've fathered your dragonscales for you, I'll go to Mum and ask her to give you accelerated membership, with all the advantages attached. Once you have dragons in your population, your membership of the Galactic Empire is immediate.'

27

General Maxwell, the Prime Minister, Richard and I stayed on the ship while everybody else returned to Earth in the pod. Marque provided us with tea and a variety of sweet and savoury finger food, and we sat at the table beneath the glowing Earth.

'What is this?' the Prime Minister said, raising one of the biscuit-like pastries Marque had prepared for us.

'It's a variation on Eniotimian night food that I thought you might like,' Marque said.

'What's in it?' she said. 'Not bugs or anything gross like that?'

'It's completely vegan, no animal products at all. On Eniotimia they grow a type of succulent plant that –'

'I don't think they need to know more than that,' Shiumo said. 'All of the food is synthetic – replicas of foodstuffs that Marque has sampled. It's chosen food for you that matches your chemistry, and everything is perfectly edible.'

'Thank you,' the Prime Minister said. 'I'd love a recipe; this is wonderful.'

'So what do you need to talk to us about without the King and the media present?' the general asked Shiumo.

'I'm concerned about the care and welfare of my offspring on your planet,' she said. 'I'll need some guarantees.'

'Of course, anything you like,' the Prime Minister said, still munching on the pastry.

'Within reason,' the general added.

'My children – all my children – are the most precious beings in the world to me. Of course they should stay with their mothers after they're born – they need to learn to be human – but once they reach maturity, I want them to come to a secure facility I will set up for them so they can learn to be royal citizens of the Empire.'

'Understood,' the general said.

'I would like Richard, with Jian's assistance, to select the prospective mothers of the first generation,' Shiumo said.

Richard's expression filled with shock, then understanding.

'I know you want to remove Jian and Richard from my so-called "mind control",' Shiumo said to the general. 'But they are the humans I trust the most. Jian is psi, and can assess the emotional state of the candidates. Richard already has a great deal of experience in selecting the best of the best for the *Britannia* project.'

She turned her head on her long neck to speak to Richard. 'Please do this for me. We will have as little contact as possible while I impregnate the women, but I want you to be the one who selects them.'

'And when you leave – what happens to Choumali and Alto then?' the general said.

'It's their choice.' Shiumo gazed at Richard. 'I don't want you to think for one second that I am influencing you. If you have any doubts at all once the mothers are chosen, then stay on Earth. I won't force you, my love. If you want to go with me, I will take you. If you don't, I will leave.'

'I understand,' he said.

Shiumo turned to me. 'Jian, will you care for my children for me?'

'Up to General Maxwell,' I said. 'She's my commanding officer.'

I'd prefer not to be a glorified babysitter, I added to the general.

'I think it's a brilliant idea,' the Prime Minister said through a mouthful of pastry.

The general's expression became stern. 'I'd like to discuss this with my people before we make a decision.'

Shiumo rose. 'I'll take you back down to the surface so you can discuss this with Jian and Richard in private. Where would you like me to drop you?'

'The lawn in front of the Houses of Parliament,' the Prime Minister said with satisfaction. 'The constituents will *love* seeing me chauffeured around by alien royalty.'

'The parade ground in front of New Whitehall it is,' Shiumo said. She gestured with one claw towards the aft of the ship. 'This way.'

'No, I meant –'

Shiumo cut the Prime Minister off. 'I know exactly what you meant, but I won't play your games. Madam?'

The Prime Minister harrumphed with a smile on her face, took two more of the pastries, then headed towards the pod.

*

The Prime Minister's car and security detail were waiting for her.

'I don't think I'm needed for the rest. You can handle it, Charles,' the Prime Minister said. 'Anything else you need?'

'No, ma'am. I'll talk to Choumali and Alto, and we'll begin the screening process.'

The Prime Minister juggled the pastries she was holding to shake hands with Richard and me. 'Well done, people – we made it. Just need to make sure she follows through. Good job.'

'Thank you, ma'am,' I said.

She hurried to her car, still clutching the pastries.

The general gestured with her head and we followed her into Whitehall. She stopped in the entry hall and glared at the floor. 'Marque, if you are present, please give Lieutenant Choumali and Commander Alto some privacy while we work out the logistics,' she said. 'Wait outside if you like. You can return to watching them when they leave the building.'

'I understand, General,' Marque said from above us. 'I'll wait outside. I respect your privacy and will not listen in on any conversations you have in the building.'

The general looked up at the sphere. 'Thank you.'

We followed her through the offices, and down in the lift to the secure area.

'I don't believe a word it said, but nothing we're about to say is classified,' the general said when we reached the conference room. 'Well done, Choumali. As the Prime Minister said: you did it.'

'To be honest, Shiumo required hardly any convincing,' I said.

'How do you feel, Alto?' the general said.

'Twenty years younger,' Richard said.

'And the mind control?'

'I had no trouble leaving her, and I don't miss her right now. I'm not even feeling unwell any more. Maybe I'm becoming resistant. Jian, are you upset about being separated from her?'

'Absolutely not,' I said.

'It could be resistance, or it could be that she's backed off on the mind control,' the general said. 'Either way, we have thirty days until the task is done. Can you do it? Say the word and I'll pull you out now.'

'I've sacrificed so much to do this,' Richard said. 'I want to see the job to completion. Humanity comes first. I can work with her for thirty days if you promise to pull me out at the end of it.'

'Same here,' I said. 'I'll leave her when we have ninety pregnant women.'

'She's determined you'll care for the children,' the general said to me.

I winced. 'Not my style at all.'

'And she thinks you'll go with her when she leaves for good,' she said to Richard.

'I know.' Richard sounded hesitant. 'But she's said I can stay here if I want. Just extract me when the job's done so I can make a decision about my future with a clear head.'

'I'll give you an office to vet the volunteers,' the general said. 'Choumali, do you want to return to Shiumo's ship now?'

'I'd prefer to stay here and help Richard. It's a huge job. As Shiumo said, I can assess the women's emotional suitability.'

'Very well,' the general said, and rose. 'Let's set you up and move this mission along.'

*

It took us a week to get the thousands of women who'd volunteered down to five hundred, using a similar system to the one Richard had used to select crew for the *Britannia*. These women were the best and brightest, leaders in their fields, scientists and professionals.

We invited them to an informal lunch on the space elevator island's grassy lawn before we began the final selection process. They were permitted to bring their spouses and families. Although we'd preferred single women, most of these high achievers were already in a relationship.

Richard gave a speech very similar to the one he'd given to the *Britannia* recruits. I zoned out through most of it, sitting behind him on the podium with Shiumo. It was strange to be back on the island where I'd gone through so much in the hope of being on the *Britannia*, and then again for the Wolf colony. I had a darkly humorous thought: maybe I was jinxing every project I'd been involved in.

I tuned back in as Richard wound up his speech.

'You are all exceptional examples of humanity,' he said. 'In the next week, five hundred will be reduced to the ninety who will be the grandmothers of a new generation of starship pilots.' He smiled at them. 'This time on the island is a "get-to-know-you" period. Don't rush to talk to Shiumo; she'll be interviewing each of you individually over the next week. Instead, mingle and meet the other candidates.'

The women began to chat together at the round tables that filled the lawn. The prevailing emotional tone was one of intense awkwardness, particularly as many of them had their spouses present.

'Are you sure inviting the spouses was a good idea?' I asked Shiumo.

'The emotional health of the spouse is as important as that of the candidate,' she said. 'If the woman's spouse doesn't agree to the impregnation, we can't go ahead. Both of them will be looking after my child, after all.'

We left the podium to sit at our own table on the lawn. Shiumo had a special couch to lie on. The wait staff placed plates of food in front of us.

I pointed to a plate. 'There you are, Shiumo. Potatoes. These are –'

'French fries! Yes, I know,' she said. 'They smell *wonderful*.' She removed the thick transparent gloves she wore when walking four-legged, picked up a potato chip and inhaled its scent. 'That is *exquisite*. Rich and nuanced.'

'Normally we wouldn't have French fries on a formal menu like this,' I said, 'but we knew you wanted to try potato. You can also eat it boiled, mashed –'

'Yes, I looked it up,' she said, and popped the chip into her mouth. She froze, her silver eyes wide, then chewed a couple of times. She raised her snout as she swallowed, her eyes closed, then turned to see me. 'And you called that *bland*.'

'Pretty tasteless, yeah,' I said, cutting into the steak. 'We sometimes add additional flavour, like vinegar or garlic salt, or sometimes essence of –'

'You humans really are completely nose-blind, aren't you?' she said. 'I mean, it's obvious because of your strong odours, but –'

'We don't smell that strong, do we?' Richard said.

'Not so much you as the chemicals you douse yourselves in,' she said.

'I remember,' Richard said, amused. 'The deodorant those soldiers were wearing made you sneeze for ages.'

'Some of the men are so ... *fragrant* they make my eyes water,' Shiumo said.

'They're covering their body odour,' Richard said. 'If we sweat we become *extremely* fragrant.'

'But it's like covering a scar with a searchlight!' she said. 'Besides, human sweat is not as bad as you think. A sweaty human smells warm and comforting.'

I gestured towards her plate. 'So, the potatoes are good?'

She put another chip in her mouth and spoke around it. 'I've never eaten anything like it before. It tastes of sunshine and warm air and the blue skies of summer. It tastes of the clean brilliance of the stars and the cutting cold of the emptiness of space. It tastes like the tenderness of a new child and the joy of a first love. It's pure pleasure, infinitely nuanced, deep and complex, and different every time I chew on it. No wonder the cat was willing to kill every colonist for it; I can't really blame it.' She looked up at Marque. 'You can't duplicate this, my friend. It's way too complex.'

'Let me see,' Marque said, and a chip flew up into its sphere. 'Good lord, I've never seen anything like this before. It's complex and changing, and the flavours are fractal in their nature – every time I think I have them identified, they gain another level of sophistication.' Its voice softened with awe. 'You're right, Shiumo. I can make a rough approximation, but I'll never be able to duplicate this.'

'I want to try all the potato dishes. I want to try sweet potatoes and yams,' Shiumo said. 'I want to try them with cheese; that's another wonderful flavour unique to humanity. The two together must be *amazing*. I want to try them baked. More French fries! Where can we get more?' She put her claw on my arm. 'Jian, more potatoes, please! Now!'

'I'll see what I can do after the reception,' Richard said.

'They're not rare and expensive, are they?' Shiumo said.

'Common as mud,' I said. 'More of a filler food than anything – tasteless, and mostly carbohydrates.'

'You are the most nose-blind race I have ever encountered,' she said. 'I wonder why you rely so much more on sight than any other ...' Her voice trailed off and she looked up. 'Oh.'

'Oh?' I said.

She gestured towards the half-moon shining in the daylight sky. 'You're hardly ever in full darkness, are you? Even at night, the moon lights your way. That's why you've evolved to be more sight-dependent. A large satellite like that is extremely rare.'

'So our sight is better than average?' I said.

'Nope. You're just nose-blind.'

'I suppose we are,' Richard said. He turned as a tall good-looking man approached us – one of the women's spouses. 'I'm sorry, can you wait until after lunch? You'll have plenty of opportunity to talk to Shiumo later.'

The man's emotions were locked down tight over hard tension. 'Dragon Princess,' he said to Shiumo. 'I know they said not to rush to speak to you, but –'

Shiumo raised one claw. 'I see your concern, sir. If you're not sure you want your partner to be in the program –'

She exploded in a wet cascade of body parts. The psi blast knocked my brain into the side of my skull and I rocked backwards. I fell out of my chair and sat on the ground, dazed.

'What the *hell*?' Richard yelled. 'Jian? Jian! Marque!'

I couldn't see – everything was fuzzy – and my ears thumped with pain against a background of screams and shouts.

'It was a psi blast,' Marque said, its voice strangely calm. 'He was psychokinetic.'

'Is he unconscious?' Richard said.

'He killed himself,' Marque said. 'Jian, how's your head? The blast hit you hard.'

'I can't see,' I said. My head felt like it was split open. I rested it on my knees. 'Is Shiumo dead?'

'In a way. Hold on, there's a sphere coming to take you up to the ship.' Marque raised its voice. 'Don't try to approach. There's an energy barrier around us. Stay back.'

There was a shriek.

'Stay back!' Marque repeated.

'Oh god, Shiumo,' Richard moaned. 'She's all over us.' He gagged.

'Found it,' Marque said with grim satisfaction. 'The sphere's here. Richard, help Jian – she's blinded.' It raised its voice again. 'Do not approach us. I'm taking them up to Shiumo's ship. Stay here, everybody; we'll return shortly.'

The air filled with the buzz of loud conversation and wails of grief, but I couldn't sense any emotions. A dark blob grabbed my arm and I pushed it away, blindly trying to defend myself.

'It's me,' Richard said. 'Let me help you up. We're getting out of here.'

'Follow me,' Marque said. 'I have the stone; everything will be all right. Come on, this way.'

The grass was a hazy green blur and Richard was a darker blur as he guided me. Then he grabbed me under the arms like a child and lifted me into darkness.

'We're inside a large Marque sphere,' he said. 'Sit on the floor.'

I sat, and felt the curved floor of the sphere beneath me. I rested my forehead on my knees and touched my scalp, expecting to find lacerations, but there were none. I was soaked with blood, and realised it must be Shiumo's.

'She's dead,' I said. 'She's gone. The dragons will destroy our entire planet in revenge.'

'No, they won't,' Marque said.

'Even if they don't, we'll all be dead in a hundred years when the atmosphere fails,' Richard said. 'What a stupid thing to do. *Why* did he kill her?'

'He may not like aliens. He may not like the fact that his wife will be having sex with an alien. He may not like the breeding program. There's plenty not to like about the whole thing,' I said. I leaned back. 'God, my head hurts. He was a powerful kinetic. I've never seen anything like that before.'

'He was drugged to increase his strength,' Marque said. 'It's possible his death was unintentional.'

'Drugged?' I said. 'There are no drugs that can increase a psychokinetic ...' I trailed off as I realised.

'So he had alien help – to assassinate Shiumo,' Richard said. 'Oh lord, she's really dead.' His voice became strangled with emotion. 'My Shiumo's gone.'

'I know,' I said, and wiped my eyes. My hands were a red blur. My whole face was wet with blood, but I didn't seem to be injured.

'What happens now?' I asked Marque. 'Will you take her ship back to the dragon homeworld? Let us come with you so we can apologise on behalf of our species.'

'You can apologise to Shiumo yourself when we get up to the ship,' Marque said. 'She'll be pissed beyond belief. She hasn't backed up her memories in at least forty-eight hours so she'll have lost all that time.'

'Wait,' I said. 'You can bring her back?'

'She's still dead,' Richard said. 'You could create a copy or a clone, but my Shiumo is dead.'

'See this?' Marque said.

I tried to clear my vision but everything was still a blur.

'Yes ...' Richard said.

'It's a soulstone,' Marque said. 'Attuned to Shiumo's soul. It takes five years for the stone to become attuned, but once it is, it connects her soul to her body. There is a cloned body ready for her back on the ship, but it won't have her consciousness – the spark of life – until I attach the stone.'

'So she's effectively immortal?' I said.

'Pretty much.'

'How do you know it's Shiumo's soul, and not someone else's?' Richard said. 'What *is* her soul anyway? It could just be the body's consciousness.'

'No,' Marque said. 'Each soulstone is unique, and once it's attuned to a particular soul the connection is permanent. You'll see when we get to the ship. The body will be alive and fully functional, but brain-dead. When I attach the stone, the body will tune itself to the frequency of Shiumo's soul, and she will reinhabit it.' Its voice softened. 'It's wonderful to see.'

'The *frequency* of her soul?' I said.

'We're here,' Marque said. 'Just a minute – we're entering the ship. All right, come with me and let's bring Princess Shiumo back to life.'

As Richard guided me out of the sphere, I tried again to clear my vision and failed.

'Am I permanently blinded?' I asked Marque.

'I'll put you into the table, and see if I can repair it,' it said. 'Ready?'

I nodded. Richard held me around the waist, and the floor fell away from under us.

Marque lifted me onto the table, removed my clothing, and put the mask over my face. Without Shiumo's mild sedation I had a moment of panic as I sank into the thick warm liquid; it felt like I was drowning.

I forced myself to relax, imagining I was in a warm comfortable bath.

Can you hear me? I said.

'You're speaking telepathically; I can see it.' Marque said. Its voice seemed to be right next to my ear. 'Keep quiet while I work on you, there's a great deal of bruising and swelling here – I need to reduce the pressure. I'm having a look at Richard at the same time to see if he was injured. *And* I'm checking the status of Shiumo's frozen spares – she had some particular specifications for her next body. Keep your eyes closed.'

The liquid receded and I felt a chill over my naked body.

Marque lifted the mask off my face. 'All right, open your eyes.'

I could see, but everything was still blurry. Richard was a fuzzy dark shape on the other side of the white room.

'I can't focus,' I said.

'That's from the swelling. It will take about half an hour for it to go down. How's your head?'

I sat up. 'Not hurting any more. Thank you.'

'You are most welcome.' A jumpsuit emerged from the table between my feet. 'Put some clothes on, and let's resurrect Shiumo.'

I had to peer at the jumpsuit to see where everything went, but once I had it on I felt much better. My eyes appeared to be clearing slowly. I could see the back of Richard's head as he stood facing away from me.

'Stand still while I lift you,' Marque said, and the floor rose so we were in the main area. 'Shiumo's spares are in the belly of the ship, next to my main storage. Come this way.'

A sphere emerged from the back of the ship and we followed it. It stopped at the entrance to the pod room, and a piece of the floor dropped again to carry us down to a large black-walled hall. Marque kept us behind a hazy energy barrier as we descended.

The room appeared to comprise a large proportion of the bottom half of the ship, its walls curving to match the dimensions. My eyes were clearing quickly, and I could see more detail as I looked around. The room was mostly empty, with strange installations protruding from the floor and walls that made it look like a postmodern-art gallery. The smallest was half a metre tall, and the largest stretched from the floor to the ceiling high above us. Some were simple white cubes, and some were complex black shapes carved with beautiful curling decorative designs. Others were complex multicoloured mazes of pipes and gears, moving incredibly slowly and ranging from small in size to enormous. There seemed to be no pattern to the objects' placement or size.

'This way,' Marque said, leading us to a featureless black wall with a large table in front of it. 'I'm pulling up Shiumo's specs. I want to make sure the body's exactly as she ordered.'

A drawer emerged from the wall above us and floated down to land on the table. The sides fell away to reveal a three-metre-long red dragon. It was the same colour as our Shiumo, and the face had definite similarities – but it had two leathery wings as well as four legs, and a large fin on its tail. Cold radiated from it, turning the surrounding air to vapour, and a rime of ice started to form on its scales.

'The specs are good,' Marque said. 'I'll imprint the brain with the stored memories.'

I expected Marque to open the body's brainpan to make the transfer manually, but nothing happened.

After five minutes of silence, during which time the body gradually warmed, the ice melting from it and flowing into the table, Marque said, 'Successfully restored. I'll fit the soulstone, and finish defrosting the body. It'll take another five or ten minutes.'

A clear transparent gem, colourless as glass, detached from the dragon's forehead and floated away. Shiumo's silver gem – the one that was sitting in her forehead when she was alive – floated out of the sphere and lodged itself into the depression on the dragon's forehead.

A soft black couch emerged from the floor behind us.

'Take a seat while we wait for her to come around,' Marque said. 'In the meantime, I'm sure you have plenty of questions about this process.'

'You said the soul is a frequency – of what?' Richard said. 'Sound? Light?'

'The electromagnetic band, but the wavelength is hyper-long. Hundreds of metres long. The scientists suspect it's a pulse wave bouncing through the universe that was created by the Big Bang itself.'

'Our souls are *echoes of creation*?' I said.

'Got it in one,' Marque said. 'Your bodies are receivers; your souls are like a signal – the body receives and interprets it. The soulstone is like ... a tuner, so to speak. It tunes the body to a particular wavelength – in this case, the wavelength of Shiumo's soul – and ensures the body contains her specific signal.'

'So all our souls are identical ... the same broadcast?' Richard said.

'No, it's an analog signal. Infinite variation. Each soul is a slightly different frequency.'

The ice had completely melted from the dragon now. It took a huge breath, then blew water vapour out of its nose. It took two or three more deep breaths, then shifted slightly, its breathing settling to a normal rhythm.

'Excellent,' Marque said with satisfaction.

'What if two people are tuned to the same signal?' Richard said. 'They'd have the same *soul*?'

'Doesn't your species have a legend about people who share a soul? You call them soul mates,' the dragon said, her eyes still closed. 'Haven't you met people who are *perfectly in tune* with each other? You even say in your language that people can be *on the same wavelength*. It's a rare and treasured thing when two people share the same soul frequency. In seven hundred years I've yet to meet anyone with the same frequency as me.'

'The ancients were right,' Richard said softly with awe.

'About reincarnation?' Marque said.

'Ugh. The brain connections aren't finished yet. Give me a minute,' Shiumo said – and it was Shiumo. Her mind felt the same, even though the body was different. She hoisted herself onto four legs on the table, then opened her eyes and stretched her wings. 'Oh good, I've been wanting them back for a while. How much did I lose, Marque? Where were we?'

'Forty-eight Earth hours – two Earth days. After the backup, you went to the island to vet the candidates for impregnation. One of the spouses wasn't happy about the situation. He blew you up with a psi blast.'

'Humans aren't strong enough to blow someone up,' Shiumo began, then stopped. 'Are you sure he's human?'

'He was human – the blast killed him. He was using drugs to boost his power,' Marque said. 'Must have had non-human help.'

'Ouch. Did you get a sample to trace the drug?'

'Yes. I'm analysing it now but am coming up blank on the source. We may have to visit Dragonhome to do a wider search.'

'Jian and Richard are safe, which is all that's important,' Shiumo said, and turned her head to look at us. 'I am sorry you had to go through that. It's not something we normally share early in a relationship. Some races go a little ... strange when they find out the true nature of the soul.'

'The ancient people of India knew all along,' Richard said. 'Hindu ... Buddhist ... both philosophies are based on the belief that souls transition from body to body. Reincarnation.'

'Where does your family name come from, Richard?' Shiumo said as the Marque sphere buzzed around her. It moved in close to her face and used energy to open her eyes and mouth. 'Your genetics say you are descended from the Indian subcontinent, but your name is extremely rare and not Indian at all.'

'My family have tried to track it down, but the paper trail ends at British immigration,' Richard said. 'When my great-great-something-grandfather arrived as an immigrant, he'd trained as a classical singer at the Delhi Conservatorium of Music. Apparently his name was too long, or too ethnic or something, and the immigration official saw his occupation – vocal, counter-tenor – and asked him what it was. "It's the male equivalent of being a contralto," my great-great-something-grandfather said, and that's how the name came about.'

'That's hilarious,' Shiumo said. 'You guys have even gendered your *vocal ranges*. I bet you've even assigned a gender to me.'

'Well, you sound female,' I said.

'Marque doesn't help. It refers to you as "she",' Richard said.

'Don't listen to her. If a species is gendered, she assumes the gender identity of whichever sex produces the babies,' Marque said. 'It's a conscious choice.'

'So you could sound male if you wanted to?' Richard said. 'That might have changed the way I related to you right from the start.'

'See? So gendered!' Shiumo said.

'My ancestor was lucky,' I said. 'The immigration official could pronounce "Choumali" so he was allowed to keep his name.' I smiled. 'It annoyed the hell out of my father, though; he had to keep telling everybody he was Welsh, not African. I have the same problem.'

'Good to go, Shiumo,' Marque said.

'All right. Back off and let's see,' Shiumo said, and spread her wings.

'I have you,' Marque said.

Shiumo beat her wings, hitting us with a rush of air. She rose ten metres, then flew around the enormous room.

'No way,' I said. 'No *way*. She is much too heavy to fly with those small wings. Is her body hollow or something?'

I'm quite capable of flight when the gravity is low, she said.

'You're carrying her?' I asked Marque.

'More like I'm reducing her personal gravity. She carries herself.'

Would you like a ride? she said, hovering above Richard with minimal flaps of her wings. He smiled up at her and they shared a moment of joint appreciation.

She lowered herself to land next to us, hind legs first and then front legs.

'You're the living embodiment of my home nation's emblem,' I said.

'Which nation?' Shiumo said. 'African Commonwealth? China?'

I snorted with exasperation. 'I just told you. Wales!'

'Of course. I remember that statue your spouse gave me. Marque, have you notified the Earth authorities that they don't need to prepare for conflict with my people?'

'General Maxwell needs proof you're alive,' Marque said.

Shiumo focused on us. 'Will I pass as myself? Or will the general think I'm a different dragon?'

Richard and I shared a look.

'Depends how much of this process you want to explain,' he said.

She lowered her head. 'I know I've been saying full disclosure out of respect for our new ties, but this is different. A human just tried to kill me. If he'd survived, he may have tried to destroy my soulstone – and they can be destroyed. Crush my soulstone and there is no way of bringing me back.'

'They call it the Real Death,' Marque said, and I heard the capital letters.

'So what do we tell the Earth authorities?' I asked them.

'Please don't tell them about the soulstone,' Shiumo said, gazing into my eyes.

'I won't,' I said, and she relaxed. 'But why don't you make a backup? Attune an extra stone, and store it just in case? It's dangerous only having one – what if it's damaged or destroyed by accident?'

'We can only have one soulstone, and it must be on our forehead at all times. If you remove the stone for storage, it loses its attunement,' she said. 'I think it is our only weakness.'

'Do the cats know about it?' I said.

She made a hissing sound of distaste. 'They *collect* our soulstones. They take them from us whenever they can, and trade them, and display them as trophies.' She thrashed her finned tail. 'Our souls are *trinkets*!'

'Why don't you go and get them back?' I said. 'I'd fight them to reclaim such treasures!'

'The stones they collect lose their attunement quickly,' she said, radiating misery. 'If a cat takes your stone, it's the Real Death. Waste of time trying to recover it.'

'Shiumo, a cat ship just pinged one of me at the edge of this system,' Marque said, its voice full of urgency.

'There's the source of the psi drugs,' Shiumo said with grim humour. 'Obviously the human was supposed to destroy me, and then my stone – but instead he died. How far away is the cat?'

'On the other side of the asteroid belt, heading in fast. Do you want me to stop it?'

'No. We don't want to aggravate it. You know what the cats are like. Piss it off and it might destroy Earth in retaliation. Ask it what it wants.'

'It's ignoring me. It's just landed on the surface where you were holding the reception for the reproductive candidates.'

'We have to get down there!' I said. 'And we need to be armed. I won't give one of those bastards another chance at us.'

A small black weapon, similar in appearance to a revolver, floated out of Marque and into my hand.

'Just in case,' it said.

'Only use it as a last resort, dear Jian,' Shiumo said as I tucked the weapon into the back of my waistband. 'Cats can be brutal when provoked, so diplomacy all the way.'

We put our hands on her shoulders and she folded us back down to the island.

28

The cat ship had landed on the lawn a hundred metres from the stage. The five hundred women and their families were being moved into the elevator building. A couple of Richard's staff were facing off with the cat on the stage, and nearly collapsed with relief when they saw us. Shiumo led us up to the stage to join them.

This was a different cat from the one that had destroyed the colony. It was covered in black fur and wore a dark grey jumpsuit.

'Good day, humans,' its translator box said in a cultured voice without an accent. It bowed to us. 'I wish to initiate trade relations with you. *Without*,' it bared its teeth at Shiumo, 'the interference of the evil dragons.'

'You are not welcome here,' Richard said. 'The dragons have never hurt us, but your kind have killed many of us. We are not interested in trading with you. Leave now.'

'I am not responsible for the actions of others of my kind. If they have hurt you, I sincerely apologise,' the cat said. 'They must have misunderstood your actions and reacted wrongly.'

'It attacked us without provocation and killed nearly a thousand of us,' Richard said.

'Then that was a tragedy. But not as much of a tragedy as what is about to happen on this island.' The cat stared, unblinking, at

Richard. 'I have watched your broadcasts, and see you are starting a breeding program with this dragon. Do this and your species will be extinct within ten generations. The dragons eradicate other civilisations by breeding them out of existence. I am here to stop the dragon and save your species.'

'Don't be ridiculous,' Shiumo said. 'That would only happen to animals that have no control over their reproduction. And these gentle sentient humans are not animals!'

'You lie so easily,' the cat said, its voice silky. 'We have seen it happen again and again. You conquer through reproduction.'

'You steal *children* to use as *toys*!' Shiumo snapped.

'We never steal them,' the cat said with fierce dignity. 'We pay their full value – and we value intelligent and cunning children very highly.'

Richard and I shared a shocked glance.

'They are an important commodity for many species. Such trade with us has made those species rich.' The cat glanced around. 'Your own children appear to be agile and smart. They would be an extremely valuable trading resource.'

'You torture children to death,' Shiumo said. 'Individual cats travel through space and steal children to sell. Whole species have been wiped out.'

'We never take them by force,' the cat said. 'And we never take more than can be replaced. It works well for everybody. We are honest in our motives and dealings – unlike you dragons, who breed entire civilisations out of existence as you lie to them about *your* motives.' It turned to Richard and me. 'Trade your children with me, and I will give you warp ships that are far superior to – and safer than – allowing the dragons to breed with you.'

'You're the one telling lies,' Shiumo said. 'Your warp ships come with a contract that forces any planet who buys them to join your Republic.'

'I am only here to trade,' the cat said. 'Warp ships for children. Give me fifty children, and I will give you three ships. If you refuse to trade, and continue to relate with this evil dragon, I will report you to my homeworld. We will be forced to welcome your planet into the glory of our Republic – for your own protection.'

'You will not!' Shiumo said. 'Invasion and occupation – that's all you think about! I *love* these people and I *will* protect them.'

'Bring the children to my ship. I am waiting,' the cat said, and walked back to its ship a hundred metres away.

'If we fight it, what are our chances?' Richard said.

'If you show it violence, it will retaliate with everything it has. It will blow up your planet, just like they did the Nimestas' home,' Shiumo said. She lowered her snout slightly. 'The best option is to do as the cat asks.'

'We will *not* give it our children!' Richard said.

'It's the sacrifice of a small number of children for the safety of your entire population, my love. You don't have a choice.'

I watched the cat as it walked back to its ship, casual and in control. 'Marque, how far away is their homeworld?'

'Thirty-seven light-years from here. There are a few independent non-aligned systems out here on the rim. The cats are one of them.'

'So if this cat sends a message home it will take thirty-seven of our years to reach its planet? And if they return here by warp – even though it's a short time for them, it will still be thirty-seven of our years?'

'That's right.'

'And they travel alone, right? They're like our Earth cats – fiercely independent?'

'Exactly.'

'Then we have seventy-four years to prepare for the war. They are not having our children.'

I kneeled, took careful aim with the energy weapon Marque had given me, and shot the cat in the back. I continued to shoot as it fell, until there was nothing left of it but a smoking hole in the ground.

'I can't believe you did that,' Shiumo said, her voice weak with shock.

'You killed it!' Marque said. It flew to the cat's body and hovered over it. 'If we –'

'Attempt to resuscitate it and I will shoot you too,' I said. 'It's the only one here, and it's a long way from home. If it sent a transmission, it will take more than seventy years for its fellow cats to find out what happened and come for us. I just gave us time to prepare.'

'Well done, Jian,' Richard said softly.

'That was so brutal,' Shiumo said. 'What sort of people are you?'

'People who are willing to do anything to protect their own,' I said.

There was a high-pitched wail from the cat's ship. A black cat – naked and furry, and only a metre tall – stood in the hatchway, screaming.

I lowered the weapon. 'Oh, shit.'

The little cat shouted something incomprehensible in a hissing, high-pitched voice.

'Goodness,' Shiumo said. 'That was the last thing I expected it to say after you killed its parent.'

'What did it say?' I said.

'It said, "I needed that servant",' Marque said. 'I'll translate.'

A mass of gold-coloured fur charged out of the ship, knocking the baby cat over in its haste. Its fur rippled as it galloped towards us on four legs, looking like a small long-haired bear.

'Dragonfather! Dragonfather!' it shouted in a deep gravelly voice.

'Hey, that's my *toy*!' the cat shouted, and stormed after the furry alien. 'Come back here. You're *mine*!'

The furry alien hid behind Shiumo. 'Take me home, Dragonfather. I'm grown up now. I can go home.'

'You're mine. Get back to the ship!' the little cat shouted. 'Move! Right now, or I'll *thrash* you.'

The furry alien took a few steps back as the cat approached us, then hid behind Shiumo again. 'Dragonfather, please – they promised. I'm all grown up and I can go home.'

'Return to the ship, and I'll take you both back to your homeworlds,' Shiumo said.

'No,' I said.

'We can't return the cat. It'll tell the other cats we killed its parent,' Richard said.

'You can't keep them here!' Shiumo said.

'We'll look after them,' I said. I turned to the furry alien. 'What's your name, little one?'

'I'm not little, I'm mature!' it said. 'My name is ...' It made a soft howling sound completely without consonants.

'And it's *mine*!' the cat shrieked.

'Give it a name in your own language – we all do that,' Shiumo said. She gazed down at the furry alien. 'Were you sold or stolen, child?'

'I'm not a child!' the furry alien said. 'I'm an adult and I can *go home*.'

'Marque?' Shiumo said.

Marque zipped around the furry creature, checking it over. 'Found the chip. Definitely sold. Not mature, so still the cat's property. By law we should return both of them to the Cat Republic.'

'I'm not going back!' the alien wailed. 'They promised that when I grew up I could go home, and I'm grown up now!'

I put my hand on its back. 'We won't send you back. We'll look after you.'

It cringed away from me.

The little cat stormed up to us and slapped the alien across the head. 'You're still mine, and we're going home!'

It made to hit the alien again, and I grabbed its hand to stop it. 'Oh no, you don't.'

The cat shook its hand free, and kicked me. 'You killed my parent! This is *my* toy.' It glared at the furry alien. 'You're coming back on the ship with me *right now*, and we're going home to claim my parent's property.'

'You have to stay here while we work out what to do,' Shiumo said.

'No, I'm going home!' the cat shouted, and raced back towards the ship.

I chased it, but it was much faster than me, moving with effortless grace. It leaped into the ship.

I stopped, then ran back towards the group. Everybody scattered as far from the ship as possible, concerned it would use a flammable fuel to take off. When we were all at least a hundred metres away, we stopped and waited. The hatch didn't close and the ship didn't move.

'It would make sense that its parent hasn't taught it to fly the ship, or given it access to the controls,' Shiumo said. 'I don't think it would hesitate to strand its parent if it had the chance, and head home by itself.'

Richard checked his tablet. 'The general's on her way. She says to stand by until she gets here. It'll take a couple of hours.' He looked at the cat's ship. 'Would it know how to use the cat's weapons?'

'I doubt it,' Shiumo said. 'Again, safety of its parent.'

I went back to the ship, and up the stairs. Its interior was different shades of dark grey, with soft fabric covering the floor and platforms on the walls. The little cat squatted on a carpet-covered platform, desperately thumping at a control panel that was a sheet of blank black glass.

'Take me home!' it shouted, and thumped the panel again. 'I am going to kill everybody!'

It saw me and scrabbled at the side of the panel. 'Give me a gun!'

It gave up and launched itself at me. It landed on my torso, dug its teeth painfully into my breast, and clawed my arms and thighs. I put one hand around its throat, and used the other to grab it by the scruff of its neck. I had the advantage of size, and it hung from my hands, spitting and attempting to scratch me. When it realised this was ineffectual, it clawed at my hands, leaving deep scratches.

I carried it outside by the scruff of its neck. 'Put it in an energy bubble before it flays me completely, Marque.'

The cat lifted away from me, still hissing, and Marque enclosed it.

'I guess you're *my* toy now until *you're* mature,' I said, shaking my stinging hands and spattering the grass with my blood.

The cat stopped hissing and struggling, and stared at me.

'Hold your hands up, Jian,' Marque said. It cleansed the wounds, and covered my hands with opaque white gloves. 'Leave those on for three days. They'll deaden the pain and help the scratches heal cleanly.'

'Can you take me home, Dragonfather?' the furry alien asked Shiumo.

'They won't want you, little one. If I return you, they will just give you back to the cats.'

The furry alien lowered its head. 'They said I could go home when I'm grown up. I am!'

'No, you aren't,' Shiumo said gently.

'Both of you are staying with me,' I said. 'I'll look after you.'

'Obviously not very well,' the cat spat, and slammed the energy bubble with one hand.

'Will you send me home when I'm grown up?' the furry alien said with hope.

'Absolutely. And nobody will hurt you any more. I'll be kind to you.' I turned to the cat. 'Both of you.'

'I just suggested you die horribly in a violent way that cannot be accurately translated,' the cat said, scowling. 'I want to go home.'

'So did your toy,' I said, pointing at the furry alien.

The cat squatted and glowered at me.

*

'Don't bother talking until we're inside,' General Maxwell said when she arrived, and stormed past us and up the hill. 'Shiumo's still here?'

'She is, ma'am,' Richard said.

'Good. Show me the way.'

We led her to the main conference room, where Shiumo and Marque, together with the little cat and the golden bear alien, were waiting. The room had a table large enough for ten, and posters of the *Britannia* ship and the Wolf colony's dome on the wall. Marque had made an energy cell for the cat in the corner of the room, and it squatted inside it, sullen, next to a puddle of its own urine. Every time Marque cleaned it up, the cat made a new puddle.

The general frowned when she saw the aliens, and the frown deepened when she saw Shiumo's new body.

'It's really me, I'm still Shiumo,' she began, but the general cut her off.

'Can you still impregnate our volunteers? It's vital that the program goes ahead.'

'Don't you think we should take some time to consider the implications of what just happened?' Shiumo said.

'No,' the general said. 'We made the trade. We let you heal Alto; now you must keep your side of the bargain. Ninety half-dragon children by the end of thirty days. Fulfil the agreement.'

'That's cold, Charles,' Shiumo said, her voice soft with awe.

The general smiled grimly. 'Princess – or whoever you are, which is really beside the point – my job is to make strategic choices that maim and kill the bright young men and women under my command. You haven't even begun to see the cold I'm capable of.'

'I made the agreement. I'll stand by it,' Shiumo said, gazing up at her.

'Excellent.' The general studied the cat and the furry alien. 'And now we have these two to care for, as well as the dragon babies.'

'I'll care for them,' I said. 'They're my responsibility.'

'But you said –' Shiumo began.

'This is different,' I said. 'I'm responsible for their current situation. I have to do what's right by them.'

'Well done, by the way, Lieutenant,' the general said, flashing me a tight smile. 'You're in line for another medal after what you did. Lightning-fast thinking on your feet, and you gained us nearly eighty years to prepare.'

'I would prefer not to receive a medal for shooting someone in the back, ma'am.'

'You dishonoured yourself to do what was right. You doubly deserve it.' The general turned back to Shiumo. 'You will impregnate our volunteers, and the babies will stay here. *Your* babies will stay here. And in seventy-four years, when the cats come to find out what happened,' her smile filled with satisfaction, 'you will assist in our defence.'

Shiumo opened and closed her mouth. 'This was a setup.'

The general scowled. 'Of course it wasn't. Don't be ridiculous. But if you're telling the truth about your maternal instincts, I know you'll help us.'

Shiumo lowered her head. 'My mother is going to kill me.'

'Then I suggest you head directly home – *after* you've fulfilled your contract – and talk to her about how you're going to protect the planet where your precious children live.'

'This isn't how it's supposed to turn out!' Shiumo protested.

'Tell me, Princess, how *is* it supposed to turn out?' Maxwell said with biting aggression.

'Love should be free,' Shiumo said.

'Feel free to love your children,' the general snapped back. 'Now go and make them. Alto will finish the selection process within ten days – and then you'll be experiencing a great deal of free love.'

*

General Maxwell stood with Richard and me, radiating tension. Her daughter hadn't been one of the original selections for impregnation, but a volunteer had dropped out and Linda had been a reserve. She was the last woman to be with Shiumo. Four others, who had been with the dragon over the past couple of days, waited with us to help her recover from the experience.

Linda came out of the room, flushed and glowing. She was taller and more slender than her mother, and shared the same blonde hair. She radiated the sexual satisfaction that Richard had shown after his first time with Shiumo. Every woman who'd been with Shiumo had come out with a smile that didn't fade for days.

'You all right?' General Maxwell said, touching her daughter's arm.

'I'm okay. That was a unique experience.' Linda looked at the other women. 'You should have warned me,' she said as she straightened her shirt. She raised her hand. 'I know – you did warn me, but I still wasn't prepared.' She glanced back at the room where Shiumo was. 'That was ...' She shook her head.

'You sure you're okay, Linda?' General Maxwell said. 'I can arrange help for you ...'

'No, I'm fine,' Linda said. She turned to Richard. 'I'd be taking her up on her offer to travel with her if I were you, Commander Alto. Having *that* for the rest of your life? Worth any sacrifice.'

'I'm not so sure about that,' Richard said, and handed her a tablet. 'Sign this, please.'

She signed the tablet and passed it back, then smiled at the other volunteers. 'I'm glad you guys are here.' She nodded to the general. 'I appreciate you being here, Mum, but I need to talk to them.'

'I understand,' General Maxwell said. 'You've all said that. I expected it.'

'Come and share with us,' one of the volunteers said. 'You can't discuss it with anyone else, and we understand.'

'Do you need me for anything else, Commander Alto?' Linda said.

'No,' Richard said. 'Thank you for helping humanity.'

'Mum?'

'Go,' the general said. 'I'll wait. Come back when you're ready.'

Shiumo came out, and Linda went to her and crouched in front of her. 'Thank you, Shiumo. I feel special.'

'You are special, dear Linda.' She rubbed her cheek on Linda's. 'Thank you for a generous time of mutual joy and pleasure.'

Richard and I shared a look. Shiumo had said that to every volunteer after they'd finished. It appeared to be a polite form of words.

Linda nodded to us, then joined the group of volunteers, who took her away to unpack the experience.

'I'm starving,' Shiumo said. 'Please come up to the ship for dinner. I want to talk to you about what happens now.'

'Alto and Choumali can go. I need to write my report,' the general said. 'The project's complete; both of you are due some leave. Go talk to Shiumo.' Richard passed her the tablet and she accepted it. 'I suppose all we have to do now is wait until the babies are born.'

'I can't wait to see what they look like,' Shiumo said.

She folded us up to the ship, and we sat at the dining table. Marque provided us with our favourite meals. I felt a moment of sadness: this was probably the last time we'd eat together in her magnificent ship.

'The first thing I want to discuss is the facility Marque will build,' Shiumo said. 'I've sent plans for it to your tablets. Marque, show them?'

A glowing three-dimensional model of an organic mushroom-like structure floated above the table: a flat-topped oval on a slender stalk, with vegetation growing between the small round-windowed buildings on its top. The entire structure was a pale rosy shade of pink.

'It will hold all ninety-six dragonscales children,' Shiumo began.

'Wait,' Richard said. 'You know already that some of them will be twins?'

'Yes, and one set of triplets,' she said. 'I've also added suitable accommodation for your son David, Jian – he can attend the facility as well if he wishes. And also your two new alien children. Marque will teach them about their home species. This will be an important study. No cat has ever been raised outside the Republic, and it will be interesting to see how much of their assholery is built-in and how much develops as a result of their awful social structure and unforgiving indoctrination.'

I studied the model for a long time, torn by indecision. I didn't want to be foster mother to so many children – it wasn't what I'd planned for my military career. But the education that Marque could provide for my two alien foster kids was more appropriate than anything I could give them. And the dragonscales wouldn't be moving into the facility for fifteen or sixteen years, so I had time to build my career. I tilted my head. The facility – a pink cloud of beauty floating in the sky – looked welcoming and idyllic.

'I can see you thinking about it,' Shiumo said. 'If you decide not to do it, I understand. I will provide you with all you need to teach the children what they should know.'

I nodded. 'Thank you.'

Shiumo turned to Richard. 'I'll be back in a week. If you decide you want to travel with me, to be with me, I would love it. I love you dearly, but I want you to be sure. If you're still here on this island when I return in a week, we will go off together. If you aren't here, I will understand and I will never speak to you again. I will give you whatever you want.'

'Then remove the cloned body parts and return me to Earth,' he said.

Her head shot back on her long neck. 'What?'

'Take them off. Take me back to what I was.'

'Why?' she said, astonished.

'Because the job is done. Because you *made* more than half of me. The minute I stepped off that table I was in love with you again. I'm not my own man any more.'

She rolled her eyes. 'This again.' She looked up. 'Can we do it, Marque?'

'Sorry, Commander, not without killing you,' Marque said. 'Your body wouldn't survive the trauma. The fatigue, the pain, the headaches, the tremors, all the neurological symptoms you've experienced over the past twenty-five years – that was your body saying "enough". You've been living on borrowed time, and if we do any more to you, your time will be up.'

'Do it anyway,' Richard said.

'Richard …' I said softly.

'No, Jian. I don't want to be anything but one hundred per cent human. One hundred per cent *me*.'

'You *are*,' Shiumo said.

'Remove the cloned parts. I want to be what I was when I was born, not a fabrication. I choose death. Respect my wishes.'

'This is so sudden,' she said, her eyes wide. 'You seemed happy while we were working on the project. I thought you loved me. I thought we would travel together … Why didn't you tell me you felt this way? Talk to me!'

'You said you'd give me anything I want. This is what I want.'

'Can you do it, Marque?' Shiumo said.

'No,' Marque said. 'I'm programmed to preserve life. I can't knowingly kill you, Richard.'

'Then return me to Earth and never speak to me again.'

'One condition,' Shiumo said.

'If you love me there should be no conditions,' he said sharply.

'Answer this: do you love me?'

'Take me back down,' he said. 'You've ruined my life quite enough.'

She lowered her head and closed her eyes. 'I am sorry, my love.'

*

Shiumo dropped us back outside New Whitehall. Richard walked into the building without saying a word to Shiumo. She watched him go, her emotions full of grief. I hesitated, awkward.

'Thank you, Jian,' she said. 'He's whole again, and you helped me give him that. Please consider raising the dragonscales children for me. You're the only one I trust.'

'I need to think about it,' I said, keeping my gaze on the Whitehall building.

'I understand,' she said, her voice breaking, and disappeared.

Richard and I took the elevator down to the conference room. The general was already there waiting for us.

'So you were pretending to love her until the project was complete?' she said.

Richard didn't reply.

'This proves she doesn't have control over you, Alto.'

'I wasn't pretending. I still love her,' he said. 'It took an enormous effort of will to free myself, but I did it. I never want to be near her again.'

Maxwell studied each of us in turn. 'We tried again to provide alternative people to work with her, and again she said no. It's you two or nobody. And we need people on the inside.'

'So you want me to go with her?' Richard said, his voice flat.

'Of course we do. Report back on where she goes and what she does. This information is vital.'

'What if I share classified Earth information with her?'

'You won't have any.'

'I see. Am I discharged?'

'Absolutely not. We're assigning you the vital task of travelling with her and finding out as much as you can about the Dragon Empire.'

'No you aren't,' Richard said. 'You're cutting me loose because the job's done, more than half of me was created by her, and I'm severely compromised. You're hoping there's enough humanity left in me to help you out, but you want me off-planet because you're not sure where my loyalties lie.'

I made a soft sound of sympathy.

The general didn't reply, her gaze stern.

'I chose death, Charles,' Richard said. 'You did this to me against my will. All of you did.'

'You joined up to serve and, if necessary, to sacrifice yourself for the good of humanity,' the general said. 'It's my job to put you in the line of fire. Your sacrifice is honoured, soldier.'

'My sacrifice was *against my will*.' Richard pulled off his insignia, tossed it on the table, and stalked out.

The general pressed a button on her tablet.

'Ma'am?' an aide said.

'Arrest Commander Alto and put him in a cell on level twenty-four.' She hesitated. 'And put him on suicide watch.'

'Ma'am.'

She turned the comms off.

I moaned quietly. 'If I'd known I would never have done this to him.'

'You did the right thing.'

'I destroyed him.'

'No, I destroyed him. You followed orders and completed your mission,' she said. 'Alto submitted a report at the end of the project, saying that you are an intelligent, reliable officer whose loyalty to humanity is above reproach, and he recommended you be promoted.'

'After what I did to him,' I said with misery.

'He doesn't blame you, Choumali. He blames me, and with good reason.' She put her tablet down. 'You said that Shiumo had less control over you this time? You didn't tell her that we'd ordered you to start this breeding program?'

'That's right. Her control of me isn't complete.'

'That makes you even more important than Alto. She wants you to look after the dragonscales. She won't take anyone else. She says if she can't have you, Marque will raise them. If you stay with the children you won't be with her every hour of the day – but you'll still have a great deal of access to information, particularly as you'll be assisting with their education about the Galactic Empire.'

'I know it's the logical thing to do,' I began.

'It's the most important thing to do,' she said. 'This is absolutely vital.'

'Am I being ordered to do it?'

'Yes, you are.'

I saluted. 'Ma'am.'

'No argument?' She gestured towards Richard's insignia. 'No storming out?'

'Not from me, ma'am. I know how important this is.' I sighed. 'This is not where I thought I'd be at this stage of my career, but I have two alien children to care for now – and I want to make sure we get our own dragons. The extra information I can gather in Shiumo's facility is worth it. We need to travel to the stars.'

'Another reason why it's so important you do this.'

'And Richard? What we just did to him is …' I searched for the word.

'Heinous,' she said. 'Absolutely unforgivable. Shiumo contacted me immediately and told me he demanded that she remove the body parts even though it'll kill him. She's confused and upset – he seemed happy enough while the project was ongoing, then he turned around and wanted to die.'

'She obviously doesn't know him very well,' I said. 'The project came first. Richard will make any sacrifice for the good of humanity.'

'That's why I locked him up. He'll think about his decision for a while, and then agree to go with her and spy for us. Alto is one of the most exceptional officers I've ever served with. He's never hesitated to do what's right, no matter how much he might suffer.' She lowered her voice. 'And the mind control be damned – he deserves some happiness. She can give it to him. He's suffered enough.'

*

General Maxwell and I stood outside the space elevator building waiting for Shiumo to return a week later. The wind swept across the treeless island, and I shivered, then took a deep breath, enjoying its freshness. I remembered Nelly telling me this would be the last fresh air we'd breathe before we headed to Wolf. That seemed a lifetime ago.

Shiumo folded onto the lawn in front of us. 'Hello, everyone.' She looked around, then lowered her head. 'He's not here. I suppose I shouldn't be surprised.'

'He's here,' the general said, and gestured towards the building behind us.

A couple of guards emerged, escorting Richard, who was in handcuffs. His face was rigid and I could sense his deep humiliation from ten metres away.

'What are you doing?' Shiumo shouted, and folded directly to him. 'What is this? Let him go!'

'They'll remove the cuffs when you take me up to your ship,' Richard said.

'Why? Why are they doing this to you?' She turned to speak to the general. 'Is this because of me? What happened? Why are you doing this to him?'

'Because he's an alien artefact and we can't trust him,' the general said. 'Take him and go.'

'He is one hundred per cent human, and I do not have control of him!' Shiumo shouted. She returned to Richard. 'Marque, remove these stupid restraints. What an insult to an intelligent man who has more integrity than anyone else on this island.'

The cuffs fell away from Richard's wrists.

'Give him a weapon.'

A similar weapon to the one I'd used to kill the cat floated from the Marque sphere above us.

'Take it, Richard,' Shiumo said.

Richard stared at it. 'No.'

'Good. See?' she said to the general. 'Now. Take that weapon, Richard, and shoot the general – the person who's exiling you from your own planet. Shoot her right between the eyes, right now.'

'Don't be ridiculous,' Richard said.

'Now can you see that I have no control over you?'

'That's beside the point,' he said. 'I'm fatally compromised, and I'm no longer welcome here.' He shrugged. 'Can I come with you? This isn't my home any more.'

'Oh, Richard,' she said with compassion, and hoisted herself onto two legs, putting her front claws on his shoulders. 'Always. Always!'

He nodded to her. 'Thank you.' He glared at General Maxwell. 'You destroyed my life, my career and my autonomy. I hope I never see you again.'

The general nodded to him. 'Live a long and happy life, Richard. I wish only the best for you.'

He turned his back on her, and spoke to Shiumo. 'Can I help you set up the facility for your kids?'

'Absolutely,' Shiumo said. She turned to me. 'Come on, I have to choose a site. I want somewhere nice and warm with some ocean nearby so they can swim. You can help me.'

'Go, Choumali,' the general said. 'Let me know when the site has been chosen. The Mediterranean would probably suit Princess Shiumo's requirements.'

'Ma'am,' I said, and went to Shiumo.

'Let's go,' she said, and we put our hands on her shoulders. Richard and the general shared a meaningful look as the island dissolved around us.

29

The base station and Shiumo's facility were located on a five-kilometre-wide island; a cluster of buildings on top of a cliff overlooking the Mediterranean's clear blue water.

Six months after we'd begun setting up, Commander Stewart Blake and I waited for the Maxwell family at the rotocopter pad. Commander Blake was taller than me and heavily built, with light brown skin, greying black hair, and a square heavy-browed face that made him appear deceptively ordinary until you saw his sharply intelligent eyes. We both wore the new dark blue uniforms of the Space Corps; he'd made a special trip from his office in New London for the first gathering of the dragonscales babies.

The 'copter landed, and General Maxwell stepped out with her daughter, Linda, who was carrying her dragonscales baby. The one-month-old baby behaved like a six month old, even though she was only twenty centimetres long: she was holding her head up, and was alert and inquisitive.

The babies had been born after only twenty weeks, and the doctors had panicked that they were all premature. It was impossible to predict how long it would take a dragonscales child to develop; and Marque hadn't been able to provide the doctors with concrete predictions until the children were close to term.

But they were robust and healthy babies, their eyes already open and focusing, and each with a cluster of small red scales on their temples.

Linda said something to her mother, and headed for the other scalesmothers and their families, who were arriving at the civilian ferry terminal at the base of the cliff.

The general approached Commander Blake and me. 'Stewart,' she said, saluting Blake, then shaking his hand. 'Any word?'

'Not yet, Charlie,' Commander Blake said. 'We're expecting them soon though.'

'Good to see you, Choumali,' she said to me. 'I trust the commander's treating you well?'

'Can't complain, ma'am. I think I've been lucky with my commanding officers. All of them have been a pleasure to work with.'

'You need to give the lieutenant more to do if she's not complaining, Stew,' the general said.

Linda waved to the general from the group of scalesmothers, and the general waved back. She spoke to us without looking away from the scalesmothers with their baby slings and buggies. 'I'd like to see the alien children first. I read the reports and I want to see for myself.'

I winced. 'The confinement is for their own protection, ma'am.'

'I want to see if you're being too soft on them,' she said.

'Oh.' I gestured towards the base station. 'This way.'

Scaleshome seemed to float on its slender stalk above us. A Marque sphere was guiding the scalesmothers up the lift to the Scaleshome platform, and they were talking excitedly among themselves.

I led the general and the commander into the admin section, which was constructed of the same smooth pink ceramic-like material as Scaleshome. They followed me through the office where my small team were updating the dragonscales' records, and down the corridor to the secure rooms where I was keeping the aliens. Marque had made a small apartment for each alien, with a bedroom, living room and bathroom.

'Shiumo assures me that it's considered an honour to give aliens a name in our own language and to use it,' I said. 'I've named the cat Oliver, after my grandfather.'

'Fuck your name!' Oliver shouted from inside his room.

'They're learning English?' the general said.

'No. There's an integrated translation program in the facility. They refuse to learn our language – they refuse to have anything to do with us. This is Georgina's room.' I rapped on her door. 'Georgina?'

'Go away!' she shouted from inside.

'Can I come in?'

'Fuck off!' Oliver shouted from his room across the hall.

'I'm coming in, Georgina,' I said.

Her footsteps galloped across the floor and an internal door slammed.

I opened the door, and put my arm out to stop the general and commander from entering too quickly. When Georgina didn't make a break for it, I led them inside. Georgina was nowhere to be seen.

'She's locked herself in the bathroom,' I said. 'She won't come out as long as we're here.'

'Charming,' the general said.

'Georgina, General Maxwell is here,' I said. 'Do you remember her?'

Georgina didn't reply.

'Shiumo will be here soon. Don't you want to see her?'

We heard her moving around inside the bathroom.

'I'm going to kill that dragon!' Oliver shouted from his room. 'She did this to us.'

'Exceptional hearing,' General Maxwell said.

'I can hear your heart beating,' Oliver said loudly. He lowered his voice. 'I will tear it out and eat it.'

'Will Shiumo take me home?' Georgina said.

'Why don't you ask her yourself?' I said.

'You're mine until you're mature, personal slur,' Oliver shouted. 'Even if the dragon took you home, they'd have to give you back to me. You're *mine*.'

'And the psychologists are doing their best?' the general said, gesturing for us to leave Georgina's room.

'Yes, ma'am, with Marque's help. They won't give up.'

'I'm going to eat their hearts too,' Oliver said with menace. 'Your torture and brainwashing will *fail*. I am loyal to the Republic. I have property back home and I *will* find a way to get it.'

'Can we see him?' the general said, nodding towards Oliver's room.

'He'll just attack you, ma'am. He's not cooperating at all.'

'I will resist your torture and kill you all!' Oliver shouted.

'Maybe we *should* torture him if he wants it so much,' General Maxwell said with amusement.

I slapped my forehead. 'Thanks a lot, General.'

'I knew it!' Oliver shrieked. 'You hear that, Ee-yi-oh-ue? They're going to *torture* us. Are you ready for it?'

'I want to go home!' Georgina wailed. 'Let me out!'

'Let's go see if Shiumo's here yet,' Commander Blake said with resignation.

'I see the problem,' the general said as we walked back through the corridors to the elevator that led up to Scaleshome. 'If you keep them confined, they won't trust you. If you release them, they'll run away and hide.'

'They jump off the cliff into the ocean,' I said. 'Georgina's nearly drowned three times. She says she'd rather be dead than here. Oliver's a strong swimmer, and made it close to the mainland twice before we caught him.'

'Maybe Shiumo can help you win their trust.'

'I sincerely hope so, ma'am. Everything we've tried so far has failed. We just need one small breakthrough to move forward.'

Commander Blake stayed at the terminal to supervise the arrivals, while I took the general up in the elevator and onto the surface of Scaleshome.

Marque had cleared the main square for the visitors; usually it was covered in ceramic beams that Marque was using to build residences for the dragonscales. Some of the edges of the square were finished with perfectly smooth stone in a soft shade of pink. A few residences were complete: ten-metre-wide dome-shaped pink buildings with round windows and planter boxes around their edges.

'Is the colour an attempt to honour the old-fashioned "pink for girls" thing?' the general said. 'Since all the babies are girls?'

'No, it's Shiumo's livery, her representative colour,' Marque said. 'Any visiting member of the Dragon Empire will see the colour and immediately know that the facility and the children belong to a member of Shiumo's red clan.'

'Send me a report on this clan business,' the general said in an aside to me.

'Nothing to it really, General,' Marque said. 'Each of the Empress's daughters is a different colour, and all their children match that colour. This shade of red identifies the children as related to Shiumo.'

'And the second generation, when they're a mix of two colours?' the general asked, intrigued.

'Then it depends on what colour their scales are,' Marque said.

The general nodded. 'Makes sense. Estimated time to completion of the facility?'

'Another six months. Based on the children's development in the last four weeks, I'd say they'll be ready for their first Scaleshome retreat when they're five years old.'

'How long before they can have babies?'

'Damn, you're blunt,' Marque said. 'Working from their enhancements to the human baseline, I'd say about sixteen to eighteen years old. They'll be the human equivalent of twenty-five.'

'Good.'

I showed the general through one of the completed houses. It had a living room, bedroom and bathroom similar to Georgina's residence.

'How long did it take Marque to build this?' she said.

'Each of the residences takes a week,' Marque said.

'Some of our refugees would love housing like this.'

'Pick a site, General. When I'm done constructing the facility, I'll come and build some for you.'

'Appreciated.' She checked her tablet. 'Shiumo will be here soon. Let's go wait for her.'

Commander Blake met us in the square as the last of the scalesmothers came up in the elevator. We all stood together in the square, the babies quiet and alert in their mothers' arms or in their buggies.

'They look human until they start acting like this,' the general said, softly enough for only Blake and me to hear. 'Little Veronica's already close to walking.'

'How do her brother and sisters feel about her?' I said.

'They adore her; they call her their "ray of sunshine". She's always happy, hardly ever cries, and she has the biggest blue eyes and knows how to use them.' She made a soft sound of amusement. 'She appears to have inherited a great deal of charm from her dragonfather.'

One of the babies started to cry. Her mother quickly pulled on a sling, lifted the baby with her husband's help, and put her on her breast.

'I can hear her sucking from here,' I said with wonder.

'Their mothers say it feels like they're eating for three,' the general said. 'Linda has trouble keeping up.'

'At one month old,' I said.

'The scientists can't wait to get their hands on them,' the general said. 'But because the babies arrived sooner than expected, they still haven't finished the ethical guidelines. They're panicking that they're losing valuable research time while they sort out the paperwork.'

'If it keeps the babies safe and unharmed, they can take as long as they like,' I said.

'Hear, hear,' Commander Blake said softly. He checked his tablet. 'Any word, Marque? She's ten minutes late.'

'You know she's never on time,' Marque said.

'She can travel instantly and she's still always late,' I said with amusement.

'Has she pinged the edge of the solar system?' the general said.

'The ping would take three hours to reach us anyway. She'll probably arrive before it does,' Marque said.

The commander checked his tablet again. 'Is there any way for us to know if something's happened to her or she was waylaid?'

'No,' Marque said.

'I wish I still had that scale,' I said.

'Six more months, Jian. You're first on the list for when she grows a new one,' Marque said.

'I know.'

A few of the babies became restless, and their mothers took them for walks around the side of the square, showing them the buildings. More time passed, and I tried not to become concerned. Marque was right: Shiumo was always late. I checked my tablet; she was twenty minutes overdue.

Chairs floated out of the construction warehouse, and Marque placed them around the square for us. The mothers sat, and a few of them fed their babies as they waited.

The general sat too, and checked the feed on her tablet.

'There's no plan B if she doesn't show,' Commander Blake said. 'All we can hope is that if something has happened to her, she managed to contact the other dragons first.'

'Don't forget that she's effectively immortal,' I said. 'The only way she could be destroyed is if she runs into a cat ship –'

Shiumo's black pod appeared in the middle of the square and she shouted telepathically: *Help me! They're hurt.*

The pod opened. A group of Japanese colonists were slumped inside, and the air filled with the smell of burned flesh.

'Synching,' Marque said. 'The cat that attacked you on New Europa found the Japanese colony. We need medical attention for them immediately. There are more up on the ship – about fifty altogether.'

'Contact Major Irina Sorovich in New Whitehall,' the general shouted to Marque. 'Tell her the situation.'

'Sorovich here, General,' Marque said in a woman's voice with a crisp New London accent.

'We need meds for fifty severely wounded colonists from New Nippon. They were attacked by that damn cat,' the general said as she checked the colonists in the pod. 'Severe burns. Amputations. They're in a bad way, Irina. Do you have space for them?'

'We'll make space, General. Bring them to QA3,' the major said.

The general called to Shiumo. 'Can you transport them to Queen Anne III Hospital in Euston?'

'Show me where it is, Jian,' Shiumo said. She was still sitting on top of the pod.

I gave her directions telepathically.

'Understood. I'll take them directly,' Shiumo said.

'Tell Major Sorovich they're on the way,' the general said to Marque.

'Already done,' Marque said.

As we exited the pod, one of the women woke and screamed in Japanese, 'They took my baby!'

'Oh lord,' I said softly.

'My son. My son!' she shouted. 'It took my son. It took our children!'

'What did she say?' the general said.

'The cat took their children.'

'Oh *fuck*,' she said.

*

Shiumo reappeared with the pod twenty minutes later. 'They're all safe at the hospital, but I want to go back and check I didn't miss anyone in the dome. Jian, I need your psi ability to sense them – you're human. Come and help me, please.'

The general gestured for me and Commander Blake to enter the pod. 'Go see if there are any more of them.'

I sat on the floor of the pod and showed Commander Blake how to prepare for the journey.

The pressure changed, and the door opened to reveal Richard standing in the corridor of Shiumo's ship, holding breathers for us. He was wearing a silky deep gold shalwar kameez, and his skin glowed with good health above the mandarin collar.

'Stay in the pod – she's taking us straight to the colony,' he said. 'There isn't much chance there are more survivors, but we want to be absolutely sure. If they had a panic room or extra breathers, more may be alive.'

'Good to see you, Richard,' Commander Blake said, shaking Richard's hand.

'Likewise, Stewart. This isn't how I was expecting to meet you again,' he said with grim humour. He nodded to me. 'Good to see you as well, Lieutenant. I hope Stewart's looking after you.'

'Can't complain, sir.'

Prepare for fold, Shiumo said.

Richard passed us the breathers – they were smaller, slimmer and lighter than our Earth ones – and the door opened onto the surface of Kapteyn-b – New Nippon.

The soil was a copper-rich green, but under Kapteyn's red light it appeared black and streaked with red tones that looked like blood. The Japanese dome had collapsed over the structures that had been inside it. The greenhouse, similar to ours on New Europa, was still standing, but the edges of its skin fluttered where the cat had torn it open.

I had a flash of disorientation: I was back on New Europa and needed to check my colleagues. Then I remembered with a pang that they were all gone, and I was seeing that massacre all over again.

'Stay put and let me open it up first,' Marque said.

Its sphere flew to the dome, cut the skin, and peeled it back to reveal the bodies of the colonists. They were the deep blue of asphyxiation, the red light making them appear a mottled purple.

'Jian, see if you can sense any life,' Shiumo said. She launched herself off the top of the pod and flew over the collapsed dome. 'I don't feel anything.'

I nodded, and walked carefully over the collapsed skin of the dome, avoiding the lumpy shapes beneath it. My breathing echoed inside the mask as I sent out my empathy. All I could sense was the rage and grief of my colleagues.

You need to tone down your emotions, I told them telepathically. *They're getting in the way. I hate to say it, but please attempt to find a happy place, and take your mind away from this situation.*

'I don't think I can,' Commander Blake said over the comms, his voice hoarse with pain.

Asking them to hold in their emotions made the interference worse. I tried to ignore it as I walked among the dead. Marque peeled more skin away from the dome so everyone could check each body carefully.

'Anything?' Shiumo said above me.

'Nothing.'

After I'd covered the dome, I went to the greenhouse. It was chaos inside: the hydroponics racks had been overturned, and storage bins spilled their contents everywhere. Six colonists wearing overalls the colours of botany and security lay dead. The cat had ripped out all the potatoes, and left everything else.

There was a large burn hole on the far side of the greenhouse. Outside, in the soft dust, were tracks that looked like something had been dragged across the ground. I realised the cat must have put the children into a net or bag to get them to its ship.

My stomach fell when I saw a small dust-covered lump on the ground. I ran to it. It was a child of about a year old, lying on his back. I had to take my breather off to wipe the tears from my eyes – he was the same age as my son David. His breather had slipped from his face, and he hadn't been old enough to adjust it. He'd suffocated; his cheeky face was mottled and purple in the star's red light.

I sent my senses out further and traced the path the cat had taken with the children to its ship. I found three more small bodies where the ship had been – burned beyond recognition by its launch blast.

'I wonder how many children it managed to steal,' I said, almost to myself.

'You can find out from the survivors,' Shiumo said above me. 'They're sure to know how many children were in the colony.'

'Can you carry us to find this cat ship?' Commander Blake asked her. 'I would like to have words with it.'

'And get the children back,' Richard said.

'It's already left the system,' Shiumo said. 'Space is huge, and the ship is tiny. The chances of finding it are infinitesimal. Even if you do find it, you can't enter the warp field to interact with the ship. That would be like the dimensional stretching that happens if you're not close enough to me when I fold. You'll have to find the ship, then wait until it comes out of warp before you "have words" with it. That could take years with the dilation effect.'

'So the children's parents will have grown old, while the children remain the same age,' I said. 'That makes it even worse.'

'Do you have any idea which way the ship was headed?' Commander Blake asked Marque. 'Did it go in towards Earth, or out towards the American and African colonies, or did it head home to cat space?'

'No idea. Sorry, Commander,' Marque said. 'Once again the cat destroyed the colony's spheres. I have no idea what happened.'

'We have to work out how long it will take to reach Earth or the other colonies,' Commander Blake said. 'And be ready for it.'

'How can we defend ourselves against it?' I said.

'We'll find a way,' Commander Blake said grimly.

*

When we returned to Scaleshome, Oliver and Georgina were waiting for us in the main square, accompanied by General Maxwell and a Marque sphere. None of the scalesmothers were present.

I walked forward to speak to the aliens. 'Thank you for coming out of your rooms. It's good to see you.'

'I want to see what happened,' Oliver said.

'He doesn't believe me,' General Maxwell said. 'He wants to see for himself.'

'I need to see,' Oliver said.

'There are dead children there, Oliver. Are you sure?' I said.

He just gazed at me with his bright green eyes.

I turned to Georgina. 'What about you?'

'I have to go and explain to him how it works,' Georgina said. 'If I don't, you'll fill him full of propaganda and turn him against his species.'

'Where are the dragonscales babies? Are they okay?' I asked Marque.

'I put them all in the training centre in Scaleshome. Right now I'm giving the mothers a lecture on what to expect in the first twelve months of development.'

'Thank you.' I turned to Shiumo. 'Can you take us back to the colony?'

'This is a very good idea,' she said. 'Jian, Oliver, Georgina, put your hands on my shoulders. We'll collect some breathers, then go see.'

'Me as well,' General Maxwell said, and I nodded.

The Japanese colony was still deserted, the wind whistling over the destroyed dome.

Oliver trudged around the collapsed skin, stopping a few times at the bodies of the fallen.

'There are no children here,' he said. 'Marque lied.'

'The massacre of the adults means nothing to you?' the general said, irate at his apathy.

'If these people refused to sell their children, they deserve everything they got,' Georgina said. 'Civilised people appreciate the wealth that children like me bring to their families.'

'The children are on the other side,' I said, and gestured for Oliver to follow me. 'Is it important for you to see that your people killed children?'

He didn't reply, but his emotions were full of misery and regret.

'You didn't know this happened?' I said.

His misery deepened.

'Your people regularly —'

'Shut up!' he shouted at me. 'Where's the child?'

'He's on the other side of the greenhouse,' I said. 'You don't have to look if you don't want to.'

'I have to see,' he said grimly.

He went through the greenhouse to where the small corpse lay in the dust, and kneeled next to the little boy. His face was expressionless, but his emotions were full of turmoil.

'My mother told me that we never steal,' he said. 'Ee-yi-oh-ue was bought and paid for.'

'The cats never deliberately kill the children when they raid a planet — they're too valuable,' Georgina said. 'One or two losses are unfortunate but normal.'

Oliver rounded on her. 'Could you just *shut up* for one second and stop making excuses for my people?'

'It's called Stockholm syndrome,' I began.

'I know what that is – your psychologists explained it to me!' Georgina shouted. 'And I *don't have it*! The wealth my family gained from selling me to the cats means none of them will ever have to waste their lives in the mines again. It was worth it.'

'Just shut up,' Oliver said.

The general sidled up to me. 'Let's go back to Earth; this isn't achieving anything. He doesn't care at all.'

He does. It just doesn't show. He's messed up right now, and expressing it as anger. She's the one who isn't really concerned about the deaths, I said.

The general nodded.

I led them to the cat ship's landing site, where the three children had been incinerated.

'What a horrible way to die,' Maxwell said softly. 'Those poor children.'

'Shut up!' Oliver shouted at her.

'Yeah, be quiet!' Georgina said, and Oliver raised his hand to slap her. She cringed away. 'Sorry. Sorry!' Her voice lowered in pitch and her emotions filled with terror. 'I just want to help you!'

Oliver stopped mid-action and stared at her, then at his hand. He lowered it and turned away. 'I've seen enough. Take me home.'

'I want what's best for you, Oliver. But if we send you home, your people will do this to us,' I said, indicating the carnage.

'No, they won't. They'll blow up your planet, and you'll deserve it,' Georgina said.

'They really destroy whole planets?' Oliver said, the realisation of the truth filling his emotions.

'The cat that destroyed this base also destroyed the Euroterre base on Wolf 1061, killing nearly a thousand of us,' I said. 'I was one of the few survivors. You're only in Scaleshome because your mother was threatening to destroy Earth and take our children.'

Oliver remained completely unmoving, but his emotions were a mess.

'I think you're the only one in the galaxy who didn't know what the cats do,' Georgina said.

'Take me back to Earth,' he said to Shiumo. 'I've seen enough.'

'Pathetic,' Georgina said with scorn. 'Shiumo, take me back to my people. If Oliver releases me from my contract, I'll be treated like a princess back home.'

'You're not mature, so they'll just give you back to the cats,' Marque said. 'The contract lasts for as long as you're immature.'

'You want to stop me from telling the cats that Jian has Oliver,' she said.

'Can you blame us?' I said. 'The cats will blow up Earth with both of you on it if they find out.'

'So you won't take me home?' Georgina said.

'I'm sorry,' I said. 'We can't.'

She ripped off her breather and ran away, loping on her four legs across the dust.

'I have her,' Marque said, and set off after her.

After fifty metres, she collapsed on the ground. Marque encased her in a bubble, lifted her and returned her to us, then put her breather back onto her face.

'You'll probably need to keep her confined until she comes to her senses,' it said.

'Let's go home,' I said.

'Not our home,' Oliver said, and stayed quiet all the way back to Earth.

30

Twelve months later, I rushed down to the ferry terminal to meet Victor. He had our son, David, in a buggy and was holding the baby bag over his shoulder. David was nineteen months now – a big toddler with Dianne's dark brown skin and close-cropped curly hair. He grinned broadly when he saw me, and struggled against the buggy restraints, trying to get out.

'I appreciate this,' Victor said, breathless. 'It was so sudden! Took me completely by surprise.'

'You shouldn't be surprised; it's about time you received some recognition. Your work is amazing. And this exhibition is the chance of a lifetime.'

He touched my face. 'Your work is amazing too.' He kissed me, then pulled back and smiled. 'Remember, there's always a place for you in our little house, darling Jian. I know what you're doing is important, but we still love you.'

I kissed Victor back and squeezed his hand. 'You know how much I have to do here.'

The announcement of the ferry's departure filled the hall, and Victor passed the baby bag to me. 'Everything's in here. He's walking now!' He glanced down at David, who was grunting with the effort of pulling against the buggy restraints. 'We'll let you out in a minute, you little barbarian!' He turned back to me. 'You're saving humanity and we're super-proud.'

'Go!' I said, pushing him away, and he turned and sprinted for the departing ferry.

David started to squall and I crouched in front of him. 'Wait till we get you home and then I'll let you out, okay?'

'Now!' he shouted.

I shook my head, and got up to push the buggy. 'No. When we're home.'

I took David up in the elevator to the base station, and then through to the Scaleshome elevator entrance. His wails changed to a chant of 'Marque! Marque!' as we went up the elevator. He adored the AI and spent a great deal of time tormenting Marque during his regular visits.

Marque came out to meet us in a female android body that appeared in its early fifties, short and slightly overweight. She smiled when she saw David, and his efforts to escape became even more frantic. 'Go, I have him,' she said, releasing him from the restraints and lifting him to sit on her hip. He hugged her and she held him close. 'Go do your thing and leave the bag here.'

'Keep a close eye on him; he's nearly walking,' I said.

'I have eyes everywhere,' she said.

They followed me to the rotocopter platform, where Commander Blake was waiting. 'Emergency childminding sorted?' he said, sounding amused.

'All fixed. It's a huge opportunity for my ex to have a whole gallery to himself,' I said. 'And David's other mother is in Frankfurt giving a keynote at a symposium.'

'I'll take David for a walk around,' Marque said, and before I could reply she was gone, pushing the buggy with one hand and holding David with the other.

'Are you sure your son's safe with the ... thing?' the commander said.

'I should be offended,' Marque said from a sphere above us.

'He's probably safer with Marque than he is with me,' I said. 'I have too much happening and can't keep an eye on him all the time. Marque can.'

'But he knows who his mum is,' Marque said. 'He keeps asking me to bring him back to see Jian. Oh, the dragonscales children are here.'

The girls emerged from the ferry terminal elevator and came up the hill towards us, holding their parents' hands and talking to them. They were already walking at only thirteen months. I'd seen them onscreen, but real life was another matter. Although David was six months older than them, their developmental acceleration was obvious. They appeared around five years old.

The rotocopter landed and General Maxwell came out, accompanied by her daughter, Linda, and dragonscales granddaughter, Veronica. Veronica was wearing a pretty blue dress that accentuated her blonde hair and red scales, and appeared even older than five.

They came over to me and we did the usual saluting.

'Hello, Marque,' Veronica said. 'Is my room all ready?'

'Ready and waiting for you, Ronnie,' Marque said. 'With guest quarters for you as well, Linda.'

Both Linda and the general controlled their expressions, but I could tell they were disturbed at being the guests in the house of a thirteen-month-old child.

'I understand you have a cat here,' Veronica said to me. 'You can't let him go home because the cats will come back and destroy Earth. How old is he?'

'Marque says he's about four years old.'

'That's only slightly older than us,' Veronica said. 'Can we include him in the orientation that Marque's doing for us? We're all aliens together, after all.'

The general's expression slipped and she looked concerned.

'Don't worry, Nanna, it's just because we grow up fast,' Veronica said without looking away from me.

The general shared a look with her daughter.

'What do you think, Lieutenant? Marque?' Veronica continued. 'Would it work? And what about Georgina – has she stopped running away?'

'It's worth a try,' Marque said. 'You can share experiences. And Oliver will need the same basic education as you dragonscales.'

Veronica lit up with a huge grin. 'Good. It's settled. We need a boy to talk to anyway – we're all girls.' She turned to her mother and grandmother. 'Let's go check out my little house. I can't wait to see it now it's finished!'

After two hours of looking around the facility, all the dragonscales gathered in the square for Commander Blake to speak to them. It was slightly uncanny to see such a large group of pretty young girls all the same age, especially as they'd all chosen to wear their long hair in pigtails.

Oliver stood at the front of the group, with a girl either side holding his hands. Georgina sat on her haunches next to him, sullen and miserable.

Marque's nanny form stood to one side of the group holding David, who struggled to be let down to walk around. She took him a short distance away to look at the gardens.

'Welcome back,' Commander Blake said. 'I have a few notes before we begin the orientation. Marque says there are still some construction zones. They're cordoned off so please stay away from them. We don't want you to get hurt. Dinner will be in the main lecture hall at seven –' Blake was interrupted by a commotion to my left.

A couple of the girls were fighting, shouting and pulling each other's hair. Their astonished parents tried to separate them. Another girl joined in, shouting at the two already fighting. One of the girls went down, and another sat on top of her, screaming in her face. The parents tried to pull them apart, furiously apologising for their behaviour. The nanny Marque rushed to help.

'You are all exceptionally bad parents!' Oliver shouted, and I turned to look at him. He was holding David in his arms and radiating fury. David was crowing with delight. 'Your little boy nearly ran off the edge of the platform! I had to stop him. Why weren't you looking after him?'

I turned to the nanny Marque with the same question. 'Why weren't you minding David?'

'I was distracted,' she said, gesturing towards the fighting girls. 'And I was watching him. Nothing would have happened.'

She reached for David. He cringed away and clutched at Oliver, stroking his fur.

'He nearly ran right off the edge,' Oliver snapped. He turned away. 'We're going for a walk. I'll mind David better than the stupid AI.' He stormed off, David laughing with delight in his arms.

The girls instantly stopped fighting, got up and brushed themselves down. They shared a smile.

'So that was just –' I began.

'That cat has really big ears,' Francine said loudly, like a small child announcing something important.

'You girls apologise right now,' Marque said sternly from a sphere above us.

'Sorry, Francine,' Ingrid said.

'Sorry, Ingrid,' Francine said.

'Don't worry, Jian, it won't happen again,' Ingrid said. The girls embraced, then held hands. 'You were telling us about dinner?'

Oliver was now sitting on the ground with David in his lap, both of them radiating warm affection for each other. Mai-Lin, one of the dragonscales, was showing them how to play peek-a-boo. Georgina was with them, and Mai-Lin took her paw-like hand and showed her how to stroke David's hair. David put his hands on Georgina's face and Georgina radiated surprise and delight.

'There's no chance that Oliver will suddenly decide to use David as a toy?' I asked Marque. 'I know how strong his instincts are. Make sure you keep a better watch over them.'

'The familial instincts are stronger than the predatory ones, particularly with an infant, even one of another species,' Marque said as it accompanied me back to the podium. 'His mother planned to give Oliver a baby brother. They'd talked about it for a long time before you killed her.'

'Thanks a *lot*,' I said quietly.

'David's established himself as a surrogate sibling; Oliver should treat him well. Georgina's warming to David too. Don't worry, I'll keep an eye on them, but they appear to have connected.'

'You should have warned me about your plan.'

'You wouldn't have let us do it,' Marque said. 'David was nearly off the edge of the platform.'

I put my hand on my chest as I felt a sudden surge of anxiety at the thought of David tumbling from the platform.

'See? That,' Marque said.

*

Victor appeared onscreen almost immediately when I called him later that evening. 'David's okay, isn't he?' he said. His face was full of concern.

'David is perfectly fine and has made quite a few new friends,' I said.

He visibly relaxed.

'How's the exhibition going?' I said.

He lit up. 'The space is wonderful. The opening's in five days – I hope we have everything installed in time. You know that big piece, the steel one?'

I nodded.

'We may have a buyer for it already. One of the big multinationals wants to set it in front of their headquarters.' He was obviously excited. 'This is so good!'

'Victor …'

'Yes?'

'Did the gallery owner mention anyone from Scaleshome talking about you? Nobody called from here to suggest that they exhibit your work?'

'No,' he said, bewildered. 'You didn't, did you? You know I want to be successful on my own merit –'

'Not me,' I said. 'I know you do. Nobody else?'

'Not as far as I know.' He grew even more confused. 'Why do you ask? Did someone from Scaleshome want one of the sculptures? I have a few that would suit …'

I hesitated, then said, 'No. It's fine. Congratulations. Send me lots of photos of the opening!'

'I will!'

31

Fifteen years later

I fussed around my office, putting the finishing touches on the welcome packs for the dragonscales. They were about to arrive for the final part of the project, where they would produce Earth's own dragons. Everyone on the planet had been preparing for this moment, chafing under the restriction of having only Shiumo's irregular visits to help carry our interstellar colonists and diplomatic delegations. Having ninety dragons would bring an exponential increase to the amount of trading and diplomatic ties that humanity could develop. The whole Earth was watching us.

Oliver entered my office and sat across from me, full of excitement. He was eighteen now, and wearing a pair of tan-coloured shorts and a blue-and-white T-shirt stretched over his lanky form. His soft black fur stood up around the edges of his clothes.

'The first ones are about ten minutes away!' he said.

I didn't look up from sorting through the data packs. 'Believe me, I know.'

'Any word from Shiumo?'

I shook my head, then looked up at him. 'Where's Georgina?'

He shrugged, a gesture he'd learned from me. 'Off sulking somewhere.'

'She's your sister, Oliver.'

'She's a passive-aggressive bag of rejection,' he said. His ears twitched. 'Marque? I hear something.'

David charged in. 'They're here!' He fist-bumped Oliver. David was wearing an identical outfit to Oliver, shorts and a matching T-shirt, in solidarity with his brother. David's ginger-tinged dark brown hair was a breezy cloud around his head; a deliberate provocation to his military short-back-and-sides second mother.

I sorted through the rest of the data packs, huffed out a breath, then straightened my uniform. 'I'm ready for them.'

'There are some dragonscales at the base of the elevator,' Marque said. 'They'll be here soon.'

'Excellent.' Oliver threw himself out of the chair and jiggled next to David. 'This is so exciting! I cannot wait. This party will be *amazing*.'

'Seriously!' David said. 'Thanks for letting me stay an extra week, Mum. I appreciate it.'

I wagged my finger at them. 'Just don't –'

'Cause trouble!' they said in unison, and laughed.

Georgina appeared in the doorway. She eschewed clothes in a deliberate salute to her Eh-Ay-Oyau heritage. 'May I speak with you, Jian?'

'I'll leave you to it, Mum,' Oliver said. He came around the desk, embraced me, and kissed me on the cheek. He towered over me now. 'You'll do great. Stop looking so worried.'

'Thanks, Oliver.'

David saluted me with a grin, and both boys went out.

'Are you all packed up?' I asked Georgina.

'I am,' she said, and formally lowered her head. 'I thank you for caring for me, Major Choumali. I will take fond memories with me of this time with you. I now ask that you call me by my Eh-Ay-Oyau name: Ee-yi-oh-ue.'

'I'm sorry it worked out this way, Ee-yi-oh-ue. I hope your people treat you like a princess. You deserve it.'

'I would have been a princess much sooner if it wasn't for you,' she said, and walked out.

'Shiumo's here,' Marque said. 'How about that – she's actually on time.'

I went out of my office and through the gardens, and found Shiumo and Richard standing in the main square. Shiumo was still in her four-legged, winged red body, and Richard was wearing a kaftan-like robe in muted shades of tan and gold that contrasted with her red scales. They both smiled broadly when they saw me.

I embraced them. 'So good to see you, Shiumo. And, Richard, you haven't aged a bit.'

He smiled down at Shiumo. 'Being with a dragon will do that for you.' He held two rocks out to me. 'For you. I'll give you my journals later.'

'Thanks. I look forward to reading them.'

The two smooth blackened rocks, each five centimetres across, appeared to be fused pieces of burned glass. They were clear with a faint blue tinge where they weren't scorched. I turned them over in my hands.

'Knowing you, these aren't lumps of volcanic obsidian,' I said. 'They're probably something alien and terribly expensive.'

'They're diamonds,' Richard said, and I nearly dropped them. 'It rains diamonds on Jupiter.'

'He gave you *rocks*,' Shiumo said with scorn. 'Absolutely worthless.'

'One as a keepsake, and one to sell,' Richard said. 'I can't imagine how valuable a Jovian diamond would be to a jeweller or a collector. Hopefully it'll make you independently wealthy.'

'I'm already rich,' I said. 'I have three fantastic kids, and I live in a rose-pink palace floating in the sky.'

'You have ninety-nine kids, Jian, if you calculate dragon-style,' Shiumo said. 'We count by the number of children you care for, rather than those from your relationships or those you've officially adopted.' She turned her head on her long neck and jiggled from foot to foot. 'The first dragonscales are here. My children!'

The elevator doors opened and five of Shiumo's daughters, together with their parents and human half-siblings, came out.

The dragonscales girls were nearly two metres tall, and all had long hair in a variety of colours and styles depending on the ethnicity of their mothers. The red scales shone at their temples, and each wore a red gem in the centre of her forehead that Shiumo had fitted when they were five years old. They were sixteen now, but appeared about twenty-five, and were androgynously beautiful and lithely graceful. It was incongruous to see them wearing ordinary teenage clothes – jeans and T-shirts, or simple dresses.

Two of the girls squealed and raced to embrace Shiumo, then Richard. The rest held back, waiting their turn.

'Are we the first? We're the first!' Jessica said.

'Told you we'd be early,' Regina said.

'It's so good to see you both,' Shiumo said, obviously moved.

The rest of the greetings took place, the dragonscales children laughing and sharing jokes with their families and Shiumo.

Jessica looked around. 'Did you enlarge Scaleshome again, Marque?'

'By about thirty per cent since last year's meeting,' it said. 'Since you'll be here more than just a couple of weeks this time, I've made bigger quarters for you all, and extended the study halls and library.'

'Awesome,' Regina said.

The lift doors opened and more dragonscales arrived. They shared greetings, laughter and hugs with each other and Shiumo.

I sidled up to Richard, who was smiling indulgently as Shiumo welcomed her children. 'Travelling with Shiumo seems to agree with you, sir.'

His smile widened. 'I am loved, I love, I travel – every day is new. But most importantly, I am still of value to humanity.' He grew more serious. 'Are the journals really useful? I feel like I'm just writing down the interesting things I experience.'

I raised the diamonds. 'The journals are worth any number of these. You have no idea how much we appreciate the information.'

'Good.' He looked around, admiring the tropical gardens that flanked the pale pink walls of Scaleshome. 'This facility is more impressive every time I see it, Jian. The kids will be very happy here.'

'Thanks, but Marque did most of the work.'

'How are Oliver and Georgina? Did Georgina decide to go home?'

'Yes. She'll be treated like royalty now that her contract's finished and she survived it; of course she'll go home.' I sighed with feeling. 'Her people can probably provide better care for her mental health issues than I ever could.'

'That's not fair, Jian,' Oliver said. As usual, he'd approached silently on his bare feet. 'Hi, Richard.' He wrapped one arm around Richard and gave him a quick half-embrace. 'Marque knows her psyche inside out but Georgina refuses its help. It's not your fault she's like this; it's mine. I tortured her for years.'

'You only had her as a toy for a couple of years. I've kept her a prisoner for more than a decade,' I said. 'I hope she finds peace on Eh-Ay-Oyau.'

'I'm betting she'll last six months of their sickening adoration before she begs to come back here,' Oliver said. He nudged me with his shoulder. 'And when she does, say no.'

'Don't be mean to her, she's your sister,' I said, poking him in the side and making him jump.

'Meow,' he said.

David joined us. He hugged Richard and me, then turned to watch the dragonscales. More had arrived, and there was an excited babble as they greeted each other with many hugs and small gifts.

'They're all so beautiful they hurt my eyes,' he said.

'I don't see it,' Oliver said. 'Even though I'm steeped in human ideals of attractiveness after living here for so long, human girls just leave me cold. Even the dragonscales – half-human, half-dragon – don't do it for me.'

'Don't worry, man, they scare me to death,' David said. 'Totally not my type.' He grinned at Oliver. 'Maybe if they were boys?'

'Maybe,' Oliver said, then shrugged. 'Don't think so though. I don't think I'll ever find a partner.'

'Are you attracted to your own kind?' Richard asked with interest.

'I am, sir. I'd love to meet a female cat who hasn't been on the inside,' Oliver said. 'I doubt I ever will.'

'Is there internal dissent in the Cat Republic?' Richard said 'Maybe you could join a resistance group –'

'No,' Oliver said. 'It's our nature to be selfish. It's the way our brains work. I'm the only one who's had experience outside the Republic's indoctrination. I'm better off alone.' He put his arm around my waist. 'Having Jian for a mum and David for a brother makes up for it. Jian's okay without a partner, and I will be too. I have a family.'

'Oh, Ollie love,' I said softly, and gave him a squeeze.

'Zianto and Hanako are here,' Marque said. 'You have two dragonfathers for the second generation instead of just one.'

'Excellent,' Shiumo said with relish. 'Gather them up. Let's do this.'

Small Marque spheres emerged from the sphere above us and zipped around the facility notifying the dragonscales girls. They gathered in the main square with their families.

Zianto appeared next to us, with her Marque sphere above her. She had visited Scaleshome a few times during the annual meetings and the dragonscales universally adored her. Another dragon, presumably Hanako, appeared next to her, also with a Marque sphere. Hanako was pastel green and looked similar to Shiumo, with four legs and two wings. She had a dark green soulstone in her forehead.

'All here,' Marque said.

Shiumo and her sisters embraced, brushing their cheeks against each other, then Shiumo turned to address the dragonscales.

'Hello, my lovely children,' she said, and they quietened to listen to her. 'You all know why you're here. If you don't feel right about this, approach me afterwards and you'll be removed from the program. We'll respect your privacy.'

A few of the girls shared looks with each other and their parents, but the prevailing emotional tone was enthusiasm. They were psyched to be having this experience, and looking forward to it.

'The Empress has been exceptionally generous in providing us with two Seconds. Zianto you already know. Hanako messed up her previous First Contact and wants to make up for it by helping Earth out.'

'Oh, thanks a *lot*,' Hanako said in a deep velvety voice.

There was a smattering of applause and laughter, and some small cheers.

'You've prepared all your lives for this, and we know you'll be magnificent,' Shiumo said. 'Settle into your rooms. This will be your home for the next year or so. We'll do some final health checks to make sure you'll be able to lay the eggs, then the program will proceed. As I said, you can change your mind at any time.'

The girls cheered, and many of them hugged each other.

Hanako looked around. 'This seems like it's all under control, so where are the potatoes?'

'Wow,' Shiumo said. 'You really don't mess around.'

'Marque provided me with an approximation. I cannot *wait* to taste the real thing,' Hanako said.

'I have some in my quarters,' Shiumo said.

'Let's go!' Zianto said.

'Prepare to taste the best thing *ever*,' Shiumo said. 'They're *amazing*.'

All three dragons disappeared; and the dragonscales and their parents dispersed to their quarters to settle in. Some of the girls guided their parents to the elevator to see them off, obviously content to be left to their own devices.

The lift doors opened and a man, a woman and two girls stepped out. I went to welcome them, then realised I'd never seen them before. Both girls were fully human. The man and woman radiated determination.

The woman pushed one of the girls forward to stand in front of me. 'This is my daughter Stella,' she said. 'She applied for a study exchange in America, and as part of the application she needed a blood test. She's *pregnant*.'

'Uh, okay,' I said, wondering where this was going. 'What does this have to do with us?'

'Her best friend is a dragonscales – Julia. Tell the lady, Stella.'

Stella looked down; she radiated mortification. 'Julia's the father. She's the only one that I ... we ... she's the only one.' She looked up at me. 'I knew she could do it like a boy, but I didn't think we needed to take precautions!'

I opened my mouth to dismiss her claim, then closed it again. I'd seen the dragonscales girls when they were small and their bodies had seemed standard female. But I hadn't seen any of them naked since puberty.

'Come into my office and we'll talk about this,' I said. 'Marque, fetch Julia and Shiumo, will you?'

'Shiumo's already in the office,' Marque said. 'And Julia's behind you.'

I looked back to see Julia following us, her head bowed with shame. Her parents were with her.

I closed my office door and sat behind my desk, using it as a barrier between me and the painful emotions that filled the room.

'I'm sorry, I didn't get your names,' I said to Stella's parents.

'I'm Romy. This is Ben,' Stella's mother said.

'Julia, how could you?' Shiumo said softly.

'I'm sorry, Dragonfather,' Julia said. 'I thought ...' Her voice trailed off, then she rallied. 'We're both girls!'

'Obviously you're in a difficult situation, particularly with Stella wanting to go to the Americas,' I said to Stella's parents. 'How can we make this right for you? We can arrange a termination for Stella. Marque can do it simply and painlessly –'

'Goodness, no!' Romy said. 'Terminate? No!'

'That's not what we're here for,' Ben said. 'We want to know ...' He glanced at his wife.

'If her baby will be a dragon,' she said.

'No,' I said. 'It will be dragonscales like its ... father.' It felt strange referring to Julia that way.

Julia moaned gently. Her parents broadcast mortification, and her mother wiped tears from her eyes.

'And dragonscales can have dragon babies, right?' Ben said.

I nodded. 'With dragons, yes.'

'So Stella's baby – it could be the father or mother of a dragon?' Romy said.

I understood. 'You want a dragon in the family.'

'Of course we do!' Ben said.

'Our own dragon,' Romy said with wonder.

'You're about to create the second generation of dragons, and they'll be the same age as Stella's child,' Ben said. 'Can one of the dragons father it for us when they're both old enough? Or are they too closely related? We worked it out, and they're first cousins.' He looked to Shiumo for confirmation. 'Is that too closely related?'

'Dad ...' Stella said.

'And can Julia come back and father another dragonscales on our other daughter?' Ben said.

'Dad!' Stella said, horrified.

'There are five more families here with human daughters,' Marque said. 'I let Stella's family up because Stella said she's Julia's friend and she had something important to give her, but I've kept the others at the base. I just double-checked and there are more families waiting at the Scaleshome ferry terminal. Total: forty-three human girls so far, all with their families.'

'Are all the girls pregnant?' I said.

'Checking ... Yes, they are.'

I rose. 'I'll sort this out. Everyone, could you please follow Marque and it will give you a tour of Scaleshome.'

'Please come with me, everyone, and I'll take you on a tour of the facility,' Marque said. 'Julia, I'll show you to your room.'

'Can Stella's sister share it with Julia for a while?' Ben said.

'Dad!' Stella and her sister said in unison as they closed the door behind them.

'Marque, stop any more families from coming to the island,' I said. 'And send those at the base of the tower back to the ferry terminal.'

'Understood.'

I sat in my chair again and glared at Shiumo. 'Ten generations.'

'You were there when we warned them – you helped me talk to them!' she said. 'We told them not to have sex with *anyone* until they'd given birth to the dragon children. They knew they shouldn't get pregnant, and that birth control may not work on their half-dragon metabolisms. They *knew*!'

'But did they know they could father children?'

She didn't say anything, just studied me with her silver eyes.

'Why didn't you *tell* them? Why didn't you tell *me*?'

Again she didn't reply.

'Oh, fuck me sideways, Oliver's mother was right. "Second" doesn't just mean a second generation – it means completely replacing us with dragonscales. No wonder membership of the Empire is immediate – you're replacing us with your own kind.' I pointed at the door. 'Get out.'

'We told them not to have sex!' she said again.

'Like that *has ever worked in the history of humanity*!' I pointed at the door again. 'Get out. I need to contact my superiors and tell them that you aliens just fucking *invaded Earth right in front of us*!'

'I told you that interbreeding was a terrible idea, but you insisted. You blackmailed me into doing this. This is not my fault!'

She disappeared.

I slapped my forehead. 'Ten generations.'

I called my superior at the UN and his aide answered the call.

'This is Major Choumali from the Scaleshome facility. I need to speak to the Secretary urgently – we have a major crisis here. The dragonscales girls have been fathering kids all over the place. I have nearly fifty girls here pregnant with more dragonscales. He needs to call me back immediately.'

'He's not here right now, Major,' the aide said, obviously not comprehending the urgency of the situation. 'It's the middle of the night here. Can I have him call you back in the morning?'

'This is an emergency,' I said, frustrated. 'The dragons are invading us.'

'What?'

'Alien invasion! He needs to call me back immediately!'

'I'll let him know,' he said, stunned, and disconnected.

*

I'd paced my office for ten minutes waiting for the UN Secretary to call me back when an EBC reporter appeared on my big screen, doing a vlog for the network. The caption said 'Dragon children' and with a sinking stomach I turned the volume up.

'There are over a hundred of them in this town alone,' she said, walking along a rainslick cobbled street somewhere in Britain.

'One dragonscales girl – although "girl" may not be the correct term here – has fathered a child on more than half of the girls in her school, some girls in a nearby school, and a few older women, some of whom are married. None of the women or the families of the girls she's impregnated have complained. In fact, most insist that they want the prestige and possible income from a dragon in the family. Many have gone into hiding, concerned that they may be forced to terminate their pregnancy.'

I groaned. It was out already.

The screen switched to show a couple with a teen daughter sitting on a couch in a normal suburban home.

'Well, who wouldn't want a dragon in the family?' the father said. 'With our extended lifespans, having a great-grandchild capable of earning an income as a starship engine will set us up for a grand retirement.'

'Bonnie's grandchild will be able to carry us around the Dragon Empire,' the mother said. She smiled at her daughter. 'You did the right thing, honey.'

The girl smiled but didn't speak. She had the glazed look of someone not sure they wanted to be where they were.

The transmission flipped to an academic from a British university. 'If you're right about the number of children, this is a disaster for humanity,' he said.

The reporter spoke offscreen. 'More and more pregnant women are showing up. All are claiming it was their idea and they want to keep the children.'

'If that's the case, their children – the dragonscales children – will produce more dragonscales. At this rate ...' The academic raised his tablet and a graph showing an exponential rising curve appeared on the screen next to him. He lowered the tablet and glared at the camera. 'In ten generations, humanity will be wiped out. We'll be bred out of existence, replaced by dragonscales. All the dragons have to do is move in and breed a few more dragons, and even the dragonscales will become extinct. In as little as five hundred years, Earth could be populated entirely by dragons.'

The screen flipped back to the journalist, now walking past a village pub. 'The question remains: can we control this situation? Can we stop the dragonscales from impregnating every woman around them? The value of having a dragon in the family is impossible to quantify. Everybody wants one. Birth control doesn't work on dragonscales, and somehow condoms aren't effective either.'

A man tottered out of the pub behind her, and stopped to grin at the camera. The reporter didn't see him.

'When Shiumo first arrived seventeen years ago, we were looking at extinction in a hundred years as the oxygen disappeared from our atmosphere,' she continued. 'We've saved ourselves from that. But are we about to breed ourselves out of existence instead?'

'Alien invasion!' the drunk man said, raising his arms. 'They came for our women.' He guffawed. 'Who'da thought they'd come for our women – with their own women?' He leaned unsteadily on the fence. 'Dozens of the little buggers in the village! Shame I'm a bloke – I'd be having a baby with them too. Word is the dragons will be able to charge whatever they like to transport stuff to other planets – they'll be a gold mine for their families.' His grin disappeared. 'Wish I'd been born a girl. Would've had one of them babies in a second.' He waved dismissively at the camera and staggered away muttering, 'Aliens taking our women.'

'The government has yet to respond,' the reporter said. 'In the meantime, all we can do is count the losses, and hope we can salvage our species.'

32

General Maxwell charged into my office barking into her tablet. She'd dropped her daughter and dragonscales granddaughter at Scaleshome thirty minutes before. Obviously she'd seen the report and returned immediately.

'Yes. Legislation to identify and isolate them. Round up all those at the ferry terminal. Arrange for sweeps through every neighbourhood where a first-generation child lived. We want them all.'

She folded her tablet, and shook her head. 'I'm *retired*, dammit! Where are the dragons?'

'They disappeared,' I said. 'We can't find them anywhere. Marque, did they go back to their ships?'

Marque was silent.

'We are altogether too reliant on that thing,' Maxwell growled. 'We need to deport it with its dragon masters.'

'Right now it's our only contact with them,' I said. 'Marque, where is Shiumo?'

Marque hesitated, then said, 'I don't know. She and Richard folded away. She's out of this system and beyond my reach.'

'She ran.' The general scowled. 'I believe it. And Zianto and Hanako?'

Marque hesitated again. 'They're ... visiting with –'

'They're already fucking the girls?' the general shouted. 'Holy fuck, we need to stop this!' She turned to me. 'How many weapons do you have here?'

'There's no need for that,' Marque said.

I retrieved a handgun from my locked desk drawer. 'This is all I have. I never thought I'd need it. Scaleshome is secured by the elevator.'

She took the gun from me, then opened comms on her tablet again. 'I need two squads of elite special forces at the Scaleshome ASAP. Bring them in on a 'copter. ETA on Admiral Blake?' She listened, and nodded. 'Good.'

She loaded the handgun and checked it as she spoke to Marque. 'Tell Zianto and Hanako that if they're not in this office in two minutes, I will personally shoot the dragonscales that they are currently "visiting".'

'You'd shoot your own granddaughter?' Zianto said from the other side of the room.

'Get Hanako here *now*,' the general said.

Hanako appeared next to Zianto. 'There's no need to cause a fuss.'

'You two listen to me,' Maxwell said, leaning one hand on the desk and glowering at them. 'I am putting all of the dragonscales in isolation. They are not fucking anyone. Then I am rounding up every woman they've impregnated and I'm putting them in isolation as well. If you make any attempt to stop me, I will order their execution. Every single one of your children – and your grandchildren – will die. Do you understand?'

'They're your children too!' Hanako said.

'You would really shoot your own granddaughter?' Zianto repeated.

'In. A. Second,' the general said.

'They have soulstones,' Hanako said.

'I'll crush them.'

'You're turning us all into dragons. Why? Why are you doing this?' I said, my voice forlorn. 'You don't need to – there's no reason.'

'It's just easier to deal with people who aren't too different from us,' Zianto said with casual dismissal. 'You're so primitive that even talking to you is hard work.'

'The dragonscales are half-human anyway,' Hanako said. 'They're you ... but *civilised*.'

'Wonderful – straight-up colonisation,' the general said. 'Earth, terra nullius. Fantastic.' Her tablet pinged and she opened comms on it. 'Good. Is the legislation through? Excellent.'

She lowered the tablet and spoke to the dragons. 'You are now officially expelled from Earth. Leave and do not return.'

'But your interstellar colonies,' Zianto said. 'The dragons for your spaceships ... We're helping you!'

'Not any more. Leave.'

Zianto and Hanako shared a look, then turned back to the general.

'No,' Zianto said. 'We've started this, and we'll finish it.'

'We made an arrangement,' Hanako said, and both dragons disappeared.

'Fuck fuck fuck,' the general said under her breath. She made a call on her tablet. 'How far away are you, Stew? And the specials? Good.'

She turned to me. 'Choumali, can you lock down Scaleshome? Stop them from leaving?'

I winced. 'No. Marque runs the place. It intelligently controls everything. Marque?'

It didn't reply.

'Fuck!' the general roared, and stormed out.

'Why are you helping them?' I shouted at the ceiling. 'They're going to wipe us out. I thought you were programmed to protect life!'

'Nobody's being hurt or killed,' Marque said from the air above my head.

'The dragons offered the Nimestas reproductive assistance. I thought they *preserved* species.'

'The Nimestas are dragonscales. The dragons already did them,' Marque said with amusement.

'*Did* them? This is what they do – drive species to extinction? Now they're doing it to us!'

'And isn't that ironic, human? How many species has humanity wiped out in its quest for comfort and security?'

'We'll all die, and you're helping them kill us.'

'Nobody will die,' Marque said. 'You will all live long, full and comfortable lives. I have your genome stored away; you can't become extinct. Human dragonscales will always exist. There aren't enough dragons in the universe to completely wipe you out. Your species will become larger, stronger, healthier and altogether more civilised. To be honest, Jian, I really don't see why you're making such a fuss.'

I roared with frustration, and followed the general to the main square. Some of the dragonscales had already gathered there to see their parents off. Zianto and Hanako were standing near them.

'Jian,' Marque said when I arrived.

'Not now,' I said.

'Leave Earth and take your children with you,' the general said to the dragons.

'No. They're your children. You deal with them,' Zianto said. She turned to the dragonscales. 'Go down in the elevator, and I'll have Marque move you to a place that's independently run by us. Veronica?'

General Maxwell's granddaughter stepped forward hesitantly.

'You stay right here,' the general said. 'You saw what they're planning, Ronnie – I can't let you leave. We need to lock this down.'

'Jian, this is important,' Marque said.

'Can you keep Veronica here?' I said.

'More important than that.'

'It can wait.'

'Do as you're told, Ronnie,' Linda, her mother, said. 'Stay here.'

'Go down in the elevator, dear,' Hanako said kindly to Veronica. 'Lead the others. You'll all be safe.'

Veronica looked from her grandmother to her mother and then to the dragons, her face full of uncertainty.

'Ronnie, if you try to leave I will be forced to shoot you,' General Maxwell said. 'All of you need to stay here so we can stop you from creating any more dragonscales. We need to sort this out.'

'Jian ...' Marque said.

'Marque, unless you can get rid of Zianto and Hanako and keep the dragonscales contained here, shut the fuck up,' I snapped.

Veronica took a couple of hesitant steps towards the elevator.

The general pointed my handgun at her, and Veronica stopped, her pale face contrasting with the red scales at her temples.

'Mum, don't!' Linda said, standing between Veronica and the general. 'She's your granddaughter!'

'You know my priorities, Linda.' The general's voice was hoarse with emotion. 'Move or I'll shoot you too.'

'Mum, no,' Linda said.

The general shook her head, overwhelmed with grief at the decision to shoot her own child and grandchild. 'You all have to stay here, Veronica, to protect humanity. You're too dangerous to our species. Linda, move.'

'She means it, Ronnie,' I said.

'Marque will protect you,' Zianto said. 'Go down in the lift, and we'll take you all away from here.'

Veronica nodded sharply.

The general took careful aim. 'Ronnie, I mean it. You can't leave. Dragonscales children are popping up everywhere out there. If you don't stay here, away from humanity, you'll wipe us out!'

Veronica ignored her and strode with determination towards the lift. Three of the other dragonscales followed her, then the rest.

The general's aim didn't waver. 'Move, Linda, or I will shoot you too.'

Linda followed her daughter, blocking the general's line of sight. The general made a soft sound of pain and fired. The bullet pinged off a Marque energy wall and landed on the ground a metre away from Linda's feet. The general fired again, and again the bullet didn't hit.

'Jian, this –' Marque said.

'Shut the fuck up!' I shouted at it.

The girls passed some shocked-looking parents who had remained to help their daughters settle in, and stopped in front of the lift.

A two-second blinding flash of light was followed by a blaze of heat so searing it burned my lungs and throat. There were screams, then the flash was gone.

We all stood riveted to the ground with shock and confusion.

'I suggest we discuss the extinction issue later,' Marque said. 'I've been trying to tell you: a cat light cruiser is in orbit, along with an exploration ship, and they're attempting to blow up Scaleshome, probably because they identify it as dragon-made. I can't protect us forever. What do you want to do?'

The general pulled out her tablet and made a call. 'Brian, it's me. Yes, it's an invasion – the dragonscales have been making more dragonscales babies all over the place. But this is worse ... Stop. Stop, Brian! It's worse than that. The cats are attacking us.' She paused to listen. 'Yes! That's what it is. Destroy the potatoes! Give the order.'

She turned to speak to the dragons. 'You said we had more than seventy years before the cats knew about us. And that the cat that attacked New Europa and New Nippon wasn't heading for Earth. Were those lies too?'

'No. The cats may have seen our ships,' Zianto said.

She and Hanako rapidly tapped the scales on their necks, then shared a look.

'They haven't attained non-warp FTL as far as we know,' Hanako said.

'It's only one cruiser and an exploratory ship. It should be a small fleet,' Marque said. 'They usually attack from an overwhelming position of strength. You must have forced their hand by showing up.'

'If they see our ships in orbit, they will try to intervene,' Zianto said.

'Could this be the exploratory ship that attacked New Europa and New Nippon fifteen years ago?' the general said. 'The colonies are fourteen light-years away – it would take the cats at least that long to reach Earth.'

'Checking ... Yes, it's the same ship,' Marque said. 'The cruiser must have been nearby and joined it. Dropping out of warp to join up may have delayed them.'

'They're here for the rest of the potatoes,' I said.

'They want to get them before we dragons do,' Hanako said.

'I know that,' the general said. 'All the potato growers on the planet just received the order to destroy every plant they have.'

'Don't destroy them all!' Hanako said.

'We were ready for this,' the general said. 'Where's Oliver?'

'Here, ma'am.' Oliver approached, accompanied by his own Marque sphere.

'Don't you two go anywhere,' the general told the dragons. 'We need your help to defend *your* children from this attack. And the dragonscales are safer here. Don't let them leave.'

'We know,' Hanako said.

'Two rotocopters are on their way with Admiral Stewart Blake and some special forces,' the general said. 'Let them in when they arrive, Marque.'

'No,' Zianto said. 'No soldiers. Don't let them in, Marque.'

'Dammit,' the general began, but the cats hit Scaleshome again with a blast of light and heat that knocked the breath out of us.

'General, the transmission equipment's in the admin section,' I said. 'This way.'

*

Oliver took up a position behind the microphone. I nodded to him, trying to broadcast encouragement.

The dragons stopped just inside the doorway. It was a crush with all of us in the tiny transmission room.

'They've attacked our ships, and Marque can't defend them forever,' Zianto said. 'You said you have a way to stop them?'

'We can try,' I said.

'You won't hurt them, will you? We don't want to go to war with them.'

Another attack hit us with a blinding crash.

'I can't take much more of this,' Marque said. 'I'm running out of energy to maintain the barrier. Two or three more hits and Scaleshome will be destroyed.'

'Hurting them is the least of our worries right now,' I said, and nodded to Oliver. 'Go! Go!'

He pressed the button to connect to the cat ships' wavelength and spoke to them in their own tongue. Marque translated for us.

'Stop attacking the dragon facility,' Oliver said. 'I'm one of your kind, kidnapped by the humans, and I'm inside the facility. Please stop; you'll kill me.'

The cats replied in their own language. 'You are a feral, uncivilised and not trained in the way of the true cat. You are contaminated and must be destroyed.'

Another hit, and this time the ground rocked beneath us.

'I really can't keep this up,' Marque said. 'Another hit and I'll only be able to put a few of you in energy bubbles. Many will die.'

'Tell them the rest, Ollie,' I said.

Oliver spoke again. 'The humans have destroyed every potato on the planet, and hidden all the seeds in a secure storage facility. If you don't stop now, the humans will destroy that too and we will never again taste the excellence that is potatoes.'

'Don't harm the potatoes!' Hanako said, her eyes wide.

'We will *destroy them completely* if this doesn't stop,' the general said. 'And if you don't control your dragonscales, we will destroy them anyway.'

'No,' Zianto moaned. 'This is going so wrong!'

There was another blinding flash, then another. I ducked, then looked around, surprised to be still alive.

'That was your ships, dragons,' Marque said. 'They blew them up.' Its voice filled with fury. 'I had *data* stored on those ships.'

We waited for another hit, but it didn't happen.

'They may have run out of power on their ship. If so, they could be recharging the guns from their warp drive,' Marque said.

'Do you know how long we have before they start firing again?' I said.

'For a small cruiser like that, about seventeen minutes.'

A message came through from the cats. 'Give us your potatoes and the feral now, or we will destroy a population centre. You have seventeen minutes to submit.'

The general opened her tablet. 'Stew? We have seventeen minutes until they can fire again. There are two cat ships. I'm on my way to Birmingham with the dragons. I'll infiltrate with Choumali and the specials. No, you secure Scaleshome; I'll do the cat ships. If you're in mid-air, swapping Choumali will be too complicated.'

She folded her tablet and spoke to the dragons. 'We have strike teams with a special weapon that will completely disable the cat ships. But we need you to fold us there. You take us, we drop the weapons, and leave.'

'We don't want to hurt the cats,' Hanako said.

'The weapon will disable their ships without any long-term damage,' the general said. 'We won't kill them or destroy their ships. Nothing that would give them cause to retaliate. We just want to shut them down long enough for you to drop them back home; and make it clear that every time they approach Earth we'll do it again.'

Both dragons' heads shot back on their long necks.

'You really have a weapon that can disable the cats to that degree?' Hanako said.

'We do,' the general said. 'We tested it on Major Choumali's son.'

'It completely incapacitated me for more than a day,' Oliver said. He winced, showing his long canines. 'They'll only need to experience it once, then they'll stay away forever.'

'I hope you're right, General,' Zianto said.

'Choumali, I need your psi ability to show the dragons where to go,' the general said. 'The troops are waiting at the Birmingham base. Zianto, Hanako, if you wouldn't mind transporting me and Major Choumali to the location she shows you? Let's get this moving as fast as we can. And Marque: let Admiral Blake in when he arrives. He can help the defence effort if the cats manage to land here.'

Marque hesitated, then said, 'Okay.'

*

At the Birmingham base, a dozen special forces soldiers were loading up with full gas-protection equipment.

Their captain opened a locker and gestured inside. 'Major Choumali,' she said, her voice muffled behind her mask, 'here's spare equipment for you and General Maxwell. I understand you've used it before?'

'Yes,' I said. 'When we tested it on Oliver.'

'I need a pod to carry this many people,' Zianto said. 'And my ship's been destroyed.'

'Can both of you together carry fourteen of us?' the general said, zipping up her own protective equipment.

The dragons shared a look.

'It's pushing it, but we can manage,' Zianto said. 'Just make sure to stay within three metres of us.'

The general pulled on her mask. 'You'll need to protect yourselves. I suggest Marque places you in an energy bubble as soon as we release the bombs.'

'What's in them?' Hanako said, watching the bombs being placed into a locker. Each spherical bomb was twenty centimetres across, black and unremarkable. She sneezed loudly. 'What is it?'

'Chilli,' I said, my voice muffled by my mask.

'A meat dish with spices?' Marque said.

'Hot pepper, and I told you about using American dictionaries,' I said.

'Oh, it's just a plant's chemical defence system. I fail to see how this will work. Natural products tend to be weak and ineffective.'

'Wait and see,' I said.

The specials put the lid on the bombs locker and moved into position around the dragons. Their captain gestured for me to join her next to Zianto. I put my hand on Zianto's butt, and checked my wrist tablet: nine minutes since we'd left Scaleshome.

The dragons folded us up to the bridge of the cat cruiser. I moved my head to see through my mask's eye holes. We were in a towering control centre, at least twenty metres high. Platforms housing control stations were set at varying heights above us, all occupied by cats. They sat facing the control centre's transparent front wall, which gave a spectacular view of Earth.

The cats pulled weapons and leaped down off the platforms towards us. They wore jumpsuits similar to the one Oliver's mother had worn, in different shades of grey.

'Team two with Hanako to the exploratory ship,' General Maxwell said. 'Zianto, fold outside the ship and wait for us there.'

'No, I want to stay and see,' Zianto began, but a cat shot at her. The beam bounced off the energy wall Marque had placed in front of her.

'Don't argue, just go!' the general shouted as the cats shot at us, the beams splashing onto the energy barrier.

Marque placed a location marker onto my tablet, together with a schematic of the ship, and the dragons disappeared, taking three of the specials with them.

The soldier near me tossed the first chilli bomb. It exploded with a loud *poof* that sprayed a fine mist of bright red chilli powder everywhere.

The cats screamed and fell writhing on the floor. They clawed at their faces, still screaming. Those on higher platforms dropped to the ground as well, until all of them were down.

'Good,' the general said. 'Let's go.'

We left the bridge and entered a narrow corridor, higher than it was wide, with platforms above us that the cats obviously walked along. Everything was covered in a dark grey, textured coating that was like rough carpet.

A squad of cats raced down the hall towards us, and one of the specials tossed a bomb at them.

The chilli leaked into my protective equipment and my eyes started to burn, but it wasn't so bad that I couldn't function. The cats, however, with their more sensitive noses and no protective equipment, were completely disabled. Three more raced towards us, and fell three metres away.

'You have to wonder what full-on tear gas would do,' one of the specials said.

'It overloads their nervous system and stops their heart,' I said. 'My son nearly died.'

'We should be using that on the bastards then,' one of the others said as they tossed another bomb into what appeared to be a mess room to one side of the corridor.

I wiped the red powder off the eye holes in my mask and saw that ten cats inside the room were down.

'If we kill them, the Cat Republic will destroy Earth,' I said, pointing down another corridor, which according to Marque's schematic led to the living quarters. 'This is just a warning. How many bombs left?'

'Fair enough,' the special said. 'Twelve bombs left.'

'Is that enough for the rest of the ship, Major?' the general said.

'No, but once the chilli's in the ventilation system it will shut them down completely. It only takes a few grams to incapacitate them.'

We arrived at a T-intersection and I checked the map. The crew quarters were small, oval-shaped caves in three tiers along the cross corridor, with two platforms above for the cats to enter, but no stairs from the ground up. It seemed that most of the ship's volume was taken up by the warp drive and a couple of energy cannons.

One of the specials checked her mask. 'This stuff's leaking inside – it must be super-fine.'

'It's so super-fine that no filter can completely remove it,' I said.

She looked up at the tiers of caves. 'How do we get up there?'

'We don't need to. Follow me.'

I led them along the corridor on the left, and we stopped at the end wall. Cats were emerging from their sleeping pods, then ducking back inside as they realised they were under attack. There was no general alarm sounding through the ship; the cats in the bridge had been disabled before they could turn it on.

'Toss one up every three metres,' I said, and the specials nodded.

The first bomb went up and sprayed chilli everywhere.

As we moved along the corridor, a member of the second team contacted us on comms. 'We're on the exploratory ship. It had a skeleton crew, which we've neutralised.' His voice filled with exultation. 'There are fifteen tiny Japanese kids on board. They must be the ones the cats kidnapped from New Nippon.'

'Yes!' one of the specials said, and they filled with jubilation.

'How much time remaining on the recharge, Marque?' I said. I was concerned that we hadn't disabled all of the cats and they might still fire at Earth.

'Three minutes,' it said. 'The firing controls are in the bridge, and the crew there were knocked flat. But there may be secondary controls in engineering. I suggest you go straight there.'

'You should have told me that sooner!' I shouted, and gestured for the specials to follow me.

'You're doing exceptionally well by yourselves,' Marque said dryly. 'I've never seen such an effective non-lethal disablement of any species. That chilli stuff is like magic. I cannot believe you humans actually *eat* it.'

We ran down the corridor to the T-intersection, and back up towards the bridge. The walls were stained red with chilli, and the cats were still on the floor, writhing and screaming.

Engineering was under the floor halfway back to the bridge, but when we reached the point on the map there was no visible entrance.

'Marque, open the engineering hatch for us,' I said, checking the time. The cat ship would be recharged in two minutes.

'Accessing ...' Marque said, and part of the floor opened to reveal a rough-coated ramp that went down towards the aft of the ship.

We jumped in and raced towards the engineering room. It was ferociously warm, and the warp drive was hidden by complex magnetic containment and cooling systems that wrapped around it in a massive circular nest of pipes and wires, three metres across, set into the back wall.

The cats were all on the floor screaming. Enough chilli had leaked from the floors above to disable them. The specials threw a couple more bombs just to make sure.

General Maxwell and I went straight to the warp drive's control panel and monitoring systems.

'Marque, what would happen if I shot the guts out of this?' the general said.

'Without the containment and cooling systems, the drive would probably go critical and blow up the ship.'

'Understood,' Maxwell said. 'Choumali, lead us to the extraction point. Marque, tell the dragons they can fold the ships back to the cats' own system.'

I checked the map on my tablet, and led the team up the ramp and back to the corridor above. The cats had stopped writhing and were lying still. I checked one and couldn't feel a pulse.

'Shit,' the general said. 'They're not dead, are they?'

'No, Charles,' Marque said. 'They're unconscious. The chemical's shut them down completely.'

'Good,' she said, and gestured for me to lead the way. We picked our way through the prone bodies, some still writhing, to the T-intersection where the crew quarters were. As we reached the intersection, we were all stretched impossibly thin – the dragons had folded us into cat space.

'We're at the extraction point,' I said to Marque. 'I suggest you put some sort of protection around the dragons before they come inside. The chilli may have a similarly intense impact on them.'

Zianto appeared in front of us, cried out and fell to the ground, writhing. We gathered around her and put our hands on her, ready to fold.

'I told you to protect her!' I shouted at Marque.

'Fold us out!' the general shouted at the same time.

'She's in an energy bubble. None of the chilli should have got through,' Marque said. 'Hanako's okay on the exploratory ship.'

'Zianto obviously is affected by the chilli!' I said.

Marque created a wave of water that splashed over all of us. It got into my mask and saturated the filter, making it hard to breathe. I was forced to pull the mask off, and inhaled a face full of chilli powder, but it was a mild burn, not the full-on agony the cats and Zianto were experiencing.

The other specials removed their masks as well, and shook their heads as the chilli went into their eyes, but nobody was incapacitated by it.

Fold us out! I shouted at Zianto.

She screamed inside my head, radiating intense agonising pain.

Zianto! Get us out of here!

She folded us out, and I fell two metres onto the main square at Scaleshome.

Marque doused us again with a torrent of water that didn't stop. I gasped for breath, and the water changed to a white chemical slurry that had a slight neutralising effect.

I splashed it into my eyes to clear them, and looked around. I saw with a bolt of horror that Zianto had folded inaccurately in her distress, and three of the special forces soldiers were embedded in the ground. One was dead, buried up to his shoulders. The other two were still alive – one buried from her waist down, and the other trapped up to his knees. They both writhed in agony, screaming, until I psionically knocked them out.

'The mission was a success,' General Maxwell said, running her hand over her wet blonde hair. 'Three losses out of twelve is high, but worth it.' She frowned at the unconscious half-submerged specials. 'Now we have the unpleasant task of bringing these soldiers' families here to say goodbye before we pull them out of the ground and kill them.'

'No need, general,' Marque said. 'If the dragons fold them out, I can keep them alive and grow new body parts for them.'

Admiral Blake ran to us. 'Did the chilli work?'

'Admirably,' the general said. 'Complete success. The only losses were these three. Where are the Japanese children?'

Hanako appeared with a group of children clustered around her. She disappeared, then reappeared fifteen metres away with more children. Then she collapsed and lay twitching on the ground, making a high-pitched wailing sound.

'Did you use all the bombs?' Admiral Blake said.

'Yes,' I said.

'Dammit.' He pulled out his tablet and checked it, then spoke to the dragons. 'I need your help to collect another round of bombs in case more cats turn up.'

The dragons didn't reply; they were still gasping on the ground.

Zianto? Hanako? I said.

'Broke them,' the general said with grim humour. 'The chilli's just as effective on them. Good to know.' She turned to Admiral Blake. 'Have the dragonscales been rounded up and locked down?'

'The UN are on their way,' Blake said. 'Secretary Park will be here in twenty minutes. He wants to talk to you.'

'What a coincidence,' Maxwell said, pulling her tablet out of her protective gear. 'I'd like to speak to him too. Marque, these soldiers need to be extracted from the ground before they die. Wake the goddamn dragons up and get them moving.'

'I'm trying,' Marque said. 'They're unresponsive.' Its sphere moved in close to Hanako's neck. 'I'm tapping her scales, calling for a dragon from their homeworld to help us.'

'Good.' Maxwell checked her tablet, then turned to me. 'Is there a meeting room we can use when the UN people get here?'

'Yes,' I said. 'I'll show you the way.'

'Let's lock this down and prepare for another cat attack while we work out what to do about the dragonscales children.' She smiled grimly. 'After what just happened, I have a few ideas.'

33

As the general and I were about to leave, Shiumo and Richard appeared in the main square.

'Marque says you need our help, and I need yours. The Nimestas –' Shiumo sneezed loudly and took a few deep breaths. 'What the hell is *that*?'

'Damn,' Marque said. 'Even after I've rinsed it off, Shiumo's still reacting to the chilli. That stuff is *potent*.'

Shiumo sneezed again and shook her head. 'It really hurts!'

'We were attacked by cats and we pepper-sprayed them,' I said. 'It has the same effect on dragons.'

'You pepper-sprayed the dragons?' Richard said, aghast. 'Why? What the hell's going on, Jian?'

Shiumo rounded on us. 'If you've hurt my sisters ...'

'They're not injured. They just received a full dose of that pepper stuff right in the face,' Marque said. 'I think they'll be out of commission for a while. And the cats destroyed their ships too. A couple of cat ships attacked Earth, and the pepper-spray disabled the cats long enough for us to fold them home.'

Shiumo's head shot up. 'This is a way to disable the cats and stop them attacking?'

'Yes, but we need you to help our soldiers first,' Maxwell said. 'They're stuck in the ground.'

'You can help me then!' Shiumo said. She went to the unconscious special who was buried up to her waist. 'Ouch. This pepper stuff must be awful for my sister to mess up like that. Ready, Marque?'

'Ready.'

Shiumo folded the soldier away, leaving the distressing image of half her body still in the ground. She returned and went to the second soldier. 'We need to hurry,' she said, and folded him away too.

'Where do you want me to put the poor dead one?' she asked when she returned, then she raised her head. 'I'll have to do it later. The cats found the planet we took the Nimestas to, and they've attacked. They're killing the Nimestas to harvest their saliva.'

'Their saliva?' I said.

'Apparently its scent is divine,' Richard said.

'The Nimestas refused to allow themselves to be farmed, so the cats are just killing them to take it,' Shiumo said.

'Good,' General Maxwell said. 'Here's our chance to make it absolutely clear to the cats that what we just did wasn't a one-off.'

I turned to the leader of the special forces team. 'Captain, you said all the pepper bombs were gone?'

'We have plenty more back in Birmingham, ma'am.'

'Go and collect the bombs, Choumali, then come back here,' the general said.

I moved closer to Shiumo and showed her the location on my tablet. 'Can you take us here?' Then I looked up at Marque. 'Can you shield her from the chilli? How about putting her in a spacesuit?'

'No dragon has ever needed a spacesuit,' Shiumo said, indignant.

'This time you do,' Marque said, and a glowing aura of energy appeared around her. 'I've put positive pressure in this one. Here's hoping it keeps the pepper out, otherwise it may be a short trip.'

Shiumo folded the captain and me to Birmingham, where we filled a transportable storage locker with a larger number of bombs.

When we returned to Scaleshome, the general already had her mask on. She stood next to Richard, whose emotions were a violent mixture of anger and betrayal. He hadn't known about the dragons' reproductive bullshit.

'Take us to these Nimestas,' the general said to Shiumo, and put her hand on Shiumo's shoulder. Five of the specials gathered around Shiumo too. The general nodded to Richard, and he nodded back.

'Will this pepper stuff work underwater?' Marque asked me.

'It will be even more effective in water.'

'Okay,' it said. 'I don't have time to fabricate full underwater suits for you, so I'll give you pressure suits over your protective gear. You'll have a limited supply of air, but after what happened on the cat ship I don't think you'll need more than a couple of minutes.'

The air around me grew pearlescent, with a rainbow shimmering at the edge of my vision. A heads-up display appeared in front of me, showing my remaining air and the status of the suit.

'Everybody green?' Marque said.

'Yes,' we all said, and Shiumo folded us to her ship.

We stood in the gallery of her ship looking down on the Nimestas' sanctuary. Three big cat cruisers floated above the water planet.

'Three ships against fifty peaceful Nimestas,' Shiumo said. 'The cats are such cowards.'

'Fold us onto the ships and we'll disable them,' I said.

'There are five cats on the surface harvesting the Nimestas. We have to go down there first,' Shiumo said.

'How many cats on the ships?'

'At least a hundred on each one,' Shiumo said.

'All right,' General Maxwell said. 'Surface first, then we'll deal with the ships.'

We gathered around Shiumo and she folded us into the water. A group of three cats in spacesuits were firing at an enormous Nimestas. It writhed in agony, bleeding greenish-yellow into the water. Two more cats were cutting up another Nimestas while it was still alive, tearing into its head with energy weapons.

Don't throw the bombs, I broadcast to everyone. *They may harm the Nimestas, and the cats are wearing suits.*

So how do we do this? Shiumo said.

I studied the situation. 'Can you disable their suits without killing them?' I asked Marque. 'So they get a face full of chilli?'

'No,' Marque said over my suit's comms. 'You can't have one without the other. If you disable their suits, the water pressure will kill them before they drown.'

Everyone back to me, Shiumo said. *I know what to do.*

'What are you –' Marque began, but we gathered around Shiumo and she folded us back to her ship.

She disappeared, and returned with a cat; then rapidly returned with four more, one at a time. 'Throw the chilli!' she shouted as the cats fired on her. Their weapons' beams bounced off Marque's energy shield. 'Cover them with it!'

'That won't do anything,' Marque said.

We threw the bombs anyway, spraying red chilli powder over the cats' pressure suits. Marque was right – it did nothing. The cats fired on us as well, and Marque protected us.

'I can't hold this shield for long,' it said. 'Shiumo, what were you thinking? Fold them back to the surface. We'll find another way.'

Shiumo disappeared, and reappeared behind one of the cats. She lowered her head and concentrated as she reached towards it with one claw. A half-centimetre-wide hole appeared in the cat's suit as she manipulated space in four dimensions, then closed again. The cat screamed and fell.

Shiumo folded to the next cat, and created a hole in its suit as it spun to fire on her. It quickly fell too.

The three remaining cats concentrated their fire on her, and Marque protected her.

'Marque, give me a weapon so I can fire back,' I said.

'No need,' Shiumo said, and folded behind another cat. She raised her claw to put a hole in its suit, but the hole was too big; it tore a chunk out of the cat's back. Shiumo released the hole, and folded to the next cat. A hole appeared in the air next to the side of the ship, and blood pumped out of it.

'Shit,' Shiumo said, and the hole disappeared.

She put a small hole in the suit in front of her, sending its occupant screaming to the ground, then folded to the last cat. She put her claw up to make the hole, and a small spherical piece of flesh – looking like red muscle and spongy lung tissue – appeared in front of me, then fell to the ground with a wet splat. Shiumo tried again, and the cat screamed and fell, bleeding from its nose.

'Marque, help!' she said, and collapsed, her sides heaving with effort. 'I think I put the holes inside them.'

'They'll survive until we return them to their homeworld,' Marque said.

'We need to deal with the cruisers,' I said. 'Shiumo, are you okay?'

'My whole face hurts,' she said. 'My eyes! How can this stuff get into a spacesuit?'

'Your four-dimensional stupidity probably made your suit leak,' Marque said. 'That was such a risky thing to do – you could have killed all of us. Do you need a rinse?'

Shiumo sneezed loudly. 'Yes, please! It burns.'

Marque doused her with the white slurry, and she shook her head. She went to one of the cats on the ground, touched its shoulder, and they disappeared.

'Stand by, she may need you,' Marque said. 'If there isn't enough chilli on these cats, you'll have to go into the cruisers and throw some bombs around.'

It's working, Shiumo said. *They're falling down around me.* She reappeared, put her claw on another of the prone cats, and folded it out. *This is the first time I've actively fought them. It feels good to help my loved ones and put these damn cats in their place.*

She took the last cat, and reappeared. 'There's one more ship. I'll fold you into it, and then we need to give those poor Nimestas medical attention.'

'I have a sphere on its way to the surface. I'll give them emergency treatment until you can fold them up here,' Marque said.

'To me, everyone, and I'll take you to the cruiser,' Shiumo said.

'Form up behind me,' the general said. She kneeled next to the locker holding the bombs and thumbed the fingerprint scanner to secure it.

'What are you doing? There's still one ship full of cats,' Shiumo said. 'They'll destroy the planet if we don't stop them!'

'As far as we've seen, you dragons are creatures of your word,' the general said. 'We want your word that you will halt your reproductive conquest of Earth, and stop your dragonscales from uncontrolled reproduction.'

There was a bright flash of light – the remaining cat cruiser was shooting at Shiumo's ship.

'Can't this wait?' Shiumo said. 'Only my mother can make that promise, and in the meantime the cat cruiser could blow up the planet and kill the Nimestas!'

'Pass our message through to your homeworld and obtain agreement from your mother,' the general said. 'Or we won't help you.'

'The humans are the only ones capable of handling the chilli,' Marque said. Its voice gained an edge of amusement. 'You have no choice; you have to agree to their terms. It doesn't matter how primitive they are; you can't afford to breed them out of existence.'

Shiumo tapped the side of her neck. 'There, I passed the message on. Now let's go!'

'We need confirmation that the Empress agrees to our terms,' the general said. 'Not just your word. A message from her.'

'I can't guarantee anything, but I'll try,' Shiumo said, and tapped her neck again.

A dull brown dragon in a spacesuit appeared in front of us with a Marque sphere. It sneezed violently. 'What the hell?'

The sphere projected a message from the Empress. She was sitting on a shady balcony of white stone, surrounded by a number of different aliens. 'I agree to your terms,' she said. 'Now please save the Nimestas!'

'You have what you wanted, humans,' the brown dragon said. 'You have no idea what you've just set in motion. The entire Empire is watching. Now go save our Nimestas dragonscales.' She disappeared.

General Maxwell thumbed the contact point on top of the storage locker. It opened, and she passed the bombs around.

'Remember,' she told Shiumo as we all put our hands on her. 'You can't fight the cats without the chilli. And to use the chilli you need us.'

'Let's go,' Shiumo said, resigned. 'My mother's going to *kill* me when I get home.'

*

After Shiumo had dropped all the cat ships back in their home system, she returned us to Scaleshome. A platoon of UN troops in their distinctive sky-blue combat dress were waiting for us, with a small group of dragonscales girls standing nearby and watching with curiosity. The pepper on us hit the girls, and they shrieked and attempted to run away, but fell to the ground before they could get very far. Marque lifted them and carried them towards the medical centre.

'That answers that question. We're the only ones who can deal with the cats,' General Maxwell said to Shiumo.

'I can see that,' she said. 'My mother really is going to kill me.'

The commander of the UN troops stepped forward and saluted us as we removed our protective equipment and Marque doused it in the neutralising slurry. 'Secretary Park is with Admiral Blake,' she said. 'Come this way.'

'Admiral Blake can take over,' General Maxwell said. 'I'm retired – this was just a one-off. I'm not needed any more, and we have an agreement from the dragons to halt the reproductive assimilation.'

'Secretary Park would still like to thank you. All of you,' the UN officer said.

We went into the meeting room. Richard was sitting to one side broadcasting raw, grief-stricken fury, but didn't speak.

Maxwell sat across from Secretary Park and nodded to him. 'We made the dragons agree to stop their reproductive assimilation program. I suggest Shiumo carries a diplomatic delegation to the dragon homeworld as quickly as possible so they don't have time to back out.'

'Where are Zianto and Hanako?' Shiumo said, then raised one claw. 'Never mind. They probably took off. Hanako's already in enough trouble for screwing up her previous First Contact.'

'They suddenly had other places to be,' Park said. 'Princess, will you take us to your home planet to seal the agreement?'

'I have to. I'm responsible for this.' Her voice became small. 'This is all my fault.'

'We're giving you a way to defend the Empire against the cats,' I said. 'You'll be a hero.'

'I don't think my mother will see it that way,' she said.

'I want you to act as ambassador, Charlie,' Secretary Park said to General Maxwell. 'After Choumali and Alto, you're the most experienced in dealing with these aliens, and you're also our toughest negotiator. You've worked with the dragons, and used the pepper bombs. You're the best choice.'

'I'm *retired*, Brian,' she protested. 'Surely someone else can do it?'

'You are absolutely the best person for the job,' he said.

'I would prefer Earth's representative was someone more ... diplomatic,' Shiumo said.

'See? Even the dragons are scared of you,' Park said.

'I'm a soldier, not a diplomat!' Maxwell said.

'Oh, come on, Charlie, you haven't stopped complaining about how boring retirement is. You're going to love every minute of this,' Park said amiably. 'We need you. Do it.'

Maxwell's expression became wry.

Park turned to me. 'Major Choumali, you'll accompany the ambassador's delegation as her psi, along with a couple of UN guards and the team of specials trained in the use of the pepper bombs. You're going straight to the dragon homeworld.' He studied Shiumo. 'Will you take them, Princess? The other two dragons have disappeared.'

'I'll take them,' Shiumo said, resigned. 'My scales haven't stopped tapping since we took out those cat ships. Everybody's so excited that we finally have a way to deal with the cats without full-on conflict.'

'They need to go now,' Park said. 'Are the dragons ready for their arrival?'

'They're ready,' Shiumo said. 'I'll take –'

She stopped as a couple of UN guards entered the room. They were holding a large aluminium locker at least a metre tall.

Shiumo's eyes widened. 'Is that more pepper bombs? I doubt you'll be allowed to take that many –'

'It's a gift for the Empress,' Park said. 'A selection of seventeen different types of seed potato.'

Shiumo's eyes became even wider. 'Hot damn! She'll love it.' She turned her head on her long neck to look at Park. 'Can I have some potatoes too – as a reward for taking your delegation?'

'Come back at the end of the negotiations and we'll see what we can do,' Park said. He rose. 'Now if you don't mind, we'd like to have this done as quickly as possible.'

Oliver raced into the room and skidded to halt, nearly hitting the potato locker. 'Take me too! I want to show the dragons that not all cats are bad!'

'Good idea,' I said.

'No,' Shiumo and Marque said in unison.

'Why not?' Oliver said.

'Oliver, the cats have attacked many planets at the edges of the Empire,' Marque said. 'The dragon homeworld is full of refugees, sheltered by the Empress herself.'

'There are people on Dragonhome who have lost entire families, clans, whole *planets* to cat attacks,' Shiumo said. 'They would see you, and see all they've lost. They'd kill you on sight.'

Oliver subsided. 'I want a chance to show them I'm different.'

'We'll put the word out around the Empire that you exist and that you're working with us,' Shiumo said.

'Maybe I'll make a documentary about you,' Marque said. 'The Empress will want to meet you – but going to Dragonhome is a really, really bad idea. Even I can't guarantee your safety.'

'All right,' Oliver said, resigned.

I hugged him, and he pulled me close. 'Do us proud, Mum,' he said into my ear.

I pulled back and put my hand on his face. 'Not as proud as I am of you, son. Look after your brother.'

'I will.'

'I'll bring the pod down to carry you all,' Shiumo said. 'You'll finally see Dragonhome, dear Richard.'

Richard's face was rigid with restraint, but his emotions were full of betrayal. He took Shiumo's scale out of his pocket and held it out to her. 'You lied to me. Since the first day we met, you lied to me. You came here with the intention of wiping us out, but you pretended you were helping us.'

She looked at the scale for a long time, then up at him. 'The breeding program was humanity's idea.'

'Stop lying to me! This was your plan all along,' he shouted. He shoved the scale at her. 'Take this. And. Never. Speak. To. Me. Again.'

'I still love –' she began, but he tossed her scale onto the floor and stalked out before she could finish.

'This is all going so wrong,' she whispered.

'Dragonhome. Now,' Maxwell said.

Shiumo disappeared to collect the pod from her ship.

'Good luck, Charlie,' Secretary Park said. 'I know you can do it.'

34

When we were all on Shiumo's ship, she asked us to sit around her table so she could speak to us.

'Before we proceed, I have to explain about goldenscales,' she said, quiet and cowed. 'My mother will assign you one as a liaison to help you with the protocol on our world. Sometimes a second-generation dragon isn't the colour of either of its royal parents; it's just plain yellow. We call these dragons goldenscales to make them feel special, but they're generally limited in talent and ability to fold. They love helping people so they act as personal assistants for us. Please be kind to your goldenscales. We love them dearly and want to protect them.'

Without another word she folded onto the nose of her ship, and carried us to the dragon homeworld. It appeared larger than Earth, with more land mass, which was covered in green vegetation that contrasted with its yellow and red deserts, and smaller oceans.

Shiumo reappeared next to us. 'We have to disembark onto the orbital network. I can't fold any closer than this. Follow me.'

She led us to the rear of the ship, and Marque opened a door for us that led out onto a receiving platform in a dome-shaped room. Its transparent ceiling showed space above us, with the dragon planet taking up half the sky. Gravity was set at Earth-normal. A tunnel, also with a transparent ceiling, led out of the room.

A small moon was visible near the station. It was difficult to make out its exact size, but its surface wasn't rock; it was a viewscreen of glowing dots that scrolled the message: *Welcome, representatives from Earth.*

'Is that an artificial satellite?' I said.

'I suppose it is, in a way,' Marque said. 'It's me.'

A brilliantly golden dragon entered the room with a Marque sphere floating above her. She was smaller than the other dragons, only a metre and a half long. She bowed her head. 'Greetings, Ambassador Maxwell. I'm your goldenscales assistant. I've taken the name of Miko in your language.'

'This is where I leave you,' Shiumo said. 'I have things to do.'

'I'm sure you do,' Maxwell said dryly. 'You can run, but this will catch up with you.'

Shiumo turned away to return to her ship.

'Oh, and Shiumo?' Maxwell said.

Shiumo turned back.

'Don't bother trying to win Alto back. You'll just be wasting your time.'

Shiumo lowered her head and went back into her ship.

'Keep an eye on our emotional states,' Maxwell said quietly to me. 'If we start sounding controlled, we need to get out of here.'

I nodded to her. 'Ma'am.'

'Welcome to Dragonhome,' the goldenscales said. She turned and gestured with one claw. 'Allow me to show you to the space elevator that will carry you to the surface. The Empress herself has rooms waiting for you in her palace.'

I walked at Ambassador Maxwell's shoulder, my empathy at full sensitivity. The five specials we'd brought, all with pepper bombs secreted in their armour, followed us; and the two UN guards with the locker of seed potatoes brought up the rear.

Miko guided us through the tunnel further into the orbital station. The lower walls and floor of the tunnel were a shiny opaque black, with matching black ribs that curved between the transparent upper walls and ceiling. The network of tubes connecting the stations was visible, and surrounded the entire planet.

We walked for nearly half a kilometre before coming out into an enormous room where it seemed all the corridors met. The ceiling was so high it was almost invisible, and the walls were similarly distant. Planter boxes held colourful alien plants between walkways and fountains, and there were white dome-shaped dragon buildings in the centre of the space, with different species of aliens strolling between them. The buildings closer to us were smaller, only one or two storeys high, and appeared to be shops and restaurants with tables set out among the gardens. A stunning variety of species were visible, sitting on a range of chair types around the tables, or reclining on soft mats on the ground. The buildings further away stretched all the way to the ceiling of the room, twenty storeys above.

Miko turned to face us. 'The elevator trip will take about four of your hours. Dragons aren't permitted to fold within orbital distance of Dragonhome as too much four-dimensional manipulation in such a small area can damage space-time. Marque will see to your safety and comfort while you are in the pod. Let me show you your quarters while we travel to the surface.'

She led us past a pair of blue-finned aquatic aliens floating in a two-metre-wide sphere of water. One of the aliens made a watery sound and Miko stopped. The alien extended an eyestalk out of the sphere of water and spoke to her. She replied in the same language, and the alien withdrew its eyestalk and floated away, still talking.

'What did it say?' I asked her.

'They asked if you are the ones who will help the Empire to finally break free of the scourge of the cats,' she said. 'It offers all it possesses to anyone who can defeat the cats and bring justice for the loss of its planet.'

'And what did you tell it?'

'It's not my place to tell it anything. Marque will transmit any official announcements.'

Miko took us into the village and along a small boulevard-like street. The buildings on either side were more shops and restaurants; and the ceiling two storeys above gave off a gentle glowing light like soft daylight.

'Trade in this market is by request,' she said as we walked past the shops. 'Please confirm your safety with an in-house Marque before sampling any food, beverages or mind-altering substances. The shops sell them for all chemistries and they may not match your own.'

'What does "trade by request" mean?' Maxwell said.

'Just ask for anything and they'll give it to you,' Marque said. 'I fabricate everything, so unless it's something that will require a large amount of my time or energy, you can basically have anything you want. Items that can't be fabricated, like your potatoes, are sold elsewhere.' Its voice gained an amused edge. 'There's a swimming pool here already, Major. Miko can show you where it is.'

'I like swimming,' Miko said with pleasure.

At the end of the boulevard, a hundred metres away, was an arched entrance, two storeys high. Miko led us through it, and into an oval lobby with an atrium soaring twenty storeys above us. There were stairs on three sides of the atrium, and doors – larger at the bottom, smaller at the top – opened onto the galleries on each floor. Everything was constructed from a smooth glazed substance in a soft ivory colour that shone in the mock sunlight.

'Marque has already tailored your rooms to your biometrics,' Miko said. 'Your names are on the doors. If you get lost, ask Marque which way to go.' She led us to a bright blue, raised area on the floor, ten metres across. 'Just use this lift to get to your floor.'

'They've never used one of these before, Miko,' Marque said.

'Oh,' she said, her eyes wide, and cocked her head. 'You've never used a lift before?'

'Not like this,' Maxwell said.

Miko hesitated. 'Uh ... okay,' she said, and gestured for us to stand on the blue area.

'Nobody's afraid of heights?' Marque said. 'It just occurred to me that one of you might be.'

'Afraid of *heights*? What, like being high in the air?' Miko said, shocked. 'Why would anyone be afraid of that?'

'Not so much the height as the fall,' I said wryly.

'But you never fall.' She sounded confused. 'Marque will always catch you.'

'Not where they come from,' Marque said. 'Do you need visible walls?'

'We'll get used to it,' Maxwell said. 'Don't give us special treatment. We need to learn how to do things here.'

'Understood,' Marque said, and the floor lifted swiftly and smoothly. We all moved closer together, away from the edges.

'Throw yourself against the wall to show them it's safe, Miko,' Marque said.

Miko took a small running jump at the side of the platform and hit the invisible barrier with an audible thump.

'Do it again,' Marque said.

Miko did the same thing – and this time flew completely off the edge. Maxwell gasped as Miko fell. The goldenscales rose up alongside the lift, matching its velocity, and drifted back onto the platform.

She shook her head. 'You should have warned me, Marque. You made me look silly. Only children do that!'

'They grow out of it by the time they're adults,' Marque said. 'They realise I'll never let them fall and the thrill goes out of it. I've put the barrier back up; none of you can fall off.'

I gingerly walked to the edge of the platform and put my hand out. The wall felt the same as Marque's usual energy barriers.

The lift stopped close to the top of the building, and we stepped out onto a gallery with a soft-textured floor. The centre of the atrium ceiling appeared as a sunny blue sky with white drifting clouds. Each door had a name next to it in English.

Mine was first, and I waved my hand over the door to open it. The room was identical to the one Marque had built for me on Shiumo's ship.

'We'll just wash and use the facilities,' Maxwell said. 'Then we'd like to go straight to the space elevator pod and down to Dragonhome without delay.'

Miko hesitated, and looked up at Marque, then to Ambassador Maxwell. 'I'm sorry, I obviously haven't made myself completely clear,' she said, and bowed her head. 'I sincerely apologise for my failure to communicate. This is the space elevator pod. We will arrive on the surface of Dragonhome in about four of your hours. Please use that time to relax, enjoy the facilities of the elevator, try the food and other substances. I am here if you have any personal needs. Just tell Marque that you require my services and I will come to you immediately.'

She moved her neck and head in a complicated sweeping motion that ended in a low bow. 'Welcome to Dragonhome.'

*

I used the small bathroom in my room, and went along the gallery to Ambassador Maxwell's room. I waved my hand over the door and after a moment it opened. One of the specials stood on the other side, radiating a thoroughly impressed reaction to the alien facilities.

The ambassador and a couple of the senior specials sat at a conference table in the centre of a suite that was much larger than my room. They were all nursing hot drinks.

'Good,' Maxwell said when she saw me. 'Come and sit.'

As I sat at the table, a pot of green dragon tea floated out of the wall in the suite's kitchenette and landed in front of me. I poured for myself.

Maxwell gestured at my tea. 'So everything here is tailored to individual preferences?'

'Marque registers what you like,' I said. 'You never have to ask twice, and it's aware that your preferences may change according to your mood or the time of day. Even the gravity is individually tailored for every species.'

'That's a level of comfort beyond anything I'd ever considered,' she said. 'No wonder the dragons are pacifists. They're soft from never being cold, hot, hungry or ill.'

'On the contrary, Ambassador,' Marque said. 'When your own species realised in the past that it was being too sedentary, the population quickly became focused on physical exercise. In the same way, advanced member societies of the Empire deliberately seek out uncomfortable experiences – so they aren't, as you say, soft.'

'Interesting,' Maxwell said, and sipped the drink Marque had provided for her. 'I have a great deal to learn.' She eyed me. 'And I think the best way would be to talk to the other people in this elevator pod. Are you up to a tour?' She checked her watch. 'How long have you been active? You've done a lot in the past day or so.'

I lowered my head and tried to puzzle it out. 'I greeted the dragonscales at Scaleshome about ... twenty hours ago? It's all a blur.'

'Maybe you should take a nap for an hour or two.'

I was wired on adrenaline and didn't feel tired, but she was right about the fatigue. It was definitely slowing me down.

I rubbed my eyes. 'You'll need me if you go downstairs to talk to people.'

She hesitated, and Marque broke in. 'I'll help the ambassador, Jian. You can rest.'

'Not acceptable,' Maxwell said. 'Take a ninety-minute power nap, Choumali, then meet us back here. While you're out, I'll have Marque give me an overview of the culture, economy and social structure of the dragon capital.'

'I can tune your brainwaves to give you a better –' Marque began.

'No,' Maxwell and I said in unison.

'I'll be back in ninety minutes,' I said.

*

I didn't feel rested when I returned to Maxwell's suite. The guards and specials were all listening to Marque's briefing with varied expressions of incredulity.

Maxwell rose when she saw me. 'How long were you living on Shiumo's ship? How comfortable are you in the dragons' culture?'

'Marque?' I said.

Maxwell raised her hand. 'Don't answer. Just the fact that you turned to Marque is all the answer I need.' She straightened. 'Marque says we've been invited for coffee, and I want your opinion on it.'

'As I was telling the ambassador,' Marque said, 'you've been pinged by a member of a species with an unpronounceable name that would like to have social contact with you. Their species enjoys introducing others to the Empire, and this individual would gain a great deal of pleasure if you permitted it to show you around.'

'Any weird shit?' I asked Marque.

'No weird shit,' it said.

'Is that a code?' Maxwell said, amused.

'Yes. Marque's studied our broadcasts and understands our social taboos,' I said. 'Richard worked the code out with it after a particularly bad First Contact episode during his travels with Shiumo.'

'The alien that wants to meet you is very similar to your species. They even meet socially over food and drink,' Marque said. 'Practically indistinguishable from humans.'

'Let's go and speak to Mr Unpronounceable,' Maxwell said.

'They're hermaphroditic, and this individual's name is Hrim,' Marque said.

'Indistinguishable,' Maxwell muttered as we went out.

*

Hrim was a four-metre-long horse-like alien, with three tiny hoofed digits at the end of each of its six slender legs. Its body was covered in brown scales with soft, feathered edges; and its long, narrow head had two normal eyes, with a soulstone between them, and a third bulging, faceted eye above the soulstone.

'Generally, yes, the dragons will negotiate in good faith,' Hrim said as we sat together in a café. 'The cats are a danger to us all, and finding a way to deal with them that doesn't mean going to war is a massive breakthrough. If you can also stop the dragons' reproductive assimilation program,' it gestured with one of its hoofs towards the purple scales on its forehead either side of its faceted central eye, 'you'll be doing everybody a favour. We've been asking the dragons to cut it out forever.'

'We'll do our best,' Maxwell said. 'I'll let you know how it turns out.'

'You won't need to,' Hrim said. 'We will hear everything the Empress says to you during the negotiations, and the entire Empire will hold her at her word.'

'Everything we say to her will be broadcast?' Maxwell said.

'Absolutely. The dragon administration is open and transparent. They have to be, or nobody would tolerate their reproductive bullshit. The advantages of being part of the Empire outweigh the disadvantages – particularly when the alternatives are torture and genocide by the cats. I hope you're successful.'

'Thanks for all your help,' Maxwell said.

'My pleasure. If there's anything else you need, ask Marque and it will put you in contact with me. My people enjoy introducing new species to the ways of the Empire. And if you guys can stop the damn dragons' reproductive assimilation, we'll all be in your debt.'

Miko approached us.

'I guess we need to change the topic,' I said.

'Wouldn't hurt,' Hrim said. It pulled itself onto all six feet and towered at least five metres above us. 'She's here to tell you that we're about to arrive. See you around Sky City, humans. As I said, I'm always here to help.'

'Contact us later and we'll arrange for you to receive some potatoes,' Maxwell said.

'I would like that very much,' Hrim said, and it tossed its head and wandered away.

35

'I hope you are all rested and comfortable,' Miko said. 'We are arriving at the base station. If you will come with me, I'll guide you down to the surface.'

We joined the throng of people who were headed in the same direction, away from the central buildings. They kept a respectful distance from us when they saw Miko.

The exit door led out onto a black shiny platform stretching away from us for nearly a kilometre, with the pale blue sky of high atmosphere above it. There was nothing beyond the edge of the platform, just clouds. We still appeared to be high above the surface of the planet.

The Marque satellite flashed messages across its surface in a number of different languages, together with projections of the Nimestas we'd rescued receiving medical treatment, and footage of what appeared to be another cat attack on a desert-like planet.

'This way,' Miko said, and led us across the platform to a bus-sized ovoid structure. Its side opened to show seats in a circle, all facing inwards. The top half of the oval was transparent, and the lower half was white.

Other aliens were entering vehicles of a variety of sizes and shapes; and some went to the edge of the platform and jumped off.

'The people jumping off are being carried by Marque, right?' Maxwell said.

'Yes,' Miko said. 'But it's easier to talk if we all travel together.' She gestured towards the vehicle. 'If you don't mind.'

We climbed in, and put the potato locker in the centre of the circle of seats. The seats were a hard, plastic-like substance, but they moulded themselves softly to our butts when we sat on them. The door closed, and the vehicle lifted off and took us down through the clouds.

As we dropped below them, Sky City became visible. It was so big that the edges of the floating city weren't visible; it appeared to be at ground level. A vast number of trees with colourful foliage in all shades of the rainbow, from blue to brilliant purple, were interspersed with trees a dull brown or grey colour. The vehicle levelled out and soared over a wide plaza, at least a kilometre each side, paved with shining white tiles and dotted with grassy areas containing more of the colourful and duller trees. There were so many aliens gathered on the plaza that my perception shut down and I couldn't tell one from the other.

'Goodness,' Miko said. 'That's unusual. Why are there so many people on the square, Marque?'

'To hear the negotiations firsthand. If the dragons accept the humans' terms, these people's families may finally be safe from the cats.'

'They're all there for *us*?' Maxwell said.

'Precisely,' Marque said.

'Which building is the Palace?' I said. 'There are two.'

'That one is Parliament,' Marque said, and an arrow appeared on the glass, pointing at a large blue-white building in a swooping wave-like shape. 'The Palace is at the other end of the plaza.'

We swept over the throng towards the Palace, which was built from a shining white material. Its basic shape was the standard dragon dome, but with many spires and towers, some transparent, others opaque white, and many with long silky pennants of different colours snapping on top. A ten-metre-wide terrace with no balustrade ran all the way around the outside of the Palace, five metres above the square.

The aliens crowded into the square kept their distance from the building. There weren't any guards or obvious markers, but there was a definite line the aliens wouldn't cross, ensuring a clear area in front of the Palace.

'It looks like something from a fairytale,' Maxwell said.

'Except the princess is the dragon,' I said wryly.

'The pennants indicate which of the Empress's children are in residence,' Miko said. 'Each princess has her own hue.'

'What about the plain brown and grey pennants?' Maxwell said, pointing at some towers on the left. 'Does that mean the princess isn't home?'

'Brown and grey?' Miko said, confused.

'You can't see those colours; they're outside your visual range,' Marque said.

'Oh, yes,' Miko said. 'That sometimes happens with our visitors. Every species sees the world differently.' She clasped her front claws together. 'Isn't diversity wonderful?'

'Yes, it is,' Maxwell said, her voice heavy with sarcasm, but Miko's rapt expression didn't change.

She isn't being callous. She's completely unaware of her species' activities, I said to Maxwell. *The naivety isn't feigned.*

'Makes for a delightfully harmless tour guide,' Maxwell said.

'I am glad you find my services satisfactory,' Miko said, bowing her head. 'Here we are.'

The vehicle swooped over the front of the Palace and landed in a courtyard under the towers. The side opened, and we climbed out onto the red grass-like lawn. A four-metre-tall crystalline sculpture sang quietly in the centre of the courtyard, with a pair of bright blue, lion-like aliens basking in the sun beneath it.

'This is Princess Shiumo's tower,' Miko said. 'Your guest quarters are here.'

'Is Shiumo around?' I said as Miko guided us to the base of the tower. Its gleaming white contrasted with the red grass covering the courtyard.

'She is currently off-planet on diplomatic business,' Miko said. 'Five of her spouses live in the tower and she plans to visit them soon.'

'Five,' Ambassador Maxwell said under her breath.

One of the blue lions rose and padded towards us. It was slightly smaller, and longer and narrower than an Earth lion, about half a metre high at the shoulder.

'Richard?' it asked me.

I stopped, confused, then realised what it was asking. 'No, I'm not Richard. None of us is.'

It went back to lie under the sculpture without replying.

'Richard is a favourite with the other spouses,' Miko said. 'They find his jokes very entertaining.'

'His jokes?' Maxwell asked me as a set of double doors opened to let us into the tower.

'Apparently they find some of the things he says funny when he doesn't intend them to be,' I said.

'Wonderful,' she growled.

There was a red lift circle in a room next to the base of the tower. We stood nervously on it.

'Don't worry, you're perfectly safe,' Miko said.

A hole in the ceiling opened and the lift propelled us up through the open air – way too fast to be comfortable. I sensed that Maxwell and the rest of the group were in various stages of panic.

'Blank it out, Marque,' I said, and the walls went opaque.

Maxwell straightened her jacket. 'Thank you.'

There was no feeling of deceleration when we stopped. The side of the lift opened onto a transparent-walled room, high in the tower, with soft lounges and red cushions scattered around the floor. The transparent walls gave us a glimpse of the rest of the Palace before they turned opaque pink.

'Leave the walls transparent, Marque,' Maxwell said. 'We have things like this back on Earth. I don't think anyone will have a problem with it. But if they do, we'll ask for it to be changed.'

The walls became transparent again. We were spectacularly high, with other Palace towers visible around us. The city stretched away into the distance in each direction, seemingly forever. Through a bank of curving windows on one side of the tower, we could see the space elevator platform, nearly as big as the Palace itself.

Four doors led from the main room to more rooms containing cushions; probably bedrooms.

'As it is nearly night-time, the Empress will see you in the morning, in seven of your hours,' Miko said. 'Captain Shudo, head of the Imperial Guard, will escort you into the Empress's presence. Is there anything I can do for you in the meantime? Do you require food or entertainment or any other personal services before you see the Empress?'

Marque spoke to her in the dragon language, and she listened attentively.

'That's extremely rude,' I said to it.

'It's more efficient,' it said. 'Dragons use fewer sounds to convey greater information. I'm telling her what your species usually does at night – the usual meal, sex, hygiene, sleep thing.'

'No sex!' the ambassador said, alarmed.

'We're quite capable of communicating our own needs,' I said. 'Make a meal for us, fabricate some fresh clothing for tonight and tomorrow, and we'll be fine. Does this apartment have a bathroom?'

'Some steps will appear on the other side of the room in an hour, leading up to individual bedrooms and bathrooms for you. I'm making them on the next floor up right now.'

I bowed to Miko. 'Thank you for your kind attention, Princess –'

Her eyes widened. 'Not Princess!'

'Goldenscales,' Marque said.

'Goldenscales Miko,' I said. 'We'll be fine; Marque will look after us. Will we see you tomorrow?'

'Probably not until it's time for you to leave. Captain Shudo will look after you tomorrow.' She lowered her voice. 'It is not my place to act on behalf of her Imperial Majesty.'

'I understand. Thank you for your assistance. We'll be fine.'

Miko looked around at us, then bowed her head. 'I am honoured to have served.' She stepped onto the lift platform, radiating mortification, and the doors closed.

'She's horrified that we called her Princess, and convinced she messed up,' I said. 'Marque, reassure her that she did a great job.'

'I'll do my best, but all the goldenscales are extremely insecure,' it said.

'We don't have time to worry about her feelings right now, Choumali,' the ambassador said. 'We have strategies to prepare for when we meet the Empress.'

'Ma'am,' I said, and sat next to her on the couch.

36

We were ready the next morning when the Imperial Guards arrived. They were a group of different species, all wearing similar outfits of blue trimmed with silver, and stared curiously at us with a variety of coloured and shaped eyes.

One of the guards stepped forward. 'I have taken the name of Captain Shudo in your language,' he said. His Marque-translated voice sounded male. He was short, only up to my waist, and plump, with bright pink fur that grew long enough to obscure his face, and blue scales that peeked between the fur on his temples. He said something in a growling tongue that sounded like the dragons' language, and Marque replied the same way.

Shudo led us into the lift room. Again, there was no sensation of movement as it swept us down to the ground. The doors opened onto the red-grassed courtyard, and the singing sculpture in the middle had changed from a faceted crystal to a spherical transparent blob.

We followed Shudo to a long breezeway through the gardens, passing plants and flowers of a variety of bright colours and delicate scents, and came to a paved forecourt in front of the Palace's main doors. Each door was twenty metres tall, and etched with a symbolic dragon in blue and silver.

The doors swung open silently and the captain gestured for us to go in. We entered a hall with a ceiling as high as the doors. Its smooth white floor was inlaid with blue and silver dragon motifs, and the hundred-metre-long side walls were decked with different-coloured banners that swept from the ceiling down to the floor, each with a motif at the bottom that could have been a single alien letter or symbol.

'Do the banners represent the Empress's children?' I said.

'Correct,' the captain said. 'The Empress has one hundred and fifty-three children at the moment.' His voice gained an amused edge. 'The Empress can control how many kids she has, but her children seem to have difficulty with the concept. I'm glad you'll be talking to her about it.'

'Does the Empress support her children's assimilation activities?' I said.

'She claims she's too lazy to deal with primitive species, and assimilation is just easier,' the captain said.

'That's what Zianto said.'

'By the time the new species is aware of what's happening, it's usually too late,' the captain said. 'Here we are. We would like to check the gift you are bringing for the Empress before you go in, if that is acceptable.'

'Of course,' Maxwell said, and gestured for our guards to open the locker.

The Imperial Guards stepped forward with obvious interest, and spoke quickly to each other in the dragon language. Captain Shudo gingerly picked up a yam, breathed in its scent, and staggered back in awe. He passed it around and the guards made similar sounds of appreciation.

Shudo placed the yam back in the locker, and glanced up at Maxwell. 'Is this all you brought?'

'Yes,' she said.

'Are these foodstuffs rare on your planet? How long do they take to grow?'

'They're common vegetables,' she said. 'Very quick and easy to grow.'

The guards had a quick discussion among themselves again.

'I suggest you limit their availability,' the captain said, his tone amused. 'Everyone has tried the Marque approximation, but the real thing is ...'

'There isn't a word in your language for how exceptional he said they are,' Marque said.

'You may finally be the leverage we need to control the dragons,' the captain said. 'Everybody appreciates their assistance with interstellar travel, but turning us into dragonscales is a very high price.'

'I hope we are successful,' Maxwell said. 'But isn't it treason to criticise the dragons like that? You won't be punished?'

The captain stared at Maxwell, then blinked a few times. 'That is a unique way of looking at the world,' he said. 'Welcome to the Royal Palace. The Empress awaits. She has configured her conference room to something you'll be familiar with. I'll shut up and let you talk to her.' He grinned at us, revealing three rows of bright purple pointed teeth. 'Give her hell.'

We all straightened our uniforms as the enormous doors at the end of the hall opened towards us.

The Empress's reception hall was even larger than the room we'd come from. The vaulted ceiling was higher, and made up of a network of arches, their edges embossed with twining silver filigree that shone in the light coming from the bank of windows overlooking the square.

The Empress reclined on her throne at the end of the hall, with three bright green, mantis-like aliens crouched on their many jointed legs next to her. She looked similar to the recording we'd seen of her during First Contact: her body was a shining pearl-white silver, and her eyes and soulstone were a deep sapphire blue. She was larger than I'd expected – at least twice as long as Shiumo, but with the transient nature of dragon bodies it was possible that her size was a conscious choice.

The Imperial Guards took up positions around the hall, leaving us to approach the throne.

We stopped at the base of it and hesitated, unsure about the correct protocol. Maxwell broadcast mortification; she was military, not foreign affairs, and hadn't thought to ask Marque about how to greet the Empress. Eventually she bowed, and we followed suit.

'Honoured Empress,' Maxwell said, and waved forward the guards holding the locker. 'I come in goodwill from Earth. I believe we can solve your cat problem, and I have a gift for you.'

The guards opened the locker to reveal the potatoes.

The Empress's blue eyes went wide when she saw them. 'Welcome, people of Earth, and thank you.' She gestured with one claw towards the three insect-like aliens standing next to her. 'These are one of my current Imperial dragonspouses, Terrclick. Terrclick is a shared consciousness in three bodies. Take care when moving close to them. They are in a bubble of lower gravity and methane atmosphere.'

The central insect spoke in a clicking language, its mouthparts moving swiftly. Marque translated at the same time. 'Hi, all. We hear that you have a solution for this assimilation business. We hope you do; our species is all dragonscales and these asshole dragons won't change us back.'

'Quiet, bugs,' the Empress said.

'Word outside parameters,' Terrclick said, and rapped the Empress's shoulder with one of its front claws.

'Later,' she said. 'Terrclick is also here as an advisor. Their species is expert at this sort of negotiation and I could use their input. We're making history here, and I want to do it right.'

'I'm honoured,' Terrclick said.

The Empress changed to a two-legged form: a majestic black woman, twice as tall as me, with broad shoulders and slim hips, small breasts and long legs. She picked up a bright blue robe from behind the throne, wrapped it around herself and stepped down to our level. Her dark skin and long floating hair reflected the light around her, and her bright blue eyes were huge and expressive.

The soldiers behind me made soft sounds of awe.

Don't let her appearance sway you, I said to them. *It's an illusion.*

'Ma'am,' one of them said.

'Let's do this,' the Empress said. 'Human-style table and chairs, please, Marque, so we can speak to our guests.'

A conference table and chairs for us emerged from the floor, as well as a larger chair for the Empress, and a soft pad for the three Terrclicks. The Empress sat, and the Terrclicks positioned themselves next to her.

'Marque showed me the effects of your pepper bombs,' she said to Ambassador Maxwell. 'It seems we can finally deal with the scourge of the cats and protect our dominion without descending into war.'

'Yes,' Maxwell said. 'But in return you have to stop assimilating other species. Vow that you won't make more than half the population of any species into dragonscales, and we'll provide you with as many pepper bombs as you need.'

'Stopping assimilation would be a major change to the way we do things,' the Empress said. 'It will have huge ramifications from one end of the Empire to the other. I'm not sure we're ready for the aftermath of something so drastic.'

'No restrictions, no pepper bombs,' Maxwell said, her tone clipped.

'But it's such a huge change!' the Empress said. 'What do you think, Terrclick? Is this a good idea? Could you handle the aftermath, Marque?'

'Of course I could,' Marque said. 'It's about time you quit this nonsense and grew up, Silver.'

'Yeah, stop this bullshit of breeding species out of existence,' the central Terrclick said. 'People have been telling you forever to cut it out. So do it.'

'Are you *sure* you can handle the consequences of this, Marque?' the Empress said. 'It will be an immense strain on your resources.'

'Now you're just being offensive,' Marque said.

'Promise me you can handle it.'

The Marque sphere went red and floated directly in front of her face. 'I can handle it!'

'All right then,' the Empress said. 'We'll agree to stop the assimilation program under one condition.'

'No conditions,' Maxwell said, broadcasting determination. 'We provide the bombs, and you stop the assimilation.'

'I understand, but we dragons – and our dragonscales – have never fought in war. It has always been unthinkable to us; we are a peaceful species. We are unskilled, while you humans, as well as being immune to the effects of these pepper bombs, have been at war for millennia.'

'Yes ...' Maxwell said, not sure where this was going.

'Can we make use of your expertise, Charles? Will you come and lead the defensive operation for us? Your species has turned this around from reproductive assimilation to negotiation on your own terms in a frighteningly short time. We need your skills.'

'I won't be mind-controlled by you,' Maxwell said.

'Don't worry, we'll ensure that you aren't dragonstruck,' the Empress said.

'You have a *term* for it?' Maxwell said.

'It's an unfortunate side effect of being with us. I'm surprised that Jian isn't completely in Shiumo's thrall, and wasting away when she's apart from her.'

Maxwell shot a sharp glance at me, but I was too shaken to respond. I'd been lucky.

'Probably because Jian left before the bonding process was complete, and went to your Wolf colony,' the Empress said. 'Refusing sexual contact with Shiumo would have been a factor as well.'

'I knew it!' Maxwell said under her breath.

'Refusing sex with a dragon,' Terrclick said with awe. 'I admire your willpower, madam, if you aren't an asexual member of your species.' Its mouthparts moved on all three bodies, making a soft grinding sound. 'Even if you are asexual, it is remarkable.'

'So, Charles, will you help us?' the Empress said. 'We'll put the Empire's resources at your command.'

'How big are your armies?' Maxwell said, still suspicious. 'Will we humans be a minority in your armed forces?'

The Empress shrugged. 'We don't have armies. We run from conflict; we don't fight. We're hoping that humanity will be our army. You are probably the only species that can handle the pepper bombs.'

Maxwell hesitated, and I could almost hear her mind running through the possibilities. If humanity became the dragons' army, we could use the pepper bombs against them, giving us the power to overthrow the entire Empire. Alternatively, the dragons could be planning to enslave us with their mind control and use us as battle fodder. Her emotions went dark; she was obviously thinking of a way to extract us from this situation.

Be ready for a firefight, I said to the guards, and they all shifted into readiness, putting their hands on their concealed pepper bombs.

Terrclick's three bodies all raised one front claw. 'Wait, Silver. You're thinking too much like a dragon, my love.' Its triangular heads all nodded in unison, and one of the human guards made a soft sound of disgust. 'Ambassador, this agreement probably sounds too good to be true. You must suspect that the dragons are planning to use mind control on you, since this weapon disables them as well as the cats. The dragons have no control over the dragonstruck process. It happens to those who love a dragon, and anyone who is struck and wants to leave the dragon concerned, receives a scale to keep them safe.'

'Tell that to Commander Alto,' Maxwell growled. Then her expression softened. 'Shiumo did give him a scale.'

'The dragons don't do it deliberately, and it won't happen to you if you're careful,' Terrclick said. 'We – the citizens of the Empire – won't let them control you. We'll make sure you are treated with honour as you provide us with this vital service.' Its mouthparts moved silently. 'We need you desperately.'

'In return for your military skills, we will stop the reproductive assimilation and provide you with backup and support, as well as full membership of the Empire with all that entails,' the Empress said.

Maxwell was torn by indecision.

'Is it a good deal, Marque?' I said.

'I work for the dragons, Jian. I'm not the one you should be asking. Ambassador Maxwell needs to make this decision herself. But I suggest you clarify with the Empress what full membership of the Empire grants you.'

'Of course,' the Empress said. 'Your home planet will immediately receive a full-size orbital Marque, which will ensure the safety and comfort of every member of your species living on-planet. Disease and accidental death will cease. What else? Oh, yes. The Marque will synthesise anything you need; and assist you in controlling your tradeable resources – such as these potatoes – until you have your own dragons. I understand you were in the second stage of the breeding process? So you have dragonscales ready to produce your own dragons?'

Maxwell nodded.

'I will give you one of my daughters to carry your colonists to nearby stars until you have your own dragons,' the Empress said. 'And as we already agreed, the reproductive assimilation will be severely curtailed. Marque?'

A star map of the Earth neighbourhood appeared around us. A boundary was illuminated, enclosing at least a hundred nearby red dwarf stars.

'These red dwarfs aren't ideal for your species, so if you like we can convert them to yellow stars similar to your own,' the Empress said. 'We can build planets around them if there aren't any there already. There are no restrictions on population growth and expansion inside your own district, so you'll be able to create a stellar community in no time.'

'Holy fuck,' Maxwell said under her breath.

'Did I miss anything?' the Empress said.

'Soulstones,' Terrclick said.

'Holy *fuck*,' Maxwell said, more loudly. 'Seriously? Immortality for all of humanity?'

Our team whispered to each other behind us, unable to restrain their excitement.

'Absolutely,' the Empress said. 'We will fit them on you after you've done the mandatory awareness training of the repercussions of effective immortality on you as a species. There are some side effects.'

'I'm sure there are,' Maxwell said wryly. She spoke side-on to me. 'Are you sensing any duplicity from them, Choumali?'

I hesitated, then said, 'No, ma'am.'

'It's an offer in good faith?'

I hesitated again. The entire future of humanity could rest on my answer to this question.

'Shiumo said that only dragons and dragonscales could be fitted with soulstones,' I said.

'Perhaps she was mistaken or you misunderstood her –' the Empress began.

'No,' I said, cutting her off. 'Shiumo lied. She never told us about being dragonstruck – mind control – even though we suspected that it was happening. She vehemently denied it the whole time she was with us.'

The Empress watched me with her deep sapphire eyes.

Maxwell's emotions darkened.

'I couldn't tell that she was lying,' I said. 'And I'm not sensing any duplicity right now. When it comes to dragons, I obviously can't tell the difference between truth and lies. They've been lying to us right from the start, Ambassador, it's been one deceit after another. I hesitate to trust them now.'

'Everything I've told you is the truth,' the Empress said. 'You're the only ones who can handle the pepper weapons. We need you.'

'Again, it sounds like she's telling the truth, but I can't be sure,' I said to Maxwell.

Maxwell linked her hands behind her back and looked down. 'Let me think about it,' she said. 'I need to liaise with my superiors back on Earth. Give us some time.'

'Very well.' The Empress rose, removed her robe, and returned to dragon form. 'Take all the time you need. Marque, return them to their quarters in Shiumo's tower. Ambassador, perhaps you would like Marque to show you around Sky City and introduce you to other member species.'

'Speak to the member species,' Terrclick said. 'They will tell you whether the offer is made in good faith.'

The Empress focused her brilliant blue eyes on Maxwell. 'I hope you can help us, Charles, because your skills can save millions of lives.'

She nodded to the rest of us, then said, 'Show them to their guest quarters, Captain.'

Captain Shudo waddled towards us and stretched out a furry arm. 'This way.' When we were some distance from the Empress, he said to Maxwell, 'I hope you take the Empress up on her offer, ma'am. We dragonscales always inherit the peaceful nature of our dragon parents. Having a warlike species in charge of this project would be hugely beneficial.'

'I wouldn't call us warlike,' Maxwell said.

'You have been at war since the start of your known history,' Marque said. 'There has never been a time when Earth has been free of armed conflict. You're one of the most warlike species we've ever encountered.'

'Yeah, you're perfect,' the captain said. 'So steeped in war that it never occurred to you to use a less wasteful method of culling your excess population of violently territorial young males. Every couple of generations you throw them against each other until very few are left.'

'That's not what we –' Maxwell began, then smiled wryly. 'I guess that's what it looks like from the outside.'

Shudo led us out of the audience hall and back onto the breezeway. Marque didn't follow us.

'Oh, don't tell us the Empress was right and you're choking,' the captain said to it.

Marque didn't reply.

'Delightful,' the captain said. 'Give it a minute to reroute the processing. We need it to carry us up to the top of the tower.'

'I made the mistake of creating the equivalent of ... an email box for you,' Marque said. 'Standard procedure when a new species arrives on Dragonhome. Everyone just saw your interaction with the Empress and wants to talk to you about it.'

'How many requests for them to fight the cats?' Shudo said.

'Ninety-four billion. Ninety-five. Hold on, I really need to reroute some processing into orbit.' It was silent a moment. 'All right, I have it under control. The Empress was right: this change has repercussions throughout the Empire. It's gone completely wild out there – everyone on the planet wants to make an appointment with you. Well done, humans. For a small, primitive, blind and relatively dimwitted race, you've done yourselves proud.'

'Thank you very much,' Maxwell said, her voice heavy with sarcasm.

'Ignore it when it's being rude like that,' Shudo said. 'It's embarrassed about its failure to think ahead.'

'This gives you an idea of how major this is for the rest of the Empire,' Marque said. 'It's a really big thing, guys.'

'Please say yes, Ambassador,' the captain said. 'This way.'

37

Back in our quarters, Maxwell sank onto one of the couches. 'I need to send a message to Earth.'

'Of course,' Marque said. 'Give it to me, and I'll pass it to the scales network to be folded to your people.'

Maxwell pulled out her tablet, and thought for a moment. Then she swiftly tapped out a message. After five minutes, she stopped and read it through.

'That's it. Can you send it for me?'

'I've passed it to the scales transmission control room,' Marque said. 'It's being sent to one of the dragons to fold to your command centre. The name on the top is the recipient?'

'Correct,' Maxwell said.

'The first few characters don't seem to make sense.'

'That's the confirmation code to identify me,' Maxwell said.

'I see. All right, it's sent.'

Maxwell rose and went to the window to look out. I stood next to her. The space elevator platform behind the Palace complex was a flat grey area with multiple cables around its edge, each the size of a large pillar.

'Do you think they'll say yes?' I asked her.

'I don't know, Choumali. Frankly, the whole thing sounds too good to be true.'

'I have a response for you,' Marque said.

'Already?' Maxwell sounded suspicious. 'That was too quick.'

'Shiumo is on Earth, and relayed for me,' Marque said. 'She's trying to talk to Richard.'

'Unsuccessfully?' I said.

'The message is on your tablet,' Marque said, ignoring me. 'It starts with a code that Secretary Park said to copy exactly.'

Maxwell went to the coffee table where she'd left her tablet, picked it up and read the message. Her face went grim.

'What does it say, ma'am?' one of the guards said.

Maxwell read the message aloud. '*You're the one on the ground, Charlie. You're more informed than anyone here. Make the decision, and we'll support you.*' She tossed the tablet onto the table. 'Thank you *very* much, Brian. I will never forgive you for this.' She sighed. 'I suppose we should talk to some citizens of the Empire. But the ones I really want to talk to are those who've chosen not to be a part of it.'

There was a tapping at the window and we looked up. The Empress and the three Terrclicks were floating on the other side of the transparent wall.

'May I come in?' the Empress said.

Maxwell nodded for her to enter, and the wall disappeared. She floated through and landed softly on the floor.

'If you don't mind, I'd like to speak to you privately,' she said.

Maxwell gestured towards the guards. 'Whatever you have to say, you can say it in front of my team.'

'No, I don't mean them; I mean the Empire. Put us on private, Marque.'

'Done,' Marque said.

'I couldn't talk about this until Parliament gave me permission,' the Empress said. 'It's a highly classified piece of information that will change the entire power dynamic of these negotiations.'

'In your favour,' Terrclick said.

'What is it?' Maxwell said.

'Remember that we need you desperately, and we don't want to see you harmed,' the Empress said. 'Will you let me fold you to my ship, Ambassador, and share some information that will change everything? You can bring your guards with their pepper bombs.'

'I thought nobody was allowed to fold within orbital distance of Dragonhome,' Maxwell said.

'This will be the first time a dragon has folded here in over a thousand years,' the Empress said. 'That shows you how extremely important this is to us. Please come.'

'Very well,' Maxwell said.

She waved the soldiers and UN guards closer, and we all clustered around the Empress, who folded us up to her ship.

The interior was shining white with silver accents, and a transparent top half like Shiumo's ship, but much smaller. The Empress disappeared, and reappeared on the nose of the ship; and the dragon planet, with its network of orbital tunnels and stations, vanished.

Space reappeared around us, and we all stared in shock. We weren't far from a star that filled up half the sky – a red dwarf. There was another glowing object next to the star; it was shaped like a vertical many-legged starfish, made up of thousands of glowing dots that were black around the edges and glowed brilliant white in the centre.

The Empress folded her ship so we were between the red star and the starfish-shaped object. The change in perception gave us an idea of the size of the glowing object: it was at least half the size of the red dwarf star.

The ship folded again so we were directly in front of the starfish-shaped object, and close enough to see a hundred of the dots at the end of one arm. Each dot was dark at the edges and bright in the centre, and the light emanating from them merged together.

The Empress moved the ship closer again, so one of the glowing dots filled our vision.

Ambassador Maxwell took a step back. The glowing dot was a cat cruiser, bigger than any we'd seen before.

'How big is that thing?' she said.

'Four kilometres long,' Marque said.

'Good lord. And how many of them are there?'

The Empress moved her ship back so we could see the entire formation again.

'Sixty-four thousand,' Marque said. 'The cats are so confident of their strength that they make no effort to hide themselves.'

'Holy fuck,' Maxwell said under her breath. 'And this is when you tell me they're headed for your home planet?'

The Empress appeared in the gallery next to us. 'Only member planets of the Empire know about this, but we've already started to evacuate. As I said, we dragons don't fight; we run.'

I spoke quietly to Maxwell. 'If we joined forces with the cats, we could help them conquer the dragons. Our pepper bombs are just as effective on both species.'

'I know that,' she said, watching the cat ships. She glanced at the Empress, then back at the fleet.

'We're putting a great deal of trust in you by showing you this,' the Empress said. 'You could destroy us all if you joined forces with the cats.'

'Both species are lying genocidal assholes,' Maxwell said, almost to herself. 'You dragons use mind control and sexual slavery to commit reproductive genocide on other species.'

'I know. We agree to stop if you'll help us,' the Empress said softly.

'The cats just use straight-up genocide, killing everything in their path, and kidnapping children to torture and murder.' Maxwell glanced at me. 'Including their own children if they feel like it.' She turned back to the cat fleet. 'Both of us have children who are threatened by the cats, Choumali. You have Oliver, and I have Veronica.'

'You were ready to kill Veronica to protect Earth,' I said.

'I knew damn well that wouldn't work. I was just trying to scare her.' She sighed. 'The dragons are assholes, but the cats are worse.'

'Not by much,' I said.

'I know.' She muttered under her breath: 'Sixty-four thousand ships full of these bastards. Do we even have enough soldiers on Earth to deal with this?' She shook her head. 'It would take us some time to be able to launch a surprise attack. We've only recently started to rebuild our population after the last war, and here I am committing us to another one. A much bigger war.'

'We can't attack the cats until they're out of warp,' the Empress said. 'We have to wait until they reach their target.'

'How long?'

'Thirteen of your years. Once they reach Dragonhome, they will exterminate all of us. If we evacuate Dragonhome, they will follow us to our new location. They will not rest until every dragon in existence is dead and our soulstones crushed; and they've killed all our spouses and every generation of our children. Even if we evacuate Dragonhome, they will not stop until every planet that has a dragonscales on it has been destroyed. And we don't have enough dragons to evacuate every planet.'

'Change to two-legged form,' Maxwell said without looking away from the cat fleet.

The Empress changed into the same tall black female form from earlier.

Maxwell turned to her and put out her hand. 'You have a deal, Empress. Restrict the creation of dragonscales, stop the forced assimilation of other species, and we'll drive the cats out for you. I only hope they don't find a way to resist the pepper bombs before we're finished.'

'So do I.' The Empress shook Maxwell's hand. 'I give you my word of honour that we will fulfil our part of the bargain.'

She turned to the rest of us. 'Thank you, humans. You just saved the lives of billions. Let's head back and tell the rest of the Empire.'

38

Six months after our agreement with the dragons, I took David and Oliver for a long-overdue visit to my mother. My small vehicle soared over the new farmland at the base of the Welsh mountains, the train line a grey mark slicing through the blooming green fields of potato crops. David and Oliver swooped through the air alongside my vehicle, carried by Marque, and the sound of their laughter lifted my spirits.

The capsule made a gentle landing, and I stepped out onto the rough gravel drive leading to my mother's transportable temporary residence in the middle of her farm. It was a plain steel box with windows set into the side, larger than her old cottage up on the mountain.

Oliver and David landed next to me, still laughing, then raced each other to the door, shouting 'Nanna!'

The door opened and my mother was there: tiny and thin, but glowing with good health, her eyes bright beneath her red soulstone. The boys embraced her, and she lit up. She ruffled David's hair and kissed Oliver on the cheek.

I went to her, hugging her too.

'My little family,' she said, and her eyes sparkled with tears. 'Come in. We have a long six months worth of news to catch up on.'

She led us into the rectangular living room where her original battered couch stood, and gestured for us to sit.

'Where's Dad?' David said. 'He said he'd be here.'

'He's in town collecting some steel for his latest work. He'll be back later today,' Mum said. She stood in the middle of the room with her arms crossed. 'Before any of you get the wrong idea, Richard Alto's here.'

I stared at her, then couldn't contain my smile at the thought of two wonderful people who I cared for dearly finding happiness with each other, especially after both had lost so much.

'Woot,' David said softly.

Mum scowled at him and shook her head. 'Not like that. Richard's heart is broken. He really loved that stupid dragon. He spent *years* with her without realising that she was invading other species. She'd always make some excuse to leave him on the ship when she did the really nasty stuff. He's beating himself up because he believes he should have known.'

I scowled back. 'He's right.'

She gestured dismissively with one hand. 'It's part of being dragonstruck – they can't see or think clearly.' She studied me. 'You should know that, Jian. You were really lucky.'

I looked down. 'I know.'

'Anyway, Richard's here trying to work through it. He spends most of his time helping me change from growing apricots to growing potatoes.'

'You're growing potatoes?' Oliver said, excited. 'What sort?' He grinned. 'Fresh potatoes straight out of the ground. Damn!'

'Of course I am,' Mum said. 'Earth's the only place they grow, and they're worth a fortune. Everybody on the planet's growing potatoes.'

'Can we go see Richard?' David said.

'Sure. Tell him to come in – lunch is nearly ready.'

'Yes, ma'am,' I said with mock severity and saluted her, then followed the boys out.

The land was flat and her parcel was small enough that Richard was visible some distance away, next to the few remaining apricot trees. The boys took off running towards him, and I followed at a more sedate pace. Richard was shirtless, wearing a plain pair of khaki pants and a battered straw hat that my mother had made for herself many years ago. He was muscular and tanned, and the sheen of sweat on his dark skin glowed as he struggled to uproot an apricot tree.

'I could do that for you, you know,' Marque said as we grew closer.

'I told you to piss off,' Richard said. He raised his head and saw us, and his face lit up. 'Well, look who's here. Connie told me you were coming.'

Oliver took one of the seed potatoes out of the basket and eyed it hungrily.

'Don't you dare eat that,' Richard said sharply. 'It's treated with insecticide. Wait until we're back in the house – your nan's made you some potato dishes for lunch.'

Oliver tossed the potato back into the basket. 'Nan says come now because lunch is nearly ready.'

Richard raised his hat to wipe his brow, then shoved his pick into the ground. 'Connie's looking after me far too well,' he said, and patted his firm abdomen. 'She'll make me fat.'

'Not as long as you continue to perform completely unnecessary physical tasks,' Marque said. 'You should let me do that! You're way too slow –'

Richard cut it off. 'We had this argument before, and we decided I need the therapy.' He slapped me on the back. 'I won't hug you – I'm soaked. Let's go back to the house.'

'Potatoes!' Oliver said, excited. His ears twitched. 'What's that?'

'We deaf humans can't hear anything,' I said as we walked over the heavily ploughed earth towards the house. 'What does it sound like?'

'A missile!' Oliver shouted. He tackled me and David to the ground, and threw himself on top of us.

'It's not a missile,' Marque said.

'It's me,' Shiumo said.

I couldn't see her with Oliver on top of me. I tapped him to let me up, and brushed the damp soil from my clothes.

'I don't know what you're doing here,' Richard began, then stopped. 'Is that …?'

'An egg?' David said.

'Is that *your* egg?' Oliver said.

'Mine and Richard's,' Shiumo said. She raised it in both front claws; it was thirty centimetres tall, with a lumpy red shell.

'I did not give you permission,' Richard began, but stopped when the egg tapped.

'Let's take it up to the house,' Shiumo said. 'You're about to be a father.'

'I did not agree to this,' Richard growled. He stood with his arms folded over his chest. 'You did this without my knowledge or permission, Shiumo. This is *wrong*.'

'That's beside the point, Richard. It's about to hatch,' she said.

He glowered at her, his arms still folded. The egg tapped again.

'We need to take it up to the house,' she said. 'We only have ten minutes before the baby starts to come out, and we need somewhere *clean*.'

Richard went back to the apricot tree. 'Go up to the house then.'

'This is your child!' Shiumo said.

He ignored her.

The egg rattled.

'Can you warn your mother?' Shiumo asked me. 'We need a clean surface and some towels. The fluid inside will be messy.'

We left Richard in the field and walked back to the house. Shiumo flew above us, holding the egg in both front claws.

Mum scowled when she saw Shiumo. 'You stay away from him.' Then she gestured towards the living room floor where she'd laid out some towels. 'Put the egg on these.'

Shiumo carefully set the egg on the towels, and stood back. Its shell rattled and shook as we watched.

'Wow,' David said softly.

'Richard should be here,' Shiumo said, her voice sad.

'You really can't blame him,' I said. 'You lied to him. How does he know this is his child? You could still be lying.'

'You'll know when you see it,' she said.

'What will it look like?' Oliver said, crouching to watch the egg as it shifted on the towels.

A spiderweb of cracks appeared on one side.

'You'll see,' Shiumo said. 'We may have to help it – some weaker hybrids need assistance to break out.'

A hole was punched through the shell and a little hand – a human hand – waved at us. A second hand appeared and pulled at the shell to enlarge the hole.

A child's cheeky face became visible in the gap and we all made soft sounds of wonder. She looked like a toddler, but only thirty centimetres tall; and had Richard's dark brown skin and eyes, and a mass of soaked black hair with red scales on her temples.

She smashed away the last of the shell, looked around, then held her arms out towards the door behind us. I turned to see Richard standing there, his face full of indecision.

'She's yours, Richard,' Shiumo said gently. 'Our love in physical form.'

'I did not consent to this,' Richard said.

'I know,' Shiumo said, watching the child as she stretched towards Richard. 'If you don't want to care for our child, I'll take her with me.' She turned her silver eyes on him. 'But I wanted to give you this gift. You have lost so much because of me.'

'I don't –' Richard began, then stopped when the baby burst into tears.

He went to her and lifted her out of the egg, then wrapped her in a clean towel. She quietened as soon as he held her. She was covered in slimy, blood-tinged fluid, and an umbilical cord ran from her to a placenta-like mass at the base of the eggshell.

'I need more towels, Connie,' Richard said softly, and Mum ran to fetch them.

'Let me cut the cord,' Marque said, and Richard moved the towel out of the way. Marque severed the umbilical cord and pinned it shut. 'It will drop off in about a day.'

Mum passed Richard an old towel, and the child snuggled into him as he gently wiped her clean.

'She looks like my mother,' he said, and glanced up at Shiumo. 'This is emotional blackmail. Haven't you abused me enough?'

'I'll take her with me if you choose,' she said.

'You have to – you're her mother. You have to feed her.'

'She'll eat solid food, the same as a two-year-old human. She can stay with you if you want, or I can take her.'

Richard was still broadcasting indecision. 'We have no baby food.'

'There's a supply ten minutes away,' Marque said. 'Say the word and I'll deliver it.'

Richard sat holding his daughter and gazing at her with wonder. The child smiled up at him and touched his cheek, then snuggled into him. He bent over her, his shoulders shaking.

'Bring her up to my ship,' Shiumo said. 'Let's parent her together. We'll be so happy.' She lowered her voice. 'Come back to me, Richard.'

He didn't reply.

'Please, my love.'

Richard stroked the child's back and still didn't speak.

'Is that a yes or a no?' Shiumo said.

When Richard's voice came it was hoarse, and he spoke without looking at her. 'Go away. I'll arrange for you to visit the child if you want, but I don't want to see you ever again. Leave me, dragon, and never return.'

Shiumo lowered her head and closed her eyes. 'I understand. I'll always be here for you.'

'Just go,' he said.

She nodded, and I followed her out of the house.

'Will you talk to him for me, Jian?'

'Yes,' I said. 'And if he ever thinks of returning to you, I'll stop him.'

'I really messed this up, didn't I?'

'I'll be returning to Dragonhome in six weeks to take up my commission in your army,' I said.

She lit up.

'Be warned, dragon,' I said. 'And pass this on through your network. If you dragons do anything like this again, if any more people suffer the way Richard has – we will leave you to the mercy of the cats' armada. And if you try any of this shit again after the cats are dealt with, we have the power to stop you.'

She gazed at me for a long time. 'I understand,' she said.

'Now fuck off.'

She disappeared.

'Food for the baby will be here in eight minutes,' Marque said. 'She can eat with the rest of you.'

'Good,' I said, and went inside to my family.

Loved SCALES OF EMPIRE?

Look out for

GUARDIAN OF EMPIRE

the next book in the epic Dragon Empire Trilogy

coming June 2019

Earth has joined the Galactic Empire, a vast interstellar society ruled by dragon-like aliens where everybody is immortal. Pain, famine and disease have been eradicated, but this doesn't mean the end of conflict.

A cruel alien Republic has been watching from afar and wants to take the Empire's progress for its own. Jian Choumali, ex-British forces and now Colonel in the Imperial space force, must fight to keep her friends, family and fellow citizens in the Empire safe. A brutal battle of skill and wits begins as Jian and her human colleagues attempt to combat the invaders — but with all their technology, enhancements and weapons in the hands of their enemies, the odds are stacked against them, and there is the very real threat of the destruction of the Empire itself.